BIRTHDAY GIRL

PENELOPE DOUGLAS

BERKLEY ROMANCE
New York

BERKLEY ROMANCE
Published by Berkley
An imprint of Penguin Random House LLC
penguinrandomhouse.com

Library of Congress Cataloging-in-Publication Data

Names: Douglas, Penelope, 1977– author.
Title: Birthday girl / Penelope Douglas.
Description: First Berkley Romance edition. | New York: Berkley Romance, 2023.
Identifiers: LCCN 2023016619 | ISBN 9780593641965 (trade paperback)
Subjects: LCGFT: Romance fiction. | Novels.
Classification: LCC PS3604.O93236 B57 2023 |
DDC 813/.6—dc23/eng/20230414
LC record available at https://lccn.loc.gov/2023016619

Birthday Girl was originally self-published, in different form, in 2018.

First Berkley Romance Edition: September 2023

Printed in the United States of America
17th Printing

Book design by George Towne

When you grow up, your heart dies.

—Allison Reynolds, *The Breakfast Club*

Dear Reader,

This book deals with emotionally difficult topics, including power imbalance and misogynistic language. Anyone who believes such content may upset them is encouraged to consider their well-being when choosing whether to continue reading.

PLAYLIST

"Addicted to Love" by Robert Palmer

"All She Wants to Do Is Dance" by Don Henley

"Bad Medicine" by Bon Jovi

"The Distance" by Cake

"The Girl Gets Around" by Sammy Hagar

"Glory Days" by Bruce Springsteen

"Guys My Age" by Hey Violet

"Hurts So Good" by John Mellencamp

"I Love Rock 'n Roll" by Joan Jett & the Blackhearts

"I'm on Fire" by Bruce Springsteen

"Jessie's Girl" by Rick Springfield

"Pity Party" by Melanie Martinez

"Poison" by Alice Cooper

"Pour Some Sugar on Me" by Def Leppard

"Run to You" by Bryan Adams

1

Jordan

He's not answering. This is the second time I've called in fifteen minutes, and I've been texting without any luck, too. Was he planning on still remembering to be here at two?

I end the call and glance up at the clock above the bar, seeing it's nearly midnight now. Still two hours before my boyfriend thinks I'm off work and need to be picked up.

And here I thought we got a lucky surprise tonight, me getting off early.

Shit.

I need to get my car running. I can't keep relying on him for rides.

The music fills the air around me, customers laughing to my right and one of the other bartenders filling the cooler with ice to my left.

Unease pricks at the back of my neck. If he's not answering, then he's either asleep or out. Both could mean he'll remember me after it's too late. He's not always unreliable, but this wouldn't be the first time, either.

That's the problem with making your friend your boyfriend, I guess. He still thinks he can get away with murder.

I grab my shirt and school bag out of the cabinet underneath the taps and slide my phone into my pocket. I pull on a flannel over my tank top, button it up, and tuck the front of the hem into my jeans, covering myself. I'll dress a little sexy for tips, but I'm not about to walk out of here like that.

"Where are you going?" Shel asks, peering at me as she draws a beer.

I glance over at my boss, her black hair with blond chunks piled on top of her head and a string of tiny hearts tattooed around her upper arm.

"There's a midnight showing of *Evil Dead* at the Grand Theater," I tell her as I close the cabinet and slide the strap of my leather satchel over my head. "I'll go kill time and wait for Cole there."

She finishes pouring her beer and looks at me like there are a million things she wants to say but she doesn't even know where to start.

Yeah, yeah, I know.

I wish she'd stop looking at me like that. There's a good possibility Cole won't be here at two a.m. considering he's not answering the phone right now. I know that. He could be three sheets to the wind at some friend's house.

Or he could be at home sleeping with the alarm set to come get me at two and his phone left in another room. It's not likely, but it's possible. He's got two hours. I'll give him two hours.

Besides, my sister is at work, and no one here can leave to drive me home. Work is slow tonight, and I got cut early because I'm the only one without a child to support.

Even though I desperately need the money just the same.

I grip the strap of the bag over my chest, feeling like I should be older than eighteen.

Well, nineteen now, I think, almost forgetting what today is.

I take a deep breath, pushing the worry away for tonight. A lot of people my age struggle for money, can't pay bills, and have to bum rides. I know it's too much to expect that I'd have everything figured out by now, but it's still embarrassing. I hate looking helpless.

And I can't blame Cole, either. It was my decision to use what was left of my student loan money to help him fix *his* car. He's been there for me, too. At one time, we were all the other one had.

Turning around, Shel sets the beer on the bar in front of Grady—one of the regulars—and takes his cash, shooting me another look as she enters the sale into the register. "You don't have a functioning vehicle," she states. "And it's dark outside. You can't walk to the theater. Sex slavers are just looking for hot teenage girls with blond hair and shit."

I snort. "You need to stop watching Lifetime movies."

We might be an easy distance to some larger towns, and Chicago is only a few hours away, but we're still in the middle of nowhere.

I lift up the partition and walk out from behind the bar. "The theater is right around the block," I tell her. "I'll make it in ten seconds if I run like I'm being graded."

I pat Grady on the back as I leave, the gray hair of his ponytail swaying as he turns to wink at me. "Bye, kiddo," he says.

"Night."

"Jordan, wait," Shel shouts over the jukebox, and I turn my head to look at her.

I watch as she pulls a box out of the cooler along with a single-serving box of wine and pushes them both across the bar at me.

"Happy birthday," she says, smirking at me like she knows I probably think she forgot.

I break into a smile and lift the small Krispy Kreme box lid and see half a dozen donuts.

"It was all I could pick up in a hurry," she explains.

Hey, it's cake. Kind of. I'm not complaining.

I close the box and lift the flap of my leather bag, hiding my loot inside, wine and all. I didn't expect anyone to get me anything, of course, but it's still nice to be remembered. Cam, my sister, will no doubt surprise me with a pretty shirt or a sexy pair of earrings tomorrow when I see her, and my dad will probably call me sometime this week.

Shel knows how to make me laugh, though. I'm old enough to work in a bar but not old enough to drink. Enjoying the wine she's sneaking me, off the premises, will be my little adventure tonight.

"Thank you," I say and hop up on the bar, planting a kiss on her cheek.

"Be safe," she tells me.

I nod once and spin around, heading out the wooden door and stepping out onto the sidewalk.

The door shuts behind me, the music inside now a dull thrumming, and my chest caves, releasing the breath I didn't realize I'd been holding.

I love her, but I wish she wouldn't worry about me. She looks at me like she's my mom and wants to fix everything.

I guess I should've been so lucky as to have a mom like her.

The welcome fresh air washes over me, the late-night chill sending goose bumps up my arms, and the fragrant scent of May flowers wafts through my nostrils. I tip my head back, close my eyes, and breathe in a lungful as my long bangs tickle my cheek in the light breeze.

Hot summer nights are coming.

I open my eyes and look left and then right, seeing the sidewalks are empty, but cars still line both sides of the street. The VFA parking lot is also full. Their bingo night usually turns into a bar scene this late, and it looks like the old-timers are still going strong.

Turning left, I pull the rubber band out of my hair, letting the loose curls fall down, and slip the band around my wrist as I start walking.

The night feels good, even though it is still a little crisp out.

There's too much liquor in every crevice in the bar, seeping up into my nose all night.

Too much noise and too many eyes, as well.

I pick up the pace, excited to disappear into the dark theater for a while. Normally, I don't go alone, but when they're showing an older eighties flick like *Evil Dead*, I have to. Cole is all about special effects and doesn't trust films made before 1995.

I smile, thinking about his quirks. He doesn't know what he's missing. The eighties were fantastic. It's a whole decade of just good fun. Not everything had to have a meaning or be deep.

It's a welcome escape, especially tonight.

Rounding the corner and making my way up to the ticket booth, I see I'm a few minutes early, which is great. I hate missing the trailers at the beginning.

"One, please," I tell the cashier.

I fish out the wad of tips that I made tonight from my pocket and dole out the seven-fifty for the ticket. Not that I have money to spare with rent coming due and a small pile of bills on Cole's and my desk back at our apartment that we can't pay yet, but it's not like seven bucks will make or break me.

And it's my birthday, so . . .

Walking inside, I bypass the concession stand and head for the next set of double doors. There's only one theater, and surprisingly, this place has survived for sixty years even in the wake of the bigger twelve-theater cinema centers built in the surrounding towns. The Grand had to get creative with midnight showings of classic movies like tonight, but also dress-up events and private parties, too. I don't get down here much with my school and work schedule, but it's a nice, dark place when you want to get lost for a while. Private and quiet.

Stepping through the doors, I check my phone one more time to see that Cole hasn't called or texted yet. I turn my ringer off and slide it back into my pocket.

Some ads loop on the screen, but the houselights are still on, and I quickly scan the room, seeing a few loners spread out. There's also a couple sitting in the back row to my right, and a small group of guys is in the middle—young by the sound of their inconsiderately loud laughter. Out of about three hundred seats, two hundred eighty-five are still available, and I pretty much have my pick.

I walk down five or six rows, finding an empty one, and slide in, taking a seat midway in. I set down my bag and quietly pull out the purple box of wine, reading the label in the dim light.

Merlot. I was hoping it was white wine, but I'm sure Shel needs to get rid of this stuff. We only serve it when there's an outdoor event and we don't want glass outside.

Unscrewing the cap, I sniff the pungent scent, not sensing in the least any of the fancy aromas that sommeliers seem to grasp from wine. No hint of oak with a "bold aroma of sweet cherries" or anything like that. Sliding my tray in front of me, I take advantage of the empty row ahead and bend up my knees, fitting my Chucks in between the empty seats on the armrest.

Setting the box down, I slip my phone out of my back pocket, just in case Cole calls, and plop it on the tray next to the wine.

But instead, it spills off the tray. It falls down between my legs and onto the floor, and I jerk up my knees to try to catch it, but they bump the tray and send the open box of wine spilling to the floor.

My mouth falls open, and I gasp. "Shit!" I blurt out in a whisper.

What the hell?

Planting my feet on the floor again, I push the tray off to the side and dive down to the floor, feeling around for my phone. My fingers dip in the spilled wine, and I flinch at the mess. Glancing up over the seats, I see the group of three guys a few rows down, dead ahead of me and right in line with the oncoming winefall.

I groan. *Great.*

A light layer of sweat cools my forehead, and I stand up, yanking my scarf out of my bag to dry off my fingers. I hate to ruin it, but I don't have any napkins.

What a mess.

So much for escaping for two hours.

I look around for an usher with a light, pretty positive this theater doesn't employ them, especially at this time of night, but the only flashlight I have is on my phone, and the floors are dark.

Seeing no one, I take my scarf and bag and travel down to the next row, bending down and peering under the seats to see if I can see my cell. When I find nothing, I move up to the next row and then to the next, pretty sure I heard it slide a ways. Since the rows of seats are on a decline, it could've gone far, too. *Dammit.*

Moving up to the next row, I set my stuff down and drop to my hands and knees, peering under the rows to my left and right, feeling with my hands. A pair of long, jean-clad legs sits ahead, and I look up, seeing a man sitting in the seat with fingers full of popcorn halfway to his mouth. He stares down at me with raised eyebrows.

"I'm sorry," I whisper, tucking my hair behind my ear. "I dropped my drink and my phone went sliding down here somewhere. Do you mind . . . ?"

He hesitates a moment and then blinks, sitting up. "Yeah, sure." He moves his tray aside and stands up, digging something out of his pocket. "Here."

He turns on the flashlight on his phone and squats down, shining it under the seats.

Immediately, I spot my phone under the seat next to his and snatch it up. *Thank goodness.* We both stand up, and my shoulders relax. I can't afford a replacement right now. I smooth my fingers over the screen, making sure I don't feel any cracks.

"Got it?" he asks.

"Yeah, thank you."

He kills his flashlight but reaches over, swiping his fingers over the bottom of my phone, and brings them to his nose, smelling.

"Is that"—he winces—"wine?"

I glance down at the floor, seeing he's standing in the drink I spilled three rows up.

"Oh, geez." I look up at him. "I'm so sorry. Is it everywhere?"

"No, no, it's fine." He lets out a chuckle, his lips curving more to one side with his smile as he steps out of the mess. "I didn't realize they sold alcohol here."

I grab my scarf and wipe off my phone. "Oh, they don't," I tell him quietly so I don't disturb the others in the theater. "I just got off work. My boss gave it to me for a . . . um"—I shake my head, searching for words—"to, uh . . . celebrate."

"Celebrate?"

"Shhh," someone hisses.

We both look to the guy one row back and far to the right who's shooting us a glare out of the corner of his eye. Neither the trailers nor the movie has started yet, and we're not in his line of sight, but I guess we're disturbing him. I move away, back toward my bag.

The man helping me picks up his drink and popcorn and follows, the faint scent of his bodywash hitting me. "I'm just going to scooch over, out of the mess," he says.

He sits a few chairs down and glances up at me and then back to where I was sitting when my phone and wine fell. "You're welcome to sit." He gestures to the seat next to him, probably figuring out I'm on my own tonight, too.

"Thanks," I tell him. "I'll just go . . ."

I don't finish. I back away and pick up my bag, turning to head to my own seat, when I see a guy and girl enter the theater. I freeze, watching them veer left for the back row on the other side of the room and plop down in the seats.

Shit.

Jay McCabe. The only boyfriend I've had other than Cole, and he makes Cole look like a prince. Unfortunately, he still loves to take a bite out of me any chance he gets, and there's no way in hell I'm dealing with him tonight.

"You okay?" the guy with the phone light asks when I don't move. "I promise I'm not making a pass at you. You're too old for me."

I shoot him a look, forgetting about Jay and the girl for a moment. *Too old for him? What?* I take in his more than six feet of height, the outline of muscles visible through his T-shirt, and his corded right forearm with a full sleeve of tattoos disappearing up his shirt. I've seen plenty of guys in the bar, and he doesn't look like any nineteen-year-old I've ever seen. He's got to be at least, what? Thirty?

He snorts. "I'm kidding," he says, his mouth spreading in a wide smile that makes my face fall a little. "If you don't want to watch the movie alone, you're welcome to sit. That's all I meant."

I dart my gaze to Jay and whomever he's with, but then a group of guys suddenly push through the double doors, making a lot of noise as they enter the theater. I see Jay look away from the girl and toward the commotion, and I drop down in the seat next to the guy on instinct, not wanting Jay to see me.

"Thanks," I tell the guy next to me.

I feel my ex's presence in the theater, and the old memories surface, reminding me of how helpless I let him make me feel at one time. I just want one night where I'm not thinking about everything.

I sit back and try to relax, but then I peer out of the corner of my eye, the close proximity of a guy I don't know sitting next to me suddenly like a blazing bonfire and impossible to ignore.

I turn my head, eyeing him with apprehension. "You're not a serial killer, are you?"

He pinches his eyebrows and looks at me. "Are you?"

"They're usually antisocial Caucasian men."

Good-looking male here all alone? Hmm . . .

He arches a sharp brow. "And they look just like everyone else," he adds, suspicion in his voice as he looks me up and down.

The light from the ads on the screen plays in his eyes, neither of us flinches, but I can't take it anymore. I break into a quiet chuckle.

I finally hold out my hand to him. "I'm Jordan. Sorry about the wine."

"Jordan?" he repeats, taking my hand and shaking it. "Unusual name for a girl."

"No, not really." I relax into the seat and fold my arms over my chest, lifting my knees and planting my shoes in the crevice between the two empty seats ahead of me. "It was the name of Tom Cruise's love interest in *Cocktail*, remember?"

His eyebrows rise in question.

"*Cocktail*?" I repeat. "Nineteen eighty-eight movie about flair bartending?"

"Oh, right." But he has this unsure look in his eyes, and I'm not sure he knows what the hell I'm talking about.

"Do you like eighties movies?" I ask, gesturing to the film that we're about to watch on the screen.

"I like *scary* movies," he clarifies and holds the popcorn over to me. "This one's a classic. You?"

"I love the eighties." I take a small handful and put a piece in my mouth. "My boyfriend hates my taste in movies and music, but I can't resist. I'm here whenever they show something from the decade."

I feel awkward slipping in a random mention of a boyfriend, but I don't want to give the wrong impression here. I quickly glance down at his left hand, thankfully not seeing a wedding ring. It would be wrong to sit here with a married guy.

But he just looks at me knowingly. "*Breakfast Club* is your favorite, right?" he says. "And every other John Hughes creation?"

"You have something against *The Breakfast Club*?"

"Not the first ten times I saw it, no."

A smile pulls at my lips. It *is* on TV a lot, I guess.

He leans in. "The eighties was the age of the action hero," he points out, his deep voice close and hushed. "People forget that. *Lethal Weapon*, *Die Hard*, *The Terminator*, *Rambo* . . ."

"Jean-Claude Van Damme," I add.

"Exactly."

I bite the corner of my mouth so I don't laugh, but my stomach shakes anyway, and I let out a snort.

He frowns. "What are you laughing at?"

"Nothing," I reply quickly, nodding. "Van Damme. Great actor. Very relevant films."

I can't keep the laughter off my face, though, and he furrows his brow, knowing I'm full of shit.

Just then I hear a giggle somewhere behind me, and I turn my head to look over my shoulder, seeing Jay turned away from the screen and leaning into the girl, both of them full-on making out now.

"You know them?" the man next to me asks.

I shake my head. He doesn't need to know my business.

We fall silent, and I finish the popcorn in my hand, letting my head fall back as I look up to the high ceiling and the antique gold arches overhead. He sits next to me, and I breathe in and out slowly, despite the hammering in my chest.

Why am I nervous? Is it Jay?

No, I'm not even thinking about him at the moment.

People chat around us, waiting for the movie to start, but I can't hear what they're saying, and I don't really care. My skin feels warm.

"So, what are you studying at Doral State?" he asks.

I shoot him a surprised look. How does he know where I go to school?

Serial killer.

But then he gestures to my bag on the floor, and I see the key chain hanging off it with the university emblem emblazoned on the face.

Oh, duh.

I sit up. "Landscape design," I tell him. "I want to make outside spaces pretty."

"That's nice. I work in construction."

I flash him a half smile. "So, you make inside spaces pretty, then."

"No, not really."

I laugh at his forlorn tone, like he's so bored with what he does.

"I make them *functional*," he corrects me.

He turns hazel eyes on me, warm and piercing, but then his gaze drops to my mouth for a split moment, and a flutter hits my stomach. He quickly looks away, and I drop my eyes, having a hard time catching my breath.

Clearing my throat, I bend down and pull out the box of donuts from my bag and place them on the tray, swinging the little table in front of me and lifting the lid.

The sweet scent immediately hits my nose, and my stomach growls.

I glance back at the projection window, wondering if the movie is starting soon, because I was saving these for that, but now I'm starving.

I feel the guy's eyes on me, and I glance at him, explaining the donuts. "It's my birthday. In addition to the wine, my boss gave me the only cake she could get at a drive-thru."

I pick one up and lean back, putting my feet back on the armrest in front of me.

"You're going to eat all six donuts?" he questions.

I stop the pastry two inches from my mouth and glare at him. "Would that disgust you or something?"

"No, I'm just wondering if I get one."

I smile and wave at the box, telling him to help himself.

He picks up the plain glazed, and I'm not sure if he's the no-frills type or just trying to save the special sprinkle ones for me, but either way, I kind of like it. We sit back and eat, but I can't help stealing glances at him every once in a while.

His brown hair is light, and his eyes look blue, green, or hazel depending on what kind of light is flashing across them from the screen. He has a little stubble on his oval-shaped face and a sharp nose, and my gaze is drawn to the way his angular jaw flexes as he chews. There's the faintest of lines around his eyes, so he might be more than thirty, but it could just be all his time working in the sun, too. He's tall, strong, fit, and tan, and his eyes suddenly flash to the side as if he senses me staring. I turn my eyes forward again.

Dammit.

That's okay, right? It's normal to find other people attractive. It happens. I mean, Scarlett Johansson is attractive. That doesn't mean I'm interested in her.

I take another nibble of my donut, my gaze darting to the side again, taking in his arms and the various tattoos. Black gears and bolts, like a robot skeleton, some tribal work that definitely says he was a nineties kid, and I can just make out what I think is a pocket watch that looks like it's trying to break free of his skin. It's like a hodgepodge without any discernable theme, but it's beautiful work. I wonder what the story is behind them.

I take another bite, the pink glaze and rainbow sprinkles sending electric shocks to the back of my jaw and making me crave the whole damn thing in my mouth at once.

"You know, I really kind of want abs," I say, chewing, "but these are really good."

He breaks into a laugh, looking at me and chuckling.

"What?"

"Nothing. You're just . . ." He looks away as if searching for words. "You're just kind of, like, interesting or . . . something?" He shakes his head. "I'm sorry, I don't know what I mean." And then he blurts out, "Cute," as if just remembering. "You're cute, I mean."

My stomach flips, and heat warms my cheeks like I'm in fifth grade again, when it was such a compliment for a guy you like to tell you you're cute. I know he means my personality and not how I look, but I kind of like it.

He finishes the donut and takes a sip of his soda. "So, what are you?" he asks. "Like twenty-three, twenty-four?"

"Sure, eventually."

He breathes out a laugh.

"Nineteen," I finally answer.

He takes a deep breath and sighs, something far off in his gaze.

"What?" I take the last bite and brush my hands together, slouching and leaning my head back on the chair.

"To be that young again," he muses. "Seems like yesterday."

Well, how old could he be? Nineteen couldn't have been that long ago for him. Ten years? Maybe twelve?

"So, you'd do some things differently if you could go back?" I inquire.

He quirks a tight smile and looks down at me, his eyes serious. "Let me tell you something. . . . A little advice, okay?"

I listen, looking up at him, my gaze locked with his.

"Hit the ground running," he tells me.

Huh?

He must see the confusion on my face, because he goes on.

"Time passes by you like a bullet," he says, "and fear gives you the excuses you're craving to not do the things you know you should. Don't doubt yourself, don't second-guess, don't let fear hold you back, *don't* be lazy, and don't base your decisions on how happy it will make others. Just go for it, okay?"

I stare up at him, and unfortunately, that's all I can seem to do. I want to smile, because my heart is swelling, and it feels good, but I'm also filled with something I can't place. It's like a dozen different emotions flooding in at once, and all I can manage are short, shallow breaths.

"Okay," I whisper to him.

I'm not sure if what he said was what I wanted to hear or needed to hear, but I feel my shoulders square a bit more and my chin rise with readiness. For however long it lasts, I'm a little braver, and he's my new hero.

I watch as he pulls out a small box and proceeds to light a match, the small flame burning bright. He sticks it in one of the donuts, all the pink frosting Shel asked for, because she knows it's my favorite color, glowing in the light. I feel my heart warm at the gesture.

Taking my feet down, I lean forward, close my eyes, and ask for what I want in my head, and then I blow out the flame.

I didn't wish for what I usually wish for, though. My mind is suddenly blank, and I'm not remembering all the things I need and want right now outside of this theater. Just the only thing I can think of.

We both sit back and settle in, each having another donut as the lights finally dim and the surround sound hits us from both sides of the theater.

Over the next ninety minutes, we eat and laugh, and I hide my face a couple times when I know something's coming. I jerk here and there and laugh at him when he does, too, because he looks embarrassed. After a while, I notice my head lies inclined toward him, and he has his foot up on the empty chair ahead of us with his head laid back, as well, and we're completely comfortable. It hasn't even occurred to me to keep a certain distance.

I don't watch a lot of movies with other people. I'm not used to just sitting in silence with someone else. Cole's and my schedules don't always mesh; my sister, Cam, doesn't have any free time anymore; and most of my high school friendships didn't last past graduation about a year ago. It's nice to hang out.

By the time the credits roll, I'm not sure I remember much of the movie. But I haven't been this relaxed in a long time. I laughed and smiled and joked around and forgot everything that's going on out there, and I needed that. I don't really want to go home yet.

The lights start to come up, and I slowly sit up, bringing my feet back to the floor as I swallow the lump in my throat and glance over at him. He sits up, too, but he barely meets my eyes.

Standing up, I hook the strap of the bag over my head and pick up my garbage.

"Well, they're showing *Poltergeist* in a few weeks," he says behind me, rising and taking his trash with him. "If I see you, I'll make sure to sit at higher ground."

I laugh under my breath, thinking about the wine. We both exit the row and walk for the doors, and I notice Jay and his date aren't in their seats anymore. They must've left already, but truth be told, I forgot they were here a long time ago.

Poltergeist. Does that mean he'll be here then? Is this his way of nonchalantly letting me know in case I just happen to want to come, too?

But no, he knows I have a boyfriend.

I can't help but think, though, if for some reason Cole and I didn't make it another month, would I come to the movies then, knowing he'd be here?

I blink long and hard, guilt washing over me as I trail up the aisle. I'd probably be here. There aren't a lot of "catches" in this town, and I had fun tonight. This guy is interesting.

And good-looking.

And employed.

I should set him up with my older sister. How he's gone undetected by her radar all this time is a mystery to me.

We push through the door, the last ones out of the theater, and stop in the lobby, tossing away all our trash.

I look up at him, my heart skipping a beat at seeing him in the brighter light and standing tall in front of me. Hazel eyes. Definitely hazel. But more green around the outsides of the irises.

His hair is styled with minimal product and just long enough to run your fingers through, and I drop my eyes to his smooth, tan neck. I can't see if there's a tan line under the collar of his T-shirt, though. Is he like that all over? An unbidden image of him hammering and hauling lumber without a shirt on flashes in my mind and I . . .

I close my eyes again, shaking my head. *Yeah, whoa, okay.*

"Um, I better head back," I tell him, gripping the strap of my bag. "Hopefully my boyfriend is waiting at the bar to pick me up by now."

"Bar?"

"Grounders?" I answer, thinking he probably should know the place. It's one of only three bars in town, although many favor Poor Red's or the strip club over the dive I work at. "I got off a little early tonight—unexpectedly—but he's my ride, and I couldn't get ahold of him. He should be there now, though."

He pushes the door open, holding it for me as I leave the theater, and follows me out.

"Well, I hope you had a good birthday, despite having to work," he says.

I move to the right, toward where Grounders is, and he veers left.

"And thanks for keeping me company," I tell him. "I hope I didn't ruin the movie for you."

He gazes at me for a moment, his breathing growing heavier as a torn look crosses his face. Finally, he shakes his head, averting his eyes. "Not at all," he says.

A moment of silence passes, and slowly, we both steer farther apart, but neither of us turns our back on the other.

The silence gets longer, the distance farther, and finally he raises a hand, giving me a little wave before hooking both hands in his back pockets. "Good night," he says.

I just stare at him. *Yeah, good night.*

And then I turn away, my stomach twisting into a tighter knot.

I didn't even get his name. It'd be nice to say hi if I run into him again.

I don't have time to dwell, though, because my phone rings, and I slide it out of my pocket, seeing Cole's name on the screen.

I stop on the sidewalk and answer it. "Hey, you at Grounders?" I ask him. "I'm almost there."

He doesn't say anything, though, and I pause, calling his name. "Cole? Hey, are you there?"

Nothing.

"Cole?" I say louder.

But the line is dead. I go to call him back, but I hear a voice behind me.

"Your boyfriend's name is Cole?" the man from the theater asks. "Cole Lawson?"

I turn around to see him slowly walking back toward me.

"Yeah," I say. "You know him?"

He hesitates for a moment, as if coming to terms with something, and then he holds out his hand, finally introducing himself. "I'm Pike. Pike Lawson."

Lawson?

He pauses a moment and then adds, "His father."

My lungs empty. "What?" I breathe out.

His father?

My mouth falls open, but I clamp it shut again, looking up at this man with new eyes as realization dawns.

Cole has talked about his father in passing—I knew he lived in the area—but they're not close, from what I understand. The impression I had of Cole's father from his son's brief mentions doesn't match the guy I talked to in the theater tonight. He's nice.

And easy to talk to.

And he hardly looks old enough to have a nineteen-year-old son, for crying out loud.

"His father?" I say.

He gives me a curt smile, and I know this is a turn of events he wasn't expecting, either.

I hear his cell vibrate in his pocket next, and he digs it out, checking the screen.

"And if he's calling me now, he must be in trouble," he says, staring at the phone. "Need a lift?"

"A lift where?"

"Police station, I'd assume." He sighs, answering the phone and leading the way. "Let's go."

2

Jordan

I don't think this is a good idea," I tell Cole, pulling out my stacked milk crates from the back of his car. "I feel like a freeloader."

My boyfriend brandishes that quirky tilt to his lips where you only see the left side of his teeth. "So, what are you gonna do, then?" He looks up at me, sliding my collapsible drafting table toward him and lifting it up. "Stay at your parents'?"

His blue eyes are hooded, probably from the lack of sleep, as we both walk over and set our loads on the porch steps to Pike Lawson's house.

Our new home.

The past few days have been crazy, and I can't believe that guy is his father. What are the chances? I wish our first meeting had ended a little differently. Not driving down to the police station at two o'clock in the morning to get his son—my boyfriend—out of jail.

"Come on, I told you," Cole says, walking back to the car for another load. "My dad was the one who offered to let us stay here. We just chip in on chores, and this gives us a chance to save up for a new place. A better place."

Right. And how many kids move back home to do just that and

end up staying for another three years instead? His dad had to know what he was opening himself up to.

I'll make every effort to be gone as soon as possible, but Cole doesn't save money. Setting up a new place, with a deposit—which we lost at the previous apartment due to minor damages to the carpets—and utilities will take substantial cash. Once we get a place, Cole can help pay for it, but actually getting in there and setting up will be on me.

It's been three days since the theater and meeting Pike Lawson. Once we got Cole out, I came home to find our apartment completely trashed. Apparently, he was trying to throw me a late birthday party at our place, but our friends—his friends—didn't wait to start the festivities. By eleven, everyone was drunk, the pizza was gone, but hey, they saved me a piece of cake.

I had to go into the bathroom so I wouldn't cry in front of them when I saw the place.

Apparently, a fight started during the party, neighbors complained about the noise, Cole mouthed off, and he and another one of his buddies were taken in to cool down. Mel, the landlord, stated in no uncertain terms that he'd had enough and Cole had to go. I was welcome to stay, but there was no way I could pay for everything by myself. Not after I'd already drained my savings helping repair his car last month.

And thank goodness the cops let him go without bail this time, because I didn't have a hundred bucks to squeeze out of anywhere, much less twenty-five hundred.

"You're his son," I remind Cole, grabbing my floor lamp—one of the only big things we didn't put into storage, since Cole's dad already had one of the spare bedrooms furnished. "But me staying here, too, with him paying all the bills? It's not right."

"Well, I don't think it's right for me to have to go without this every day," he teases with a cocky grin as he pulls me to him and wraps his arms around my body. I release the lamp and smile, indulging his playfulness even though I'm feeling out of sorts. It's been some time since I've been at ease long enough to forget the stress hitting us at every turn. We haven't smiled together in a while, and it's starting to not come naturally anymore.

But right now, he has that boyish glint to his eyes like he's just the most adorable tornado and *Don't you just love me?*

He plants his forehead on mine, and I thread my fingers through the back of his blond hair and look up into his dark blue eyes, which always give the impression that he just remembered he has a whole pie waiting in the refrigerator.

Taking my right hand in his, he pulls both up between us, and I clasp his in mine, already knowing what he's doing. Our fingers wrap around the other's hand, our thumbs side by side, and he holds my eyes, the same memories passing between us.

To anyone else it looks like an arm-wrestling grip, but when we look down, we see our thumbs side by side and the small, pea-size scar we both have and share with only one other person. It's silly when we tell people the story—a friend's little brother's Nerf gun that was too small for our hands, and we got skinned when we tried to use it, all three of us laughing when we realized we had the same exact scar at the heads of our metacarpals.

Now it's just Cole and me. Just the two of us. Two scars, no longer three.

"Stay with me, okay?" he whispers. "I need you."

And for a rare moment, I see vulnerability.

I needed him, too, once, and he was there. We've been through a lot, and he's probably my best friend.

Which is why I'm too forgiving with him. I don't want him to hurt.

And which is why I let him talk me into this. I really don't want to move in with my dad and stepmom, and it's just until the end of the summer. Once my student loans come in for the fall, and I've saved up from working this summer, I can afford my own place again. *I think.*

Cole holds me tight and remains quiet. He knows I'm still mad at him about getting arrested and the damage to the apartment, but he knows I care. I'm starting to wonder if it's one of my faults. Definitely my weakness.

He reaches down and cups my ass, diving into my neck and kissing me. I gasp as he presses himself into me, and I laugh, squirming out of his arms.

"Stop!" I scold in a whisper as I glance nervously to the two-story house behind me. "We don't have privacy anymore."

He smirks. "My dad's still at work, babe. He won't be home until around five."

Oh. Well, that's good at least. I look up and down the neighborhood street, though, seeing house after house, curtains open, and kids playing here and there. It's not like the apartments where everyone sees your business but doesn't really care, because you're transient and won't stick around long enough for anyone to think you're worth their attention. Here, in a real neighborhood, people invest their time in who lives next door.

I take a deep breath, soaking in the smell of grills and the sound of lawn mowers. It's a really nice neighborhood. I wonder if this could be me someday. Will I find a great job? Have a nice house? Will I be happy?

Cole bows his forehead to mine again. "I'm sorry, you know." He doesn't look at me, staring at the ground. "I keep screwing up, and I don't know why. I'm just so restless. I just can't . . ."

But he doesn't finish. He just shakes his head, and I know. I always know.

Cole isn't a loser. He's nineteen. Impulsive, angry, and confused.

But unlike me, he never had to grow up. There's always someone taking care of him.

"You know who you're meant to be," I tell him. "Committing to it is a different process for everyone, but you'll get there."

He raises his eyes, and a moment of hesitance crosses his gaze like he's going to say something, but then it's gone. He flashes his cocky little grin instead. "I don't deserve you," he says, and then he slaps me on the ass.

I jerk, holding in my annoyance as we let go of each other. *No, you don't. But you're cute, and you give good massages.*

We finish unloading the car and make several trips back and forth, carrying everything into the house. I drop off the few groceries I bought earlier in the kitchen and then carry one last box through the living room and up the stairs to our room, first door on the left.

I inhale a deep breath through my nose as I round the doorway into our new bedroom, unable to hide my smile at the smell of fresh paint. From the looks of the house we're moving into, Cole's father is renovating. Although it seems like the bulk of the major work is done. There are gleaming hardwood floors downstairs, matching crown molding in every room, granite countertops in the kitchen, with all new-looking chrome appliances, and the black-and-glass cabinetry kind of makes my heart flutter a little. I have never lived in a place even remotely this nice. For a construction worker, Pike Lawson isn't a bad designer.

It's definitely a nice house. A really nice place, in fact. Not that it's a mansion—just a simple two-story craftsman with a small walk-up porch leading to the front door—but it's redone, beautiful, and well-kept, and the front and back yards are green.

I set the box down and walk to the window, peeking between the blinds. *An actual yard.* Cole's mom's living situation wasn't always great, so it's nice to know he has a clean, safe neighborhood here whenever he needs. I wonder why he always made it seem like he needed someone to take care of him when he had this anytime he wanted. What is up with him and Pike Lawson?

Someday I'm going to have a place like this, too. My father, unfortunately, will die in that trailer I grew up in.

Cole walks in, swinging a couple suitcases onto the bed, and immediately leaves again, digging out his phone on his way out.

"Do you think your dad will mind if I use the kitchen?" I call, following him out of the room. "I got stuff to make burgers."

He keeps walking, but I hear his breathy laugh. "I can't imagine any guy, even my dad, is going to say a woman can't use his kitchen to make him a meal, babe."

Yeah, right. I shoot a look at his back as he takes a right into the living room and heads outside. I keep going straight, into the kitchen.

I used to like doing things for Cole. Being there for him better than my mother was for my father. Keeping a clean house—or apartment—and seeing him smile when I made his life a little bit easier or made sure he had what he needed. It's gotten one-sided over the past few months, though.

His father is doing a lot for us, though, and cooking a few nights a week is part of the arrangement, so I have no problem keeping my end of the deal. Well, *our* end of the deal, but Cole isn't going to cook, so I'll leave the yard work to him, which his father also stipulated was his responsibility to keep up.

Pike Lawson. I've had to make an effort to not think about the theater the other night. It's still hard to wrap my head around the randomness of the whole situation.

I keep thinking about the matchstick in the donut and the pep talk he gave me about going after what I want. Part of me, though, feels like he was saying those things to himself, too. Experience and maybe a little disappointment laced his tone, and I want to know more about him. Like what he was like as a young father.

And so I thought he was cute. So what? I think Chris Hemsworth is cute. And Ryan Gosling, Tom Hardy, Henry Cavill, Jason Momoa, the Winchester brothers . . . It's not like I had sexual thoughts, for crying out loud. It doesn't have to be awkward.

It can't be. I'm with his son.

Walking over to one of the chairs at the kitchen table, I dig my phone out of my bag and start my music app, "Jessie's Girl" immediately playing where it left off after my run this morning. I do a scan of the kitchen, as well as a quick peek back into the living room, making sure none of our things are lying around. I don't want his dad inconvenienced any more than he already is.

I walk to the fridge, running my hand over the island countertop as I pass by. While the other counters are a tan granite with accents of black, the island top is made of butcher block. The smooth wood is warm under my fingertips, and I don't feel any grooves from carving. The whole kitchen looks recently redone, so maybe he hasn't used the cutting board much. Or maybe he isn't a big cook.

A practical, bronze metal light fixture hangs over the island, and I do a little twirl before reaching the refrigerator, laughing under my breath. It's nice to be able to move without bumping into something. The only thing this kitchen needs that would make me go from an impressed nod to fanning myself in heat would be some backsplash. Backsplash is hot.

Reaching into the refrigerator, I pull out the ground beef, butter, and mozzarella, kicking the door closed as I turn around and set everything on the island. I pick up the two onions I left on the counter before and bob my head to the music, sliding and swaying, as I grab a butcher knife from the block and start chopping both into thin slices to make fried onion rings.

The music in my ears builds, the hair on my arms rises, and I feel a burst of energy in my legs, because I want to dance, but I won't let myself. I hope Pike Lawson is okay with eighties music in his house from time to time. He didn't say he didn't like it in the theater, but he also didn't bank on us living with him.

I stick to lip-syncing and head banging while I form five large patties with my hands and start to add them to a clean pan, already heated and layered with melted butter.

My hips are rolling from side to side when I feel a tickle making its way around my waist. I jump, my heart leaping into my chest as a gasp lodges in my throat.

Spinning around, I see my sister behind me. "Cam!" I whine.

"Gotcha," she teases, grinning from ear to ear and jabbing me in the ribs again.

I pause the music on my phone. "How'd you get in? I didn't hear the bell."

She walks back around the island and sits on a stool, resting her elbows on the butcher block and picking up an onion ring. "I passed Cole outside," she explains. "He told me to just come in."

I arch my neck, peering out of the window and seeing him and a couple of his friends circle my grandma's old VW, which Cole's dad paid to have towed here since it doesn't run right now. I couldn't leave it at the apartment, and Cole looks like he's finally making good on his promise to fix it so I can have a car.

The sizzle of the meat frying in the pan hits my ears, and I turn around, flipping the burgers. A speckle of grease hits my forearm, and I wince at the sting.

I know Cam's here to check up on me. Old habits and that.

My sister is only four years older, but she was the mom our mom didn't stick around to be. I stayed in that trailer park until I graduated from high school, but Cam left when she was sixteen and has been on her own ever since. Just her and her son.

I glance at the clock, seeing it is just after five. My nephew must be with the sitter by now, and she must be on her way to work.

"So, where's the father?" she asks me.

"Still at work, I suppose."

He'll be home soon, though. I transfer the burgers from the pan to the plate and take out the buns, opening up the package.

"Is he nice?" she finally asks, sounding hesitant.

I have my back turned to her, so she can't see my annoyance. My sister is a woman who doesn't mince words. The fact that she's guarding her tone says she's probably having thoughts I don't want to hear. Like why the hell am I not just taking the higher-paying job her boss offered me last fall, so I can stay in my apartment?

"He seems nice." I nod, casting her a glance. "Kind of quiet, I think."

"You're quiet."

I shoot her a smirk, correcting her. "I'm serious. There's a difference."

She snickers and sits up straight, pulling down the hem of her white tank top, the red lace bra underneath very well visible. "Someone had to be serious in our house, I guess."

"In our house" growing up, she means.

She flips her brown hair behind her shoulder, and I see the long silver earrings she wears that match her glittery makeup, smoky eyes, and shiny lips.

"How's Killian?" I ask, remembering my nephew.

"A brat, as usual," she says. But then she stops like she remembers something. "No, wait. Today he told me that he tells his friends I'm his big sister when I come to get him from day care." She scoffs. "The little shit is embarrassed by me. But still, I was like, 'Whoa, people actually believe that?'" And then she flips her hair again, putting on a show. "I mean, I still look good, don't I?"

"You're only twenty-three." I top the burger with shredded mozzarella, add another patty, and top that, as well. "Of course you do."

"Mm-hmm." She snaps her fingers. "Gotta make that money while I can."

I meet her eyes, and it's only for a moment, but it's long enough to see the falter in her humor. The way her bemused smile looks like an apology and how she blinks, filling the silence as her awkward words hang in the air.

And how she pulls the hem of her top down to cover as much of her stomach as she can in the presence of her little sister.

My sister hates what she does for a living, but she likes the money more.

She finally turns her attention back to me, her tone sounding almost accusing. "So, what are you doing, by the way?"

"Making dinner."

She shakes her head, rolling her eyes. "So not only do you *not* cut loose the male you're with, but now you're waiting hand and foot on another one?"

I place a couple onion rings on the first double cheeseburger and top it with a bun. "I am not."

"Yes, you are."

I glare at her. "We're staying here—in this fabulous neighborhood, mind you—rent-free. The least I can do is make sure we keep our end of the bargain. We clean up and share some of the cooking duties. That's all."

Her right eyebrow arches sternly, and she crosses her arms over her chest, not buying it. Oh, for crying out loud. I actually think we're making out better in this bargain than Pike Lawson, after all. Central air, cable and Wi-Fi, a walk-in closet . . .

I reach over the counter and pull the blinds up, barking to get her off my back, "He has a pool, Cam! I mean, come on."

Her eyes go wide. "No shit?"

She pops out of her chair and scurries over, peering into the backyard. The pool is perfect. It's shaped like an hourglass, the multicolored tiles on the deck are Mediterranean-style, and it has a walk-in entry with a mosaic floor. Cole's dad must still be working on it, because there's a display on the far end of the pool with flowerless flower beds and spouts for mini waterfalls that aren't yet running. There's a table and chairs placed haphazardly around the perimeter, and the rest of the grassy backyard has various lawn furniture not yet set up in any discernable way. A table umbrella lies to the right, next to the hose, and a barbecue grill sits covered with a tarp to the left.

My sister nods approvingly. "This is nice. You were always meant to live in a house like this."

"Who isn't?" I shoot back. Everyone should be so lucky.

Although it still feels wrong being here. I care a lot about Cole, though, and I'd rather be with him than at my dad's.

I finish up the burgers, while she turns around, gripping the counter at her sides, and stares at me. "You sure all he wants is a little cleaning and cooking?" she presses. "Men, no matter the age, are all the same. I should know."

Yeah, you can shut up now. I can take care of myself. If high school boyfriends and working in a bar haven't taught me that by now . . .

But she speaks up again, moving into my space and stopping me. "Just listen to me for a second." Her tone turns firm. "It's a nice house, a safe neighborhood, and yes, you can save up a little money. But you don't have to stay here."

"It's not Dad and Corinne's, so there's that," I argue back. "And I can't stay with you. I appreciate the offer, but I can't be on the couch in everyone's way and be able to study with a four-year-old trying to be a kid in his own house."

I have a summer class on Thursdays, so I need some space to work.

"That's not what I meant," she quickly retorts. "You could've stayed in that apartment. You could've afforded it."

I open my mouth but shut it again, turning around to slip the burgers into the oven for a few minutes.

Not this again. When is she going to give it up?

"I can't, okay?" I tell her. "I don't want to. I like my job, and I don't want to work where you work."

"Of course you don't." She gives me a bored look. "It's beneath you, right?"

"That's not what I said."

I don't think less of my sister because of her job. She feeds and clothes her kid. She swallowed her pride and did what she had to do, and I love her for it. But—and I would never say this to her face—it's not a career she would've picked for herself if she'd had other choices.

And I'm not out of choices yet.

Cam has been dancing at The Hook since she was eighteen. At first, it was just a temporary job to get through her boyfriend leaving her and to support their son. But juggling college and her child became too much, and eventually she quit school. It was the plan to get back on track once Killian started kindergarten, but that'll be soon, and I don't think she has immediate plans to quit anytime soon. She's gotten used to the money.

Nearly a year ago, her boss offered me a job bartending there, and she's been on my ass to take it ever since. I could make more than enough to support myself, after all, and maybe not have to take out so many student loans, either. *A few years and that's it*, she'd said. I'd be out.

But I know bartending is just the job her boss gets girls to take while he works them over to get them to start dancing onstage.

And I'm not doing that. I'm not watching my sister do that every night, either.

My body is private. It's personal to me and whom I want to show it to. I'll stay at Grounders, thank you.

"I'm fine where I am," I tell her. "I got this."

She sighs. "All right," she says, giving up for now. "Just be prepared if this doesn't work out, okay?"

This, meaning Cole and me living in his father's house.

I move around her to pull some lemonade out of the fridge and suddenly hear the low rumble of an engine growing closer. I stop, peering toward the window, and see the corner of a black truck pull into the driveway. The same '71 Chevy Cheyenne I rode in after the movie the other night to get Cole at the police station.

My heart thumps in my chest, but I ignore it and quickly close the fridge.

"His father's home," I tell her, grabbing her purse from the counter and shoving it at her. "You need to go."

"Why?"

"Because this isn't my house," I bite out, pushing her toward the laundry room and the back door. "At least let me wait a week before I impose on his space with all my friends."

"I'm your sister."

I hear a car door slam.

I keep pushing her out toward the back, but she's digging in her heels. "And you better keep me posted," she says. "I'm not letting *you* let some beer-bellied, middle-aged pervert who was only too happy to let a hot pair of teenage thighs move into his house start demanding a little extra from his new tenant."

"Shut up." But I can't help laughing a little.

Yeah, he's not beer-bellied, middle-aged, or a pervert. I don't think, anyway.

She turns around, jabbing me in the stomach playfully and lowering her voice to a deep, husky tone. "Come on, honey." She squirms up to me, trying to wrap her arms around me seductively. "Time to work off your rent, baby."

"Shut up!" I whisper-yell, laughing and trying to nudge her out of the kitchen. "God, you're embarrassing. Get out!"

"Don't be scared," she continues, pretending she's some creepy old guy as she slobbers up her lips and tries to get a kiss from me. "Little girls take care of their daddies."

And she mock thrusts into me, jutting out what beer belly she can muster with her twenty-two-inch waist.

"Stop it!" I plead, flaming with embarrassment.

She paws me up and down my hips, smiling as I try to shove her out of the kitchen.

But then she stops suddenly, her face falling and her eyes focused on something—or someone—behind me.

I close my eyes for a moment. *Great.*

Turning around, I see Cole's father standing in the entryway between the living room and the kitchen, paused and staring at us. Heat rises up my neck at the sight of him again.

I hear my sister suck in a breath, and I move away from her, clearing my throat. I don't think he heard anything. At least, I hope not.

His eyes dart between us and finally come to rest on me. His short hair is just a little messy, and I can see the sweat from his workday still dampening the sides, and the five-o'clock shadow coming in across his jaw. Black marks scuff his forearms, and the tendons in his tanned hands flex as he grips his tool belt and lunch container.

He inhales a deep breath and moves forward, setting his things on the island. "All moved in?" he asks me, running a hand through his hair.

I nod. "Yeah," I blurt out. "I mean, yes."

My heart is doing that thing again where it feels like it's riding on ocean waves inside my chest, and I can't remember what I'm supposed to be doing. So I just nod again, blinking until my sister comes into view at my side and I finally remember what's going on.

"Pike. Mr. Lawson," I correct myself. "Sorry. This is my sister, Cam." I gesture to her. "And she was just leaving."

He glances over at her. "Hi."

And then to my surprise, his gaze moves back to me for a moment before he sees the mail on the counter and begins flipping through it like we're not even here.

I blink, slightly confused.

Cam's a carnival ride. She might be younger than him, but she's certainly a woman, and most men let their eyes linger on her, her long legs, and the perky and expensive handfuls she has under that tank top. He doesn't.

"Yeah, nice to meet you," she says back. "Thanks for taking her in."

He spares us a quick glance and a half smile before grabbing all the envelopes and stuffing them in a mail holder.

Cam starts to walk out of the kitchen, and I follow her as she enters the laundry room.

Once she's out of his line of sight, she spins around, mouthing to me, "Oh, my God," with a mischievous gleam in her wide eyes.

I clench my jaw, jerking my chin to keep her moving. She's going to be over here every other day flirting with him now.

I hear Pike behind me, opening one of the ovens, and I turn around.

"I was making dinner," I tell him. "For the three of us. Is that okay?"

He closes the oven, and I see a hint of relief on his face. "Yeah, that's great, actually." He sighs. "Thank you. I'm starving."

"It'll just be fifteen more minutes."

He reaches into the refrigerator and takes out a Corona, sticking the cap under an opener nailed under the island that pulls the top off, the cap dropping into the trash. "Enough time for a shower," he replies, glancing down at us. "Excuse me."

And then he walks out of the kitchen, the bottle hanging from his fingers as he clears the entryway by only half a foot. I pause as it hits me again how tall he is. This is a good-size house, too, but it will be impossible to not notice him in a room.

"Now I get it," my sister whispers tauntingly in my ear. "And here I was, worried you'd be suffering unwanted advances from a sweaty old fat fart."

"Shut up." I close my eyes in exasperation.

I hear the back door open and humor laces her voice as she teases, "You take care of your *men*, now."

I whirl around to slam the door closed in her face, but she squeals, pulling it shut before I have a chance.

"Oh, I don't like onions."

I stop at Pike's words and stare down at the barbecue sauce drizzled all over my onion-ring-stacked masterpieces. They're an Instagram post just waiting to happen. If I take off the beautiful golden onions it'll just be a Pinterest fail.

"Try a bite?" I venture with a timid smile. "You'll like this. I promise."

In my experience, men will eat what's in front of them.

He seems to think about it for a moment and then closes the fridge and meets my gaze. His expression softens. "Okay."

He probably feels like he owes me a bite, since I made dinner, so I'll take it. Topping the burger, I hand him the plate and he carries it over to a stool, taking a bite before he even sits down. I spare a glance over my shoulder. His jaw stops moving and he blinks a few times, the muscles in his cheeks flexing. And then I hear a groan.

I turn back around to the stove so he can't see my smile.

"That's good, actually," he says. "Really good."

I just nod, but I feel a small pinch of pride.

"When you eat cheap growing up," I tell him, "you find your own ways of adding a little gourmet to it."

He doesn't say anything for a few seconds but follows with a quiet "Yeah."

I'm not sure if that means he's just listening attentively or agreeing with me. If he's found out my last name, he must know who my father is. Everyone in town knows Chip Hadley, so he would have an idea of how we lived.

I don't know much about Cole's family, though, or if they've always lived in this town. Pike Lawson isn't wealthy, but he's certainly not poor, by the looks of his house.

"It's really good. I mean it," he says again.

"Thanks." I turn around and place a plate on the island perpendicular to his seat for Cole, and my own at the stool next to that one.

We fall silent, and I wonder if he feels weird, too. We talked so easily the other night when we didn't know who the other one was, but it's changed now.

I hear movement from the living room and glance around to see Cole coming into the kitchen. I smile. He has grease all over his shirt already and a streak under his lip. He can misbehave like it's his job, but he can also flaunt some boyish charm like nobody's business.

He grabs the hamburger off his plate in one hand and tucks some dirty, rusted car part under his arm, tipping his chin at me. "Hey, babe. We're working on your VW. You don't mind if I eat outside, do you?"

I stare at him.

Is he serious? I shoot my eyes between him and his father. "Yes," I reply quietly, trying to say more with my eyes. I don't want to eat alone with his dad.

"Come on." Cole cocks his head, trying to work me with his playful expression. "I can't just leave them out there. You could come and sit outside with us."

Gee, thanks. I purse my lips and turn back to the refrigerator, yanking out the pitcher of lemonade. It's rude to just leave. His father's not our meal ticket. I should make some effort to get to know him.

But before I can tell Cole to just go and eat outside, his father speaks up. "Why don't you sit down for ten minutes? I haven't seen you in a while."

Relief hits me, and I'm thankful for the backup. I finally hear Cole release a breath and the legs of one of the island stools scrape across the tile as he takes a seat in front of his plate.

I make sure the oven is off, grab my drink, and follow Cole's father as he sits down, leaving the seat between him and Cole empty. I take it, reaching over the island and pulling my plate to me.

"So, how's work?" Mr. Lawson asks, and I assume he's talking to Cole.

Cole's right hand finds my thigh as he uses his left to lift the burger to his mouth, and I glance at his father, seeing his eyes downcast and looking at Cole's hand on me. His jaw flexes as he looks back up.

"It's work." Cole shrugs. "It's a lot easier now that the weather has warmed up, though."

Cole's been doing road construction since we moved in together about nine months ago. He's gone through a lot of jobs since I've known him, but this one has lasted.

"Thinking any more about college?" his dad probes.

But Cole just scoffs. "It took everything I had to finish high school. You know that."

I raise the lemonade to my lips and take a sip, my stomach tight and not wanting food at the moment. Cole's father chews and sets his burger down, lifting his bottle next.

"Time moves a lot faster than you think it will," he replies quietly, almost to himself. "I almost joined the Navy when I found out . . ." But he trails off, finishing instead, "When I was eighteen."

But I think I know what he was going to say. *When I found out I was going to be a dad.* Pike Lawson doesn't look old enough to be the father of a grown son, so he had to have been pretty young when Cole was born. No more than eighteen or nineteen himself. Which would put him at thirty-eight? Give or take?

"I just couldn't wrap my head around the fact that I was giving up several years of my life to the military," he goes on. "But those years came and went pretty fast. Securing a good future takes an investment and a commitment, Cole, but it's worth it."

"Was it for you?" his son shoots back, tearing off a bite of burger, his hand lightly squeezing the inside of my thigh. It's a subtle gesture I actually love despite the building tension in the room. It's his way of letting me know he might be angry, but he's not angry with me, and he hates that I'm probably uncomfortable right now.

Cole's father takes a drink from his bottle and calmly sets it back down, his tone now harder. "Well, I've had the money to bail you out of jail," he points out. "Last time. And the time before that."

Cole's hand tightens around my thigh, and my neck is so hot all of a sudden that I wish I had a hair tie. A thousand questions whirl around my head. Why don't they get along? What happened? Cole's dad seems okay, from what little I know about him, but Cole has erected a wall between them, and his dad has almost as short a fuse as his son.

Cheeseburger in hand, Cole shoves his plate away from him and pushes his chair back, standing up. "I'm eating outside," he says, releasing my leg. "Come join us if you want, babe. And leave the dishes. I'll do them in a bit."

I open my mouth to speak but stop myself, clenching my teeth instead. Well, this is going to be fun.

Cole turns and walks out of the room, and moments later I hear the front door slam shut. Muffled voices carry in from outside, and a horn honks down the street, but it's suddenly so quiet in the kitchen that I stop breathing. Hopefully Pike Lawson will forget I'm here.

How the hell am I supposed to live here? I can't take sides if they're going to do this.

But Pike speaks up, softening his voice. "It's okay," he says, and I see him turn his head toward me out of the corner of my eye. "You can join him if you want."

I turn my head, meet his eyes, and fix him with a close-lipped smile as I shrug. "It's hot out," I tell him.

I'm already burning up with the tension in here.

Besides, Cole's friends aren't my friends, and outside won't be any better.

"I'm sorry about that," he says, picking up his burger again. "It won't happen a lot. Cole's good about avoiding anywhere I am."

I nod, not knowing what else to say. I have a gut feeling I won't be here long anyway. I already feel like I'm on a tightrope.

I force myself to eat, because this won't taste this good as left-overs tomorrow. Music drifts in from outside, the rumble of a lawn mower sparks to life in the distance, and the scent of grass hits the back of my throat as it wafts through the open windows, the simple tan curtains of Pike's house billowing in the breeze coming in. Chills spread down my arms.

Summer.

A phone rings, and I see Pike reach over and grab his cell off the counter. "Hey," he says.

A man's voice grumbles on the other end, but I can't hear what he's saying.

Pike gets up, carrying his plate to the sink with one hand and holding the phone with the other, and I steal glances while he's distracted. Cam's teasing about him keeps coming back to me, warming my cheeks, but it's not like that.

Pike's kind of a mystery.

I saw pictures of Cole in the living room—as a baby and as a kid—but other than that, the house doesn't have a lot of his father in it. I know he's a single guy, but there are no coffee table books displaying his interests, no souvenirs from vacations, no pets, no art, no knickknacks, no magazines, no paraphernalia indicating his hobbies, like sports, gaming, or music. . . . It's a beautiful home, but it's like a showcase house where a family doesn't really live.

"No, I need another digger and at least a hundred more bags of cement," he tells the guy, tucking the phone between his shoulder and ear and pulling his sleeves up more as he turns on the water.

I smile to myself. He's doing the dishes. Without being asked? I heave a sigh and rise from my seat. I guess he normally does live alone, after all. Who else would do them?

He chuckles at something the guy says and shakes his head as I scrape off my plate into the garbage.

"Tell that idiot I know he's not sick," he says into the phone, "and if he doesn't get off whomever he's on by morning, I'll come and get him myself. I want to stay ahead of schedule."

I come up beside him and quietly set my dishes down on the counter before putting the lemonade and condiments back in the fridge.

"Yeah, yeah . . ." I hear him say as he rinses off plates and puts them in the dishwasher. "Okay, I'll see you in the morning."

He hangs up and puts the phone down, and I cast another quick glance at him. "Work?" I inquire.

He nods, swishing water in a glass and dumping it out. "Always. We're putting up an office building off 22 right before you reach the state park." He looks at me. "No matter how much you plan and budget, there are always surprises that try to throw you off track, you know?"

Highway 22. Same road I take to get out to classes at Doral. I must've passed his worksite lots of times.

"Nothing ever goes according to plan," I muse. "Even at my age, I know that by now."

He laughs, the corners of his mouth turning up in a grin as he looks over at me. "Exactly."

I suddenly falter, déjà vu hitting me. For a moment, I see the guy in the theater again.

I blink, trying to look away. His hazel eyes look greener under the light fixture hanging overhead, his hair has dried from his shower, and all of a sudden he looks more like Cole's older brother than his dad. I tear my eyes away from his smile, just catching a glimpse of the cords in his arm that are flexing as he works in the sink.

I snatch up my phone off the counter and turn to leave, but then remember something.

"May I have your phone number?" I twist back around and ask. "Like in case there's a problem here or I lose my key or something?"

He looks at me over his shoulder, his hands still in the water. "Oh, right." He shuts off the faucet and grabs a towel, drying himself. "Good idea. Here."

He grabs his phone and unlocks the screen, handing it to me. "Put yours in mine, too, then."

I give him my phone and take his, entering in my first name and my cell number. I'm glad I remembered, actually. Anything could go wrong with the house. The basement could flood, packages could be delivered that aren't mine, I might not be able to handle dinner on one of Cole's and my nights and need to alert him. . . . This isn't my place, where I get to make all the decisions, anymore.

I give his back, and he hands me mine, but music starts playing from mine, and he does a double take at my screen. My music app must've been up and he accidentally hit something.

Shit.

George Michael's "Father Figure" starts playing, and his eyebrows shoot up as the suggestive chorus starts.

My mouth goes dry, the lyrics registering.

I snatch the phone back and turn it off.

He breathes out a laugh.

Awesome.

Then he straightens, clearing his throat. "Eighties music, huh?"

I run my fingers through my hair, sliding the phone into my back pocket. "Yeah, I wasn't kidding."

After a moment, I look back up and see him staring at me, the hint of a smile in his eyes.

His gaze flashes to the side, and he bends over, picking up one of the home-and-garden magazines I didn't realize had dropped from my bag at the kitchen table.

"And it's Pike," he says, handing me the magazine. "Not Mr. Lawson, okay?"

He's standing so close, and my stomach flips. I take the magazine and nod, unable to meet his eyes.

He turns back to his task, and I start to walk away but stop and look back at him.

"You don't have to do that, you know?" I tell him, referring to the dishes. "Cole said he would."

I see his body shake with a laugh, and then he bends down to drop some silverware into the dishwasher before glancing over at me. "I was nineteen once, too," he replies. "'In a bit' means eventually, and eventually doesn't mean tonight."

I snort, my shoulders easing a little. *True.*

I don't know how many times I woke up the next morning to a sink full of dishes. Of course, it wouldn't make me happier with Cole if his father was carrying his weight with the chores, but I brush it off as "not my problem."

As long as I don't have to do it.

"Thank you," I say, quickly darting over to the fridge for a bottle of water to take with me.

But then a thought occurs to me.

"Do you have any other kids?" I ask. I guess I need to know if there will be other people coming in or out of the house.

But when I look over I see his jaw tense and his brow furrowed, looking a little too serious.

"I think Cole would tell you if he had siblings, wouldn't he?"

Against my will, my spine instantly straightens. His tone is chastising. Of course Cole would tell me if he had siblings. I've known him for long enough.

"Right," I reply in a rush, shaking my head like I was in a fog and that was why I asked such a dumb question.

"Besides, I've never been married," he adds, his Adam's apple moving up and down. "Having multiple kids from multiple women wasn't a mistake I wanted to make."

I remain still, watching him and kind of feeling bad. Cole was completely unplanned and, even to a small degree, unwanted by his teenage parents. Some of the mystery of their poor relationship starts to come into focus.

But I also appreciate his pragmatism. It didn't take a young Pike Lawson long to learn that making babies with just anyone wasn't what was right for him. That was a consequence I never wanted to experience, not even once.

He seems to realize what he said and how it probably sounded, because he stops and looks over at me, thinning his eyes in an apology. "I didn't mean it . . . like that. I—"

"I know what you meant. It's okay."

I jerk my thumb behind me and back away. "I'm going to go study. I'm taking a few credits this summer, so . . . night."

He turns back, loading the dishwasher with soap and starting the machine.

"Thank you again for letting us stay here," I say.

He glances at me. "Thank you for dinner."

And before I leave, I step over to the table where I left a scented candle burning. I should've asked him about that. He might not like frilly scents in his house.

Leaning over the table, I close my eyes, take in a breath, and make my usual wish: *Let tomorrow be better than today.* And I blow, almost instantly smelling the pungent stream of smoke curling into the air from the extinguished wick.

It's always the same wish. Every candle. Every time. I want a life I never want to take a vacation from. That's my goal.

Except for the match I blew out at the theater. I made a different wish that night.

When I open my eyes, I see Pike watching me. He quickly straightens and turns away.

And as I leave the kitchen and head toward the stairs in the living room, I drop my magazine on the end table next to the couch.

Now someone lives here.

3

Pike

I blink awake, my eyelids heavy and slow as the dim room comes into view.

It's still dark. I don't normally wake up before five thirty. *Why am I . . .*

No, wait. I grunt, opening my eyes a little wider and noticing the faint glow dancing across my bedroom wall.

Raindrops. Ah, shit. It's not dark out. It's cloudy.

I turn over onto my back and squint at the ceiling as I wait a moment and listen. And then, almost immediately, I hear it. The pitter-patter of little dings bouncing off the rain gutters outside.

I let out a sigh. *Goddammit.* Not good. I dig my palms into my eyes and rub away the sleep before I glance at the clock on my bedside table. Five twenty-nine.

Yep. Like clockwork.

I stopped needing an alarm clock years ago, my body just getting used to waking up at the same time every day. I still set it, though, just in case. Reaching over, I feel for the switch on the side and nudge it over two spots, turning off the alarm before it goes off.

The rain could really set us back today. I don't need to be at the site for another hour and a half, but half the guys will probably try to call in, thinking we won't be able to put in a full day anyway, so may as well stay in bed.

Not gonna happen, though. We're working on something today—anything—because I don't feel like sidestepping my kid's bad mood and foul looks all day if I stick around this house. I'd rather be at work.

When he was younger, it was different. He was mine. We did things together and talked and he wanted to be around me, but now . . .

She's gotten to him. My kid is the only hold anyone could ever have over me, and man, his mother knew how to use that. She pushed him around like a chess piece until he believed everything that came out of her mouth and that she was the victim in every situation, and I was the enemy. She could do no wrong, and I could do no right.

After a while, I just decided to be there for him. Eventually he'll wise up, and we'll get through this. He'll see through her lies, and I just need to hang on. No matter the patience it's going to take or the arguments in the meantime.

At least Jordan is pretty great. She'll be a welcome buffer between us.

Even if I was knocked on my ass when I found out who she was.

I close my eyes, resting the back of my hand over them and thinking back to that night.

I had fun hanging out with her at the movie theater. Her comebacks, her humor, how easy it was to talk to her . . . The way she just relaxed next to me during the movie, and it was so fucking comfortable and natural.

The way her smile felt on me . . .

I wouldn't have asked her out. She's way too young, and I knew she had a boyfriend.

But it was hard not to entertain the idea for a little while. She's cool.

And then when I found out who she was, I was almost angry.

I remember hearing her on that phone call and clenching my teeth so hard my jaw ached as realization hit. I was angry, because in that moment, I was jealous of my son. I was jealous of any guy who's nineteen and gets a chance to be with her.

Her flawless skin and pert nose. Her gorgeous bottom lip, which I think she caught me staring at.

The way she tipped her head back, put her feet up, and could just be next to me.

Everything felt easy.

But the girl of my dreams is off-limits. She's Cole's, and she's nineteen. There's no way.

She's a kid, and my brief, sordid thoughts will stay hidden in my head.

My phone vibrates on the nightstand, and I reach over and grab it, looking at the screen.

And I groan. *Not now.*

But I swipe the green button anyway and close my eyes, holding the phone to my ear. "A little early for you, isn't it?"

Lindsay, my ex, laughs softly, the sultry sound of her sexy voice well honed by now. The woman is used to getting what she wants from anyone.

Almost anyone.

"Not when you haven't been to bed," she taunts.

I keep my snicker to myself. Some women who become young mothers later feel as if they've missed out on their youth by jumping into parenthood so early. Lindsay Kenmont, mother of my child, didn't miss a damn thing. She didn't let being nine months pregnant hold her back any more than she let Cole hold her back when he was a toddler.

"How is he?" she asks.

I throw off my covers and sit up, swinging my legs over the bed and yawning. "Warm, fed, and safe." I rub my hand over my scalp.

"That's about all I know right now." But then I add, "I'm surprised you're okay with this, by the way."

"So that's why you offered to let them stay with you? Because you didn't think it would actually happen?" she presses. "I'm fine with him staying with you. It's about time you took on some responsibility with him."

It's about time I . . . Jesus. I laugh under my breath and shake my head, standing up. "You're not how I like to start my day, Lindsay. You know that. Now, what do you want?"

She's quiet for a moment, and then I hear her smooth voice return to its teasing tone. "Oh, you know what I want."

And despite the disdain I feel for her now, blood still rushes to my groin, much to my displeasure. We had some fun, after all. Back in the day.

And my body remembers.

Plus, I haven't been laid in a while.

But I'm not desperate enough to be used. Not yet, anyway.

"So that's it?" I tuck my phone between my shoulder and ear as I pull my jeans off the bench at the end of the bed and slide my legs in. "You think I'm going to just be ready to go every time you break up with a guy, get drunk, and want to get laid?"

"Why not?" she shoots back. "No matter who comes into your life or walks out of mine, there was always one thing we did really well together, right?"

"Sure, Lindsay." I don't bother hiding the sarcasm from my tone.

"Well, you're not seeing anyone, are you?" she inquires, but she already knows I'm not. "And it's not like we haven't jumped into bed together over the years to blow off a little steam from time to time. I don't remember you ever not liking it."

"Yeah." I let out a hard sigh. "It's called a lack of options. Small town and all?"

"Asshole."

I chuckle despite myself. I have to hand it to her. The woman can roll with any insult.

The truth is, she's right. After the breakup when Cole was two, we still hooked up from time to time, but what I said is true, as well. The sex was good, she still has a great body, and bed was the one place we never hated each other, but I only kept going back because it was easy. Every other woman in this town is someone's sister or daughter, and you can't just screw around with them without them expecting a ring at some point. And I wasn't ready for that. Not after the mess I found myself in becoming a father at nineteen. If I ever get another woman pregnant, it'll be my wife, and my wife is going to be someone I can't get enough of.

And I do want more kids. I've always wanted more. But since I'm thirty-eight—two years shy of forty—it's likely Cole will be my only kid now. I'm getting too old to start over again.

"Come on," she prods. "What have you got to lose? I know you remember, and I know you like everything you remember, Pike. That summer when I was seventeen? Still the best memories of my life."

Yeah, but not everything that came after it.

"You and me going at it under a blanket on the couch with my parents sleeping right upstairs?" she tells me as if I don't remember. "I know you still have a very healthy appetite."

Heat rises to my skin, and I pause.

"So get over here and fuck me, then," she says.

I hesitate for only a moment, but then I shake my head. It's tempting. My body wants it. And if I only admit it to myself, I am kind of fucking lonely when I slow down long enough to let myself feel it. There are so many mornings I hate waking up alone.

But no. My pride is sick of taking a hit every time she thinks I'll be ready to go at her beck and call.

"Gotta get to work." I hang up the phone before I have a chance to think about it more or, worse, reconsider. I slide my cell into my back pocket and walk over to the dresser for a T-shirt. My phone buzzes again.

"She's fucking relentless," I grumble and pull it back out of my pocket.

But this time, I see Dutch's name on the screen.

I answer it, holding it to my ear. "What?"

"It's raining."

"Really? No shit?" I chuckle, pulling my shirt over my head. "You're a genius."

"Look outside."

I pause, every muscle instantly tightening. *Dammit.* By his tone, I know what I'm going to see, but I walk to the window anyway and pull open one of the curtains, peering out into the morning storm.

"Shit."

The street outside is lined on both sides with rapids of rainwater, all racing for the storm drains, the whitewash crashing into the curb before sinking into the sewers. The street itself is an orchestra of white noise, the drops bouncing off the ground or pummeling hoods of cars, the rain so thick I can barely see the houses across from me.

"I'm meeting the guys over at the shop," Dutch tells me. "We'll load up tarps and sandbags and meet you at the site."

"I'll be there in twenty," I say, and we both hang up.

Grabbing some socks out of my drawer, I slip my phone back into my pocket and walk into the bathroom, doing a quick sweep with the toothbrush before I leave the room. I walk down the hall, past the empty bedroom, the main bathroom, and then a closed door, the other spare bedroom, quickly remembering it's no longer empty.

But as I hit the top of the stairs, a sweet and heady scent hits my nose, making my skin buzz, and I stop to breathe in. A slight hunger pang hits my stomach, and I flinch. The girl blew out a candle yesterday. Did she leave another one burning all night? We might have to have a talk. Not only is that unsafe, but I'm really not into this whole aromatherapy thing where your body is tricked into thinking there's blueberry muffins in the house when there's really not.

I head down the staircase, the house creaking under my weight, but when I reach the bottom, I look around, noticing the living room lamps are on and there's soft music coming from the kitchen.

Stepping in, I spot Jordan sitting at the island in the dark. Her laptop is open in front of her as she warms her hands around a cup of coffee.

I hesitate for a split second, taken aback by how different she looks at the moment. The light from the screen makes her eyes glimmer as the steam rises from the mug in front of her face. Then she purses her lips and blows, trying to cool the drink, while strands of her blond hair fall around her face from the messy bun piled on top of her head.

The narrow slope of her jaw, the long lashes, the soft point of her little nose, and . . . My eyes drop before I can stop them, and I take in her flawless smooth and tanned legs, visible because she's still wearing her sleep shorts. Heat stirs low in my stomach, and I turn away, digging in my eyebrows.

They can't be the same age. My kid is a kid, and she's . . .

A kid, too, I guess.

It's just weird. Last time I met one of his girlfriends, the chick had braces. It's off-putting to think of him dating girls now that were my type back in the day.

"Morning," I say as I walk past her to the Keurig.

I see her pop her head up out of the corner of my eye. "Oh, hey. Morning."

Her voice is small and cracked, and I hear the laptop close as I stick a K-cup in the machine and a metal travel mug under the spout. I look over my shoulder to see her quietly sliding off the stool and gathering up her computer and notebook.

"You don't have to leave," I tell her. "I'm on my way out anyway."

She gives a small, tight smile but doesn't look at me as she tucks her things to her side and picks up her coffee again.

"Have you been up a while?" I ask.

"I'm a light sleeper." She finally raises her eyes and laughs at herself. "Thunderstorms are hard for me."

I nod, understanding. The heat is the same way for me. The AC needs to be set at sixty-five degrees every night for me to be able to sleep. It's on the tip of my tongue to ask her if the temperature bothered her last night, but there's really no point. I need to sleep, I'm not changing it, and she knows where the extra blankets are if she needs some.

We stand in silence for a moment, and then she finally blinks and gestures to the stove behind me. "There's, um . . . blueberry muffins if you're hungry," she says. "They're just out of a box, but they're pretty good."

I twist my head around, and sure enough, a muffin pan I don't own sits on top of the stove, each cup overflowing with a golden-baked muffin. I reach over and grab one, hiding my smile. So, no scented candles raising false hopes, after all. I think I like her.

She turns around and starts to leave the room, but I call out. "Do you think you could wake Cole up real quick, please? The rain really screws with my timetable at work, and we're still setting the foundations, so I need help sandbagging today."

She looks at me over her shoulder, curious. "Foundations?"

"For the site I've been contracted to build," I clarify. "We can't work today with the weather, but we have to make sure the basement level doesn't flood. I could use Cole's help."

Realization hits and the confusion on her face vanishes. "Oh, right. Sure." She nods and quickly leaves the room, her footfalls hitting the stairs with purpose.

If she hadn't already been up, I probably wouldn't have thought to ask Cole to come help, but the opportunity to go through her instead was too good. If I ask, it'll piss him off. If she asks, it might go over better.

And besides, he knows this is part of the agreement. He and Jordan clean up after themselves, help with the cooking, do the yard work, and help with anything else I might need, and I'll pay bills while they save up enough to get back on their feet. It's not too much to ask.

I fix the lid on my travel mug and go through two more K-cups to fill my thermos before carrying both to the front door, where my work boots sit. Sitting on the bench next to the door, I set my stuff down and pull on my socks and shoes, grab my keys, and take my black pullover rain jacket out of the entryway closet, pulling it on.

I pick up my mug and thermos. "Cole!" I shout, ready to leave.

The ceiling above me creaks, and I hear quick steps. Then there's a thud before a door slams shut, and I can tell he's finally coming down the stairs.

I grip the door handle and look over my shoulder. "I've got extra coffee. We can hit a drive-thru if you want something to eat real quick."

But it's not him who comes around the corner. Jordan is dressed in tight dark blue jeans, rolled at the bottom, with Chucks, and she's pulling her hair up into a ponytail while trying to hold a yellow raincoat under her arm.

I narrow my eyes on her. "Where's Cole?"

"He's, uh . . . not feeling too well," she tells me, pulling her jacket on. "I'll come and help you, though."

Not feeling well. Code for "hungover"?

"No, that's okay," I tell her. "Stay here. It's . . . safer. Thanks, though."

Her eyes shoot up, focus on me, and then narrow. "Safer?" she questions like I just said I'm going out for a pedicure. "Or are you just worried you'll spend more time holding my hand than getting any work done?"

I try to keep a straight face. She's pretty smart.

Okay, yeah, sorry, honey, but yes. At least Cole has some experience—a little, mind you, but some—helping me during summers and weekends. I don't need to get sidetracked explaining directions instead of giving them today.

"Tell you what . . ." She buttons up her raincoat, her sweet, shy demeanor slowly being replaced with a squarer set to her shoulders. "If the little lady can't handle some rain in her hair or mud under her fingernails, then she'll go back into the truck and wait for you. Where it's *safe*. Okay?"

And then she arches an eyebrow at me like I shouldn't even go there.

I don't even know how to respond, anyway, because my brain is now blank, and I'm kind of forgetting why I have a thermos in my hand.

I shake my head to clear it and yank the door open. "Fine. Get in the truck."

This damn storm came out of nowhere.

I always watch the weather because sometimes it determines if we can work at all that day, so it's kind of important. Especially in the summer.

I thought this one was missing us and swinging north, though. I shut off the engine and pull up the zipper of my jacket, squinting out the front windshield. The downpour is blurring everything beyond the glass, but I see a flash of orange and a yellow hard hat floating a few yards ahead and know some of the guys are here already.

Jordan pulls up her hood next to me, but I don't look at her or instruct her on what to do. She can follow my lead if she wants to be here.

I hop out of the truck, hard raindrops instantly pummeling the top of my head and shoulders, making me instinctively duck a little as I slam the door and jog for the building. My boots splash through small puddles, and I dash over to the bed of a company truck, immediately pulling down the tailgate and piling up as many sandbags as I can load into my arms. Bright yellow appears at my side and, without a word, Jordan does the same, quickly loading more bags into her arms and following me around the side of the building to where the guys are waiting.

I drop the bags and glance through the steel frame of the structure, noticing the uncovered pallet of cement in the lower level. *Son of a bitch.* Nine men, including my best friend, stare at me, waiting for instructions. The wind blows the rain into the back of my jeans, soaking the material to my skin. "I want these bags around the entire perimeter!" I shout over the storm. "Three high! You got it?"

Quick nods follow.

"And get that cement covered, goddammit!"

I jerk my chin at the uncovered pallet getting ruined below. Rain or not, that always needs to be covered, just in case, and someone dropped the ball last shift.

Dutch, my best friend since high school, casts his brown eyes next to me, his expression instantly softening. I glance over to see Jordan, her hair tucked into the hood of her raincoat, but thankfully she doesn't stick around to be introduced. Heading back to the truck, she pulls more sandbags out of the bed, and I turn back to Dutch, who eyes me curiously.

I just shake my head. *Not now.* It's not weird my son's girlfriend wants to pay her way and be helpful, but it is weird that he's not here, too. Does he know she took his place, helping out this morning? What kind of man is okay with that? I taught him to fulfill his obligations, goddammit.

Or maybe he just didn't want to come with me.

I need to do something about him, but I don't know what. This whole waiting-and-seeing tactic isn't working. He needs a kick in the ass.

The men get to work, carrying stacks of three bags and setting them along the sides of the building, while I grab my utility knife out of the toolbox in the truck and slice rectangles of blue tarp to staple around the first-floor frame. Before I know it, an hour has passed, the tarps are up, the sandbags are doing their job, and aside from me, everyone has seemed to vanish.

I toss my knife and staple gun back into the truck and slam the door, looking around the site for Jordan.

I haven't seen her in a while. Regret starts to wind its way into my stomach. I should've given her some kind of direction out here. She probably doesn't know her way around. It's easy for people to get hurt if they aren't trained.

Walking around the side, I see all the bags lined up as they should be, the tarps still intact, even with the wind, and the pallet of cement neatly covered. I hear voices and trail around the back, instantly spotting Jordan helping carry window inserts to the trailer, one of the guys making sure they're covered, as well.

She's smiling. Like crazy.

Like, eyes gleaming with excitement and she's about to bounce on the balls of her feet, for crying out loud.

Is she having *fun*?

Her hood has fallen down, and her ponytail hangs drenched while strands of hair stick to her face. Her shoes are soaked, her jeans are muddy, and thank Christ she's not wearing a white T-shirt, because the raincoat is doing very little to keep the guys' eyes off her as it is.

I look over at Dale, Bryan, and Donny, who are carrying equipment to the trailer as they cast looks her way, smile, and then turn to each other, laughing at something I can't hear.

"Hurry up," I bark at them, and they jerk to attention, carrying on.

Jordan walks over to where I stand next to the building and squats down, tucking the tarp under a beam.

"So, you're the boss, then, huh?" She looks up at me inquisitively. Something about her expression seems softer than it did earlier this morning. Happier. More at ease.

Didn't Cole tell her I own a construction company? Does he talk about me at all?

Hurt winds its way through my gut.

"Well, he tries to be," Dutch jokes, answering her question.

I throw him a look, but I'm tempted to smile. Bantering is our thing, but I wish the asshole wouldn't do it at work. It undermines me, dammit.

"Shit!" Jordan suddenly exclaims.

I jerk my eyes back to her and see rainwater crashing down on her head like a waterfall. The tarp has torn away at the top of the frame and spilled all the water it collected in its crevice. She pops up, escaping from the downpour, and reaches, trying to put it back in place.

But she can't reach it.

Coming up behind her, I reach in front of her and grab it, holding it in place as I turn my head and jerk my chin at Dutch. He nods and walks off to retrieve the staple gun again.

Jordan lets go of the tarp and slides out from between my arms, stepping to the side and chuckling to herself.

"Are you okay?" I ask.

She nods, wiping off her face and shaking out her jacket. "Yeah. I guess the raincoat was useless, though, huh?"

I drop my eyes to her shirt, seeing the soaked navy blue T sticking to her body, tight and molded to every inch of her chest and stomach. A sliver of her hips and tummy peek out just below where the shirt is pasted to her. Her skin is flawless, her curves beautiful. I swallow the lump in my throat and turn quickly away.

She definitely has a body I don't remember nineteen-year-olds having when I was that age, but she is still only nineteen.

And she's Cole's. *Not mine. Don't check her out again.*

Dutch comes up and hands me the staple gun, and I start refastening the tarp. She steps back up under my outstretched arms, placing her hands underneath mine and inching in to take over holding it while I staple.

Something warm courses under my skin, but I shake it off. "Do I, uh . . . need to get you home?" I ask. "Don't you have class or anything today?"

"Summer schedule," she replies, glancing up at me. "I only have one class this term, but it's not until tomorrow. I do have to work at the bar later, though."

I wonder how she gets back and forth to work—or school, for that matter—since Cole starts his day at ten and doesn't get off work until six. She has no working vehicle. Which reminds me . . . I'll grab a few tools before I leave here that I don't have at home. Maybe I can help Cole work on her VW today.

After about another hour, everything is as tight as we can make it, the equipment is secured and put away, and everyone is soaked to the bone. I let the guys take off. I hate losing time, but summers are rainy, and we've done what we can.

Hell, not even half of them showed up anyway.

I climb back into the truck with Jordan and pull off my wet jacket, while she fastens her seat belt next to me. I start the engine and wait for the lot to clear a little before finally pulling out, both of us riding in silence.

It's so quiet all of a sudden, and I realize the rain had been so constant for the last few hours that I hadn't been able to hear a voice unless it was shouting. Or a movement, unless it was my own. Now, my ears instinctively search for anything to grab onto.

The rain hitting my truck like rubber bullets. The grind of the leather on the steering wheel in my fist. The slosh of the rain under the tires as I charge down the highway, my engine rumbling like a lullaby.

But still, it's so quiet.

She draws in a deep breath through her nose.

Her raincoat squeaks as she slides her hands underneath her thighs.

I hear a soft clicking sound and dart my eyes to the floor, where she's gently tapping her Chucks together.

She licks her lips, and I fucking wince. *Jesus.*

Reaching over, I turn on the radio. Anything to distract.

I don't know why I'm so irritable today. *No, I know.* I woke up to Lindsay on the phone. She's the last person I want to deal with first thing in the morning.

It isn't hard to miss how happy I was at Cole and Jordan's age, having fun with whatever I could get my hands on and not forcing myself to think too hard about any decisions I was making. But not long after I met Lindsay, the bill for all that fun came due. I made a kid with a girl I barely knew. A pathological liar, someone who manipulates like it's a fucking sport.

And when I left, I left him with her. Cole never had a chance.

I took her to court, of course, trying to get custody, but judges back then often saw the mother as the better option, and she knew how to solicit sympathy. She wanted Cole because Cole meant child support. And she certainly got that out of me.

It was like being in prison, having to take him back to her after my weekends with him. She twists things into knots, and that's what she did to him. By the time he was ten, he was putting himself in front of her if I needed to say things to her, and I was always in the wrong.

By the time he was fourteen, he stopped wanting to visit every other weekend, and now we barely know each other. He won't even call unless he needs money.

I shake my head, clearing it. "Want to put in a tape?" I suggest to Jordan.

I don't meet her eyes, but I can see her head snap in my direction. "A tape? Like a cassette tape?"

Her gaze suddenly flashes to my car stereo and her eyes go wide, surprise lighting up her face. I almost laugh.

She didn't notice it on the drive here?

"Is that an actual tape deck?" she blurts out.

She reaches out and touches the old car radio like it's a precious vase and pushes *Eject*. Out pops a clear cassette tape with white lettering that I've never listened to.

She removes it, cupping it in her hand and reading the title. "Guns N' Roses." Her hand goes to her mouth and she looks like she's about to fucking cry. "Oh, my God."

Darting for the glove compartment, she opens it and stares at the line of tapes neatly set up.

"Deep Purple," she reads, "Rolling Stones, Bruce Springsteen, John Mellencamp, ZZ Top . . ."

Then she seems to spot something that really excites her, because she reaches in and plucks out the black Def Leppard case. "*Hysteria*?" she exclaims, reading the album title. "They don't make that album anymore. All you can get is the live version!"

I raise my eyebrows, not sure why this is all so exciting. "I'll take your word for it," I say, a little amused at her excitement. "This truck was my father's. Those are his tapes. I just never got around to clearing them out after he . . . passed away a few years ago."

It occurs to me that she's the first one to touch the Guns N' Roses tape since he put it in the player.

She looks back at the collection. "Well, that's good, I guess," she mumbles. "You clearly don't know what you have here and these would've wound up in the bottom of a trash can, for Christ's sake. Your dad was a cool guy."

I smile, agreeing. She carefully places the Guns tape back in its case and removes the Def Leppard tape.

"May I?" she asks, gesturing to the tape deck.

I laugh under my breath and shift into a higher gear as we charge down the road. "Go for it."

We listen to two songs on the way home, entering town and taking a shortcut past the railroad bridge on the river to our right.

"Wow, look at that," she says.

I slow the truck and follow her gaze to the right, out her passenger-side window, and see the river has risen considerably. Instead of the normal twenty feet of clearance between the bridge and the water, the water now rushes like a threat just below the bottom of the bridge. Thankfully, the rain has slowed, so it shouldn't get any higher.

I step on the gas again, taking us home.

"That was fun," she said. "Today, I mean."

I raise my eyebrows and glance at her.

"I mean . . ." She blinks, correcting herself. "I don't mean it was fun. I mean, I hope you didn't get set behind or lose any money, but . . ." She inhales and exhales, turning her eyes back out her window. "A couple times I nearly felt like my life was almost in danger."

She sounds entirely too pleased about that, too, and I can tell by her tone that she's smiling.

"And that's fun?" I question.

She turns her eyes back out the front windshield and shrugs, amusement pulling at the corner of her mouth.

I chuckle. "Yeah, it was fun. Thanks for helping. I'll be sure to let you know when the next storm's about to roll in, so you can get in on the action."

"Cool."

I continue driving down the highway and into our quiet town, turning left and then a sharp right into my neighborhood, content for the first time today. She's a good kid. I hope Cole doesn't screw it up, because I can already tell this is the kind of girl who would make a good mother and work by your side, building a life instead of draining you dry.

And for some reason it pleases me that she enjoyed herself today. No one in my family ever took much interest—or pride—in what I do for a living. My mother loves me, of course, as did my dad before he died, but they pushed so hard for me to go to college, and that was the plan until Cole came along.

It was always a disappointment that I stayed in this town and worked a job they thought required more brawn than brains.

When I started Lawson Construction—my own business—and built my own home, they still always looked at me like they wanted better but knew it was useless to say anything. They'd given up.

It wasn't that they hated what I did or were unhappy with the man I've become. They mourned my missed opportunities and still worried about their son's happiness. What they didn't realize, though, is that I have my own son now, and his happiness comes first.

And I actually love a lot of things about what I do. I get hours of fresh air every day, the sun, exercise. . . . It's a good life. I sleep well at night. It's nice to see someone else enjoy it like I do.

"My day is ruined now," Jordan says. "Nothing will beat that."

"Beat what?" I reply. "Getting doused in the rain?"

"And playing in the mud."

I grin, shaking my head as I turn into my driveway. "That's not playing in the mud."

She turns to me. "Oh, you mean mudding? Is that why your truck looks all nasty?"

I scoff and turn off the car, shooting her a look. "Kid, if you can tell what color the paint is, then you're not using your truck right. You got that?"

She rolls her eyes and opens her car door. We both hop out and make our way to the porch.

Come to think of it, if she didn't mind getting wet and dirty today, she'd probably love mudding. I haven't been in a long time. My truck only looks nasty because I never wash it. That's not natural.

"Have you ever taken Cole?" she asks, climbing the steps.

"A few times while he was growing up, yeah."

I reach out before she gets to the door and open it, holding it wide for her to enter first.

But she turns around, looking up at me before she goes in. "Maybe you can take both of us next time you go," she suggests. "As long as I can drive. You're not super possessive of your truck, are you?"

"No. A truck is made to be abused. Go for it. I'll just wear my seat belt."

She smiles softly and stares at me for a moment, something I can't decipher crossing her face. Did I say something?

I stare back for a moment, noticing how her eyes look almost like a watercolor. Midnight blue but growing lighter the closer they get to the pupil. I look away, clearing my throat.

"Jordan!" Cole suddenly bellows from upstairs. "Baby, you home? Come here!"

I meet her gaze again, and she pulls away, flashing me an apologetic smile. "Gotta go get ready for work. Thanks for letting me help today."

I nod but stay in the doorway, watching her cross the living room and disappear up the stairs. A strange feeling comes over me as I stare after her. What is she like with Cole? What is he like with her? Is he good to her?

I stand by the front door, hearing the bedroom door close upstairs and knowing she's in the bedroom with him. The house suddenly feels heavy. Stuffy and thick, and I can't breathe. I don't want to go in, no matter if I need dry clothes or not.

I dump my keys on the table to my left and see her VW key lying there. I grab it and step back outside, closing the door before I head back down the porch steps and to the garage on the right of the house.

"Got some houseguests, huh?" I hear someone call.

I look over and see Kyle Cramer standing on his front porch with a coffee cup in his hand, covered from the rain, which is now a light sprinkle.

I jerk my chin, acknowledging him, but I don't reply. I never liked the guy and never cared to be friendly. Which he must realize by now.

I don't care, though. Just looking at him irritates me. And it's nothing specific that I hate. Just little things that have added up over the years. How he treated his wife. How he cheated and was never home. How he kept the house for himself after the divorce and sent her and their kids off to an apartment to live. How he constantly hires babysitters when his kids are supposed to be spending time with him for the weekend.

Eh, who knows? Maybe he tried to get custody and maybe she cheated on him first. You never really know what goes on in someone's house. Look at me and how my kid was raised, after all. Who am I to judge?

I just still don't like the guy. He thinks his white-collar career and triathlons make him a hero.

And now I sound fucking jealous. *Great.*

Punching the code into the panel on the side of the garage door, I step back and let it open. I don't keep any cars in here, so there's room for it to serve as more of a shop and workroom.

There are tools, an air compressor, an extra refrigerator, a couple workbenches, and an entire table filled with car parts that just kind of got dumped here over the years. Jordan's car is in the driveway, but I know I'll need to get in here for a few things after I pop that hood. Cole isn't bad with cars, but I know it's going to take money to get that thing running again—money they don't have. I'll at least take a look, so I can see how bad it is.

"Hey, man."

I look over my shoulder and see Dutch walking up the driveway. He has dry clothes on and a beer in his hand. Not unusual. He keeps a cooler in the back of his truck.

"Hey." I pull my still-damp T-shirt over my head and toss it on a workbench. Pulling a jack out from under a table, I walk back out of the garage and toward the faded green VW. Dutch pulls a lawn chair out and carries it to the grass next to Jordan's car.

"Five tomorrow?" he asks.

"Yep."

Since we lost time today, he knows I'll want to start early tomorrow.

"So the guys were thinking of hitting Grounders in a bit here. Grab some beers, listen to some music . . ." he tells me. "There's nothing else to do in this weather."

I twist the wrench but glance over at him. "Grounders? Since when do you go there? Did Poor Red's close down?"

"No," he answers, shrugging. "They just realized there was some fetching eye candy at Grounders now."

I look over at him, and he's smiling and jerking his head toward the house and who's inside it.

"Yeah, shut up." I squeeze the wrench. "That's my kid's girl. You guys leave her alone."

"I'm not going to do anything!" He holds up his hands in defense. "I'm married."

"I don't even want y'all looking," I state, standing up straight and tossing the tool down.

Granted, I've been looking, but I didn't know who she was when we first met.

I wipe my hands with the shop cloth. "You got that? Leave the kid alone."

He just scoffs, slouching in his seat and laying his head back. "*The kid*, I'm sure, has dealt with lots of male attention already, working at that bar. And I'm sure she wouldn't mind a little extra business tonight."

He makes her sound like a prostitute. But I guess he's right. Fending off unwanted attention has to be a skill by now, especially working at a dive like that.

I still can't see it, though. The girl has a mouth on her, but she's pretty innocent and sweet, too. Picturing her in that environment is impossible.

"Hi," a female voice chirps.

I lean over and look around the hood, seeing the same young woman who was here last night. What was her name again?

"Pike, right?" she says, putting a hand on her chest. "Cam, remember? I'm Jordan's sister."

Dutch is staring at her, his mouth hanging open just slightly.

"I'm just here to give her a ride to work," Cam tells me, and then her eyes fall down my torso and arms. "And nice ink, man."

Her eyes light up as she nods her approval. I notice she has some, too, down her upper arm, and a phoenix on the side of her torso. Which I can see only because she's wearing almost no clothes, dressed in a black miniskirt and a black tank top cut off just under her breasts.

Where the fuck is your father? Seriously . . .

Behind her, a newish white Mustang convertible sits parked at the curb, the car filled with two other women, both looking similarly dressed from what I can tell. They have big hair, and I can feel the breeze from their eyelashes when they blink all the way from here.

But then something occurs to me, and I look around the hood again. "You all work together? With Jordan?"

"No, we work at The Hook."

Dutch makes a gargled sound, and I realize he's choking on his beer. He coughs and laughs at the same time as he clears his throat.

Cam nods and teases, "Yeah, you know The Hook."

He chuckles, and I swear I see him blush. "I may have been familiar with the place back in the day."

The Hook is a strip club downtown, not far from Grounders, where Jordan works.

"Jordan doesn't work there, too, does she?" I ask. I mean, she could have two jobs, I suppose, but if I can't picture her behind the bar at Grounders, I really don't want the mental image of her at The Hook.

But thankfully, Cam rushes to respond. "Oh, no, but my boss did offer her a job bartending, though," she says. "He's been trying to wear her down for a year now. She's shy, though."

She says the last with a little wink, and I'm not sure what that means. Shy about what? Would she have to wear something similar to the dancers to work behind the bar there?

Yeah, no. Picturing her at The Hook, dealing with the guys who come in wanting one thing, will stress me out. Does Cole know about the job offer? I can't imagine he'd want her working there.

I don't have time to think about it more, though, because Jordan comes down the front porch and walks across the lawn to her sister.

"Stop talking about me," she warns her, clutching the strap of her bag over her chest, but Cam just shoots her a playful look.

Jordan responds with an eye roll, but I barely notice it. My heart is pounding painfully, taking in her attire.

I look away.

For some reason, the judgment I dealt Cam for her clothes doesn't transfer to Jordan, even though she's a few years younger. Her dark blue jean shorts, low on the hip and high on the thigh, aren't cut off but rolled up, and her loose black T-shirt shows off her stomach and hangs off one shoulder. Her hair hangs down her back in big, loose curls, and her eyes are rimmed in dark liner and dark eye shadow, making the midnight blue in her eyes pop like a stream of moonlight on a night sea.

I wonder if she's wearing her Chucks again, but that would mean getting past her legs, and I'm having a hard time doing that, so I keep my gaze averted and continue working on the car.

Guilt rips through me. *She's Cole's.* He kisses her. He holds her. He makes her smile. It's not my place to have any opinions about her, especially territorial ones like where she bartends or how she dresses. I just still keep feeling like I did in the theater. She's a young woman I met and had fun talking to, and no one else had anything to do with it. Part of me keeps feeling like I knew her first, even though I know I didn't.

"I have a double shift today," she says, and I guess she's talking to me, "so I'll get off late, but I have my key."

I nod and refit the oil cap, not looking at anyone.

There's a short silence before she starts to move away. "Okay, see you both later," she says.

"Thanks for the help today, sugar," Dutch calls out to her.

He raises his arm high and waves at the girls, and I hear some giggles before the car takes off. I keep going with what I'm doing, not thinking about how unsafe that area of town is at night or about how the perk of working behind a bar is that customers can't get their hands on her, which is nice. Her job is great, actually. It's better money than she'll make at Burger King or being a telemarketer. She and Cole will be out of the house in no time.

But no wonder that asshole Mick is trying to get her to work at The Hook. For Christ's sake. Done all up like she is tonight? Men pay a lot of money for young and hot, but even more for young-and-hot farmer's daughter.

I'm unscrewing, cleaning, and refastening things I already fastened when I realize my hand is aching and the muscles are tired. I stop and stand up straight, cracking my knuckles.

But then I see Dutch watching me out of the corner of my eye, and I look over at him, meeting his stare.

"What?" I ask.

Why is he staring at me?

But he just gives me a small smile and shakes his head. "Nothing."

4

Jordan

Can I have a Fuzzy Navel?"

I glance over and see April Lester standing at the bar between Grady Jones and Rich Hensburg and staring at me expectantly. I nod and finish stacking the rocks glasses I've just washed, then reach over and grab the bottle of schnapps.

"So, you coming home with me yet?" Rich asks April, giving her a skeptical little scowl.

Grady chuckles softly, while I smile to myself. April just turns away, looking annoyed.

All these people are regulars. April usually doesn't go home alone, and everyone knows it. Rich only half jokes to save face when she constantly refuses him, though. Old, it seems, is her only hard limit. Anyone else is fair game. It doesn't hurt for him to keep trying, I guess. Might get lucky one of these nights.

Not that I begrudge her. What do I know? She's a good customer, and she tips well, after all. I just can't help but keep an eye on her when Cole is around. I've seen her go after married men, so someone's boyfriend certainly won't faze her.

I finish pouring the orange juice and set out a napkin before placing the drink on top of it. She grabs a straw and takes her glass.

"Thank you," she singsongs and immediately turns around, taking a sip as she walks back to her booth.

I watch her go and see her slide in with two other men I've seen around before.

Sometimes she makes me think of my mom. I'm not sure why; they look nothing alike. My mom was a blonde—*is* a blonde—and April is a brunette. Hair so dark brown it almost looks black.

But they'd be around the same age. April has to be pushing forty and dresses like I remember my mom dressing. Short skirts, billowy silk tank tops, jewelry, and six-inch heels.

Like Cam. My sister inherited my mom's sexy style.

I wonder if my mom has settled down with someone or if she still needs that freedom she craved so much when I was four. I don't miss her. I barely remember her. But I do still wonder about her.

Reaching behind me, I mark a tally on April's tab for her drink and grab a towel to finish drying the glasses.

But then the front door swings open and a voice booms, "Shit, it's dead in here."

I look up, the hair on my arms instantly standing on end. My boyfriend enters with a few of his friends in tow, but it's the all-too-familiar voice leading the pack that makes my skin crawl.

Jay McCabe, my ex-boyfriend, walks in, slowly and taking his time, entering the room like the star quarterback he was in high school and still waiting for a fucking round of applause. It's funny how he got less good-looking the more I got to know him. My spine goes steel-rod straight, and awareness makes heat spread up my neck.

Cole strolls in behind with a couple guys, Elena Barros trailing them, and I see his arched brow and the slight snarl on his face as he glances at Jay and then looks over to me.

They don't hang out, but they will find themselves at the same parties sometimes. My guess is Jay headed here with his pack and Cole followed to make sure I'm okay.

Jay scans the room and then his eyes lock on me, a little smile curling the corner of his mouth. I immediately avert my gaze, my stomach rolling.

I try to pretend he's of no consequence anymore, but I think he knows he won. He should be in fucking jail after what he did to me, and he's not, because two years ago, I was scared and pathetic.

I wish someone would hurt him.

And even better if that someone turns out to be me.

Cole strolls over while his friends walk around, chatting up people they know. He swings up the partition and comes behind the bar, an apologetic look on his face as he comes up behind me, wrapping his arms around my waist.

"What are you doing?" I ask, my fist wrapped in a towel and wiping the inside of a glass.

I feel him shrug. "Haven't seen you. Just missed you."

I breathe out a laugh, trying to relax my stiff body. "I'm okay. You don't have to worry about me at work."

He nuzzles my neck, and we both know he's just worried about Jay being here.

I put my hand over his, feeling the small scar on his thumb, and inhale his clean scent. He looks fresh and good-looking, a lot better than he did this morning. No one can shake off a hangover like him.

"You know, it's bad for business if her boyfriend is hanging around," Shel warns, walking by in front of the bar and setting down a tray of glasses.

Shel fancies herself like the bar owner in the *Coyote Ugly* movie. "You are to appear available but never be available" type thing. The problem is this is a dirt bar in a small town, so either way, the tips won't set any records. Whether or not my boyfriend is here.

Cole snuggles my neck, and I smile, feeling safe against the wall of his body. His friends' voices carry as the level of noise heightens in the room, and I glance up at the clock, seeing it's nearly midnight.

And it's Wednesday night. Cole has work in the morning.

I draw in a breath, turning my head to look up at him. "You know, we couldn't really afford for you to lose those hours today," I tell him.

And if he's out tonight, chances are he'll call in tomorrow and lose more pay.

We still have bills from the old apartment that need to be paid, and I'll do my fair share, but he's damn well helping. If he misses another day, I'm going to get loud.

But he just gazes down at me thoughtfully. "I'm not stupid, babe," he assures me. "I already know everything you want to say to me, okay?"

"And you know you're damn lucky to still have your license, right?" I jab at him some more. A DUI on his record is the last thing we need, and he tempts fate constantly.

Especially after everything that's happened. How can he be so careless?

I glance down at our scars again, remembering.

"What would I do without you?" he says, his breath tickling my ear.

I jerk away. "Your own laundry, probably."

But he just laughs, tightening his hold around me. "I'm sorry I'm a loser."

"You haven't always been."

He cocks an eyebrow at my dig and walks me back into the bar, a smirk playing on his lips. "I'm good at a few things, though, aren't I?"

He tips my chin back and dives into my neck, his hot mouth kissing and biting.

Chills spread up my arms, and I gasp. "Cole . . ."

Okay, yes. You're not completely terrible at everything.

He's always been able to make me smile, and he's a good kisser. I just wish he'd do it at home more. He hasn't been touching me a lot lately.

And now he's going out again tonight.

I turn my head, kissing him and hungry for the connection, but then I quickly pull away, pushing him off with a grin. "Not here," I scold.

I twist around and clear a couple beer bottles off the bar, tossing them away.

"I am really sorry, you know?" he says in my ear. "I didn't mean to get us kicked out of there and in this situation with my dad."

I nod, pretty sure he means it. He's good people, and I've seen him at his best. Right now, he's in a rut, but he stood by me when no one else would, so I want to believe he'll get on track.

I glance over at Jay, remembering how Cole was my only friend left after I broke up with that asshole. Everyone else took Jay's side.

"So is my dad being nice to you?" he asks, pulling away and releasing me.

"Of course. Why wouldn't he be?"

He shrugs. "Just making sure. He used to be kind of a dick back in the day. Cheated on my mom a lot, which is why we don't get along." He pauses and then adds, "Just to explain the tension you're probably feeling between us."

Cheating? Why didn't he tell me this before? *Jesus.*

That doesn't seem like Pike at all, though. He doesn't strike me as that shallow.

But people grow up and change. Maybe he was a different guy twenty years ago.

But wait . . .

"I thought you said your parents broke up when you were two," I say.

If he was that young, how would he remember that?

"Yeah." He starts walking back for the end of the bar. "I just know what she's told me. It wasn't pretty, apparently, so don't take any shit from him. He likes to push women around, which is probably why he's still single."

Well, his dad did look dumbfounded earlier today when he tried to tell me to stay home and I got back in his face. I think he's used to people following his orders. Cole's last statement kind of rings true.

"We're going to hit The Cue," Cole tells me, swinging open the partition and walking through to the other side of the bar. "I'll see you at home."

"Don't be too late," I say quietly.

His shift doesn't start until ten tomorrow morning, but I want to see him when I get home. We didn't get much time together today.

He and his friends trickle out the front door, heading to The Cue to play some pool, but Jay casts a look back at me as he heads out the door, too, putting his arm around Shawna Abbot. His eyes drop down to my chest and then come back up, leering at me with one part desire and three parts threat.

And for two years it's been just that. Me taking whatever gross looks he throws my way for fear of pushing him into action again. He's left me alone otherwise, so I just avoid him and pretend he's not there.

Both groups leave, deciding to find their fun elsewhere, but before the front door has a chance to close, my sister saunters through, a couple of her coworkers trailing behind her. Every eye in the room turns their way, taking in the hot women in their tiny tops and high heels.

Sammy Hagar's "The Girl Gets Around" plays on the jukebox, and Cam heads for the bar, holding on to the edge and doing a little dance while lip-syncing to me.

She's a trip.

"All done already?" I ask over the music, glancing at the clock on the wall. "I'm not off for at least another hour."

"That's fine." Cam waves me off as she reaches around and grabs the rum out of the well and the clean rocks glass in front of me. "We need to chill out before we head home to bed anyway."

She pours one shot, replaces the bottle, and takes the soda gun, filling her glass with Diet Coke.

I pluck the scoop out of the ice bin and add a few cubes to her glass before I move down the bar, checking on the customers.

I replace Grady's and Rich's beers, get a refill for Shel's husband, who is playing video poker, and mix up three Cosmos for a few ladies who left their editions of Deepak Chopra's *The Book of Secrets* back at their booth. They bring books every week so their husbands think they're actually in a book club meeting.

"You want to jump behind here?" Shel shouts to Cam. "I need to restock beer."

She shoots Shel a look, but she gets up and comes behind the bar. Shel charges down the hallway to the cooler where the beer is stored.

"Empty out the tips and start the jar over," I call out to my sister at the other end. "You don't get a share of mine."

She laughs, looking at me smugly as she puts her hands on her hips. I turn to mix a Screwdriver for another customer, and the next thing I know there's a fat roll of cash in my face.

"Like I need your dimes and nickels, babe," she replies.

My eyes go wide, and my mouth hangs open as I gape at the wad. "What the hell?" I grab it out of her hand and fan the bills, seeing lots of ones but an impressive number of tens and twenties, too.

"That's what making your rent in one night looks like, honey." She snatches it back out of my hand. "We had a bachelor party."

Lots of drunk guys showering money. I watch her slide it back into her back pocket and frown at the gleam in her eye. It makes sense that she makes a hell of a lot more than me. I work in a bar. She works in a club. She entertains. I pour drinks.

It must be nice, though, to go home at night knowing you can pay your bills tomorrow. That you can go to the grocery store and put whatever you want in your cart.

I look up and meet her eyes, and I can tell she's thinking the exact same thing. It could be easier for me, too, if I take her boss up on his job offer.

I won't make as much as my sister as a bartender there, but I'd make more than here.

But while The Hook may offer fast money, nothing about that place is easy. Men look at Cam like a free meal, and she puts up with a lot of shit.

Still, though . . . I'm tired of worrying about money every damn day.

I go back to work, but I can feel her eyes on me. She thinks I'm a hamster on a wheel.

"Just shut up," I mumble.

She snorts. "I didn't say anything. Not one single thing."

"Thank you," I say, climbing out of Cam's Mustang just over an hour later. I fold up the front seat and grab my bag from the back, quickly glancing over my shoulder to see if Cole's car is in the driveway.

It's not. Just Pike's truck.

I shake my head.

"You don't work tomorrow, right?" Cam asks.

I turn back. "No, but I do Saturday night. I'll text you my schedule later."

"Okay."

I slam the door and dig in my pocket for the house key. "Love you. Bye," I call out.

"Oh, I bought something for you, by the way!" Cam shouts through the open passenger-side window. "Look in your backpack when you get into your room. Test it out. See how it feels."

I stop, turning halfway around and thinning my eyes on her. "Not another vibrator . . ." I whine.

She throws her head back and laughs at the present she gave me for my eighteenth birthday last year. It wouldn't have been so bad if she hadn't let me open it in front of a party full of people.

"Not that," she says. "But it's definitely something you and Cole can enjoy together." And then she jerks her chin toward the dark house behind me. "Or, um . . . perhaps the *man* of the house might like it, too. The *other* man of the house, I mean."

She wiggles her eyebrows at me, and I shoot her a dirty look. "I don't even want to open the package now."

"Night!" she taunts and pulls away from the curb.

Jerk. I love my sister, but she knows how to embarrass me.

After unlocking the front door, I step inside, push it shut behind me, and twist the lock again, looking around the dark living room. It's tidy, and I walk past the entrance to the kitchen, taking in the single, small stove light left on the way I appreciate. The sink is empty of dishes from what I can see, and I exhale, loving the feeling of coming home to a clean house.

I trail up the stairs, the house giving off an eerie silence around me. Walking down the dark hallway, I lift my head and see Pike's bedroom door straight ahead of me. It's closed and no light shines from under the door.

I swing open the first door on the left and flip on the switch, discovering what I already suspected. The bed is empty. Cole's still out.

I drop my bag, closing the door quietly and pulling my phone out of my back pocket.

I'm home. Where are you? I type and wait for the three little dots to pop up, showing me he's replying.

But after a few moments, nothing happens, and I toss my phone down on the bed.

He has to be at work in eight hours, and he better be going. Otherwise he's not coming with me when I save enough to get out of here.

I kick off my shoes and head toward the bed, ready to plop down and get off my tired feet, but I stop, remembering the "something" my sister said she put in my bag. Turning around, I pick up my satchel and unzip it, setting it on the bed. And there, right on top, is a pink-striped shopping bag I didn't put there. It's from Victoria's Secret.

Unrolling the package, I reach inside and instantly fill my hand with fabric. I suppress a groan, my wishful thinking dying. I pull out the lacy, cream-colored panties and matching camisole, which doesn't look big enough to cover much. The neckline is low, and the top's not even long enough to cover my stomach.

It's definitely pretty. And sexy. But it's skimpy as hell. Cole would have a field day, coming to bed to find me in this.

No foreplay. He'd be on top of me in a second.

But why did she buy me this? It's not like I don't wear sexy underwear. I don't need lessons in how to keep a guy interested, thank you.

But then I notice a piece of paper lying on the bed that must've been in with the clothes. I pick up the half sheet and read the flyer.

AMATEUR NIGHT!
GET WET! (YOUR T-SHIRT, ANYWAY)
MAY 27 AT 9 P.M.
THE HOOK ON JAMISON LANE
GRAND PRIZE $300!!

"Great." I laugh under my breath and drop the flyer and the clothes, shaking my head. My own sister is trying to turn me out. What the hell is the matter with her?

I'm not showing every old skeeze in town my boobs for a chance to win three hundred bucks. I can work at Grounders, because I do enjoy some of the people, listening to music, and having a job where I earn tips so I have a little cash on me after every shift, but there's nothing about a wet T-shirt contest I'd enjoy unless I was drunk. Maybe.

I make sure the blinds are closed and pull off my T-shirt and unbutton my jean shorts. Letting everything fall to the floor, I reach behind and unsnap my bra and then reach into the bureau for a T-shirt.

I stop, though, and eye the new lingerie lying on the bed. Cole might be sorry he stayed out when he comes home to see what he missed.

Pulling off my panties, I reach over and grab the new underwear and gently pull on everything. My coffee cup of pens and pencils sits on top of the dresser, and I reach over and pull out the scissors, cutting the tags off everything.

Standing in front of the mirror, I fluff my hair and comb my hands through it, adjusting the fabric on my hips and my breasts in the wireless cups. I turn around, looking in the mirror over my shoulder.

I can't help the smile that peeks out. Cam isn't stupid, is she? It's the perfect color on me, my base tan already in full swing. The panties sit perfectly on my hips, and even without much support in the top, my breasts sit perky and flattering. I run my hand over my smooth, flat stomach and up the curves of my waist, wishing someone was here to appreciate the view and make me smile.

A pool of warmth settles between my thighs, and I can't help but think how a simple change of clothes can make you feel a world of difference. I brush one of the straps off my shoulder, loving how sexy I feel. The pulse in my clit starts to throb, and I'm definitely in the mood now.

Hooking the strap back on my shoulder, I grab my phone and text Cole again, noticing he still hasn't texted back.

I kind of need you right now, baby. *wink wink*

I wait, but the three dots still don't pop up. I start the Spotify app on my phone, playing "Run to You," careful to keep the volume low as I fall onto the bed.

I'm wide awake now.

And turned on.

Closing my eyes, I let the music course under my skin and slowly drift through my fingertips, down my thighs, and back up the inside of my leg, tickling the flesh until goose bumps rise. Gently cupping myself between my legs, I roll my hips and rub, my blood starting to heat up and my heart pumping faster as my clit tingles.

I moan, feeling my hardened nipples chafing against the lace. My other hand takes a breast and squeezes it as I twist my head to the side, my hair falling in my face.

Sometimes I wonder if I could ever do what my sister does. When I see all the money she brings home, and I'm tired of the worry and the stress, could I just do it?

I flip over and push myself up to my knees as I lean over with my hands on the bed between my thighs. I press my arms into my breasts, forcing them together, full and about to pop out of the top. I roll my head and my hair caresses my back as I keep my eyes closed and start to grind to the music.

No, I can't do what she does. I don't want lots of men watching me.

But one man? Like a boyfriend? A man who craves me and who'll watch me with possessive eyes as I dance for him . . .

He's watching me. I'm in a dark room, a glossy white stage under me, and a soft purple light on me. I move onto all fours, crawling and biting my bottom lip as I lean forward, spreading my thighs, my knees pressing into the floor as I hump the stage.

He's in the back, so far away, but he's there. He's the only one there. I'm all for him. He hides in the shadows and leans his shoulder into the wall as he watches me. I roll my hips slowly, taunting and teasing him, and then move back onto my knees, grabbing the headboard to hold on to as I dance and grind.

The strap of my top falls down my arm, and I cup my naked breast, looking over my shoulder at him. The cigarette—or cigar—in his hand hangs at his side, burning a stream of smoke into the air. But he seems to have forgotten about it as he stares at me.

It occurs to me that Cole doesn't smoke, but the thought is gone as quickly as it comes.

I want him to see me. I want him to want me. I feel him want me, and I like it. God, I like it. *Keep watching me.* I wonder what his mouth tastes like. What do his teeth feel like? My nipples tighten and harden, craving a mouth.

I'm gonna get you off. Keep watching me. Keep watching me.

I lean back on my hands, rolling my hips faster and harder, and I can feel my skin growing wet with sweat as I rub my pussy and move my ass for him.

Only him.

"Oh, God," I whimper, feeling my orgasm crest. "I'm coming, I'm coming . . ."

But then a loud slam echoes through the house, and I pop my head up and open my eyes. *Shit!*

I freeze, listening. The floorboards in the hallway creak, and someone moves down the hallway and then pounds down the stairs. I hop off the bed in a hurry, in case it's Cole.

I wouldn't have woken his father, would I? That was so stupid! What if the bed was creaking?

Shame burns like fire on my face, and I inch toward the bedroom door, cracking it open for a peek. The hallway is still dark, but I can hear talking and then a door slams shut downstairs.

I frown. Stepping across the hallway, I quickly hide in the

bathroom and close the door. Keeping the light off, I go to the window and pull open one of the shutters.

"Yeah, don't worry about it. I don't mind being woken up for this," I hear Pike say, and I peer out to see him standing next to the pool, talking on his phone. "Babies are unpredictable. Take whatever time you need. We'll be fine for the next few days."

He's dressed in gray lounge pants but no shirt, and I see him rub his hand over his scalp as he yawns. My shoulders relax a little. The call probably woke him up.

He nods at whoever is talking on the phone. "Shoot us all a text when the kid is born. Congrats, man."

Then he chuckles, and my muscles relax, so grateful. That would've been embarrassing if he'd heard me.

I move to close the shutter again, but I see him grab something out of a dish on the garden table and put it in his mouth as he continues listening to whoever is on the phone.

I stop, my eyes widening as I watch him light a cigar butt. The hair on my neck stands on end, and my pulse races. I yank the shutter closed, not caring if he hears me.

What the hell? I haven't seen him smoke. Why would that have popped in my . . . ?

I charge back to my room, close the door, and pull off the lingerie. Donning a T-shirt and boy shorts, I turn off the music, the light, and climb into bed.

Cam and her stupid damn subliminal messages and shit. *Thanks a lot.*

Hey, Corinne. Is my dad home?" I ask into the phone.

I hear my stepmom move on the other end, a screen door creaking open. "Chip!" she hollers, her voice raspy from years of smoking. "It's Jordan!"

The door creaks shut again, and I think I hear the fryer going in the kitchen. I can almost feel the grainy linoleum under my feet from here. I'm so glad to be out of that trailer, even if it means mooching off Cole's dad.

"You need money?" she says as I wait for my dad to come to the phone. "'Cause we don't have any. Your dad threw out his back and missed some work a couple weeks ago, so things are tight right now."

I blink. "No, I . . ." I stammer, aggravated by her question. "I don't need money."

And they would be the last people I'd ask if I did. My father never has cash for more than a day before it's burning a hole in his pocket. One of the many reasons my mom ran out.

But at least my dad stayed.

"Chip?!" she calls again, but then growls at the dogs. "Get out of the way, you two."

I shake my head, the previous suspicion that a text would've been better now solidifying. If my dad does make it to the phone, I'll just hang up feeling pissed off that he's about as warm as this woman. Thank goodness she wasn't my stepmom for long under that roof. I left as soon as I could.

"I just wanted to let you all know I moved," I tell her. "In case you need my new address."

"Oh, right, right." I hear her suck in and know she's smoking. "You moved in with Cole at his dad's house. Yeah, we heard."

"Yeah, I—"

"Chip!" she screeches again, interrupting me.

I hood my eyes, exasperated already. "It's fine," I tell her. "That's all I called for, so don't bother Dad, then, if he already knows. I'll . . . talk to you later."

"Okay." She blows out smoke. "Well, take care of yourself, and I'll call in a week or so. Have you over for dinner or something."

My body shakes with a bitter laugh I hold back. It's not funny. It's sad, really. But she hangs up without waiting for me to say goodbye, and I let out a sigh, tossing my phone on the bed.

Neither my dad nor my stepmom is a bad person, although no one called on my birthday, either.

I was never hit or starved or verbally abused. Just kind of forgotten, I guess. They struggled for anything good in life, so it was too much to ask to let responsibility or concern for their children interfere with what tiny pleasure they managed to muster with their beer and bingo nights.

After Cam left and got her own place, I had no one to talk to. I was nobody in that trailer, and I never want to feel that alone again.

I pick up my notebook from the bed and resume the homework from my summer class that day. My textbook lies open in front of me, and I click my mechanical pencil to get more lead.

A knock sounds on the bedroom door, and I pop my head up, tensing.

"Come in?" I say, but it sounds like a question. Cole wouldn't knock. It must be his father. Did I leave laundry in the dryer? The stove on? I go through my mental checklist.

The door swings open, and Pike stands there, holding the knob but keeping himself planted in the hallway.

"I'm ordering pizza for dinner," he tells me. "Is Cole going to be home soon?"

I fiddle with the pencil in my hands. "One of his friends got promoted at the cable company," I explain, "so they're having a party out at his dad's farm. I'm sure he'll be pretty late."

He stands there a moment, his large frame filling the entire doorway. My eyes keep darting to the tattoos on his arms, so I just look back down, pretending to be absorbed in my work.

"You're not going?" he presses.

I hold out my hands, gesturing to the homework in front of me.

He nods, understanding. "Well . . ." He eyes me for a moment, looking uncertain, and then continues. "You gotta eat, too, right? What kind of pizza do you like?"

"No, that's okay," I tell him, shaking my head. "I already ate."

His eyes drop to the plate with the half-eaten peanut butter sandwich on the bed, and I know what he's thinking. "Okay."

He moves to close the door but then stops. "You know you don't need to hide up here, right?"

I look up, straightening my spine. "I'm not hiding." I laugh a little for good measure, but I think he's onto me.

"You're doing chores," he states. "You're paying for your right to be in the house. So if you want to use the pool or have a friend over or like . . . leave the bedroom, it's fine."

I lick my dry lips. "Yeah, I know."

"Okay," he finally says. "I guess I'm eating the pizza all by myself, then. I'll have leftovers for days, as usual."

He sighs, sounding extra pathetic.

"Don't order a large, then," I mumble, staring down at my notebook again.

But his quiet chuckle before he closes the door tells me he heard my smart-ass comment.

I'm sure he's ordered plenty of pizzas in all the years he's lived here alone. He's just trying to be nice and make me feel welcome. Which is great of him, and I appreciate it, but it still doesn't make me feel like any less of a freeloader. I can't let him buy me pizza, too.

And I think about how alone I felt growing up in my father's trailer and even how alone I've felt with Cole sometimes. Maybe Pike Lawson is tired of being alone and eating alone and watching TV alone, and I'm a guest in his home and perhaps he'd like to get to know the people living under his roof, right? It's only reasonable.

And maybe I'm tired of being alone a lot, too, and maybe I'm still hungry and pizza sounds pretty good, actually.

I blow out a breath and shove my notebook off my lap before standing up. Rushing over to the bedroom door, I yank it open and peek out.

"Joe's Pizza?" I inquire, seeing him right before he heads down the stairs.

He stops and turns his head to look at me. "Of course."

It's the best pizza in town, so it's a no-brainer. I step out of the bedroom and shut the door. "Halfsies?"

5

Pike

No way was she paying for half the pizza, for Christ's sake. I invited her, didn't I? And the point of them staying here is to save money, isn't it? I shove past her, ignoring the cash in her hand as I carry the pizza to the kitchen island.

She sighs, letting out a little growl. I chuckle. "Look, I got the pizza, okay? Just make sure I don't have any of your limpy lettuce on my half."

"Haha." She walks to the fridge and digs out two sodas.

I'm a pretty simple pepperoni man, and I can get behind taco pizza, but not that warm, droopy shredded lettuce that comes with it. She can have a ball all by herself.

We divvy up the slices on two plates, but before we trail into the living room, she drops a pile of greens on my plate with a pair of tongs.

"Uh, thanks."

"If you eat the veggies first," she points out, "you'll have less room for pizza. A little trick I picked up on Pinterest."

Pinter-what?

"You'll eat less pizza then," she continues, "consume less calories, and you'll feel better after your meal."

Yeah, okay. If I cared about consuming less calories, I guess.

Fine. Fuck it. Whatever. I stalk over to the refrigerator and grab the ranch dressing in the inside of the door.

"No," she blurts out, stopping me. "There's dressing on it already. Raspberry vinaigrette."

I straighten and fix her with a look.

She just smiles and turns away.

I take out two forks, pass her one, and carry my plate and soda into the living room with her trailing behind.

Once seated, I pick up my fork and let out a sigh before digging into the salad. I remember what my mom said about vegetables growing up. They taste better if you eat them when you're hungry. I'll get it over with and eat them first like Jordan suggested, then.

I stuff the forkful in my mouth, the bitter taste of the leaves dulled only a little by the sweet dressing.

"Good, right?" she says.

"No." I shake my head. "You're killing me."

She laughs. "Well, thanks for giving it a shot. You can stop if you want."

But I persevere anyway. It's not like I couldn't use a dose of greens, right?

And it's not like I hate vegetables. I like corn on the cob and, like . . . potatoes and stuff. Those are technically vegetables, right?

"So, what are you watching?" she asks.

I look up at the TV and realize the volume is too low. I reach for the remote and turn it up. "*Fight Club*," I tell her.

"Oh, hey. I was born the year this was made."

I arch an eyebrow but keep my mouth shut.

But I do the math in my head, remembering I saw this my senior year in high school. So yeah, that would be about right.

Shit, I'm getting old. To think of everything that's gone on in my lifetime that she wasn't around for or old enough to remember. I glance over at her, taking in her young skin and hopeful eyes.

She was just in high school a year ago.

We eat in silence for the next couple hours, engrossed in one of my favorite movies. I have no idea if she's already seen it, but after a while, her plate sits half-eaten and forgotten on the coffee table, and she's sitting at the other end of the couch, hugging her legs and watching intently.

"They make smoking look so appetizing," she finally says, watching Marla Singer on the screen.

"Appetizing?"

She clears her throat and sits up. "Well, it's like Bruce Willis," she explains. "I could watch him smoke for days. It's like he's eating. Eating a nice, succulent . . ."

"Steak," I finish for her, understanding.

"Exactly." She flashes me a soft smile. "They totally own it. It's part of their wardrobe."

"Well," I sigh, gathering up our plates and rising, "don't start smoking."

"You do."

I pause, looking down at her. I've only smoked once since they moved in, and I never smoke in the house. I don't even think Cole knows I smoke.

She clarifies, probably seeing the confusion on my face. "I noticed the cigar butt in the ashtray outside," she says.

Ah. I continue toward the kitchen, carrying the dishes around the coffee table. "On rare occasions, yes. I like the smell."

"Why?" She gets up off the couch, grabbing the empty soda cans and napkins and following me.

"I just do." I clear off the plates and put them in the dishwasher. "My grandfather, he smoked, so . . ."

It seemed natural to start sharing, but all of a sudden it feels stupid.

"So . . . ?" she presses.

But I just shake my head, closing the dishwasher door and starting the machine. "I just like the smell is all," I finish curtly.

I'm not sure why I'm having trouble talking to her. There's no mystery here. My grandpa was awesome, and I had a great childhood, but the more I grew up, the farther away I felt from that feeling when I was eight. The feeling of being somewhere I loved and feeling what I felt.

Happiness.

I smoke cigars once in a while to take me back there.

It's not the kind of thing I feel comfortable sharing with just anyone, though.

But it's funny how close I came to doing just that with her a minute ago.

I can feel her eyes on me, and the awkwardness crawls across my skin.

"You want a beer?" I ask, swinging open the fridge and grabbing two out. Anything to change the subject.

"Um . . . sure."

I pop the tops and hand her a Corona, finally meeting her eyes. Her very young, very blue, and very nineteen-year-old eyes. *Shit.* I forgot she's underage again.

Whatever. I take a drink and head out of the kitchen. She works in a bar, doesn't she? I'm sure customers have bought her shots before.

I plant my ass back on the couch, hanging my arm around the back of the seat and taking another drink. The movie still has a few minutes left, and she sits down at the other end to finish watching, but I can't seem to concentrate anymore.

And I don't think she's watching, either.

Something's changed. The conversation was easy, and then it wasn't. And it's my fault. I'm cold. Somewhere after Lindsay and the chaos, I stopped being able to open up. I got too used to being alone.

I frown. I don't want her to avoid me because I can't carry on a fucking conversation. She's Cole's girlfriend, and I don't want walls between him and me anymore. She could help with that.

"Are you planning to stay in town after you finish school?" I ask.

She glances over and shrugs a little. "I'm not sure. It's still a few years off," she says. "I don't really mind it here as long as I can afford vacations from time to time." She laughs a little. "I just don't want to be working a dead-end job forever, you know? If I can find work in the area, then it might be nice to stick around for my sister and my nephew for a while."

There's lots of construction going on here and in surrounding towns and suburbs. Which is why I found it easy to stay all these years. If she's getting into landscape design, it's very possible she'll have good prospects if she stays in the area.

"Have you ever traveled?" I ask, glancing over at her.

But then I stop, suddenly forgetting what I was saying. I drop my eyes to her ass, her body now twisted around as she leans over the arm of the couch to set her beer down. Her little shorts hug every curve, her knees are spread a little, and for a moment, I'm drawn to the dip between her thighs.

Heat floods my groin, and my cock throbs.

Shit. I look away.

I struggle for air and sweat breaks out on my neck. *What the fuck?*

She may not seem young, but she is. She's a kid. What the hell am I doing?

She sits back down, and I tip up my bottle, taking another swig to cover my nerves.

"Not really," she answers.

What did I ask her again? Oh, right. Traveling.

"I went to New Orleans with my sister when I was fifteen, and I won a scholarship to a summer camp in Virginia when I was twelve," she tells me. "That's about it."

"New Orleans at fifteen?" I joke. Must've been interesting.

A thoughtful smile crosses her face, but it falls quickly. "That's where my mom lives," she says.

Oh, yeah, that's right. Her dad is Chip Hadley. I don't pay much attention to gossip, but I know he's been married a couple times.

Jordan clears her throat, sitting up. "She left when I was four."

Four? What kind of person would leave her like that?

She sits quietly, looking like she's thinking, and an urge comes over me to have her in my arms.

Right now.

"When my sister graduated from high school, we tracked her down," she explains, "and we took a road trip that summer to visit her."

"How did it go?"

She shrugs a little. "Fine, I guess. She was waitressing, had a little apartment, and was living her life. She was pleased to see us. Now that we're grown and don't need a lot of care, I suppose," she adds.

She finally looks over at me, quirking a sad smile.

"Did you ask her why she left?" I inquire.

But she just shakes her head. "No, I used to want to know, but then when I met her, I didn't really care anymore." She pauses and then adds, "I didn't like her."

I watch her, remaining quiet. Does Cole have those thoughts about me?

"So, have you ever been married?" Her voice is light, and I can tell she's trying to change the subject.

I sit up, taking a deep breath and rolling my eyes at myself. "Cole's mom and I didn't last long after he was born," I tell her, "and I don't know . . . I got caught up in trying to build a livelihood—a future. Got used to being alone."

I run my fingers over my scalp, finally resting my head on my hand and looking over at her. But she looks skeptical, studying me with something cautious in her eyes. Like she doesn't believe that's why I'm still single.

"There were chances to get married," I say, assuring her, "but I guess even in high school I never wanted to be one of the numbers and do what I was supposed to do, you know? Graduate, get a job, get married, have kids . . . die."

I breathe out a laugh, but surprisingly, the words are coming easy now.

"My grandfather, the one who also smoked cigars," I clarify, "passed away when I was nine, but I still remember this house party my parents had when my dad finished college. He was in his thirties, the first one in the family to get a college education, so it was a big deal."

She sits back in the seat, holding the bottle with both hands and listening.

"I think I was like six years old at the time," I tell her. "My grandparents were there, and everyone was talking and laughing, but what I remember most is my grandfather, in his sixties, six foot four and two hundred fifty pounds, shaking the foundations of the house because he was dancing around to 'Jump' by the Pointer Sisters."

She breaks into a smile. Yeah, you can just picture it.

"My grandmother watched from the table, laughing with everyone else with this look of joy." I swallow, remembering the huge smile on her face. "Everyone was just so happy, and even at their age, they kept growing, having fun, being silly . . ." I trail off. "I don't know. I liked that, I guess."

"You *want* that," Jordan says quietly.

I think about my grandparents, constantly making each other smile, and all the women I've been with, and how I never felt that. Not even with Lindsay. I was probably incapable.

"It just didn't look forced, you know?" I go on, turning to her. "They set a high standard. It's hard to find that one person who speaks your language."

She drops her eyes, looking deep in thought.

I keep going, changing the subject. "What about you?" I broach. "Any ideas about how you want your life to be someday? Your marriage, the wedding, the perfect day, the perfect dress . . . ?"

She just sighs and takes a drink from the bottle. "I really don't care about the wedding," she says, staring back at the television. "I just want the life."

The life.

Those words hit hard, and I don't know why.

Maybe because I'm still waiting for the same thing.

Over a week later, and the house has settled into a routine, thanks to our pizza and movie night.

Jordan is usually already up when I come downstairs in the morning, and I notice there's a nicer sheen on the tabletops and countertops that wasn't there the evening before. The floors feel clean, the refrigerator is magically free of bad food and three-day-old leftovers, and the appliances shine.

Everything smells fragrant, too, and sometimes it's because she made muffins or pancakes, and sometimes it's because of the scented candles I no longer mind her burning in the house. She uses a French press for coffee, and I've stopped using my Keurig in favor of it.

Anything Cole left lying in the living room the night before, like shoes or soda cans, is suddenly gone, and I can't remember the last time I had to unload the dishwasher.

And I don't, for one moment, believe it's thanks to my kid. He's become pretty damn lazy, it seems, and I hadn't realized how he'd changed.

The more he grew up, the less time he wanted to spend with me, and I see hints of how his mom was with me in how he treats Jordan now. He's neglectful, and I find myself grinding my teeth to keep my mouth shut and my opinions to myself.

I love my kid, but it's hard to see why he deserves her.

He's hardly ever home except to sleep, and when he is, Jordan's at work until two in the morning. I was worried I'd walk in on them having sex on the couch or something when I offered to let them live here, but thank God, their schedules don't mesh well so they're hardly here at the same time. And if they are, I'm at work, and I don't have to hear or see anything.

Still, though, she's alone a lot. He won't even stay home on her nights off, and I wonder why the hell she puts up with it. She seems capable and strong-willed. A girl who can handle herself. What brought them together? She doesn't seem to have anyone but Cole and that sister of hers, in fact. No friends or other family members have dropped by here to see her that I can tell.

Either way, though, I'm enjoying having her around, even if I do wish Cole was home more. I break into a smile as soon as I walk through the door every afternoon, hearing her eighties music carrying through the house and somehow making it feel even more like summertime in here. It's nice not to come home to an empty house for a change, and I even find myself leaving work on time every day, because I actually enjoy being home now.

She and I have chatted more over the last several days, inquiring about how work was or how school is going for her, and the girl has an uncanny ability to get me to talk. She likes to run shit, and she's good about teasing or making jokes to put me at ease.

I can do without her eggplant lasagna, that's for sure, but if she weren't here, Cole would be avoiding me even more than he is now, and I wouldn't be holding my tongue with him as well as I am. I'm glad she's here.

Holding the bag of laundry over my shoulder, I charge down the stairs, swing around the banister, and walk into the laundry room.

After clearing my clothes out of the dryer, I move the stuff from the washer and drop a new load in, starting both machines again. I catch sight of the dust on the front of my T-shirt from working in the garage this morning and pull it off, dropping it in the running water before closing the lid.

Stuffing the bag on top of the dry clothes, I pick up the basket and head back upstairs. In my room, I dump the clothes onto the bed and sift through the pile, looking for another shirt.

But I stop, grazing my fingers over a tiny piece of red fabric I don't recognize. It lies nestled in a pair of my jeans, and I don't have to think twice to know what it is.

I stand up straight, steeling my spine.

Shit.

Hooking my finger through the little band, I eye the see-through red G-string hanging from my finger.

"What the hell?" I say under my breath, looking down at the laundry to double-check I have my clothes. "How did this get in my stuff?"

"Jord—!" I call out for her but stop, realizing how awkward it's going to look if I have her underwear. I'm going to look like some creeper, getting caught with her panties. *Jesus.*

I drop the undergarment like it's a hot pan.

It falls to the bed, and I rub the back of my neck, feeling the light sweat on my skin. My mind wanders.

It's been a hell of a long time since any woman's underwear was on my bed. Or in my bed.

And it certainly wasn't a G-string, either. An image of my son's innocent little girlfriend wearing this flashes in my head, and I round my eyes, rearing back a little. "Fuck. I'm gonna go to hell."

I gather up all the laundry again, burying the garment in my clothes to hide it, so I can take the basket back downstairs. I'll just toss the underwear on top of the dryer or something and let her find it.

Picking up the basket, though, I register the soft rumble of the lawn mower starting up outside and set the laundry back down, walking to the window.

Jordan is in the backyard, marching up and down the grass and pushing my green Craftsman lawn mower. What is she—

I lock my jaw, aggravation setting in. I told Cole to mow the goddamn grass. Helping with the yard work is his responsibility.

I watch as she bobs her head, and that's when I notice the high-pitched whir of guitars and the beats of a drum. She must be listening to music.

I quirk a smile. What awful eighties hair band is she listening to today?

Sweat darkens her gray T-shirt at the middle of her back, and even from here I can see her hair, some having fallen free from her ponytail, sticking to her neck. Her short white shorts show off the muscles in her thighs and calves, flexing as she pushes the machine. Her skin glistens with sweat, and I zone in on the small of her back, seeing her damp skin shine in the sunlight.

Heat pools low in my stomach, and my smile falls as I watch her.

I'm frozen. I don't want to look away.

But finally, I blink, averting my eyes and swallowing through the dryness in my mouth.

Doesn't she have a project or something to be working on for her summer class? She mentioned that a few days ago. Cole can do the damn lawn.

Reaching down, I lift up the window and stick my head out, opening my mouth to call her out, but all of a sudden she releases the handle, whips her head back and forth, and breaks into air-guitar mode.

I stop and watch her, furrowing my brow but damn near breaking into a laugh, too.

"Pour some sugar on me!" the Bluetooth speaker screams. "Ooh, in the name of love!"

She lip-syncs, bending herself backward, and then breaks into other moves, dancing and getting carried away in the song.

Gripping the handle again, she uses it for support as she throws her head from side to side, flipping her hair and swaying her hips. The rubber band from her ponytail falls out and the locks whip around, the beautiful kink in the strands falling in her face and making her look absolutely stunning. My lungs ache for air as desire rips through me, watching her move. God, if she's yours, how do you not touch her twenty-four seven?

I stop the thought in its tracks, though, and start to pull my head back in, but I catch sight of Kyle Cramer next door, standing on his bedroom balcony.

He stares down at Jordan, watching her dance.

My fingers tighten around the window frame.

Asshole. His kids are probably in the house, and he's leering like a fucking pervert.

I try not to think about how I'm practically doing the same thing, but I feel a protective urge to get a damn shotgun or something. *This one's not babysitting for you, dickhead.*

The lawn mower suddenly dies, and I turn back to Jordan just in time to see her walk up to the edge of the pool, breathing heavily and wet with sweat. She pushes her hair out of her face, inhales a deep breath, and then takes a step, falling into the deep end of the pool and sinking beneath its surface, clothes and all.

I stop breathing.

It's hot. It's in the nineties today, and she needs to cool off. But I jerk my gaze back to Kyle as he inches his chin up, trying to get a better view. Jordan then pops back up to the surface, floating on her back and resting there, her T-shirt molded to her body like a second skin. Hard little points jut toward the sky from under her shirt, and I see a smile curl his fucking lips.

"Fucking hell," I hiss under my breath. Swinging my head back into the bedroom, I slam the window closed.

Leaving the room, I charge down the hallway and jog down the stairs. Moving across the kitchen, I head through the laundry room and out the back door. Jordan is swimming for the edge of the pool, getting out.

I dart my eyes up and see Kyle still watching as she climbs out, her clothes plastered to her body and water running down every inch of available skin.

His eyes flash to me, and I shoot him a middle finger. He just laughs and shakes his head, going back into his fucking house.

Jordan fists her hair, bringing it over her shoulder and wringing it out. My gaze falls down her legs, water dripping down her toned thighs and her shorts melted to her ass.

I steel myself, fixing on a stern expression. "Jordan," I call.

She turns, seeing me, and hesitates only a moment before heading my way. She must have some idea that she's not completely appropriate right now, because she folds her arms over her chest.

"I thought I told Cole to mow the lawn." I try to hide the growl building in my chest.

She nods and picks up her ice water off the lawn table. "As long as it gets done, right?" And then she looks at me, inquiring, "Am I doing a bad job?"

"Of course, n— No," I reply quickly, hating how easily she can make me feel like an ungrateful asshole. "It looks fine, but you're already doing enough. More than enough. He handles the yard work. He can find the damn time."

"It's fine." She brushes me off and sets her water down, turning back for the lawn mower. "I need the sun and exercise anyway."

"I'll finish it." I stop her, walking ahead toward the mower.

But she catches me by the arm. "I got it," she maintains, anger growing in her eyes. "Seriously. We're not here on a free ride. I can handle a few chores."

"Not dressed like that, you can't."

Her eyebrows pinch together. "Excuse me?"

I inch forward, dropping my voice as I speak to her. "My neighbor has been glued to his balcony watching your every move out here," I bite out. "God knows what he's thinking."

"That's not my problem," she argues. "I was hot. I jumped in the pool. My clothes are on."

"Yeah, like a second skin," I finish for her, my teeth baring. "You can't pull that shit here. It's a family neighborhood. Not your sister's strip club."

"I'm in the backyard!" she growls, her face tensing. "What does anyone care how I'm dressed?"

"Their wives will!"

She arches an eyebrow and her chest heaves with angry breaths.

I look down at her, calming my voice. "The wives in this neighborhood don't appreciate cockteases strutting around and taunting their husbands, okay?" I state in plain English, so she gets it through her head.

But she just lets out a bitter laugh like she can't believe I'm for real. "Uh . . . yeah, wow." She nods and takes in a deep breath, lifting her chin and looking at me head-on. "Um, okay, here's the thing . . . I realize things were probably a little different back when you were a teenager—*eighty-nine years ago!*" she fires back.

"It was twenty, thank you."

"But nowadays," she keeps going, "we don't hold a woman responsible for a man's behavior." Her eyes pierce, and there's a little snarl on her lips. "If he wants to look, I can't stop him. If he wants to step off somewhere private and do a little self-lovin', hey, I'll never know. Not my problem!"

I clench my fists. *Damn brat.*

I can't catch my breath, but we don't break eye contact.

She's right.

I know she's right. She's not doing anything wrong. I just . . .

I don't like him looking.

At her.

After a few seconds, I collect myself and straighten, taking pleasure that I'm half a foot taller. "Cole does the yard work. Or me," I tell her. "Got it?"

I don't wait for an answer as I spin around, heading for the lawn mower.

But I hear her small, sweet voice behind me. "Yes, Daddy."

I blink long and hard, my hand tingling with an urge to give someone a spanking for the first time in my life.

6

Jordan

I haven't spoken to Pike since the argument yesterday. I refuse to call it a fight. We barely know each other. How can we be fighting?

I also haven't talked to Cole since yesterday, either, but for some reason, that's not bugging me. It's how we roll. He was gone yesterday, helping a friend with his car, and by the time he made it home I was at the bar. I slept in this morning, more as an effort to avoid running into Pike in the house than for any other reason, and only woke up once when Cole left a goodbye peck on my cheek before heading to work himself.

My stomach has been in knots all morning. Why the hell was Pike so angry? I thought we were getting along. I didn't do anything wrong. In fact, I was mowing his fucking grass, and the next thing I know he's ripping into me like I'm sunbathing topless on the front lawn while six-year-olds race their bikes down the street.

He's so volatile. Very unlike his son, who never takes anything seriously.

I climb out of Cole's car; he caught a ride with one of his friends this morning so I could get to the library. I grab Pike's lunch box, which he left at home, and take a look around the jobsite. It's busier than the last time I was here.

Workers move about, dressed in hard hats with brown leather tool belts hanging from their hips, and dust kicks up from the trucks moving in and out of the area. Hammers hit steel, and men with dirty boots and scuffed jeans straddle beams high in the air as they do whatever it is that they do to turn materials into a building. Not many get to see the bare-bones view. I wonder why Cole doesn't work for his father. This job has to pay well. I know some of these guys, after all. They support families off this job.

My gaze wanders, looking for someone accessible to drop off the lunch box to, but I'm kind of on alert, looking for Pike's tattoos, too. I don't want to see him, really. My plan when I saw he'd left his lunch at home this morning was to do a nice deed, drop it off, and leave the ball in his court to get over the argument by seeking me out to say thank you. I want to get over whatever awkwardness is between us.

Stepping over the dirt and debris lying around, I make my way for the structure and spot his friend Dutch bending over to pick something up just inside. He notices me and rises.

"Hey, Dutch." I smile. "Is Pike around?"

His eyes drop to the black insulated bag in my hand. "His lunch?"

"He left it sitting on the kitchen table." I hold it up for him. "Thought I'd drop it off while I'm running errands."

"That's nice of you." But he doesn't take the lunch box. Instead, he tosses a tool down into a box and gestures to me. "Come on, I'll take you up."

"Oh, no, that's okay," I tell him. "I don't want to bug him. I'll just leave it with you."

"If you leave that with me, I'll eat it. Or lose it." He chuckles and leads me toward some stairs.

My shoulders slump. *Awesome.*

We head up to the third floor, taking what I assume will be the emergency stairwell once the elevators are installed, and reach a landing with only frames for the walls, showing how the offices and work areas will be divided once it's finished.

Pike is the only one on the floor, far off on the left side and hovering over a clipboard.

He hears us approach and looks up from his paperwork, turning his head.

His eyes narrow on me, and I blink long and hard, feeling stupid.

He's wearing a navy blue T-shirt, and the color on him brings heat to my cheeks. I love how it looks against his tanned arms and the curves of his biceps.

"What are you doing here?" he asks.

He doesn't sound annoyed like I was afraid, though. Just puzzled.

I lift up the bag. "You left your lunch on the table."

His expression relaxes, and the tension in his body eases. "Oh, thanks." He walks over, and I hand it to him. "It's okay, though," he tells me. "I could've grabbed something from the food truck. You didn't have to go through the trouble."

The food truck? "Well, I couldn't let you eat crap from a food truck," I say.

And to my relief, he smiles a little. "It's basically the same stuff that's in there," he points out, setting the lunch box on a worktable.

But I'm way ahead of him. "Well, I snuck in a turkey and cheese cucumber wrap, too, in case you want something different."

His face falls.

"Don't worry," I tease. "Your lunch is still in there. I just made too much and needed help finishing the wrap."

The slight fear in his eyes dispels, and he takes a breath. "You're not going to be happy until I'm eating hummus, are you?"

I try not to laugh. "I'll build you up slowly."

He rolls his eyes, and I finally take a deep breath. I guess we're over the argument.

I stand there, feeling his eyes on me, the sounds of hammers pounding and the breeze blowing through the structure slowly fading away.

Then I realize that Dutch is still in the room.

We both look over at him, his gaze shifting between us.

"I'll go"—he swallows and clears his throat—"do something," he says and walks away, leaving us alone.

I look back at Pike, and I guess I should go, too, and leave him to it, but instead, I slide my hands into my pockets and gaze around. "The sawdust smells good," I tell him.

A smile reaches his eyes, and he nods, looking around. "Yeah. It's like home to me."

When our gazes meet again, heat pools low in my belly, and I forget to breathe for a moment. I quickly look away.

"I apologize for going off on you yesterday," he says. "You didn't do anything wrong. Cramer was leering, and it was creepy. I got aggravated." And then he clarifies, "Aggravated with him, I mean. I'm sorry I took it out on you."

"I work in a bar," I point out. "I'm used to a little leering. I can handle it."

Really, I can stand up and fight for my honor all on my own. And so can Cole. If it ever occurs to him. Pike doesn't need to feel responsible for me. I'm not his to take care of.

"Well, I'll get going," I tell him and start backing away.

But he stops me. "You wanna see?" he offers. "A little tour?"

I've already seen a great deal of the place, since I was here sandbagging last week, but I nod anyway. "Yeah, sure."

He leads me toward the back of the building, and I wonder if I'm supposed to be wearing a hard hat, but he's not wearing one, either, so I don't ask.

"It's supposed to be office space for that casino riverboat that's coming to the area," he explains. "There'll be a pavilion at the dock with restaurants and event space, but they're going to run everything from here. Hiring, finances, advertising . . ."

He shoots me a smile, and I look away again.

"It's like a skeleton," I comment. "When do the walls go up?"

"Once the plumbers and electricians get everything squared away," he replies, "I install the insulation and then we start walling it up. You'll see rooms instead of bones."

We enter a large space at the rear corner of the building, and unlike the other rooms, there's an entire wall without beams. Like it's going to be just one huge picture window there. I step into the small adjacent space and peer over the beam in front of my face.

"What's this space?"

He looks over at me. "It's a private bathroom for this office."

Must be nice. I stroll back into the office with him and walk over to the edge, looking out over the undeveloped land and green in the distance.

"Nice view." I smile and flip my hair, spinning around in my pretend office like I own the place. "Yes, Christopher, would you please get Japan on the line? We need to discuss the production line in Malaysia," I play.

He chuckles. "You have a male secretary?"

"A man can be anything," I retort. "Don't let your sex hold you back."

He shakes his head at me, amusement curling his lips.

We settle into the ease we had the other night when we watched TV and ate pizza, and I follow him around the building, letting him explain the months- to possibly yearlong process of erecting a building from the ground up. He started doing this work before Cole was born, and he eventually formed his own company, able to make his own rules and have more control over the types of projects he takes on. It has to be a lot of responsibility, though, knowing you're in charge of two dozen workers and the paychecks that support their families.

But still . . . he's helping to grow our town, bringing work in, and getting jobs himself.

"You must be so proud to build things you get to see every day," I tell him when we're back down on the first floor. "Places where people will spend their lives and earn their livelihoods."

"I never really thought about it like that." He stops at the rear of the building, looking out at the acres of empty space beyond. "It's my livelihood, too, I guess."

I look out and notice an outdoor space attached to the back of the building. It's large, and I can already see a marble fountain haphazardly placed for later setup.

"Is this going to be a courtyard?" I inquire, noting there's no roof. "That's a nice idea. Do you build that, too?"

"Oh, no," he replies. "A landscaping company will come when the building is nearly complete and take care of planting the grass, trees, and installing the aesthetics."

Right up my alley. I love the before and after, seeing an outdoor space transform.

"I'll let you know when they start," he offers as if reading my mind. "You can pop in every now and then to see the progress."

I smile. "Thanks."

I'd like that, actually. Aside from my teachers, no one else I know really enjoys stuff like this. Our eyes meet, and I realize that's something I've been missing. I don't have a lot in common with the other people in my life, do I?

We're locked on each other but only for a moment. A worker passes by, carrying lumber over his shoulder, and Pike suddenly straightens, breaking eye contact with me and nodding a hello to him.

"Well, I should"—I jerk my thumb behind me—"get going, I guess."

"Yeah," he answers. "Me, too."

I back away. "See you at home. I'll have dinner ready by five."

He just nods and turns back to his work.

Home. Not *the house*? It's not my home, after all.

I walk back to the car and climb in, feeling more out of sorts than when I came here. Dinner by five? Cole doesn't get off until six. Did I suddenly just forget he exists?

I wrap the towel around my body and gather up my dirty clothes, the bathroom still thick with steam. Cracking open the door, I peek into the hallway to make sure it's clear, and dash across to my bedroom, closing my door behind me.

I keep forgetting to take clean clothes in with me, so I can get dressed right after my shower. I'm still used to having my own place and not caring if I cross the hallway in my towel. At least I'm remembering to put on pajama shorts if I go downstairs for water in the middle of the night. Doubt I wouldn't die of embarrassment if Cole's dad caught me in my underwear and T-shirt.

Taking my brush, I comb out my wet hair and pick out something to wear to bed. I see a glow from outside and walk over to the blinds, peering through a crack. It's dark out—after nine by now—but Pike is still at it, in the driveway, working on my VW.

He's pretty awesome. Cole's been busy on everyone else's car but mine, although I suspect it's just an excuse for him to get out of the house.

A bright shop light hangs from my propped-up hood, and Pike circles the VW and leans over, unscrewing something. He's been out there since after dinner. He wanted Cole's help, but of course, he's out again. I think he's waiting for him.

A couple women walk down the sidewalk, dressed in workout clothes, and stop, smiling and calling out something to Pike.

The brunette on the left jogs in place, even though she was just speed-walking a moment ago, while the redhead puts her hands on her hips and gives him a flirty smile.

"Seriously?" I mumble. *Who the hell goes walking this time of night?* "Smooth, ladies. Real smooth."

Like they didn't see Pike out there working through their kitchen windows, shirtless with muscles flexing against his tanned skin, still looking every inch the bad-boy hottie they drooled over in high school, probably. Then they gave each other a call to hatch a plan to don their activewear and "just happen to jog past his place," right? I mean, it would be rude, after all, not to say hi, right?

I roll my eyes. Suburban housewives, bored with their husbands, looking to stir up shit like Pike Lawson is a pit stop to be used to excite them.

I release the blinds and back away.

I'm being so mean.

So they're flirting. So what?

I've taken pride in the fact that I'm a pretty levelheaded, calm person, but my behavior has been erratic lately. The move, the bills, Cole . . . I'm out of sorts, uncertain, and all over the place. I don't like it.

I start a playlist on my phone, "Pity Party" droning out to match my pissy mood as the bedroom door clicks shut behind me. I stop brushing my hair, turning my head.

Cole is suddenly standing in the room, leaning against the door and staring at me with a look in his eyes I know all too well. When did he get home?

Heat rises to my skin, and I clutch my towel, but I don't know why.

He crosses his arms over his chest as his eyes scale down my body and back up.

"What?" I ask when he says nothing.

"Drop the towel."

Now? But his father is still awake, and . . .

"Come on," I protest but try to keep my tone light and calm. "It's getting late, and I'm exhausted."

"I'll get you in the mood." He pushes off the door and moves toward me, his six feet easily crowding the small bedroom. "I never see you anymore. I miss you."

He steps up and wraps his arms around my waist, gazing down at me. I can't help but smile a little.

I bite my bottom lip playfully and grip his soft blond hair on the top of his head, bringing him in for a quick kiss. "I was home last night," I reply. "You weren't."

I pull away from him and tighten my towel around me.

"I invited you out," he points out.

"I was tired," I say, but I can feel everything that's been building inside of me for days about to bust free. "And I've had to do your chores, so . . ."

"I didn't tell you to do that."

"It had to get done."

The desire I felt for him a moment ago has faded, and there's a wall rising between us now.

But he tries to navigate around it anyway. "My dad's not going to kick me out if I'm a couple days late mowing the lawn, Jordan," he says, trying to put his arms around me again. "You take things too seriously."

"No, you didn't do it because you knew I would." I turn away. "As usual. You need to get it together and stop doing the bare minimum."

He lets out a sigh and releases me, turning toward the door.

"Where are you going?"

"I can't listen to this right now," he grits out. "You know why I'm always gone? Because of that." He points at my face. "The way you look at me. I'm tired of not feeling good enough."

"Oh, that's awesome," I shoot back sarcastically, grabbing a pair of his boxers out of a drawer and one of his flannel shirts off the chair. "I'm only here to be with you, and you're always gone. You know, I spend more time with your dad! Don't you think that's a little awkward for him?"

"You got somewhere else to go, then go if you're so uncomfortable."

My breath catches in my throat, and I glare at him. "Are you serious? You're actually saying that to me right now."

I already feel like a pathetic freeloader when I'm not the one who got us evicted. I've always been there for him. We're friends, dammit. We've always looked out for each other. I would never make him feel . . . *Son of a bitch.*

I pull on the boxers and throw off the towel, pulling on the red and brown flannel shirt and buttoning it. Tears spring to my eyes.

My sister was right. I could've sucked it up for a few weeks, worked at The Hook, and been able to stay in my place. At least I wouldn't feel like I'm not wanted.

He moves toward me again, his voice softer. "All I'm saying is it would be nice to put the stress behind us once in a while and show each other a little attention. I can't remember the last time we had sex."

And after the sex? Everything that's wrong would still be wrong.

"Maybe if I weren't doing all your shit around here and working until two a.m., I wouldn't be so tired all the time," I tell him. "And maybe if you were helping me save money, so we could get our own place again, instead of drinking your paychecks away every damn night, I wouldn't be so worried and stressed about money. I feel fucking alone. Where are you?"

He just shakes his head, and I can't help the tears from welling. But I refuse to cry. We need to talk, and he won't. He won't give me the one thing that will fix this.

He comes for me, taking my face in his hands. "Just shut up for a while and fuck me."

He kisses me, and I squeeze my eyes shut, the tears now spilling over and streaming down my cheeks. Goddamn him. He steals my breath, covering my mouth and moving over my lips hard and forceful, and I want to give in. The stress and the worry have gone on so long and been too much, and if I could just forget for a while it would feel so good.

Gripping my ass in both hands, he lifts me up, forcing my legs around his waist, and we fall back on the bed, Cole coming down on top of me.

Something holds me back, though. Like I'm back in the trailer park with my dad and stepmom. They don't see me.

Cole doesn't see me. I could be anyone right now.

I tear my mouth away and push at him. "Get off me."

"Baby, please." He kisses my neck, and I know him well enough to know that sound in his voice. He's upset, too. "Just be a girlfriend for tonight. We used to have fun. Let's just have fun."

"No." I shake my head, tensing. "I'm pissed at you. I need some air."

And I'll feel worse when it's over.

He keeps kissing me, and I growl, shoving him off. He finally lets go and falls to the bed next to me. He barely hesitates and then he's on his feet and yanking open the bedroom door, charging out of the room.

In moments, I hear his engine start, tires peel, and then he's gone.

Asshole.

But part of me can't help but breathe easier now, too.

I feel like I belong here more when he's *not* here.

He never used to treat me like that. Tears well in my eyes, but I blink, pushing them away.

Rising from the bed, I go over to the TV stand and pick up the stack of bills to be paid lying on top. A water bill from the old apartment, a doctor bill still not completely paid off from when I thought I broke my ankle last summer, a phone bill, and two of Cole's credit card bills about to go to collection. I don't have medical insurance, and every day I'm scared something is going to happen that will take me to the hospital for a twenty-thousand-dollar emergency room visit.

I have no working car, and even if I did, I can barely afford the insurance anyway, with whatever extra student loan money I'll have after my tuition is paid in the fall going to living expenses. I can take out another loan, but I don't want to be weighed down with that bill for the rest of my life, so I try not to take out much.

And every time I check the mail, there's a new, unfortunate surprise.

Opening the top drawer of the bureau, I pull out the tips I've made the last week that I haven't deposited yet and spread out the wrinkled bills in my hands.

A hundred forty-two dollars. The hole I'm in keeps getting deeper, because I'm not making enough to dig myself out.

I stuff the cash back into the drawer and pick out the wet T-shirt contest flyer I hid in there, as well, and look at it. Three hundred dollars isn't enough to make it worth it, but bartending at The Hook or . . . doing what my sister does and bringing home that kind of money might be.

For a moment, I can't help but entertain the idea. To be able to have cash in my pocket that isn't already gone the moment I earn it. To have nice things. To have a car.

But then I think of Cole and Jay and the guys I went to school with coming in and watching me, and I shove the paper back into the drawer, wanting to throw up. Strangers might not be unbearable, but I'm not dancing for the guys I went to high school with.

And bartending there would be almost as bad. The outfits I'd have to wear, the customers I'd be serving . . .

Leaving the bedroom, I head downstairs and round the banister, continuing into the kitchen, through the laundry room, and out the back door.

The air hits me, and suddenly, I can breathe again. The fragrant trees and the smell of freshly mowed grass fill my nostrils, and aside from the light illuminating the pool underneath the water and a candle burning on the patio table, it's completely dark back here.

I walk to the deep end and sit on the edge, submerging my legs in the water halfway up my calves. The cool water covers my skin like a hug, instantly easing my heated nerves.

Cole will be back late. By then, we'll both have calmed down, he'll climb into bed, I'll spoon him, and he'll layer his hands with mine, our signal to each other that everything will be fine.

I need to relax. I'm nineteen, and I have money worries and relationship problems. Who doesn't at my age? I'm too hard on myself. Pike seems fine with me being here, so I'll continue to pull my weight, and he won't have cause for complaint.

And worse comes to worst, my father would never turn me away at the door. Everything will be fine. It might not be right now, but it will be.

I smile a little, almost convinced. Looking down at the blue surface of the water, and the white light illuminating the clean bottom of the pool, I feel a sudden urge to prove it.

I can do it.

Everything will be fine.

And I take a deep breath, close my eyes, and leap, pushing myself off the edge and into the water. Bubbles pour out of my mouth as I release air and sink to the bottom of the pool. My hair floats around me, the water caressing my scalp, and the flannel billows up as I cross my legs and sit on the floor of the pool.

I don't know when I started doing this. I didn't grow up with a pool, of course, but maybe it was summer camp when I was twelve or Cam taking me to the public pool as a kid when I realized how scared I could get of the unknown. I like to challenge that part of myself, because it boosts my confidence when I succeed.

Taking my laundry down to the seedy basement at the old apartment by myself. Sleeping in the dark without even the hall light on. Driving home at two o'clock in the morning after a shift and not checking the back seat to make sure I'm alone in the car.

I look around, twisting my head and seeing nothing but water, but my vision only takes me so far and the view fogs into nothing. Anything could come swimming out of the distance and toward me. Anything could be behind me. Anything could come up from the drain or dive in from the surface.

I close my eyes.

If I can do this, Cole and I will be fine. Everything will be good, and I'll just keep trucking.

My lungs start to ache, but I keep my eyes closed and remain still. Something is staring at me. And there's something slinking through the water, heading straight for me. I feel it. It's coming for me.

I know it's my fear, so I keep my eyes shut, pressing on. I know everything will be fine. It's my imagination.

I can do it. I can do it. My lungs stretch painfully, and my throat burns, but I squeeze my fists. Just another second. One more second.

But suddenly, the water shakes around me, and I pop my eyes open, knowing that it's not my imagination this time. I look up and see Pike just as he's reaching out for me. He grabs me under my arms, and I bat at him, shaking my head.

My lungs are done, though, and I can't take any more. Pushing him away through the water, I plant my feet on the bottom of the pool and push off, shooting for the surface.

I break through, coughing, with my hair plastered to my face. I hear him spit water out next to me.

"What the hell are you doing?" I growl.

"I thought you were drowning! What the hell? What were *you* doing?"

I cough again, wheezing as I draw in a lungful of air. "Facing my fears. Damn," I grumble as I swim for the edge.

"Are you okay?"

"I'm fine." I swing my arm up and over the ledge, my muscles weak from the scare he just gave me.

"Are you sure?"

He hauls himself up and climbs out of the pool, reaching out a hand for me to take.

I ignore it and the question, pushing myself up to sit on the edge again.

If he saw me go into the water, then I guess he was probably wondering what I was doing there, but still . . .

I almost beat the challenge.

The shirt hangs on me, heavy and wet, but I can't take it off. There's nothing on underneath. I cough again, clearing my throat and catching my breath. He stands next to me, quiet.

"I heard you and Cole fighting," he finally says.

From outside? *Great.*

He squats down next to me, facing the water, too. I can't imagine what he must be thinking. I'm fighting with his son, and then I'm diving fully clothed into a pool. Yeah . . .

I take a deep breath, making sure to calm my tone to ease him. "I make deals with myself," I say to him but don't meet his eyes. "If I can do something I don't want to do, then everything will be fine. If I do something that scares me, then I can beat whatever else comes." I half smile. "I don't like to swim alone. It creeps me out. Especially at night."

I finally turn my gaze on him. He's staring down at the pool, listening.

"It's a game I play with myself," I tell him.

He nods, understanding.

"Cole doesn't want me here," I say, dropping my eyes as needles stab my throat. "I don't think he wants me at all anymore."

I don't know why I'm telling him this, but he listens. On the rare occasions we have talked, he seems to *want* to hear. It's easy with him.

"He's young," he explains. "We all do and say selfish things when we think we own the world."

"Do I?" I shoot back.

I mean, I'm no angel, but I know I treat Cole better than he treats me.

Pike doesn't say anything, but I can see him looking at me.

I'm a pushover. I walked away from my ex and my parents, but I never let them have it. I never fought back. I just ran.

Aside from my sister, Cole is all I have, and I let shit slide because he was more to me than just a boyfriend.

"Can I ask you a question?" Pike says.

I glance at him, my heart skipping a beat at seeing his eyes cast down and locked on me. The reflection of the water makes them look cloudy blue.

"How did you and Cole meet?" he asks.

And despite my aggravation, I smile a little.

My eyes drop to the scar on my thumb, and I lick my lips. "When I was sixteen, I worked at a car wash," I tell him. "No other girls worked there, but it was all I could find, so I gutted it out with a team full of guys."

I feel the heat from his body next to me, and I time the rise and fall of his chest, finding myself matching it.

"I got a lot of crap," I continue, remembering the snide comments every time I bent over or leaned into a car. "Teenage guys can be . . ."

"Yeah," Pike finishes for me knowingly, humor in his voice. We exchange a grin.

He used to be a teenage guy, too, after all, I guess.

"There was a guy named Nick who always got people off my back," I go on, remembering. "He was nice to me and talked to me. He didn't leer or act immature."

I absently rub my finger over the scar.

"One day he invites me to hang out, and he brings Cole along." I look over at Pike, the anger from earlier suddenly gone now. "We all became friends, had a lot of fun, and I think I became closer to them than I have been to anyone. Except my sister, that is."

He nods, looking like he's thinking. And then he asks, "And you and Cole started dating? How did Nick take that?"

I turn my eyes back out to the pool, taking in a deep breath. "He never knew," I say quietly.

Pike remains quiet, the tension in the air thick now. I said *he never knew*. Not *he doesn't know*.

I clear my throat. "One night, a couple years ago, before Cole and I were seeing each other," I tell him. "He and Nick were out together. Cole had too much to drink, and he passed out. Nick caught a ride home with someone else."

Tears prick the backs of my eyes, and my mouth is so dry.

"The driver lost control of his truck, it rolled, and all the kids in the back of the bed went tumbling out."

"Oh, my God," he says under his breath, dropping his head.

I finish. "Nick was caught under. He died a couple days later."

I squeeze my fists to try to keep from crying. He was the only person I knew who died. It wasn't like my mom leaving. Nick didn't want to go. He lived for video games, and his hair was always hanging over his glasses, and I miss all of his quirks.

Sometimes I wonder what happened to his little brother's Nerf gun that we all used and all skinned our thumbs on.

"Jesus Christ," Pike mumbles. "How did I not know about that? I faintly remember hearing something, but I didn't know Cole was friends with anyone in that accident."

I sit up straight and nod. "Yeah, Cole . . ." I pause, trying to find my words. "He had a hard time getting over it."

Pike's eyes narrow on me.

"He was supposed to be Nick's ride that night," I explain.

Realization crosses his face, and I'm sure he feels like he should know all this, but it makes sense that Cole wouldn't tell many people. He was ashamed.

"We didn't let each other out of our sight after that," I tell him.

I was hurting, Cole was hurting, and I was the only one who knew why he felt responsible, so I was the only one he could talk to.

And after a while, it just became habit. Us, side by side. Us, turning to each other. Us, wanting what was familiar, constant, and safe.

Us, holding on to Nick by holding on to each other. We both found ourselves desperate for one true friend. He and I hurting over Nick, but also me just getting away from my ex-boyfriend. It was so easy to dive into each other and escape. So easy.

"I'm so sorry, Jordan," Pike says. "Are you okay?"

I peer up at him.

"Sorry." He falters, looking away. "It's stupid to ask that now, I guess."

No, not stupid at all. It's nice to have someone to talk to.

"Everything's fine. Or it will be," I say. "It has to be."

He darts his gaze to me again, and I gesture to the pool.

"I sat at the bottom of a dark pool with my eyes closed until I couldn't hold my breath anymore. It has to be okay now, right?" I ask.

He snorts, his mouth turning up in a grin.

He rises and holds out his hand again, and this time I take it. He pulls me up, and we head for the house, but I notice the candle still burning on the wooden table.

Darting over, I lean across the table, close my eyes, and blow, the candle extinguishing. Turning back, I follow him up the steps.

"Can I ask you another question?" he prods.

"Shoot."

"Why do you do that?" He glances back at me.

"What?"

"The closing-your-eyes-to-blow-out-a-candle thing," he explains. "I've seen you do it a few times now."

I shrug, not realizing he'd noticed. I thought I'd gotten pretty good at doing it quickly and under the radar.

"Just a quirk." I follow him through the screen door. "Birthday wishes don't always come true, so I don't waste a chance when I blow out a candle."

7

Jordan

Hey, can you pick me up at two?" I pin the telephone between my ear and shoulder as I count out my bank and put it in the register. "Ash didn't come in. Her baby's sick, and I don't have another ride."

"Yeah, yeah," Cole says. "Of course. I'll be there."

After our last fight, the aftermath progressed exactly like I predicted. He came home buzzed and relaxed, crawled into bed, and we cuddled it out. Things have almost gotten back to normal—or what our normal is, anyway—enough that I didn't mind when he tried to pull me into the shower this morning. However, when we got into our bathroom, we discovered his dad had ripped out the sink and had started tearing away the tiles in our shower, our bathroom the next thing on his renovation list. How had we slept through that? And what time did he get up this morning?

"I'll be done at two," I state again, closing the register drawer.

"Yep, got it. Love you."

"Love you, too," I reply and hang up.

Pike has been working on my car, and in an effort to smooth things over, Cole actually helped today. I'm not sure how I'm going to repay his dad, though, because I know he's spending money on parts, even though he acts like he got the new exhaust cheap or just had those new tires lying around. I've been trying to go above and beyond in the house, doing things like making breakfast for everyone this morning and cleaning under the cushions on the couch. I even planted some flowers in the backyard, around the border, to help the aesthetic, which Pike agreed to as long as I don't bring flowers in the house. I laugh, thinking about how grumpy he can be sometimes. It's pretty funny.

Hours later, exhausted and my feet aching in my Chucks, I can't wait to get back to the house, either. Home and in bed. I'm so tired.

Tying my hair up in a ponytail, I count out the bank, put it back in the tray, and slide the tray into the safe for the next shift. After I cover the liquor bottles, finish the dishes, and turn off the lights, I peer out the window, seeing Cole's car by the curb. I smile, delighted he's on time.

I blow out the remaining candles on the bar, closing my eyes and taking a breath each time. *I hope tomorrow is better than today.* It's my go-to wish when I don't have anything else in mind, and every day that passes, I'm trying to get closer to making it come true.

I grab my book bag, stuffing my tips in the pocket, and head out the door, locking it behind me. The fresh air feels good in my lungs, and I toss my bag through the open back window before opening the passenger-side door. I slide into the front seat, turning my tired but grateful smile on Cole.

"Hey—" I stop, my smile immediately falling.

Jay, my ex, sits in the driver's seat. I look over my shoulder, making sure I didn't miss Cole passed out in the back seat, but it's empty.

My hands tremble. "Where's Cole?"

Jay cocks his head, looking apologetic. "He's wasted, babe. The guys didn't want to let him drive." His arm rests over the back of my seat, his hand inches from my hair and neck. "He's sleeping it off at Bentley's house. They told him someone would make sure you got home. I volunteered."

No. Nuh-uh. Not a chance.

I don't hesitate. Pulling the handle, I swing my door open and jump out, reaching into the back seat and retrieving my bag. "It's fine," I tell him. "I can grab a ride from Shel. She's still inside."

"No, she's not. You just locked up."

I knew he would challenge me. Nothing gets by him.

An eerie calmness laces his voice, but I know it's only skin-deep. "Come on, I'm already here," he presses. "You don't want me to have come out here for nothing, do you?"

I lean down, glaring into his dark brown eyes as I simultaneously fish the bar keys back out of my back pocket. "I didn't ask *you* to come. And like I said, I have another ride."

Turning around, I hurry for Grounders' entrance and quickly unlock the door.

"Jordan!" I hear him bark.

I yank the door open and step inside, casting a stern look back at him as he still sits planted in the car. "Go home."

And I pull the door closed again, twisting the lock and backing away like he's going to try to bust it down. I stay there, breathing hard and shaking.

He won't let that slide. He won't do anything tonight, because he would've been out of the car faster than I could make it to the bar door if he was going to try, but he'll be pissed enough to not forget.

He was a six-month-long mistake I made in high school, but I won't be that stupid again. My guard is up now.

And he didn't come to give me a ride home tonight. Not directly, anyway. Maybe after he was done with me.

I close my eyes, trying to drown out the memory of him pounding on my car window one night as I frantically tried to get my key in the ignition. I can still feel the fire on my scalp from where he yanked my hair.

I turn away and open my eyes, pushing away the thoughts. After a moment, I hear the engine roar past the bar and the tires screech down the street.

He's gone.

I set my bag down on the bar and run down the hallway, past the bathrooms, and check the locks on the back door, untwisting and retwisting, yanking the handle to make sure it doesn't give, and then I jog back up front and check the front door again and the windows.

Taking my phone from my bag, I sit on a barstool, clutching it in my fist. Who do I call?

Jay's probably telling the truth. Cole is drunk again. Why would he do this? He knew I was counting on him to be here. I'm positive he doesn't know Jay was the one who came instead, but still . . . I could fucking kill him.

I swallow down the sickness rising up my throat.

I call my sister, but as suspected, it goes to voicemail. She's probably just getting out of work or home asleep already.

My dad? Stepmom?

They haven't even called since I called them a week ago. They can't do anything without acting like it's a huge imposition. Asking them for anything is owing them. It's a burden.

I'm a burden.

Pike crosses my mind. I have no doubt he'd come.

But it would just piss Cole off if his father found out he dropped the ball tonight, and I don't want Pike to know, either. It's embarrassing. We're adults, and we've made our beds. He's taking care of me enough, and I'm not waking him up when he has work in the morning. It makes me a burden.

The only other person I could call is Shel, and her home is on the other side of town.

I don't want to call Cole, because, of course, he can't drive, but maybe he could send another friend.

But no. I'm not calling him. I'm too pissed right now.

And this town doesn't have cabs, either.

I eye the pool table, the overflowing ashtrays sitting on the edges, and the scratch marks all over the filthy felt.

Well, fuck. It'll be light out in a few hours. I can walk home then. Time to suck it up. I'm not asking anyone for shit.

Hopping off the stool, I make my way behind the bar again and dig out two stacks of clean white bar towels and carry them to the pool table, one by one fanning them out and covering the dirty surface.

I kicked off the air conditioner hours ago, so it's a comfy seventy-five by now, but I pull out my hoodie from my bag in case I want to cover up later. Grabbing my phone, I leave the hallway light on and climb on the table, scooting down enough so I have room to lie down. Tucking my arm under my head, I yawn and check the volume and battery on my phone, making sure I have enough power to last in case something goes wrong while I'm alone here all night.

Like Jay coming back.

I find my app that makes a box-fan sound and play it in hopes I can get a little sleep, but I'm not optimistic. I don't feel secure, so I can't relax.

Closing my eyes, I feel the weight of fatigue on my lids and the pleasant sensation of exhaustion. It's the kind you know you deserve, because you worked your ass off that day.

But after twenty minutes, my mind is still racing. My body is done for the day but not my brain.

When my cell rings, I'm pretty sure it's a sign I'm not meant to sleep tonight.

I bring it up to my eyes, squinting at the bright light.

Pike.

I knit my brow. "Hello?" I hold it to my ear, yawning again.

"Hey," he says as if he didn't expect to reach me. "I . . . uh . . . I just saw it was after three, and no one's home, so I just wanted to check in. Make sure everything's okay."

I turn on my side, still using my bottom arm as a pillow, and hold the phone to my ear with the other hand.

"I'm fine." I smile at his concern and joke, "Do I have a curfew or something?"

"No," he replies, and I can hear the humor in his voice. "You guys stay out and have fun. Do your thing. I just . . ." He pauses for a long moment and then continues. "You know, you don't worry about things you're not aware of. When Cole didn't live with me, I didn't always know where he was or what he was up to, so I didn't think about it all the time. You two living under my roof now, I seem to be worrying constantly." He breathes out a laugh. "That bar is shady. I just wanted to make sure you got out of work safely and everything's cool. I'm just . . . checking in."

I don't take offense at his remark. It's not my bar, after all, and yes, it is a dump.

I'm tempted to see if he wants to come and get me after all, since he's awake, but my pride won't let me. I don't want to be a problem. And I definitely don't want to be responsible for making waves between him and Cole. I can fight my own battles.

"Yeah. Everything's cool," I lie, adding some tease to my voice. "I'm not a kid, you know?"

"You kind of are."

I snort. Well, kid or not, I guess it's nice to have someone looking out for me.

"Did you call Cole, too?" I ask.

But he doesn't answer. Instead I hear a loud slam and some shuffling. "Shit," he barks.

My eyes open wide, alert. "What's the matter?"

"The damn microwave doesn't work right," he growls. "I knew

I shouldn't have replaced it just to match the other new appliances, dammit. It won't pop popcorn."

I narrow my eyes, but I want to laugh so badly. He gets so worked up. "There's a *Popcorn* button," I remind him.

"I pushed it!"

"Twice?"

"Why would I have to push it twice?" he retorts like I'm stupid.

"Because the size of the bags you use takes three-point-five minutes of cooking," I point out.

"I know that."

"Well, on your new microwave, pushing it down once only gives it *two* minutes of cooking. For the smaller bags," I clarify. "You need to push it down twice to get the right time."

There's silence and then I hear a mumbled, "Oh."

I press my lips together to keep from laughing. His random helplessness is pretty amusing. I wish I was there.

"Well," he says after a short silence, "I guess I'll let you go, then."

"Hey, wait," I say, stopping him.

I pause, unsure of how to word this.

"Do you mind if I ask you something?" I finally say.

"No, I guess not."

I wet my lips, hesitating. I don't want to offend him, but I'm curious.

"Where's all your stuff in the house?" I ask.

"Huh?"

I inhale a deep breath, forging on. "There's furniture but not much else. It doesn't look like you live there. Why?"

The other end of the phone is silent, and I stop breathing, afraid I'll miss him speak.

Was the question insulting? I didn't mean it to be. I just realized he knows so much about me, and I hardly know anything about him. He knows who my parents are, what happened to Cole's and my friend, that I love eighties stuff, I grew up without a mom, what I study in college . . .

But he's still such a mystery.

"I'm sorry if that sounded bad," I tell him when he doesn't answer. "It's a beautiful home. It's just that Cole mentioned that you and his mom met in high school, where you were kind of a baseball star. You must love the sport. I'm just curious why I don't see trophies or pictures or anything like that in the house. There's no recent photos of you and Cole, either, no music, no books . . . Nothing that describes you or what you like."

He draws in a breath, clearing his throat, and a cool sweat travels up my neck.

"It's all packed in the basement," he tells me. "I guess I just never dug it out after I moved into the house."

"How long have you been in that house?"

"Uh . . ." He trails off as if thinking. "I guess I bought it ten years ago."

Ten years?

"Pike . . ." I say, trying not to snicker.

He breathes out a laugh in my ear, and I smile, shaking my head.

"Guess it sounds weird, huh?" he asks.

That you still haven't unpacked everything? *Yeah.*

I flip onto my back, keeping my arm tucked under my head. "I understand we do away with certain things as we get older," I tell him. "But you've had a life since you moved into that place, haven't you? I don't see anything of your personality. Places you've visited, trinkets you've picked up over the years . . ."

"Yeah, I know, I, uh . . ."

He hesitates again, letting out a sigh, and the sound of his breath vibrates across my ear, sending tingles down my spine.

I wish I could see his face. It's so hard to read him over the phone. All I can picture is the way he drops his eyes sometimes, like he doesn't want someone to know what he's feeling, or the way he nods like maybe he's afraid of what he'll say if he speaks.

He finally continues. "Cole became more important," he admits. "Somewhere along the way, who I was and what I wanted became irrelevant."

I kind of understand. When you have kids, your hopes transfer to them. Your life takes a back seat to what they need. I get it.

But Cole is an adult now, and Pike has been on his own for a while. What does he do when he's not at work?

"I'd love to see some of the stuff," I broach. "If you ever want to unpack it, I'll help."

"Nah, that's okay."

I knit my brow at how quickly he shoots me down.

"You mean I can't even see old yearbooks and if you and Cole were twinsies at the same age?" I tease.

He lets out a quiet chuckle. "God, no. Back when the only important thing I had to do was my hair?"

I grin, but of course, he can't see it. Was he a one-girl kind of guy back in high school, or did he have lots like Cole did before me?

I remember what Cole said about his father cheating on his mom, but for some reason it doesn't ring true.

"The truth is, Jordan," he says, "when you're young, you can be really stupid. I don't care to remember that time in my life. I want to move on."

But you're not moving at all, by the looks of it.

"You need some spice in your life," I jab at him. "You should get a woman."

"Yeah, and you should get back to your friends now," he retorts.

I laugh. "Oh, come on."

"What makes you think I don't already have a woman, Jordan?"

His voice taunts, and I can feel it all the way down to my toes.

My mouth goes dry. "Do you?" I ask.

I mean, I was just joking. Wouldn't it be awkward to have two women walking around the house? I already have my chores down, and I do most of the cooking. That butcher block island and I have a relationship now. I might get a little jealous if another woman touches it.

"You haven't known me long," he plays. "My needs do have to be taken care of once in a while. I am human, after all."

My stomach flips, and I shoot my eyebrows up. *His needs?*

An image of what he looks like when he has to get those needs met flashes through my mind. I push it away.

Um, yeah. Okay.

All of a sudden, he laughs. "I'm kidding," he says. "Yes, I do go out from time to time, but I'm not seeing anyone now. You don't have to worry about running into some woman you don't know in the house."

"Or *women*," I say. "Right?"

He scoffs, and I can just picture his face. "Do you honestly see me being able to juggle more than one female? Ever?"

"No, you like your me time."

"Exactly."

My heart warms, and I knew I was right. Cole's mom fed him bullshit to turn her son against his father.

It's on the tip of my tongue to say something about Cole, but if Pike confronts him about the lies his mom probably told, Cole will see it as me betraying his trust. And it might embarrass Pike. They're not my family. It's not my place.

A yawn stretches my face, and I let out a little moan, my eyes growing heavier.

"Well, I guess I'll let you go," Pike says. "You both have fun, okay? Be safe."

"We will." My lids fall closed, his voice lingering in my ear. "And remember," I tell him. "Push the button down twice."

He snorts. "Yes, ma'am."

"Later," I say.

He pauses a moment before replying. "Good night, Jordan."

He hangs up, and I set my phone down, yawning again and not bothering to turn my box-fan app back on.

A smile still curls the corners of my lips. How can a thirty-eight-year-old man not know how to make microwave popcorn? It's literally idiot-proof.

I chuckle, my lids resting heavy and sleepy as I forget about Jay and Cole and how uncomfortable this pool table is or how exhausted I'll probably be tomorrow. Pike drifts through my mind and everything he said and how deep his voice was when he told me "good night, Jordan" and how it made goose bumps spread up my arms.

And how this is the third night this week he's been the last person I speak to before I fall asleep at night.

8

Pike

The next morning, I'm surprised to see I'm the first one up. Jordan is usually moving about, showering, or working on her laptop before I'm even downstairs, but the house seems empty. I open the front door and notice Cole's car isn't in the driveway, either.

It's Sunday morning. He wouldn't be up already. Did they not come home, then?

I go about my business, carrying on with my morning, but as it reaches ten, I want to get going on the main bathroom, tearing out the old tub and prying up the floor tiles, but it's going to be a lot of noise. I knock on Jordan and Cole's door to make sure they're not in there.

No one answers, and I crack open the door to see the bed still made and the bedroom empty. I guess they must've crashed at a friend's last night. I close it again and get to work.

"Hey," Cole says as he walks into the kitchen an hour later.

I shut the fridge, clutching a soda, and turn toward him as he tosses his keys on the counter. He looks haggard, his hair matted and his eyes red.

"Hey." I gesture to the cabinet to the left. "The aspirin's in there.

Get yourself some water and a shower. You can help me with the bathroom."

He nods, but he looks like he's two seconds from vomiting. His skin is a sallow green, and I actually feel sorry for him. I don't miss that feeling.

"You're drinking a lot," I say.

He ignores me, shuffling toward the cabinet and pouring himself some aspirin.

I press further. "You're drinking too much."

He still says nothing, but his jaw flexes, telling me he heard me.

I wish he'd talk to me. Even fight with me, because it's better than nothing. I want to hear about his job and his life. About the friend he lost. I shouldn't have learned something like that through Jordan.

I should've pushed harder when he started to shut me out. So much harder.

But I know who I really have to blame for the wedge between us.

"I was good to your mother," I tell him.

He sniffles, taking another huge gulp of water and still not looking at me.

He'll believe her. He's not ready to hear me yet. But I'm still saying it.

"I worked hard, I supported you both, and I was faithful." I rise from the seat and look down at him. "You can ask me questions. I won't lie."

But he just shakes his head, finishing off the glass and setting it down. "I gotta get a shower."

He turns to walk away, but I'm not done yet.

"Have I ever not done something you asked me to do?" I ask him.

He stops but doesn't turn.

Anytime he needed money, I gave it to him. Anytime he needed a ride, I was there. Whenever he wanted to go somewhere or see something or take a karate class or just be with me, I was always there for him. Pain stretches through my chest as I stare at his back.

I was a good father. When he wanted me around.

"Have you ever caught me in a lie?" I go on.

A lie she didn't teach him to believe, that is?

He looks over his shoulder at me, and I can see the struggle in his eyes. He wants to be angry at something or someone, and I was that target for a long time, but now he's not sure why anymore. He has to start seeing who his mother is and what she does to people. He needs to stop letting her do it to him.

"I'm here," I say. "Okay?"

I hear him breathe, the rise and fall of his chest heavy, and finally he nods, still looking hesitant, but it's something.

Then he turns and walks out of the room, toward the stairs, but I suddenly glance at the front door again, something occurring to me.

"Where's Jordan?" I call, walking into the living room.

He's halfway up the stairs but looks over at me again and shakes his head, still not speaking.

"Didn't you pick her up from work last night?" I question. "Weren't you both together?"

"No." He yawns and rubs his hand through his hair. "I'd had too much to drink, so I sent one of my buddies to pick her up and bring her home. She probably went out for a run, and you just missed her."

I stand there, trying to piece together my conversation with her last night as Cole trails upstairs.

So when I spoke to her last night, she wasn't with Cole. Wasn't with him at all.

And she hasn't been home. Their bed is still made.

Cole heads upstairs, and I shout after him, just remembering. "Use my bathroom!"

I'll be working on theirs for a little while longer, and my bathroom has the only other shower in the house.

I move back into the kitchen, still thinking.

Why would she lie about that? If she stayed with a friend, her sister, whatever . . . it's fine. But she let me believe she and Cole were together, which is why I called—to make sure they *both* were okay.

I sent one of my buddies to pick her up and bring her home.

Yeah, your buddy didn't bring her home. I have half a mind to be worried, but she lied for a reason.

And despite how much I like Jordan, I can't help the old feelings curling through my gut that I haven't felt for a very long time. I don't like being lied to.

Especially by women.

An hour later, I walk into Grounders and already see a lunch crowd filling the high-top tables and bar. A couple servers dressed in their jeans, tight shirts, and little aprons carry plates to bikers pit-stopping during their Sunday runs and hunters coming in from their early morning jaunts. The bar is filled with old-timers who look like they slept in their clothes last night, and the dank fluorescent lighting makes everything look dirty despite the smell of Pine-Sol stinging my nostrils.

The soles of my work boots stick to the floor with every step I take across the room. I've never understood the appeal of this place or why it's lasted so long.

I spot Jordan at the other end of the bar, her fist covered with a white towel and buried in a drinking glass as she dries it. I wasn't sure she'd be here, but when she's not at the house, this is where she is.

She's still in the same clothes I saw her leave in last night, and a yawn stretches across her face. Her hair is bound in a high ponytail, and her lips are rosy with a hint of lipstick.

She was pretty yesterday. This morning, my suspicion is blurring everything. All of a sudden, I'm twenty again and wondering where Cole's mother was all night.

But Jordan's not like that. She's a good girl.

It just doesn't make any sense she'd say she was with Cole when she wasn't.

Unless she was up to something she shouldn't have been.

I don't want Cole to go through that with Jordan. Not like I did with his mother. What if he gets her pregnant and gets stuck dealing with a person like that? I don't want him to be fucking alone forever because he thinks he wasn't enough for her.

I force my breathing to calm down. I'm jumping to conclusions. *Relax.*

She sees me approach, and her eyes light up a little. She opens her mouth to say something, but I speak first.

"Are you okay?" I ask. "Did you have a good night?"

She cocks her head, faltering a little. "Um, yeah, I guess."

So nothing bad happened, then. She's in one piece and seems happy enough.

"Did you and Cole have fun?" I press, my pulse starting to race.

She drops her head, avoiding my eyes as she sticks the glass under the bar. "Yeah." She nods.

And I flex my jaw, my temper rising. She just lied again.

"Yeah, Cole seems to think he never picked you up." I plant my hands on the bar and lean in. "He says one of his friends picked you up, but he didn't see you the rest of the night, and you didn't come home."

She stares at me, a blush crossing her cheeks. "Um . . . Yeah, it . . . I . . . I was . . ."

She stammers, flustered, and I stand there waiting for the easy, simple explanation I know will come, but . . .

It doesn't.

She opens her mouth to say something again, but then closes it, a slight wince in her eyes like she knows she's been caught.

I even out my tone, trying to sound calm. "Where were you all night, Jordan?"

Her gaze flashes everywhere but on me, her shoulders tense, and her breathing gets heavier. She can answer the question. She just doesn't want to.

"Jordan?"

"Is Cole home now?" she asks.

"Yes."

"Then we're both fine. The rest isn't your concern," she states.

I narrow my gaze on her. "And my house isn't a hotel, little girl."

She could've stayed with her sister or a friend, but why lie about that? She's hiding something.

She lifts her chin, continuing. "Where I slept last night is between Cole and me."

I keep my face straight, but all that floods my head are the images of a very young and stupid me catching my girlfriend screwing some guy in a car in front of our apartment at three in the morning. If it looks like a duck and quacks like a duck . . .

Yeah.

I push off the bar and cross my arms over my chest. "I honestly don't care what you do, Jordan," I tell her, my heart slowly icing over, "but I'm not stupid, either. Cole may be distracted, but I'm not. Whoever picked you up last night didn't bring you home, so if you're screwing around on my son, I'll take offense to that," I warn her. "And then I'll ask you to leave my goddamn house. I'm not paying to support someone like that. You understand? Don't you ever lie to me again."

Her jaw flexes like she's as angry as I am. I expect her sharp tongue to come flying back at me, and I think it will for a moment, but then it doesn't. Instead her eyes start to water, and her chin trembles as she breathes small, shallow breaths. She looks away, blinking.

"Yeah, got it," she says quietly. And then she puts the towel down and lifts up the partition, leaving the bar. "Excuse me, please."

She walks away down the hallway and out of sight. I stare after her.

I might be wrong. I could be wrong.

But I've ignored my gut so many times, and I know better now. I thought she was one of the good ones, but I'm not going to be made a fool of again. If she wasn't doing anything, she would've answered the question.

Turning around, I head back down the bar toward the door. But a voice stops me.

"Screwing around on your son . . ." a female voice mocks my words. "Your *precious* son."

I stop and look at Shel Foley, the owner, who stands behind the bar, a cigarette in her hand and smoke billowing in front of her face.

"You got something to say?"

She pushes off the back counter and sucks in another drag before snuffing the cigarette out in the ashtray and planting her hands on the bar. She glares at me. "Your dumbass kid was supposed to pick her up from work last night after she worked a ten-hour shift," she tells me. "He got drunk at a party, and guess who came to get her in his stead? Jay McCabe—her ex—who thought it was fun back in high school to smack her around after he lost a game."

What?

"She refused to be in a car with him," Shel snarls at me. "Instead, I found her curled up, sleeping on the filthy pool table this morning, because she didn't have anyone else to call last night." And then she narrows her eyes. "She didn't want *you* to find out what a loser your son is."

I remain still, unable to move.

I don't breathe, and I can't blink, rage threatening to overflow.

He hit her. He fucking hit her? My fists curl, and my lungs ache. Every muscle burns.

Motherfucker.

And Cole was at the same party? Did he send him to pick her up? What the fuck? How can he stand to be anywhere near a shitbag like that?

A vision of some cowardly little punk grabbing Jordan, hurting her, making her cry . . . I . . .

I close my eyes.

I just made her cry.

"She's a good kid with a really good heart," Shel continues. "And she deserves a hell of a lot more than the assholes in this town, including your son. I hope she leaves you all to it and never looks back."

Jesus Christ. What was I thinking?

I spin around and follow to where Jordan disappeared down the hallway. I have to talk to her now. Everything in my gut that made sense minutes ago now seems ridiculous. Why would I jump to conclusions I have no proof of?

Dammit, Cole! I can't believe him.

I trail down the hallway, seeing the restrooms, an office, and another room with the door slightly ajar. She's probably in the bathroom, but before I decide to wait, I inch open the other door to check there first.

She stands in the center of the small room with her back to me, but I can tell she's wiping her eyes. Floor-to-ceiling shelves line the walls, stocked with bottles of liquor, mixers, and juices and other supplies like napkins, straws, and candles.

I stand in the doorway and hear her sniffle.

"Jordan?" I say hesitantly.

She instantly straightens, turning just enough for me to see the side of her face. "Seriously?" she says, trying hard to harden her voice. "Just leave. You want me gone? You got it, okay? I'm gone."

I take a quiet step forward. "Jordan, I'm really sorry. I don't know what I was thinking."

"Just go."

"You should've called me," I tell her, taking another step forward. "I would've been here in a heartbeat. I'm sorry. I just—"

But she suddenly whips around, glaring at me. "You know the thing about men?" she asks, wiping her eyes with a hardness to her jaw. "They think they can treat you badly because you'll take it. But you win when you never let them do it again." She steps up to me, adding, "You can kiss my ass."

And then she swings around me and leaves the room.

I deflate. I want to follow her. I want to set the record straight and let her know that I was wrong. I want to have it out and make it right, but . . .

I don't know.

This is the second time we've argued, and both times it was my fault. We shouldn't be fighting. It's what a woman does with her boyfriend, not his father.

And that's what I am. Her boyfriend's father.

Nothing more.

But deep in my heart, the small ember growing bigger and bigger every day knows that's a lie.

It *is* more. I didn't lose my temper for Cole's sake. It was for mine.

She's become important, and for the first time in a long time, I've found myself actually enjoying talking to someone. I've started to let my guard down.

She feels good to have around.

And I just sent her packing.

9

Jordan

Shel tries to send me home early in my double shift, but after the episode with Pike, the last place I can be right now is in his house. I have nowhere else to go, not to mention I need the money.

How could he do that this morning? Barge into my work like he knows anything? I don't belong to him.

And if he has a concern, why can't he convey it nicely? Not every lie is meant to hurt someone. I was covering Cole's ass.

Yes, I understand suspicions. I get it. He doesn't know me well, and he's concerned for his son, but how can both Lawson men suck so badly at mature, adult conversation?

I rub my eyes, my mind drifting back to the moment he told me he wouldn't support someone like that and to get out of his goddamn house. In that moment, I felt unwelcome. Again. Unwelcome somewhere else. By someone else. I felt like a burden. Like I did with my parents, and even with Cole and Cam sometimes.

Why do I always let myself feel like I don't deserve better? I thought he was nice. I thought we were friendly, and I'd started to relax.

I groan, trying to keep the tears at bay. I hate that I cried in front of him.

I work until the night shift arrives at six and stay long enough to eat the other half of my sandwich from lunch as my dinner, pocket my tips, and count out my drawer before slipping on my sweatshirt and grabbing my bag. I haven't showered in over twenty-four hours, and a headache presses between my eyes from lack of sleep. I just want to sit under a hot shower and drown out everything else.

My stomach sinks a little, remembering I have nowhere to go to take that shower. I'm not taking a damn thing from Pike Lawson ever again. Not to mention I'm still pissed at Cole. He texted to make sure I was okay and to apologize again, but I didn't text back.

I wave bye to Shel and the other girls and leave the bar, stepping out into the welcome evening air. The sun has set, but there's still some light as I strap on my backpack and head left, down the street.

I need my own place. My own and no one else's. I need my own home that's all me where I can feel like me and never be pushed out or crowded or unwelcome. Where I feel safe.

And that means I need money.

Without thinking, I begin walking, my legs carrying me forward down Cornell Street and over to Lambert, the sky growing darker and the lightning bugs glowing in the trees above. The traffic has lessened, but it gets heavier over the next hour as I trail farther and farther toward the outside of town. Houses line the streets, as well as a few corner shops and gas stations, but there's less light out here, so I stick to the sidewalk and the welcome porch lights to the left and right.

After less than an hour, I see the lights from The Hook up ahead and the parking lot filling with cars. I've been here before, but I hate walking into a busy place in day-old clothes with hair that smells like smoke.

I scan the parking lot and spot my sister's Mustang off to the side of the building. Every night, one of the bouncers walks all the girls out to their cars, just in case a crazy fan decides to try to catch one of them when they're alone.

Walking into the club, I'm all of a sudden shrouded in darkness, the heavy beats of the music vibrating the floor under my feet. It's warm and smells like fog and perfume. Unlike at Grounders, there's no smoking allowed in here, and instead of ancient wooden floors with dirt lodged in all the cracks, a gleaming black floor squeaks under my sneakers.

"Hey, Peaches!" a woman calls. "What are you doing?"

I turn and see Malena through the window of the little box office. She never charges me a cover, of course. I don't come here for that.

"Cam around?" I ask.

"She just finished onstage," she replies. "She's probably on the floor somewhere now. Go on in."

"Thanks." I give her a smile and walk into the club, the little knot in my stomach tightening more. I've never bugged Cam here unless I had to. Some of the ladies' sisters or friends will sit in the back with the other dancers and hang out and socialize, but it's hard for me. I can handle seeing my sister naked, but I have a problem seeing others see her naked. Fathers of friends from school, an old boyfriend . . . even women from around town who come in packs for a girls' night out to "do something different," but I know they'll leave and just talk shit about the dancers the next day to anyone who will listen. Looking out from behind the curtain and seeing my elementary school bus driver or something would throw me for a loop. I don't know how she does it.

The room is cast in strobe lights, rotating up, down, and around, while bulbs line the edges of the stage, which protrudes out into the crowd and is surrounded by tables. It's not a big place, but there are two separate pedestals with poles and their own lights where dancers can dig deeper into the audience away from the main act.

Stopping at the bar right inside the entrance, I look around for Cam's brown hair, probably styled big enough to make any Texas woman jealous. There's a good number of patrons tonight. Loners, a few couples, booths filled with men who look like they just left the office scarfing down steak and burgers, and a larger party of young guys I don't recognize.

Gwen, one of Cam's friends, places her hands on the arms of a chair and lowers herself back into the seat.

And into the lap of the man already sitting there.

Supporting herself with her arms, she moves and grinds, rolling her hips and laying her head back on his shoulder. My skin warms, and my breathing turns shallow. I've seen her or any one of the other girls do this a dozen times. It's him who has me mesmerized, though.

Her customer looks in his late twenties, a young man in jeans and a T-shirt, but he's handsome and fit. His eyes are downcast, looking over her shoulder and down the front of her body as she moves on him. His hands, unable to touch her, clench the arms of the chair, and I look up, seeing his jaw flex.

Taunting, teasing, captivating his attention and dangling something he wants right in front of him and then yanking it away, because he can't have it . . .

In this brief moment, I wonder if I'd be that good.

"I see a few eyes on you already."

I turn my head, seeing Mick Chan, The Hook's owner, standing around the corner of the bar. Mick is a middle-aged ex-wrestler who married a stripper and decided he wanted to spend the rest of his life in a bar, so he and his wife opened this place and have lived happily ever after since.

He smiles at me, his black T-shirt stretching across his still-muscled chest. "The money we could make together," he says with a wink.

I turn my eyes back to the room, holding back my snicker. Dude should seriously start a booth at the high school career fair, so he can snatch up women as soon as they ripen to the legal age of eighteen rather than keep harassing me.

"Your sister says you don't have the head for this, and I'm supposed to leave you alone, but, Jordan—"

"I didn't come here for that," I snip. "I came to talk to her."

I finish scanning the room and am about to head to the back, but he suddenly moves toward me, his tone calm but stern.

"You see these customers at Grounders, too, right?" He glances to the crowd and back to me. "It's the same guys you serve there, isn't it?"

I lift my gaze back to the tables and booths, recognizing some. It's a small town. So what?

"Why do you think they go there at all?" he asks, narrowing his eyes on me. "I have a chef and a better menu here. Trained bartenders. Cleaner bathrooms. Why not spend all their bar time here?"

"Because Grounders is cheaper."

"Because Grounders sells sex, too," he fires back. "These boys go to Grounders for you, Shel, Ashley, Ellie . . . not the cheap beer and peanut shells all over the floor. Why do you think there are no men working there, after all? Shel hired you because of the way you look."

I don't say anything but just focus back on the stage, where I see my sister walking out from behind the curtain. Mick watches me, and I can almost feel his breath on my neck even though he's three feet away.

"Don't kid yourself," he tells me. "They're still looking at you like a piece of ass, even with all your clothes on." And then he glances up to the stage and my sister swinging around the pole. "She just makes a hell of a lot more money."

The next day my sister doesn't ask why I slept on her couch. She takes her son and me out for breakfast, and then we hit the farmer's market for some produce. We talk about the county fair coming up, what's new in the movie theaters, and what kind of party Killian wants to have for his birthday in September.

My sister likes to give me a hard time, but she's good about seeing when I'm hurting, too. She knows when to back off.

After her dance last night, I followed her to the back of the club and got her keys from her, so I could have her car and get into her house. I didn't know what to tell her about why I needed to crash with her, so I didn't explain anything. Where would I start? Cole flaking on picking me up the night before? Me alone with Jay in a car, on a deserted street in the middle of the night, for the first time in two years? Me spending the night on a pool table? Pike accusing me of screwing around on his son and taking advantage of his generosity?

Her boss putting the pressure on me again about working for him?

Cole barely acting like I exist anymore?

I feel a sob stretch my throat. I can't go back there. I'd rather sleep in my car. The three-year-old in me with pride the size of the Pacific will show him, won't she? I'll live in my broken-down car with no AC and busted door handles, because I don't need anyone, right?

Through my watering eyes, I smile a little as I drive my sister's car down the lane. It's not as bad as all that, actually. I have my dad's house. My stepmom may not want me there, but they won't turn me away.

It won't always be like this.

I turn into Pike's neighborhood, downshifting my sister's Mustang and coming up on his house.

My sister doesn't have to work today, so she let me use her car to get my things out of Pike's house.

As his place comes into view, though, I spot his truck in the driveway, and my stomach knots.

I don't want to see him right now.

I should come back later.

But no, I need my clothes and my books for school. I can get the rest another time, but I need a few things now.

I park and climb out of the car, taking the small suitcase I borrowed from my sister, and walk across the lawn and up the stairs. Taking out my key, I go to unlock the door but see that it's already open. I take a cautious step inside.

The living room is empty, and I pass the kitchen, seeing that he's not in there, either. My shoulders relax slightly. Making my way to the stairs, I grab the banister.

"Jordan."

I freeze, awareness and nerves making the hair on my neck stand up. *Shit.*

Turning around, I steel my expression and lift my chin as I face Pike. He stands between the kitchen and living room, wiping his hands with a dirty towel, his arms and fingers covered in dirt. He's wet, sweat-soaked through parts of his gray T-shirt, and his face is more tanned than the last time I saw him. Like he's been outside a lot the past twenty-four hours.

"I just need to get my stuff," I say and turn back for the stairs.

But he stops me again. "Jordan."

"Look, whatever, okay?" I cut him off, turning toward him again. "I shouldn't be here anyway, and it's not like Cole is here half the time, either, so let me just cut my losses and get my shit."

He steps forward. "Where will you go?"

I almost want to cry. "My dad's house. In Meadow Lakes," I tell him. "I'm not your problem, okay?"

There. It's done. No need to pretend that I don't have other options. I'm leaving. I hate the idea of going back to that trailer park shithole, but it won't be forever. I'll live.

I move to head up the stairs again, but he speaks up, almost in a rush.

"Please," he blurts out, stopping me. "Come here for a minute. I have something I want to show you."

He must see the suspicion in my eyes, because he asks again, firmer and resolute this time. "Please," he says. "Just for a minute."

He turns and heads back into the kitchen, and I hesitate for a moment before following him. I don't want to be curious, but I am.

I enter the kitchen and see him walking through the adjoining laundry room and out the back door. What's in the backyard that I'd want to see?

The screen door flaps shut, and I take a deep breath and straighten as I follow him.

He stands next to a rectangular parcel of land that was simply part of the yard twenty-four hours ago. Now the grass is gone, there's a border outlining the perimeter, and rich, black soil turned up in the box. There's a hose attached to some PVC pipe, which is embedded in the soil with spouts for sprinklers at several intervals.

He looks over at me, almost like he's nervous to see my reaction.

"What is this?" I ask.

He glances at it behind him and back to me again. "It's a garden," he answers. "I was hoping you'd want to help with it or something."

I'm speechless. My heart is beating so hard, and the sun feels so hot. How did . . . ? But then I remember. He knows I love landscaping. He knows I read all those magazines. He knows what I like.

An ache hits my heart. He did this all in one day?

But I'm not melting for him. I harden my voice. "Since when did you want a garden?"

He approaches me, and I cross my arms over my chest, steeling my armor.

"Jordan, I was an asshole," he says. "I jumped to a conclusion because I had it bad, and I'm old and jaded. I expect gutter behavior from everyone." He pauses and frowns. "But it was me with the gutter behavior. You're different, and I really fucked up. It won't happen again. I can't believe I said those things."

He's turning blurry, and I can't stop the tears from welling despite how hard I'm clenching my teeth.

"I want you to stay," he goes on. "I like having you here. It's nice coming home and having life in the house. Having people to talk to. It's nice having help, and . . ." His jaw flexes, and he looks angry. "And you shouldn't have been sleeping on a fucking pool table. You'll stay as long as you need, do you understand? I don't want you to leave."

My chin trembles, and I can't help it. The tears spill over, and I drop my head to hide them.

"Please don't cry again," he begs, "or I'll have to take out the pool and build you a gazebo or some shit."

I break into a laugh, sniffling and wiping my eyes. "No, don't take out the pool. I like the pool."

Wandering over to the new garden, I take in how big it is and how much work it must've taken. It doesn't make his behavior okay, but it does help knowing that he worked his ass off on something that he thought would make me happy. No one has ever done something like this for me.

I mean, my sister has bought me clothes and taken me out, but Pike did something he knew I would love. Something that's very much me.

"This is amazing," I tell him, meaning it. "But I really think it's best if I just go."

"This is your house," he tells me. "You belong here for as long as you want. You and Cole can invite your friends over, play your music, light your candles—"

"Toilet seat covers?" I tease.

"Fuck no."

We exchange a chuckle, and I gaze back at the soil. We can fit so many vegetables in here.

"I bought a bunch of seeds," he says, grabbing a bag and sifting through handfuls. "But I'm not sure how everything gets planted or how much space to allot for each vegetable, so I thought you might want to plan it out?"

I meet his eyes, and we hold the look for a moment. I think maybe he wants me around even more than he's letting on. Like maybe I'm a buffer between him and Cole, and like he said, he's enjoying having people in the house.

He hands me the bags of seeds and slowly takes the suitcase from my hand. "I'll put this in the garage," he says. "I'm going to go get a shower. Maybe we can get started planting in the morning?"

His eyes seem to search mine, and my breath catches for a moment at his gaze.

I finally nod, turning away.

He walks toward the house again and then I hear his voice from behind me. "And if we need more supplies, just let me know. I have to hit Home Depot tomorrow anyway."

"'Kay," I whisper.

And then I look at him over my shoulder. "And you're not old, you know?" I call out.

He looks at me, amusement in his eyes. "Old enough to have gotten set in my views. And that was wrong of me."

"Thanks."

The muscles in his arm flex as he holds my suitcase, and I can't help but stare at the tattoos running down the length. They look slightly faded, like he got them when he was a teen.

What was he like at Cole's age? It's hard to picture him as a . . . well, a guy, I guess. He's so serious. To a fault, almost.

But he's sincere.

"The next time you need a ride—or anything," he tells me, "promise you'll call?"

I nod again and turn back to my seeds, excited for the summer ahead.

10

Pike

Two," I tell Dutch and toss the cards I don't want back at him. Shifting his eyes from his own cards, he pushes two more over to me, and I fit them into my palm and examine the new hand. It's shit, but I do have two sevens, so it's not a complete loss.

Not that I care. I'm not a competitive man—at least not when it comes to poker—but hosting these get-togethers once a month at my house gives us something to do while we talk. I dart my gaze up to Dutch and then flash my eyes around the table, seeing Todd, one of my foremen, as well as Eddie, John, and Schuster either exchanging or rearranging cards. Everyone puts a few bucks in the middle, and Todd raises us by three more. Everyone takes the bluff . . . hoping it is a bluff.

"I am not excited about my girls growing up, I'll tell you that," Dutch says, flashing me an amused look.

"Why?"

He just shakes his head, sighing. "That noise would drive me nuts. For now, all I have to endure is the occasional sleepover with a gang of giggling eight-year-olds."

I chuckle under my breath, the pounding from upstairs starting to feel like walls caving in. I wince. It's only about nine thirty. If it's still this loud in an hour, I'll tell Cole to turn the music down or the neighborhood will be on my ass. It wasn't supposed to be a party, but I'd encouraged him and Jordan to have some friends over, so it's my own fault, I guess.

"It wasn't so long ago we liked quite a lot of noise," I mention, tossing him a grin.

The guys laugh, mumbling their agreement. We'd all graduated together, and it was a happy turn of events that a few of us now work together, although John and Schuster don't, being a cop and a roofer, respectively.

It hasn't been long since we were a lot like Cole—making messes and having too much fun in our mistakes. I was the first to get thrust into adulthood, but we still kept close over the years. Marriages, kids, a divorce—we'd all been through the wringer, and it was a wake-up call one day when I realized I'd been waiting for my life to start—my real life—only to realize that it had already happened when I wasn't paying attention.

That train I was waiting to catch raced by me without stopping. There probably wouldn't be a wife, and I would never know what it would be like to have my kids grow up seeing me every day. At this point, I'm too used to being on my own; I'm like an only child.

And an only child doesn't know how to share his things.

Todd raises another dollar, and I'm out, followed by John, Schuster, Dutch, and Eddie. Todd collects the pot, and Dutch shuffles all the cards, dealing again.

The muffled music from upstairs all of a sudden blares louder and clearer, and I hear footfalls on the stairs followed by a slammed door. Bare feet appear on the stairwell, the legs coming more into view the lower they descend.

Jordan bends down, peeking under the basement ceiling at us. "Hey, do you mind if I grab the Otter Pops out of the freezer?"

Everyone glances up at her, turning their heads, and I gesture, barely sparing a glance from my cards. "Yeah, go ahead," I reply quickly.

Liquid heat runs down my arms, and I stare at my hand, struggling to concentrate, because she's all I'm aware of now.

She hurries down the rest of the stairs, her footsteps light and quick like she's trying not to be seen or heard as she dashes over to the wall to my right and lifts the lid of the big freezer.

The room has grown quiet, and I'm not sure if the guys are afraid to talk normally because there's a woman in the room or if they're distracted. I stare at my cards and search my brain. What were we talking about a minute ago?

Oh, kids. Right.

I hear things being moved in the freezer and glance over, my gaze immediately falling to her feet. She's on her tiptoes and bent over, holding the lid up with one hand as she digs in the huge container. She seems to be aware of her shorts and that she's bending over in front of a table of guys, because she keeps straightening every few seconds and pulling her shorts down as much as she can.

Her toes are painted a soft pink, and I can tell she's wearing a bikini top under the gray T-shirt. The strings are visible tied behind her neck, and I can see more of it through the sides of her sleeveless T-shirt, which are cut out, showing off the curvy, sun-kissed skin of her waist. The muscles flex in her thighs, and my stomach swoops up and around.

I start to glance back at my cards, but I catch her pushing her hair behind her ears, and that's when I notice the little holes in the T-shirt. Up on the shoulder, by the seam.

Is that . . . ?

"Isn't that your shirt?" Dutch leans in, whispering.

I squint at it a little, and then I notice my baseball number in faded, chipped green peeking out from behind her hair. I knew I recognized those holes.

I look away. I must've left it on the furniture the other day, and she picked it up, thinking it was Cole's maybe? He was in baseball, too, I guess.

And she cut out the sides of it? I kind of want to be angry at the loss. I've had that shirt since high school, but . . .

It was too shabby to wear in public anymore, anyway. And she looks better in it than I ever did. I glance at her again, seeing the shirt drape over her smooth, sun-kissed skin, and a subtle wave of pleasure creeps in that she's wearing something of mine on her.

I shift in my chair, blinking at my cards to get past the stars in my vision.

"Need a hand?" Eddie offers her.

Flickering my gaze to Jordan, I see her bend over into the freezer, and I furrow my brow.

But Todd comments, a sly humor filling his tone. "Oh, leave her alone. She's doing just fine on her own."

The guys chuckle, unmistakably enjoying the view, and Jordan swings back upright, hefting the box of Otter Pops into the crook of her arm. She arches an eyebrow at Todd while letting the lid slam shut.

I brace myself for her smart mouth, but instead, she saunters to the table and looks over his shoulder and down at his hand. "Oh, look at that," she says, her eyes lighting up and her voice chipper. "You have all the kings in the deck. What luck, huh?"

Dutch snorts, and I can't help but shake with laughter as everyone joins in the amusement. Everyone except Todd, who throws down his cards, giving up his hand now.

She fixes a self-satisfied smile on her face and makes for the stairs again. I'm half-tempted to tell her to make sure no one gets those ice pops in the pool, but I'm trying not to micromanage her and Cole like they're kids.

"Oh, hey, can I ask you a question?" she says, stopping halfway up the stairs.

I meet her eyes.

"There's a little cake in the refrigerator," she goes on. "Cole's begging to eat it, but I didn't buy it and wasn't sure where it came from. Just wanted to check with you before he digs in."

Fuck. I keep my face straight despite my aggravation. I can feel the guys' eyes on me.

"Oh, uh, it's a . . ." I mumble, shaking my head and pretending to study my cards again. "I, uh . . . I got it for you guys . . . today, at the store . . . for both of you."

She doesn't say anything, and after a moment of completely uncomfortable silence, I glance up. She cocks her head, looking confused.

I toss three cards at Dutch for him to pass me three more, although I'm not sure which three I just discarded.

She's still looking at me. I can feel it.

I rush out with more info, hoping she'll say something and get out of here. "I was just passing Etienne's and remembered you didn't get any cake on your birthday," I tell her, acting nonchalant, "or a chance to really celebrate. I just thought you guys might like it." I grab three new cards off the stack when Dutch fails to pass me new ones. "I was passing by anyway. No big deal."

If it wasn't a big deal, I wouldn't have felt suddenly weird about it when I came home. It was stupid to get it in the first place. She's not my kid.

But for some reason, passing the window and spotting the three-layer cake with pink roses covering every inch, I thought of her. I guess I was just still trying to make up for acting like a dick the other day.

And the other night she mentioned blowing out candles, making wishes. . . . She didn't get to do that properly on her birthday—donuts don't count—so I felt bad even though it wasn't my fault. Buying it seemed like a good idea at the time.

Bringing it home felt sentimental, though. Too sentimental. I stuck it in the fridge, hidden in the pink box, waiting to see if the mood struck me again before I just threw it out.

"But yeah, it's yours, so let him go for it," I finally say, sparing her a quick glance before looking back down at my cards.

"Weren't you going to tell me it was there?"

I shrug. "I forgot about it, I guess."

The lie doesn't sound convincing, but her excited voice saves me from the heat of everyone's eyes on me.

"Well, in that case, then, no," she states firmly. "He can't have any. It's mine."

My heart warms, and I can't help it. I look up slowly. She's smiling at me as she ascends the rest of the stairs.

"Thank you!" she calls, and then I hear the door open and the music flood in before it closes again.

Pink. I bought her a fucking pink cake like she's seven. With roses on it. Did she see the cake? Does it look like a little girl's cake? Or worse, something romantic? They had cakes with balloons on them. They had plain cakes. Fuck, I'm an idiot. I didn't even think.

I throw down my cards, closing my eyes and running my hand through my hair.

"Just a minute, guys," I say, pushing back my chair and moving around the table, toward the stairs.

A few snickers and chuckles explode behind me as I leave the basement and run after the kid.

You know, it wasn't long ago I could think clearly. I wasn't constantly doubting every move I made and listing every possible outcome for a single action and how Jordan would respond to it. I haven't been this confused about anything in a long time.

Pushing through the door at the top of the stairs, I hear the blare of "I Love Rock 'n Roll" coming from the backyard and the splash of someone jumping into the pool. I'd tasked Jordan with collecting keys for anyone drinking, but if the neighbors decide to call the cops because of the noise, my safety measure to keep kids from drunk driving wouldn't save me from the illegality of letting minors drink here in the first place.

Although I have a cop downstairs, so I'm guessing the odds are on my side.

I enter the kitchen, catching glimpses of the partygoers outside, and see Jordan by the refrigerator, pulling out the pink box with the cake.

She turns around and sets it on the island, looking up and meeting my eyes. "I'm not going to eat it yet," she says. "Otherwise I'll have to share it. I just want to see it."

Apprehension creeps in as she lifts the lid, and there's an apology on my lips even as I see her break into an excited smile.

I walk to the fridge and get a soda I pretend I came up here for. "Sorry if it's childish," I tell her. "Not sure what I was thinking."

She crosses her arms and folds her smile between her teeth, like she's trying to contain herself, but it's not working. I can see the blush on her cheeks in the dark kitchen and the way her breath is trembling.

She turns her head toward me. "I don't think I've ever had a cake this pretty," she says. "Thank you for thinking of me. It's a nice surprise."

She glances back at the cake, a whimsical look in her eyes.

Great. Now I feel worse. She looks like this is the nicest thing someone has ever done for her, and wouldn't that be fucking sad?

It kind of is a pretty cake, though. The frosting is designed into roses and starts off at the bottom in white and slowly grows pinker by row as it moves toward the top, where it's finally evolved into a dark hot pink.

See, it wasn't stupid. I knew she liked pink.

"It's pink on the inside, too," I tell her. "Pink cake, I mean."

Her smile grows bigger.

And it's not made for kids, now that I remember. The cake is made with champagne, the saleslady said.

Okay, I did good. My head finally evolves into the perspective I had when I bought it, and I feel less tortured.

She dips her finger into a rose and brings it to her mouth, sucking off the sugar. My gaze freezes, watching the way her lips purse and her tongue dips out to lick the tiny bit of frosting left off the tip.

I groan inwardly, unable to stop myself from wondering how warm her mouth is.

I clear my throat. "Uh, I completely forgot candles," I admit, moving for the drawer behind me, "but I know you have to do this, so . . ."

I pick out a box of matchsticks next to the pot holders and light one, going to stick it in the center of the cake, but I stop. "Should we call Cole inside?"

She glances out the window and then waves me off. I stick the matchstick into the cake.

I watch as she closes her eyes, exhales a breath, and relaxes her shoulders, and then slowly, a small smile curves her lips. Instinctively, I smile, too, like I don't know what she's thinking, but I think I know what she's feeling in that moment.

She blows out the matchstick and opens her eyes, the stream of white smoke billowing in front of her face.

I stay by her side for a moment, not wanting to budge.

Someone should be holding her right now. Someone should be coming to stand in front of her, putting both his hands on the counter at her sides, and feeling her breath against his face.

I breathe a little faster, imagining what she tastes like.

And then I reach for the soda can I'd set on the counter and fist it until the aluminum crackles.

That's not good. Those thoughts aren't good.

I walk away, swallowing three times to wet my throat, and I grab the cassette tape container from my truck off the counter and slide it across the island to her.

"And that's for you, Birthday Girl," I say to distract from any vibe I might've just been giving off. "You're welcome."

Her eyes fall on the black container, recognizing it, and widen, her jaw dropping. "What?!" she exclaims. "Are you seri— No way!" She smiles brightly. "I can't take these! They were your dad's."

I nod, now feeling safer with the island between us. "My dad would want someone to have them who's going to love them. You'll love them, right?"

It's not like I ever play the damn things. I just listen to whatever's on the radio. She seemed pretty in awe of them, so it was the only thing I could think to give her that she'd want.

She holds up her hands animatedly and makes a face like she doesn't know what to do with me. "But . . ." She trails off, scoffing. "Pike, I . . ."

"You want them, right?" I ask.

She scoffs again, making a face. I can see the struggle in her eyes. To her, it's a valuable gift and she doesn't have a right to them. But she's also dying to take them.

"Are you serious?" she asks, cupping her face in her hands.

I can't help but laugh. She's fun to make happy.

She scoops them up and hugs them. "I have tapes. I have a collection. Shit!" she bursts out. "I feel so bad, but . . . I want them, too. So, I'll take them."

She feigns an apologetic look but laughs, which amuses me even more.

"Good," I say.

And I feel better now, too. At least I've hopefully made up for my behavior earlier in the week. With this and the garden, she seems elated.

I move away from the counter to take my leave, but she stops me. "Oh, wait."

Spinning around, she removes a tray from the fridge and walks over to me, setting a bag of tortilla chips on top and handing it all over to me. "I made an extra taco dip for you and the guys."

I look down at it, my stomach immediately growling. "Oh, you didn't have to do that." We usually order wings and pizza. But this actually looks really good. "Thank you. They'll love it."

She smiles, and for three long seconds we're locked there, in each other's stares. Almost as if the air is so heavy with something else that we can't move.

Finally, I inhale a breath and back away. "Make sure they clean up when they're done, okay?" *Not make you do everything*, I want to add but don't.

She just rolls her eyes at me and turns back to her tapes.

A loud thud wakes me from my sleep, and I jerk awake, blinking my eyes into the darkness. What the fuck? I could've sworn the bed vibrated, too. It takes a moment to place all the sounds outside, and then I hear the beat of muffled music filtering in through closed windows.

Jesus, they're still up? I look over at the clock, seeing it's just after one in the morning. I throw off the sheet and yawn, running my fingers over my scalp.

It's fucking hot in here.

I sit up, swinging my legs over the edge of the bed, and stand up.

Walking across the room, I open the door and head down the hallway and the stairs. At the bottom, I check the thermostat and kick on the AC. *Seventy-nine degrees in here.* I'm willing to compromise, but that's unbearable. It doesn't help that I have to sleep in pajama pants now that there are people in the house, but I'm afraid I'll wake in a start and forget I'm fucking naked.

I walk into the kitchen, keeping the lights off, and stop at the sink, peering out the window onto the patio. I'm surprised the cops haven't been called. It's less noisy than it was before, but it's still too damn loud for this late.

I look around the backyard for what caused the thud, and my eyes immediately go wide and I turn away. Seriously, Cole. What kind of friends pull this shit at someone else's house?

At least two girls are missing the tops of their bikinis, one of them being heavily groped by a guy I can only assume is one of Cole's buddies as they make out in the pool. The other girl is lying on a lawn chair, one arm tucked behind her head and her sunglasses on despite the fact that it's dark out.

I turn around, feeling my pants for my phone. He needs to get those little shits off my property now, but I can't go out there. Not sure if it would be awkward for them, but it would definitely be weird for me. It's a safe bet I know their dads, probably.

Where the hell is Jordan? I don't know why that thought pops in my head, but for some reason, it's instinct to suspect she'd have a problem with this, too. Where the hell is my phone?

I remember it's plugged into my charger next to my bed, and I head back up the stairs and down the hallway, entering my room and pulling it off the cord.

At least most of the party has cleared out, by the looks of it. It shouldn't be too hard to get rid of the remaining eight or so. But the backyard is a mess, and I've been more than gracious about this. He better not ask for another damn party for a long time.

Heading back down the stairs, I dial Cole on my phone as I stop just inside the kitchen. Holding it to my ear, I listen as his line rings.

But I soon hear a tinkling coming from somewhere in the living room and look behind me to see a light on the arm of the couch. It's Cole's phone lighting up with my call. *Goddammit.*

Hanging up, I tap my thumb and click on Jordan's name to dial her instead. But as I'm about to hit *Call*, I glance up and suddenly pause.

She's there. Standing in the shallow end of the pool, thigh deep, with her arms locked to the front of her body, trying to keep her top on as Cole pulls the tie at the back of her neck. He stands in front of her, staring down, as she shakes her head, trying to resist, but smiling all the same. I can see her embarrassment from here.

A flood of feelings hits me, and so many thoughts swim through my head as I try to look away but can't.

Don't look at her, I tell myself.

And my fist curls around my phone, willing Cole to leave her alone, too. She obviously doesn't like it.

And I don't like it.

But I can't keep my eyes from rising to her again, seeing the pink seashell bikini she's wearing and the thin straps slowly spilling off her skin.

God, she's beautiful.

I feel a knot wind painfully inside me, taking in her long hair falling against her bare body, and her arms, the only things holding up the scraps that cover her anymore.

I run my hand over my face, trying to rub away the shame, because if I were Cole I'd be handling her very much the same but a lot more privately. I wouldn't want anyone else seeing what I get to see.

Blowing out a breath, I drop my eyes. This night needs to end. Maybe I should cut the electricity so everyone will leave.

But before I have a chance to move, I see that Jordan is out of the pool and moving toward the window. She holds her top with one hand and slips on my old T-shirt again with the other, reaching in and retying the strings of her bikini once the shirt is on.

Her brows are furrowed, like she's annoyed, and I tilt my head, looking behind her to see that Cole has moved on, laughing and throwing a football to someone.

She heads around the house, toward the back door, and I straighten as she enters the kitchen. I connect my phone to the charger on the counter to make it look like I'm doing something.

"Oh, hey," she says, pausing when she sees me.

I glance over, clearing my throat. "Hey, everything okay?"

"Yeah, I was just going to . . ." She hesitates as if looking for an answer. "Cut up some watermelon."

I nod once and walk over to the fridge, reaching on top and grabbing the fruit for her.

She pulls out a cutting board and chopping knife, and I forget about asking her to break up the party. She doesn't seem to want to be out there at the moment.

Pulling out the other cutting board next to the fridge, I settle in at the counter next to her and slice the watermelon in half for her.

One part stays on my board, I move the other half to hers, and we both start chopping.

The remnants of the party run around the backyard, some kid catching a squealing girl who's half-naked, and I drop my eyes again, feeling fucking stupid, like this isn't my house and I'm some seventy-year-old pervert spying on teens gone wild running around my own damn yard.

I see her glance through the window in front of us and then quickly to me, probably gauging my annoyance. There are topless women in my backyard, after all, and I freaked out over her wet T-shirt when she was mowing the lawn the other day.

But instead, I resort to sarcasm this time. "Do you think Cramer next door is enjoying the view?"

She snorts, faltering in her chopping, and follows it with a laugh.

After a moment, though, I hear her taunting voice. "Are you?" she replies.

I widen my eyes a little, surprised, and look down at her. She casts me a cocky little smirk.

"You're still young," she points out, joking with me. "Still look energetic. Why don't you go out more?"

Who says I don't go out? My barhopping days are over, but I had friends over tonight, too. Sure, that's not "going out," but I'm not a hermit.

"You're not gay, are you?"

I shoot her a look. *Excuse me? Didn't we talk about my dating habits the other night?*

But she shakes her head right away, clearing it. "Yeah, never mind. Didn't think so."

Jesus.

Granted, I don't have as much of a social life as I could. I know that. I'm not even forty yet, and my downtime resembles my grandfather's retirement.

I pause a moment, searching for the easiest words to explain it to her. "I like my boring life," I tell her, my voice kind of sounding like an apology. "Most women don't."

"Maybe girls don't," she replies, a light humor in her voice that I appreciate. "I find you far from boring. You should go out more. There's a shortage of men in this town. Too many boys."

I smile to myself. She sees me as a man, not just someone's father. I shouldn't like that as much as I do.

And yes, there may be lots of boys, but there are also lots of women, and none of them are for me. Believe me, if my future wife lived in this town, I would've found her by now.

She slices one of her sections in half and turns it sideways to cut triangles in twos. I follow suit.

Outside, a young woman with a long brown ponytail scurries across the pool deck, her orange bikini making her tanned skin look darker.

I jerk my chin. "Should I go after her?"

Jordan glances up at the girl outside the window and drops her eyes again, continuing to slice the fruit. "She's too hot for you."

"You think I can't handle her?" I joke, cutting off two more triangles. "I've been around the block, you know?"

"Several times by your age, I'm sure. Need a nap yet?"

Why, you little—

I slice through the fruit, and the knife comes down, its point jabbing me right on the inside of my middle finger on my left hand.

"Shit!" I drop the knife and bring my hand up, the ache sinking down to the bone. I suck in air through my teeth. *Dammit.*

"Oh," Jordan gasps and drops her knife, too, wiping off her hands. "I'm sorry." She offers a regretful little laugh. "Here, come here."

I suck the blood off my finger, barely taking notice that she's pushed me down onto a barstool at the island as she retrieves bandages from the cabinet.

Did I put those there? I didn't put those there.

Rushing over to me, she peels a package open, and I see it's a wet wipe, probably "antibacterial" something or other.

"I can do it." I hold out my hand.

But she moves in anyway, inspecting the pea-size drop of blood balling on my finger again. "I know," she says, "I just feel bad. I didn't mean to piss you off and distract you. I was just teasing."

I hiss as whatever's on the wipe hits my open wound. "You didn't piss me off," I tell her, but it comes out as a growl. "Well, you did, I guess. You always do, but it's in a good way."

"In a good way?" Her brows furrow.

Yeah, like, you know, fun. *You're fun.* And kind of funny. And pretty interesting. I don't know how she makes my temper rise so quickly, and over stupid, petty shit, and I can't explain why, but I like it.

I don't know how to tell her that, though. It sounds weird.

When I don't answer the question, she continues, her voice quiet and serious. "You know," she says, not looking at me, "if you *are* interested in her, I can bring her around more. If you want."

The girl in the orange bikini?

"Bring her around?"

She nods, wiping my finger still. "A sleepover or something maybe. You won't have to make a move. She'll jump you."

She won't look at me, but I stare down at her nevertheless. She wants to get me laid?

I feel a warm, light sweat cover my spine as I become aware of the heat of her body standing between my legs. I watch as she blows hair out of her face only for it to fall back into the same place again.

Orange Bikini isn't the one I want jumping me.

Absently, I reach up and brush the hair out of her eye, grazing her forehead as I tuck it behind her ear for her. Her gaze rises, meeting mine as I let my hand fall down the strands of her smooth hair, and my heart skips a beat as we both stand there, locked.

I can almost feel her face in my hands. The urge is so strong to know what it's like to hold just a part of her.

Jesus Christ. I drop my hand, looking down at the small wound on my middle finger.

"So do you want me to?" she broaches quietly, almost like she's afraid of what I'm about to say.

I shake my head. "No," I finally tell her. "She's not bad, but she's not what I like."

She unwraps a Band-Aid and fastens it to my finger, slowly smoothing over the bandage again and again.

My fingers tingle where she holds them, and I watch her face, her focus still not leaving my hand.

And then suddenly, she nearly whispers, "Well, what *do* you like?"

I watch as she licks her lips, her breathing shallow, and the jolt to my cock has me feeling damn near ready to tear something apart with my teeth.

What is she doing to me?

"Women old enough to drink, for starters," I retort, pulling my hand away.

She quirks an eyebrow. "Yeah, like you're some barhopping partier yourself."

Yeah, she's right. I drink at home.

"But good." She sighs, backing up and planting her hands on her hips. "I didn't really want to set you up with her."

"Why?"

"I don't think she's your type." She tosses away the wrappers, ease in her eyes now. "Plus, I'd be jealous. I like being the only woman in the house."

"And if I had said yes?"

She shrugs, feigning an apologetic look. "Well, then you just wouldn't get your new favorite burgers the way you like them anymore."

I grin, shaking my head. So presumptuous.

But yeah, actually I do love her way of making burgers better.

She takes my hand, giving my little wound a good once-over.

"It's fine. Thank you." I stand up, forcing her back a little. "Go on out with your friends."

She turns her head over her shoulder, gazing outside, but she doesn't look in the mood to party anymore.

"What are you going to do?" she asks, walking back to the watermelon and loading a big bowl with the pieces.

"Try to get back to sleep, I guess," I tell her.

Hopefully she doesn't mess with the AC and I can stay asleep.

Making my way out of the kitchen, I rub my finger, feeling the ache of the stab.

I glance back at her and see her eyes already on me over her shoulder. She quickly turns back to her work, and I just want to stay.

After a long moment, I swallow. "Night," I say.

But before I make it into the living room, I hear her voice behind me. "What did you mean, 'in a good way'?"

Her eyes are on me again, and I lift the corner of my mouth in a small smile. I'm not sure what to say that doesn't sound completely inappropriate.

Finally, I just decide to spit out the easiest answer, turning and heading for the stairs. "I like talking to you," I say over my shoulder.

11

Jordan

I like talking to you? What have I ever said that was so fascinating? I let out a scoff, shaking my head as I peel the potatoes for dinner.

Maybe it's a lack of options. He's lived alone for so long that any conversation seems interesting? We have absolutely nothing in common.

But, the truth is . . . I loved hearing it. Why do I want him to like me so much? And why was the party the last place I wanted to be last night when I realized he wouldn't be out there, too?

I glance up and see him in the backyard through the window in front of me. He's working on trimming the tree by the fence separating his yard from Cramer's, using a long, handheld device that stretches up into the tall branches. I mentioned that not enough sunlight is reaching the garden, so he took it upon himself to solve the problem. Without even being asked.

I love the garden more than I admit to him. It's like my own little space, and it will still be there after I leave. It's comforting.

The seeds are planted, and the sprinklers dust the soil for a few minutes every morning and evening like clockwork. I've started to like hearing them kick on in the wee hours, when it's still dark and I'm the only person up and in the kitchen with my coffee.

Everything is starting to feel familiar and warm here. Like a home.

I carve into the potato skin, rough and abrasive. *Typical.* I always grow attached to things that aren't forever. The idea of my mother returning when I was little, Nick, Jay, my apartment and the desire to make a home of my own . . . I amaze myself at how absolutely pathetic I continue to be. I jab the knife into the cutting board and dig out a few more potatoes from the bag.

And to make matters worse, I haven't been able to stop thinking about last night all day, and the party is the least of it.

The birthday cake, the tapes, joking around with him . . . The way he remembered that I have to blow out a candle and make a wish. A flutter hits my heart, and I smile and then scowl, confused and not wanting those feelings.

I blew out the matchstick last night, wishing for the same thing I wished for in the movie theater that night. I loved how I felt in that moment and hoped that I could feel that way every day. That's all I wanted.

Not for something to be different or for something I didn't have, but that I would feel exactly the same the next day. And the next.

Special, remembered, happy.

He makes me happy.

Happy in a way that my boyfriend should.

Peeling another potato, I see him move outside, out of the corner of my eye, and I try to stop myself, but I look up anyway.

Raising his arms, he pulls his navy blue T-shirt over his head and slides it into his back pocket, reaching over to pick up the branch cutter again.

For a moment, I freeze. My hands pause in their task, and the sounds of the cutter, the lawn mower across the street, and the music playing in the kitchen slowly fade away.

His skin—golden and toned—looks warm and smooth; the

muscles of his stomach and the cords running down his forearms press against his skin, displaying how long and hard he's worked in his life. Sweat glistens down his neck and spine, and I can see the ripples of the muscles in his back. Even through the tattoos.

Long legs in worn jeans with his T-shirt hanging out the back pocket and covering part of his . . . I wet my lips as I tear my eyes off his behind and stare at the way his jeans hang off his hips.

Every muscle flexes as he chops branch after branch, and all I can manage are short, shallow breaths as I admire even the way his pant legs drape over his tan construction boots.

Mr. Lawson is hot. He's able and strong-bodied, and I wonder how he feels. What is he like with a woman?

I drop my eyes again.

"Oh, that's hot," I hear a voice say.

I blink and jerk my head, looking behind me. *Cam.*

She stands next to the side of the island, having come through the front door without me hearing her. She has one forearm planted on the granite, leaning casually with an amused look on her face.

I turn back to my task, my heart hammering in my ears.

It's bad enough to ogle someone who's not Cole, but it had to be her who caught me, too.

"I've never seen you look at Cole like that," she says.

How long was she standing there?

I decide to nip it in the bud. "Like what?" I snap. "Stop trying to start shit."

I hear her shuffle across the floor as she comes up to stand next to me at the sink. I cast a glance at Pike to see he's still working, oblivious to us in the house.

"You both are getting pretty cozy here," she teases, rinsing off the peeled potatoes and putting them in the pot. "He's doing yard work. You're cooking. It's like you're a couple."

"Shut up. I'm young enough to be his daughter."

"But you're *not* his daughter," she shoots back, turning toward me and leaning in. "You're a hot young piece of pussy living under his roof, and you know he's thought about that. He may be Cole's dad, but he's also a man." She turns back, looking out the window and checking him out. "And a fine, healthy-looking one, too."

"I have a boyfriend. *His* son."

That's right, Jordan. That's exactly what you should've told yourself when you were staring at him a minute ago.

But my sister just shrugs. "Even hotter."

I let out a bitter laugh. "If you like him, go for it."

"Nuh-uh." Her lips curl playfully. "I'm all worked up about the fantasy now. I want my own boyfriend's father."

Ugggggghhhh . . . my cheeks warm again.

"You're sordid. And you don't have a boyfriend," I point out.

"Well, I should get one. One who has a hot dad."

I shake my head. I'm not talking about this anymore. She's convinced I was ogling, and she thrives on naughtiness. I'm not feeding her.

"Plus, you're my sister," she states. "I don't want to make you jealous by hooking up with him."

"Why would I be jealous?" I blurt out, finishing the last potato. "Seriously. I have a boyfriend. Who Pike Lawson screws is of no consequence to me. Go for it."

Turning away, I wipe off my hands, veer around her, and grab the pot of water with potatoes and put it on the stove, starting the burner. *Pork chops are marinating. Dough for the biscuits is sitting.* I go through my mental checklist as quickly as I can to keep my mind occupied. And away from him.

He can see whomever he wants. This is his house.

"Well," I hear Cam say, "if you're okay with it, then . . ."

I remain at the stove, pretending to check the burner, but my hand tightens on the knob, fear twisting my insides.

The next thing I hear is the back door slamming against the frame, and I jerk upright, seeing that she's left the kitchen.

Son of a . . .

Walking back over to the sink, I peer out the window and see Cam heading across the lawn to where Pike is working. She tosses a look over her shoulder at me like she knows I'm watching. She smirks, and I scowl.

I wasn't serious. The thought of her hands on him . . . his arms around her . . . I don't want to see that. She's my sister.

He senses her approach and looks down at her, turning off the tool, and I watch as he listens, probably wondering why she's bugging him.

Maybe he's wondering, that is.

My sister is hot, and not many men would refuse her if she set her sights on them. Maybe Pike's attracted to her? He is a man, like she said.

And she's older, has her own place, a car, and is rooted in this town for the time being. She's still significantly younger than him, but she's not a kid.

She's not a "little girl."

She crosses her arms over her chest, shuffling her feet a little, giving the impression of modesty, and I shake my head, because Cam is not modest. At all.

Just very good at reading people. She knows coming on too strong will freak him out.

After a moment, she touches his arm, and I barely breathe as I watch her bend her neck, inspecting his ink. Then, quickly, she straightens and lifts up her arm, showing him the huge black phoenix on the side of her torso.

He watches as she lifts up her white tank and bra straps, and my stomach sinks, expecting him to blush or look uncomfortable, because uncomfortable is Pike's thing, but he doesn't. Instead, he watches her as she talks animatedly, excited, and then suddenly he smiles, his body shaking with a laugh at whatever she's saying.

Something tugs at the back of my throat, and I don't feel good.

He keeps looking at her. His eyes have barely left her since she walked out there. Does he want her? Does she turn him on?

I mean, I want him to like her, just not want her. It's not right. I don't want to hear her moaning and panting down the hall all night.

Besides, she won't like him. He's way too uptight. Pretty boring, actually.

But she'd definitely make him feel good for a while.

I close my eyes, a five-ton weight on my shoulders.

She turns and starts picking up branches off the ground, and he goes back to cutting, both of them working together in happy unison. But I see her turn to mouth something at me with a cocky little smile.

It takes a moment to register what she said.

"Jealous yet?"

I can't help the snarl that escapes as I flip her the finger and then turn around, walking away from the window. *Damn her.* She won't do anything. She thinks I like him. She's just trying to piss me off.

I pull the collar of my T-shirt away from my body, every inch of my skin feeling irritated. I need a breath.

Walking over to the stove, I turn off the burner and leave the kitchen, jogging up the stairs. I enter Cole's and my bedroom, pull some clean clothes out of the drawers, and leave, walking across the hallway to our bathroom.

But as soon as I step inside, I stop, seeing the mess Pike has made. The tub is ripped out, the valves to the sink are disconnected, and there's debris all over the white tiled floor.

He's still renovating. I forgot.

His bedroom door lies open, and I can see his bed straight ahead, the headboard against the opposite wall as I walk toward his room. Every time I've passed through here to get my showers this past week, it's felt awkward. Being in his room alone.

I don't snoop, but it's tempting.

His bed is always made. A little haphazardly, blankets just tossed back up in a rush, but I can't help but be a little taken aback. If not for my stepmom, my father's bed would never be made.

Heading for the bathroom, I see the pictures of Cole from birth to senior-year portraits lining the frame of his dresser mirror. A flat-screen hangs on the wall, its power cord dangling and unplugged. A model schooner sits on his bureau with only a light layer of dust on the white sails.

And an old watch with a worn leather band that I've never seen him wear sits in a dish on his dresser. There's no other jewelry anywhere.

Aside from the bed, the two dressers, the TV, and the bedside tables, the room is minimal. Nothing on the walls, of course, one black lamp with a gray shade, and a strong afternoon light streaming through the cracks in the partially open blinds.

I hate that he lived here alone for so long. Someone needs to spice this place up. Not my sister.

Swinging the bathroom door closed behind me, I lock it and reach into the shower, turning on the water. I set my change of clothes on the sink counter and strip down, pulling out a towel from the shelf and hanging it on the hook outside the shower.

Jealous yet? I shake my head, my ire rising again as I step into the shower and close the glass door.

I'm not jealous. I just don't want to see her push him around like I know she definitely can. So much is a game to my sister, and she hides her insecurities behind flighty behavior and sarcasm.

Pike's not like that. He needs someone calm. Someone who knows how to keep *him* calm.

Someone who can wrap their arms around his neck and make the rest of the world disappear.

Tipping my head back, I wet my hair and close my eyes, feeling the heat of the water pounding my shoulders and neck. Chills spread down my arms, and my head suddenly swims with the pleasure of the warmth.

Turning around, I plant my hands on the wall and roll my head under the spray, finally coming back up and leaning against the wall behind me as I push my hair back over my head.

My stomach curdles. If Cole wasn't in the picture and Pike came into the bar one night and sat on a stool and talked to me . . . I'd like him. I'd really like him.

I'd want him.

I squeeze my eyes shut tighter. God, my sister is right. Something is happening. *It's been happening, actually.* Does everyone else notice, too? Does he notice?

Shit.

I open my eyes, and they immediately fall on his bodywash sitting in the caddy in front of me. Cole usually uses Axe, but he hasn't pulled his stuff out of the other shower yet, probably just using his dad's Irish Spring.

I cast a quick look toward the glass, making sure I'm alone, and pull the bottle off the rack and pop the lid.

Little suds fizz around the opening from the guys' showers that morning, and I close my eyes, bringing Pike's bodywash to my nose. The musky fragrance fills my head, and tingles spread across my skin. It's cheap soap, but it's no-frills, does the job, and reminds me of jeans, lumber, and the barest bristle of a five-o'clock shadow on a man's jaw.

It's him.

My throat swells like I'm taking a gulp of water, and I swallow, feeling disappointed that nothing is there. I lick my lips, breathing hard.

I suspend reality somewhere in the back of my mind and absently squeeze a drop of the soap into my hand. Bringing my palm up to my nose, I smell again, my breath catching, my eyes falling closed, and my clit instantly throbbing.

Should I go after her? I remember his rare, cocky smirk that excited me last night. I didn't want him going after anyone, but God, I'm desperate to see what that looks like. What is he like with a girl?

You think I can't handle her? I've been around the block.

The hand with the soap falls down my neck, glides over my collarbone, and washes down my breast and over my nipple. *Handle her?* "Not her," I mouth to myself.

My fingers graze down my stomach as I lean back on the wall, and I slide my hand between my legs, biting my lip and shuddering at the touch.

I slowly start to rub myself, my fingers working little circles on my hardening clit.

"No," I whisper, opening my eyes. "Stop, stop, stop . . ."

I force Cole into my head. His hands on my body. His lips on my ear. The way he buries his face in my neck, so I can never see his eyes.

Oh, baby.

Fuck, baby, fuck.

You feel good. So good.

His hands grip my ass, and I rub the nub harder. Faster. Chasing the momentum I just had. The orgasm taunts me low in my belly and wants out so hard.

"Cole," I say, closing my eyes again. "Go harder."

I spin around, facing the wall and pressing myself into it with my hand still buried between my legs. He's behind me, demanding in. He wants to fuck.

I slip a finger inside and start moving on it. I lay my cheek against the wall, trying to go fast, so I can't think. Maybe if it's just fucking, I can come.

My finger is wet, and I slide it back out and rub my clit again. I want to come. It's right there. But I can't. The muscles in my arm strain, and my lungs ache for air.

Please.

But it doesn't come. My fingers slow, and I exhale, tears stinging the backs of my eyes.

I bite my lip again, aching so badly. I'm so wet.

And then, my mind in a fog and my will gone, I crawl inside my head where no one else but me can see.

I hide and give in, because no one but me has to know. In that moment. In my dirty thoughts and torrid little fantasy, I want him. I want to be for him. Our little secret.

Hidden.

"Such a good girl," a new voice whispers in my ear.

Pike's voice.

His body is behind mine now, larger and taller, caging me to the wall. His hand fists the back of my hair, and he pulls my head back slowly, leaning in to flick my lip with his tongue. I whimper.

"Taking care of the house the way I like," he taunts, and my hand becomes his hand in my head as he takes over fingering me. "Cooking my meals the way I like. Pretty little thing for me to look at. You're doing so well, Jordan."

I keep my eyes closed, feeling for his lips, my whole body pulsing with an electric current at the taste of his warm mouth and the water of the shower cascading over his hot skin. I can feel his cock, hard and ready behind me.

"I need you to do everything a woman does now," he instructs. "Everything a good girl does for a man. Can you do that?"

I nod, panting. "Yes."

My orgasm is cresting again, my nipples press painfully into the tiled wall, and it feels so good between my legs. I want him. I want him on me. I want to know what he feels like.

Reaching behind me, I don't think. I grab a loofah and slide it between my legs. The netting chafes my clit in a way that sends me over the edge. I roll my hips into it, wanting to feel anything, because it's him in my head and that's enough. His smell surrounds me, his mouth sucks my neck, and he's hefting me up, so he can slip inside me. It's rough and hard, his hands on my tits one minute and his mouth stealing my breath the next. God, his tongue tastes good.

The orgasm tingles deep, building and building, and Cole's father is fucking me so good.

I come, the wave washing over me, and I cry out in silence, breathing hard but making no sound. *God.* I collapse against the wall, nearly crumbling as I shudder, the orgasm drifting down my legs and making my knees weak. I squeeze my eyes shut and shake through it until it ebbs away, leaving me light-headed.

When the shower stops spinning and my breathing has returned to normal, I open my eyes, a flood of emotions rushing me.

Oh, my God. I want to cry.

What the hell is wrong with me? Why would I do that? And with his father? I . . .

I'm confused and stressed-out and seeking comfort in a guy because he's been nice to me a couple times. *Jesus.*

No matter what happens with Cole and me, Pike Lawson is off-limits. *Don't forget that.* There are hundreds of men out there just like him. He's not special.

It can't be him. Ever.

I straighten, taking a deep breath. Looking down, though, I see the loofah in my hand isn't my pink one. It's Pike's silver one.

"Shit."

A few suds are still in it from his shower this morning.

And I used it to orgasm. *Awesome.*

I groan inwardly.

Climbing out of the shower, I bury it under tissue paper in the trash can and make a mental note to get him a new one next time I'm out.

And some different bodywash, I think, too.

12

Pike

"Jordan?"

I dart my gaze left and right as I pass each aisle, having lost her nearly ten minutes ago. *Where the hell did she go?*

The guys and I finished at the site early today, and with a little daylight left, I'd come home from work to find Jordan working in the garden. She wanted to check out some chicken wire or something for the tomato plants, and I thought I'd add a stone border around the tree in the backyard, so we hopped in the truck and headed to Home Depot.

After putting in the order for the stone, though, I lost her.

I finally spot her at the end of an aisle digging in a shallow box sitting on a shelf. Standing back upright, she pulls out a sheet of tiles and holds it up in front of her, studying it. Carrying the two new yard tools I've picked out, I walk toward her, steeling myself.

She looks beautiful today, and shit keeps happening to my body every time I look at her. Like there are live wires underneath my damn skin. Black T-shirt, white shorts, hair down and free, minimal makeup—she's no-frills, and it works. Farmer's daughter and exactly my type once upon a time.

I shake my head, clearing it.

"What's that?" I ask, approaching.

She glances at me, still holding up the square sheet of tiles. "It's backsplash."

I reach out my free hand, running my thumb over the tan stone strips glued to the paper. "Backsplash?"

"You're in construction," she snips, giving me a chastising look. "Don't you ever watch HGTV? Backsplash is everything in home décor."

"Yeah, I've seen it," I assure her, dropping my hand. "I just . . . I don't know. Seems like a frill."

She rolls her eyes, her gaze resting on the stones again. "It's the little things that add personality to a house," she tells me. "An artsy chandelier, the right rug, and backsplash." She turns the sheet around, facing me and showing me. "This is you. It would look great with what you've done in the kitchen."

"*Me*, huh?" I let out a chuckle, meeting her eyes. "And what am I?"

Her smile falls and a look of surprise crosses her face.

I blink. "I didn't mean it . . . like that," I tell her.

It's not what I said but how I said it. Way too insinuating.

She seems to brush it off, though, turning the sheet around and staring down at it again with appreciation. "It reminds me of a cave," she finally says. "You're like a cave. You don't give up all your secrets at once. Who knows how deep you go, right?"

My eyebrows shoot up. *What?*

How *deep* I go? Did she just . . .

Her eyes suddenly go round, and she jerks her gaze to me, looking mortified. "I mean," she rushes out, "like . . . on the . . . on the inside. Your personality." A blush rises to her cheeks. "I didn't mean it like . . . ugh." Her shoulders sink, and she stuffs the sheet back into the box, giving up. "I'm going to drool over bathroom fixtures now. Bye."

And she walks away from me quickly, disappearing down an aisle.

My mouth quirks into a smile, and I break into a quiet laugh, staring after her.

"So, what do you think?" A young man in an orange apron steps up out of the corner of my eye.

I don't look at him, though, still staring at the aisle she just disappeared down. "We'll start off with three boxes of this." I gesture to the tiles on the shelf. "See how it looks . . ."

He moves over and starts unloading the boxes. "Wise choice. Happy wife, happy life, right?"

Happy wife, happy . . .

I watch him pull out a box and carry it away, the pulse in my neck suddenly throbbing.

He thinks she's my wife?

A smile pulls at the corner of my mouth, and I'm not exactly sure which emotion is filling my chest right now, but it feels good and there's a lot of it.

Later that evening, I slouch back into the couch with my arm tucked behind my head and a beer in my hand, watching TV. I've been in a lucid daze for a while now as one show has turned into five.

I set down my beer and pick up the remote, finally turning off HGTV and blinking, I think, for the first time in three hours. "She's right," I mumble. "They're fucking obsessed with backsplash."

In a moment of curiosity, I had clicked on the channel after we got home from Home Depot, and it's like I blacked out after that, only momentarily zoning back in to make a sandwich and try to talk to Cole.

He's out again now, though, having grabbed a quick shower and another quick exit after he came home from work and realized Jordan wasn't here. I thought we could go get a late dinner or something, but apparently, his plans couldn't be broken, again.

Or he's afraid to be alone with me. It's not like I want to fight, either. Even just watching a show together would be fine. I mean, we have managed not to kill each other in the past. He used to like me.

And where does he get all this money to party? He has to be spending everything he's making.

Not that I'm in a rush to have him save money and leave, but I guess I can now judge myself as harshly as I'd judged Jordan. *The more you do for someone, the less they do for themselves.* I'm as much to blame as she is. Cole won't grow up until he's forced to.

I down the rest of my beer and stand up, carrying the empty bottle into the kitchen.

My phone rings in my pocket, and I dig it out.

Dutch.

"Hey," I answer, tossing the bottle into the garbage.

"Hey. You should come to Grounders right now."

Huh?

"Like, *right* now," he adds before I have a chance to say anything.

"Why?"

"Because . . ." He pauses, and I hear a breathy little laugh. "Jordan is, um . . . misbehaving, I guess you could say."

I straighten, my brows pinching together. "Misbehaving?" I repeat. "What does that mean? And why do you think I care? I'm not her dad."

Music pounds in the background, and I can hear a crowd talking and laughing. One of my guys is getting married in a couple weeks, so the crew took him out tonight. We need at least one person not hungover tomorrow, so I stayed home.

"If you say so, man," he retorts like he doesn't believe I don't care. "But your son may not like what I'm seeing right now. What *everyone* is getting to see right now."

"What are you talking about?" I challenge.

"You're going to have to come to find out. I just hope you don't get here too late."

There's a click, and I think he hung up.

"Dutch," I bark into the phone. "Dutch!"

I expel a sigh and pull the phone away from my ear, slamming the trash can lid closed.

But I stop, doing a double take at something lying on top. Lifting the lid again, I pull out a pink half sheet, the pinup girl on the flyer catching my attention. Studying it, I let the lid fall closed and read it.

AMATEUR NIGHT!
GET WET! (YOUR T-SHIRT, ANYWAY)
MAY 27 AT 9 P.M.
THE HOOK ON JAMISON LANE
GRAND PRIZE $300!!

I straighten my spine, taking note of the date, and then relax a little. It's still a couple weeks away, so Dutch wouldn't mean this. It's not happening tonight, and it's not at Grounders.

It's probably Cole's flyer, anyway.

But on reflex, I flip it over and see handwriting on the back.

Make that $, girl!!

I quirk an eyebrow.

Is this Jordan's? It's from The Hook. Did her sister give this to her? Jesus, what is wrong with that girl? Who would encourage their little sister to enter a wet T-shirt contest, for Christ's sake?

Again, though, it's not tonight, and she threw it away, so that's a good thing.

But now I'm anxious.

I like the kid. I don't want her to feel like she needs to do shit like this to make money. I'm not rushing either of them out of my house, am I?

I pocket the paper and rub my scalp, exasperated. Dutch likes to mess with people, especially me, but she did sleep on a pool table because she was too proud to ask for help. She doesn't make the best choices.

I groan, knowing I'm not going to relax now. Sliding my phone into my pocket, I grab my keys and shut off the lights before leaving the house.

Climbing into my truck, I start the engine and blast the radio as loud as I can stand to distract from the worry pooling in my gut. He just has to go and start shit, doesn't he?

He did seem more amused than distressed, though, so he's probably fucking with me. He just wants me to get out of the house.

It takes less than ten minutes to get to Grounders, and I find a parking space around the corner, not too far. I can hear the music from out here, and I wonder if the local leagues had some baseball games tonight and everyone is still celebrating.

Misbehaving. I shake my head, grabbing the handle. The girl doesn't know the meaning of the word. She's as good as gold.

Taking a deep breath, I pull open the door and nearly wince at the noise. Hard to believe this was exactly my scene once.

"Addicted to Love" screeches through lousy speakers, and round high-top tables are packed with customers. The bar is filled, not a single stool vacant, and I look around, seeing that the booths are all filled, as well. A few women stand in line for the bathroom, the pool table is surrounded by bystanders, and the air is smoky and charged. I can already feel eyes on me.

I nod at Calista Mankin as her eyes light up and she waves, and I spot James Lowry out of the corner of my eye. Both people I've probably seen only five times since high school, and I already feel uncomfortable.

My gaze finally falls on Jordan as she stands at the jukebox, the pages flipping over in front of her as she scans the playlist through the glass. The crowd is thick, but I see the back of her head. I'd recognize her hair anywhere.

My shoulders relax a little. I knew it was just some asinine plot to get me here. She's fine.

I move through the people, trying to find Dutch and the guys, but then I see Jordan leave the music machine and make her way back to the bar, and that's when I catch glimpses of her through the throngs of people and see what she's wearing.

My eyes flare. *Jordan, Jesus . . .*

Her jeans fit her as snugly as always, the curves of her ass perfect, but her damn tits are threatening to pop out of her . . . corset. Why the hell is she wearing lingerie?

It's a white top, shimmering and laced up the front into a heart-shaped bodice with demure-looking little ruffles along the borders. My eyes fall down her cleavage, my head spinning with images of what'll spill out when she unlaces that top tonight.

The corset doesn't even reach the top of her jeans, but instead stops just above her hips, her trim waist and tummy drawing attention from every man she passes. The laces are pulled taut, giving her an hourglass look that's just begging for a man's hands. I fist mine.

The skin of her bare shoulders, her hair falling down her back, the sway of her hips as she walks . . . I tear my eyes away before I'm caught. She makes her way behind the bar again, and I ignore some of the self-satisfied smiles from men in the room as they follow her with their eyes, and I try not to wonder what their hushed whispers are telling each other.

A hand waves in the corner of my vision, and I shoot my glare up at Dutch sitting with the guys in a booth. I walk over.

"What the hell is she wearing?" I grumble, sliding into the booth.

Dutch turns his head toward me, his drink inches from his lips. "It's the lingerie show," he tells me. "They have it every Thursday night. The bartenders and servers don nighties or corsets and serve drinks and food. It's fun."

No, not really.

But I look around and see a few other ladies carrying out appetizers and bringing drinks, some of them in very thin attire. At least Jordan's corset looks as thin as armor.

"But Jordan's never done it before," he goes on. "That's what shocked me. Thought you should know."

"Why the fuck would I want to know?" I pull a beer out of the ice bucket on the table.

"Yeah, sorry." He turns away, mumbling into his glass, "You seem like you couldn't care less."

I shoot him a sideways look, hearing the laughter in his words.

Sticking the beer back in the bucket, untouched, I rise and head to the bar. I hear a snort behind me, but I don't care. She's kind of my responsibility, and I don't want her doing things like this because she thinks she needs money.

There's only one bartender besides Jordan. The owner, Shel. I'm sure she hasn't forgotten me, so I veer to the opposite end and catch Jordan's attention as she pops the tops from a line of six bottles of beer.

"What the hell are you wearing?" I lean in, speaking as quietly as I can.

She jerks her head toward me, meets my eyes, and quickly turns away again like I'm the last person she wants to deal with right now.

She hands over the beers, collects the cash, and spins around, punching the screen in front of her. "It's fine," she assures me. "It's just a corset, Pike."

"They are all looking at you."

She nods, smiling sarcastically. "That's the point."

"Jordan." I sigh, trying to whisper as I squeeze around some old dude at the bar. "This is a small town. What if your father were to walk in?"

"He doesn't come in here," she says, closing the register drawer and finally looking at me. "And neither do you, normally." A blush crosses her cheeks. "Besides, I'm not stupid. I wouldn't take part in something I thought would humiliate me."

She turns and hands the change back to the customer, but he waves her off, letting her keep it. She smiles and turns back around, dropping the bills into an already overflowing canister.

"What are you even doing here?" she says, starting to mix another drink. "I thought you were sitting the bachelor party out, because"—she sets the bottle down and does air quotes as she imitates my growling voice—"'there needs to be at least one sober person at work tomorrow.'"

I arch a brow at her. I don't sound like that.

Reaching into my pocket, I pull out the flyer and push it over the bar at her.

She stills, and her face goes ashen. "Where did you find that?"

She grabs it and dumps it somewhere under her. Into a trash can probably.

Taking a napkin, she sets it in front of a customer and gives him the fresh drink she just made.

"If you need money," I tell her as she turns around to mark a piece of paper, "I'll lend you whatever you need, okay?"

And she stops, slowly turning her eyes on me. Her gaze sharpens—she's angry, and she looks like she wants to yell at me, but she doesn't. Instead she whips around and barrels down the bar and through the partition, turning only quickly enough to crook a finger at me before she twirls back around and heads down the hallway.

My stomach sinks. I really don't mean to piss her off as much as I do. What did I say now?

Veering through the crowd, I make my way down the empty

hallway, finally coming to the same room she was crying in when I pissed her off the last time.

Entering through the open door, I see her standing with her hands on her hips and her head cocked at me.

"I would rather eat from a dumpster than take money from you," she bites out.

I should shut up. But God help me, I can't. "Hate to break it to you, but you already do," I tell her. "You live in a house where you pay no rent or utilities, young lady."

"I cook and clean for you!" she shouts, but I doubt anyone can hear us back here and through the music. "I pay my way, you arrogant prick!"

"All right, all right," I growl, blinking long and hard. "You're right, okay? But, Jordan, men will get ideas. They'll think they have a free pass and they can touch what belongs to my son. You're embarrassing him."

"Your son?" she mocks, laughing. "Well, you just missed him, actually. He already saw me, and he doesn't care, Pike. He thought I looked good, and then he left with his friends. He doesn't care!"

"Well, I care!"

The words are out of my mouth before I can stop them, and I freeze, almost too afraid to breathe.

Oh, shit. What did I just say?

Her mouth falls open a little, but she shuts up, probably shocked into silence by my outburst. Her eyes stay locked on mine, unblinking, with a mixture of confusion and surprise written all over her pretty face.

But instead of regret, my temper quickly rises again. How the hell can he not care?

And why do I?

Jesus, fuck.

She's grown, isn't she? And if her boyfriend doesn't mind, then who am I or anyone else to stake an investment in her decisions? It's not my place.

No, there's nothing wrong with what her sister does to support herself or how Jordan's dressed tonight. She's fucking gorgeous.

I just don't . . . want her body being for everyone.

"You're special, Jordan." I take a step closer to her. "You know that, right?"

Her eyes start to glisten, her gaze falters, and she looks away.

God, does she know how incredible she is?

I let myself take in her smooth and glowing skin and the curve of her waist in front of me, perfect for grabbing hold of. One man should see her dressed like this, and it should be the man who appreciates what he has.

"Don't do things outside of your nature because of money," I tell her. "You're perfect the way you are. Don't change."

I don't want you to change.

"It's just a corset, Pike."

"Yeah, and then it'll just be a wet T-shirt contest and a job at The Hook, right?" I fire back.

She rolls her eyes and turns around, grabbing a case of Bud Light and heaving it into my arms. I grab it just in time. Then she reaches for a case of Budweiser and leads the way out of the room, ending our conversation.

But I follow, hefting the case up onto my shoulder. "You're not working at The Hook," I tell her.

"And you're not my dad."

I nearly shoot her a dirty look behind her back, but that would be immature. Why ruin the excellent example of a levelheaded, responsible adult I've set since she's come into my house?

She plops her case down on the bar and turns around, taking the case I have, as well.

I open my mouth to try to say something—anything—to smooth over whatever damage I've done again and still try to get her to put some damn clothes on.

But she cuts me off before I can say anything. "I need another case of Bud Light," she orders me over her shoulder.

I shake my head. Damn her brass.

I turn around and walk back to the liquor closet, grabbing another case of beer. After I drop it on the bar, I head to the booth where the guys are still congregating and take out the same bottle of Busch Light I had before.

"Staying?" Dutch inquires.

I shrug, looking anywhere but at the bar. "For a bit, I guess."

I down the bottle inside of a minute, and it's not my favorite beer, but I'm suddenly too embarrassed to go to the bar and ask her for a Corona now. I should've gotten one when I was up there.

A server approaches, though, and I'm about to flag her down, but I notice she's already heading my way with a tray of shots. She's cute in her black miniskirt and black vest, but she doesn't look any older than Jordan.

She smiles. "Hey, guys." And then she starts unloading her tray, setting a round of shots in front of us. They're pink or orange on the bottom, with some kind of yellow liquid on top.

"What is this?" Jason Bryant, one of my guys, asks.

"It's called a Pineapple Upside-Down Cake," she says. "It's on the house. Jordan says they're Pike's favorite."

A round of laughter explodes around the table at the "chick" shot everyone now thinks I drink, and I shoot Jordan a look at the bar.

She grins, giving me her biggest, proudest smile.

And now we're not mad at each other anymore.

Taking the shot, I down it, the alcohol going down like a piece of candy, and while it tastes fine, I'm not sure what the point is. There can't be enough alcohol in it to feel anything.

I'm sure it will be a successful running joke if I ever decide to join the guys for a drink again, though.

After about an hour and another beer, the crowd has thinned a little, and I'm pretty tapped out on eighties music. Jordan seems fine, and I'm not sure why I thought she needed protecting.

I should just hit the road.

But just then, a Corona appears in front of me, and I look up, seeing Jordan standing over me.

"Hey," she says, her expression soft and gentle.

I'm sure it would be like that all the time if I would just stop fucking with it.

"You doing okay, sugar?" Dutch asks her.

She glances at him and smiles and then looks back down at me. "I was going to call you, actually," she tells me, lowering her voice. "I don't know if you're staying late, but I was wondering if there was any way you could bring me home tonight. I don't get off until two. Is that too late?"

Her eyes are apologetic, like she's afraid she's being an inconvenience, but of course, I told her to tell me if she needs a ride home. I'm happy to do it.

"No problem. I'll be here."

But Dutch nudges my elbow. "We gotta be at the site by five a.m., just remember."

"It's fine," I say curtly, barely looking at him.

Of course I'd love to get more than a couple hours of sleep, but this isn't a choice.

Jordan takes a step back. "Are you sure?" she asks again. "I could ask Shel. It's a little out of her way, but I don't want you losing sleep."

"It's fine," I assure her. "I'll be here."

"Well, why don't you just give her your keys?" Dutch speaks up. "I'll drop you at home, and she can have your truck. I'm getting out of here soon anyway."

Mother— What is his goddamn problem?

But Jordan rushes in, making her apologies. "No, no, it's okay. I can—"

"Fuck, I said it was fine," I blurt out, shutting everyone up. Then I glare at Dutch. "Would you shut up?"

He turns away, pursing his lips because he wants to fucking smile like he knows something.

Everyone is still for a moment, and I shake my head, pulling my keys out of my pocket. There's no logical reason to wait around for her if Dutch is offering me a ride now.

I hand her the keys. "Here you go. It works out perfectly."

"Are you—"

"Yes, I'm sure," I tell her. "It's fine."

She slides the keys into her pocket. "Thank you."

"Truck's parked just around the corner."

She nods and heads back to the bar, glancing back at me once. I check my phone, seeing it's nearly midnight, and if Dutch is giving me a ride, I'd rather get it over with now.

I take a long swig from the Corona, drinking about half. It didn't escape my notice that she remembered what beer I like, too. Pulling some money out, I toss a few bills on the table for whatever I drank and tell Dutch, "Let's go."

He hauls himself out of the booth, his scruffy buzz cut mussed as he yawns. We make our way toward the door, and I pass the bar, tossing a few bills on it in front of Jordan.

She gives me a knowing look. "Didn't we talk about this?"

"I'm just a customer."

The look in her eyes says she's not buying my reason for tipping her, but the humor in her gaze says she'll let it go. This time.

We leave and walk across the street to Dutch's Tahoe and climb in.

"You didn't really want to wait around until two, did you?" he asks as we fasten our seat belts.

Actually . . .

"No," I tell him, deciding I don't have the energy to get into it. "Thanks for the ride."

He pulls away from the curb, and I slouch down a little, moving the seat back for more legroom. His wife is usually in this seat. I lay my head back and into my hand, closing my eyes.

I feel the car make a U-turn and then he speeds down the street, heading home. It's quiet for a few minutes as he finds a satellite station, and the glare of the streetlights glows through my closed lids. It's a short drive home, but even still, I would've liked to have been the one to bring her. Who knows if that shithead ex will try to come around in the next hour? Will she be walking to the car with anyone?

I'm not just worried about her safety, though. I have this urge to make sure she's okay and taken care of, and while I've tried to morph it into a "fatherly" type of responsibility, it's not.

It never will be.

I like what I feel when I see her and talk to her and think about her. Even when we fight. And I have to admit it to myself—I am attracted to her.

I hate it, but I can't ignore it and pretend it's not there anymore. I need to deal with it.

It doesn't have to be a big deal, though. We go through life running into people we're attracted to all the time. It happens, and you can't help it. It doesn't mean I'd try anything. I just feel guilty it happened with her.

And the fact that she's in my house makes it harder.

Cole really did get the shit end of the stick with parents. What a fucking piece of work I am.

I can't help it, but I can make sure I don't act on it.

She doesn't make it easy, though, getting into it with me as easily as she does. She knows how to press my buttons. Almost as if she was made for it.

"She seems like a good kid," Dutch says, breaking the silence.

I open my eyes, the lids heavy from the long day. "Yeah." I sigh. "She's quiet. Clean. I barely know she's in the house."

"That's great." I can see him glancing over at me from time to time. "Getting along okay?"

"Yeah, why?"

I feel him shrug. "She seems nervous around you."

I chuckle. He could say the same for me if he were looking close enough.

"Well, I can be intimidating," I joke.

"Yeah, she looked like she wanted to straddle your hard, intimidating cock right there in the bar."

My eyes pop open completely, and I glare over at him. "Are you kidding me? What the fuck?"

"Oh, please," he shoots back. "You're telling me you didn't see her fidgeting and biting her lip at just the sight of you when she brought you your *favorite* beer?"

She was?

"She was like a puppy with her tongue hanging out of her mouth," he adds.

Was she?

I clear my head and look back out the window, puzzlement etched on my face.

Whatever.

"Don't talk about her like that," I tell him. "That's my kid's girlfriend, man. Come on."

Straddling my . . . I shake my head. Unbelievable.

"So, she's off-limits to you, then?"

"Yes!"

"Then why were you looking at her like you loved what she was wearing and wanted to see it on your bedroom floor tonight?"

"I wasn't looking at her like that," I grit out through my teeth.

But he just laughs under his breath.

Asshole.

"Hey, I'm not knocking—"

"Shut up," I say.

Damn it. It's not right. It's bad enough I'm looking at her like she's an actual woman and not my son's girl, but I'll be damned if anyone finds out about it.

"All I'm saying is she's exactly your type," he tells me, evening out his voice. "Did you notice that? You always went for girls like her in high school. Before Lindsay the Train Wreck, anyway."

"Just shut up."

But he doesn't. "I'm not saying you should do anything. And that's why I stepped in and didn't let you bring her home."

His tone turns serious.

"All kidding aside, Pike," he goes on, "she *is* exactly your type. You shouldn't be alone with her."

Yeah.

I know.

I just hope he's the only person who's noticed.

"Thanks for the intervention," I tell him, "but even if I were attracted to her, I'm capable of controlling myself."

"You're not seeing yourself from my perspective." He looks out the front windshield, solemn. "You look at each other like . . ."

"Like?"

He swallows, an unusually troubled pinch to his brow. "Like the two of you have your own language."

13

Jordan

I pull into the driveway, my body jostling from side to side as the headlights fall on the closed garage ahead. Pressing in the clutch, I hit the brake and park, turning off the engine.

The bar cleared out early, Shel and a couple of the other girls staying to close up, so I got out well before two tonight. Pike only left an hour ago, but he's undoubtedly in bed by now. He's not a night owl.

I look over, seeing Cole's Challenger parked in the next spot. He's home.

I knit my brow, apprehension suddenly hitting me.

The distance between us is growing, and I feel like he's miles away these days. The need he seemed to have for me a couple weeks ago is almost nonexistent now, and I wonder why I'm still here.

But I have an idea.

Guilt winds its way through my gut as I remember what happened in the shower the other day, and how my brain took a completely different turn than I wanted. Or didn't know I wanted.

It was just the stress. The moment got away from me, and Pike was a focal point. He's been nice and caring, and I've been starved for a little attention, and I zoned in on him. That's it.

At this point, though, I have almost no reason to stay here, but still, even with Cole's and my problems, I hate the idea of leaving. This house has become familiar and warm. A home. And even though Pike can certainly be an invasive ass sometimes, I do like him. He cares. He doesn't express his concerns very eloquently, of course, but I know his intentions are in the right place. It's nice to have someone looking out for me and giving a damn about what I do.

And I hate to admit it, but I like the way he makes me feel. The way his eyes look at me like I'm the only thing in the world.

Climbing out of the truck, I grab my bag with the corset in it. I changed into a T-shirt before I left the bar, and while I felt pretty exposed all night with a few more pairs of eyes on me than I'm used to, I quirk a smile to myself, thinking of the wad of tips in my pocket right now. It's not nearly what Cam makes or what I could make bartending at The Hook, but it's more than I normally earn in a week, so . . .

And I can't lie. I kind of liked the attention. I knew the moment his eyes were on me tonight when he walked in and I was at the jukebox. I could see him out of the corner of my eye when I walked to the bar, too, and I know that look. *Possessive.*

I lock the truck door, my heart thudding again as I head for the house.

I need to talk to Cole. I need to look into his eyes and take his hand in mine, look down at our matching little scars and see if I still feel this going anywhere. A few months ago, he always had his arm around me. Now I can't remember the last time he's touched me.

Entering the house, I close the door, drop my bag, and slip off my flats. I curl my toes, the ache in my feet shooting up my calves.

The living room is shrouded in shadow, and I walk to the dark staircase and stop, listening. No noise comes from upstairs, so Pike and Cole are probably both asleep. Trying to be as quiet as possible, I tiptoe into the kitchen and take a glass from the cupboard, pressing it under the water dispenser on the fridge.

But when I glance up, I see Cole in the backyard and freeze.

I drop my hand from the dispenser, the glass upending and the water in it splattering all over the wooden floor. Heat courses up my neck, my lungs empty, and I can't look away. Everything hits me at once, and I feel like I'm outside myself, watching me watch him.

Cole.

I swallow twice, barely able to wet my throat. Elena Barros is in the pool with him, her elbows resting behind her on the edge, while he leans down into her, his forehead pressed to hers like he does with me. Her naked body glistens with water and moves in a wave, matching his rhythm as he grips her ass and fucks her, her breasts grazing his chest again and again.

Absently, I take a step, coming to the sink, and continue to try to process what I'm seeing. Cole would never do this to me. He's not my ex. He's not my parents.

My chest caves, too heavy to take in more air. Nausea rolls through my stomach, and bile rises up my throat.

He cups her face, kissing her, his body moving steady and strong, and they hold each other's eyes as he enters her again and again. I can't hear her moans, but I know she's enjoying it.

Tears fill my eyes, I tighten my fist around the glass, and I clench my teeth. I'm angry with myself more than with him. I should've been the one to end it when we got evicted from our apartment. I knew he only wanted me because he didn't want to be alone. I could feel it then.

But now here we are, and he's had the last word, hasn't he?

My chin trembles, and the tears spill over. My mom, Jay, Cole . . . I am forever the most pathetic fucking person I know. I keep wishing the lousiest people want me. Why?

"Hey," someone says, but the voice sounds distant. "Home early, huh? Glad you're not wearing the corset. Did you burn it for me?"

The fridge opens, and the light pours out as someone digs in and pulls something out, but I keep staring out the window, something cold and thick slowly coating my stomach like syrup.

I can change the moment I decide to.

"Jordan?" I hear Pike say. "Are you okay?"

I finally realize he's standing next to me. The fridge door closes, and I turn to look at him, tears still wet on my cheeks.

His hazel eyes, looking amber right now, immediately narrow with concern. But then his gaze flashes to the window, and all color drains from his face.

"Oh, Jesus," he growls and grabs my arm, pulling me away.

I lose my composure and start gasping, drawing in heavy, shallow breaths as he veers around me and storms out the back door. I wipe the tears from my face, because I'm upset and hurt but mostly just pissed. And not entirely with Cole, either. I did this to myself. I always do this to myself.

"What the hell are you doing?" I hear Pike bark.

I hear a slosh of water, surprised voices, and a gasp.

"Shit!" Cole exclaims. "I thought you were asleep."

"No one's fucking asleep!"

"What?" Cole says.

No one. I think he just realized I'm home, too.

Drying my eyes, I walk across the kitchen and let my legs do the thinking.

Pushing through the back door, I descend the wooden stairs and see Elena hiding her naked body behind Cole, who is still waist-deep in the water.

"What is the matter with you?" Pike stalks over, picking up the towels and throwing them at his son.

He catches them and Elena snatches one, quickly covering herself as half the towel hits the water around her. She casts me scared glances.

"I thought she was at work until two," Cole tells him, sounding guilty and speaking to his father as if I'm not here. His head is bowed, and he's not meeting anyone's eyes.

"So doing it behind her back is okay?"

"No, I just—"

"I can handle this," I cut them both off, stepping up.

I surprise myself by how calm my tone is and how I'm not crying. I don't mind crying in front of Cole, but I'm not tearing up in front of her.

Pike looks over at me, hesitating for several seconds. Finally, he turns around, and I hear the screen door shut.

As soon as he's gone, Elena quickly runs out of the pool, tightening the towel around her as she grabs her clothes from the lawn chair.

"I'm going to go," she says, an apologetic look on her face as her eyes dart between Cole and me. "I'm really sorry, Jordan."

She ducks her head and rushes past me, toward the house and probably straight to the bathroom, so she can change.

I turn my eyes back on Cole. His blond hair is slicked back, and he looks at me with the same eyes he had right before he told me that Nick didn't make it.

I wish I was angrier with him.

Mostly, I'm just disappointed.

"It's been going on a while?" I ask.

His eyes fall, and he nods solemnly. "Since your birthday party."

You mean the one I didn't attend?

He takes a deep breath and squares his shoulders, stepping out of the pool and wrapping the towel around his waist.

"I've known you a long time," he says, "and we both needed each other a lot when this started, but you were always going to move on. You know that."

"So why did I come here at all?" I ask him. "Why keep me around?"

I could ask myself the same questions. We were both weak, hanging on to the only good thing we each had. And we ignored how by staying together we were ruining it.

I love him. He's my friend. How could he humiliate me like this?

"You weren't supposed to be like him," I tell him, tears pooling again.

He looks up, knowing exactly who I'm talking about. Jay was a piece of shit. Not Cole. Cole knew what I went through. Was he trying to hurt me?

"You were my friend first," I go on. A friend is supposed to be good to you.

But he doesn't say anything. There's nothing to say. It's not his fault it ended. It's just his fault it ended so badly.

"In our bed, too?" I ask him. "On the nights I was working?"

His silence tells me I'm right, and a wave of anger suddenly hits me. Did Pike know that Cole had her over? Or maybe other girls over?

But no—I stop myself, the knots in my stomach unwinding a little. He seemed as shocked as me just now.

I nod, also realizing Cole didn't meet Elena out alone, either. He met up with her at parties, no doubt. "And all your friends knew," I say, the betrayal becoming perfectly clear.

I'm on my own now. Aside from Cam and the ladies at the bar, I've lost my last friend.

He approaches, stopping in front of me. "I'm going to stay with Elena for a while," he says. "You stay here until you can—"

"Fuck you." I raise my eyes, saying it with the same indifference as "you're welcome."

Heading back into the house, I don't stop to see if Elena is gone or if she's waiting out by Cole's car. I pick up my bag and head to the bedroom, pulling out my cell phone and sliding down to the floor against the closed door.

I dial, the line picks up on the fourth ring, and I swipe away a silent tear as I harden my voice. "Hey, Dad."

The next day, I stare at Cole's and my bedroom, his stuff discarded where he left it and every last item of mine finally packed up.

I guess I'm glad I didn't bring much. Most of my clothes fit in the two suitcases I have—one belonging to Cam that I brought when I thought I was going to leave a couple weeks ago.

But then Pike Lawson built me a garden, and it just goes to show, no man has had to do much to get me to come running back.

I laugh at myself under my breath. I will miss the garden, though.

I carry the last box through the living room, resisting the urge to take a final look at the garden through the kitchen window, and walk out the front door, seeing Pike's truck pulling in from work.

My heart starts thumping harder. *Dammit.* I wish I could've gotten out of here before he got home. It's not even five yet. I cut out of the lunch shift early so I could get packed up and out of here in time, too. What's he doing home already?

"What are you doing?" He follows me around the truck.

I shove the box into my back seat, on top of another one, and the car is just big enough to hold everything I came with. It all fits in two suitcases and three boxes. Everything else is in storage. And I don't see me getting it out anytime soon, either. My father's "house" doesn't have room for a drafting table.

"Thank you for everything," I tell him, knowing he knows exactly what I'm doing. "You've been really amazing."

"You're leaving?" He looks confused.

I close the car door and turn to him, my stomach rolling as I swallow the lump in my throat.

"With Cole gone, and us broken up, it's not right for me to stay,"

I say. "You never had any obligation to help me, but you did, and I can't thank you enough. I really do appreciate everything." And then I can't help but force a little smile for both our sakes. "Especially my cassette tapes."

I stare at his troubled eyes, the green in the irises seeming to grow darker, and an ache hits my chest. I turn away, pretending to make sure the door's closed to have a second to collect myself.

"My dad is letting me come home for a while." I turn and tell him. "I'll be okay."

"But . . ."

"Oh, I forgot my purse." I run my fingers through the top of my hair and bolt for the house, not letting him finish as I rush away.

I don't want to argue with him, and I'm afraid if he says anything else, I'll start crying.

I don't want to leave, but I know I have no right to be here anymore, and maybe he'll come into the bar from time to time to visit, right? Maybe I'll see him around more now that I know him and I'd recognize him.

Of course, I'm upset about Cole, too. I've spoken to him practically every day for the last three years.

But I *want* to be away from him. I don't really like leaving Pike.

Who's going to make him converse with people, and who's going to sneak in the vanilla extract and cinnamon he doesn't realize he likes in his coffee now?

I blink away the sting in my eyes, growling at myself. *He'll be fine.* He survived thirty-eight years without me, didn't he?

Plucking my purse off the couch, I open it, doing a visual inventory: cards, keys, wallet, phone. . . . And I close it, doing a mental check and making sure I grabbed my phone charger, my razor and shampoo from the shower, and any remaining laundry in the washer and dryer.

Shit. I forgot to replace his loofah, didn't I? Oh, well . . .

I finally take a deep breath, realizing I have everything, I guess.

Walking back outside, I fix a half smile on my face and straighten my spine. To the left, Kyle Cramer trails inside his house with a couple kids who I assume are his, but I don't make eye contact. I don't want the neighbors getting nosy.

"Jordan . . ." Pike starts in on me.

But I cut him off. "Thank you so much again. For everything."

I head to the driver's side and open the door, my stomach knotting into a thousand little balls, each one getting tighter and tighter.

"Jordan," he calls again. "That car's not ready to go. It'll stall every time you stop."

I give him a shaky smile. "I'll deal with it. Really, I'm all panicked out. I don't think much will upset me anymore. I'll be fine."

Pulling out my keys, I climb in. "Thanks for all the work you did on it already. You definitely didn't need to do all that."

"Wait," he blurts out, sounding urgent.

I stop, unable to look at him, but I feel him take a step forward. He hesitates like he's searching for words.

I glance up.

"Just . . ." He shakes his head, looking exasperated. "Move the stuff into the back of my truck. I'll take you."

I open my mouth to argue, but he cuts me off.

"I need to finish the VW," he says. "It needs to stay here for a couple more days. And don't give me attitude about it. Can you all of a sudden afford a mechanic?"

14

Pike

Meadow Lakes. I want to laugh. There's no meadows or lakes, and there's certainly no lake on a meadow. It's a sixty-year-old trailer park full of dumps propped up on cinder blocks.

Did she actually grow up here?

I'm starting to think Cole didn't have it so bad, after all. I look around, taking in the ancient silver Airstreams mixed in with some double-wides from the eighties, broken blinds barely visible behind muddy windows, and termite-rotted exteriors, green with mildew and exposed insulation. This whole fucking place is a fire hazard. I don't want her here. She doesn't have to stay at my house, but just . . . not here.

Jordan sits in the seat next to me, slowly running her palms across each other and staring down blankly, lost in thought. I can't shake the feeling that she's trying to put off looking out the window as long as possible.

It's not dark yet, but the sun has set, and a couple kids race out from between two mobile homes, chasing a ball. I slow down in case they run into the street.

"Right there," Jordan says.

I glance over, seeing her gesture to my left, and follow her gaze to a trailer with filthy lime-green siding, and I clench my teeth.

An AC unit protrudes from the front window, a rickety old wooden fence wraps around the bottom, parts of it lying broken on the ground or sections just plain missing, and the porch is crowded with random junk, clothes, and a couple loaded trash bags. Three young guys stand on the porch, smoking and talking.

"Here?" I turn and ask her.

But she just unfastens her seat belt, preparing to get out.

"Who are those guys?" I say.

She glances up for only a moment before averting her eyes again, taking her bag. "It's probably my stepbrother and a couple of his friends."

I pull up in front of the trailer, since the small driveway is full, and turn off the engine.

"You have a stepbrother?" She hasn't mentioned him.

She just shrugs. "In the technical sense," she says, quirking a smile. "I don't talk to him much."

"But he lives here," I say, trying to get clarification.

She nods, and before I can say anything else, she climbs out of the truck, taking her purse with her.

Well, how many rooms can this place have if there's another kid living here? Does she even have a bed?

She pulls a suitcase out of the back, swings her bag over her head, and leads the way. I grab a box and follow, grinding my teeth to keep my fucking mouth in check. I don't know if I'm angry or worried or what, and I don't know if I have a right to feel those things or if any concern is justified. She'll probably be fine. This is her family. I just . . .

I feel like I'm going to explode at any second.

We walk up the few steps to the front door, and Jordan barely looks at her stepbrother and his friends as she opens the door.

"Ryan, this is Cole's dad," she mumbles. "Pike, this is my stepbrother, Ryan."

I turn to the kid, and he straightens, holding out his hand. "Hey, man."

I shift the box in my arms and manage to shake his hand. "Hi."

He's stocky and short for a guy, about Jordan's height, but he tries to make up for it with a neck tattoo and a black leather jacket.

In summer.

"So, you home now?" he says to her, taking a swig from his beer.

"Yeah."

One of Ryan's buddies nudges him. "Is this the one who's a stripper?"

I tighten my fingers around the box.

He snorts, nearly spitting up his beer. "Nah, man. That's the other one." But then his eyes take Jordan in, moving up and down her with a smirk. "This one can dance a little, too, though."

They all laugh, and I feel a lump push up my throat like a growl. Steeling myself, I turn and push the door open for Jordan, forcing her inside.

I should be more forgiving. It's not like I wasn't the occasional little prick from time to time growing up.

How the hell does he know how she dances?

I give myself a mental shake and take a deep breath. *Drop off her shit and go home. She's not my concern. This is her choice.* And if I were her, I'd do the same thing.

I'm actually proud of myself. She's no stranger to my outbursts or pushy demands, and I'm keeping amazingly quiet given the fact that I hate this neighborhood, and this entire situation is grinding my gears. I can hang on for five more minutes, right?

And if I do, then maybe I'll treat myself to Dairy Queen on the way home for keeping my mouth shut for once.

Her father, Chip, is passed out on a recliner to the left, the TV playing some sitcom at a dulled volume, while a couple ladies sit at the kitchen table to the right. They smoke cigarettes with cans of beer in front of them. A car stereo blares in the distance, and a few firecrackers go off around us outside.

"Need any help?" a lady with dark hair asks from the table. She lifts up her beer, taking a drink and barely giving me any notice.

Jordan shakes her head and veers into the kitchen, around the ladies at the table. She doesn't introduce us, and I certainly don't care if this lady doesn't. Your daughter—or stepdaughter—comes home with a guy you've never seen, and it doesn't prompt a question, at least?

I assume it's her stepmom, anyway, since she has the same small brown eyes as the guy outside.

I inhale the smell of Lysol mixed with a tinge of burritos and wet soil, like something got rained on or there's rot somewhere. We make our way down the hallway, our footfalls creating a hollow thud as we come to the first door on the left.

"There might be some laundry we tossed in there," the lady at the table calls back. "Gather it up and toss it in the washer, would ya?"

I take another deep breath. *She'll be fine.*

She pushes the bedroom door open, and I look into her old bedroom. My jaw flexes.

"Where's my bed?" Jordan calls out, sighing.

But no one answers her.

The room is littered with fucking junk. She has a dresser that's missing drawers, a beach towel hanging over her window, and cobwebs in the corner of the ceiling. I can smell the pile of dirty laundry that her room now houses and narrow my eyes at the hole in the wall.

No.

Jordan sets down her suitcase and turns to me, grabbing at the box. "Don't worry," she says, smiling at whatever look I have on my face. "I'll be fine. You know me. I'll have this place spic-and-span by tomorrow."

But I won't let her have the box, keeping it secure in my arms.

I tear my eyes away from the mousetrap sitting next to the heating vent with no grate over it to keep rodents out and jerk my hard stare down to her. "Hell, no," I growl. "I'm done with this conversation. We're leaving now."

Holding the box in the crook of one arm, I reach down and grab her suitcase with the other hand and immediately turn, barreling back out of the house.

"Excuse me?" she bursts out behind me, dumbfounded.

But I'm already gone. I ignore the women in the kitchen and don't even turn to see if her father has woken up before I push through the front door and past the guys still loitering on the porch.

"Pike!" she yells after me.

I ignore her. I know she'll follow me. I have all of her stuff.

Dropping the box and suitcase back into the bed of the truck, I dig out my keys and climb into the driver's seat. She charges around the front of the truck and opens the passenger-side door.

She glares at me. "What the hell are you doing?"

"You're not staying here." I start the engine.

"What the hell's the matter with you?" she blurts out.

I glance through my window, seeing the guys on the porch looking at us curiously. "Has that stepbrother tried anything with you?" I ask her.

"Nothing I can't handle."

"And his friends?"

She inhales a breath, and I can tell she's trying to stay calm. She's impatient with my concerns. "I'll be okay," she maintains. "I'm not your kid. My dad is here."

"Your dad isn't . . ." I bark but stop.

Insulting her won't get us anywhere.

I press my back into the seat and grind my fist over the wheel.

Her father isn't a bad guy. From what I know of him, anyway. We've even talked a few times in passing.

But he's weak.

He's a drunk, and he's a loser. He's the type who does the bare minimum in life and puts up with scraps, because he's too lazy to fight for better. He can't be there for her.

"This is stupid," I say. "You're not trading in a perfectly good home, in a nice, safe neighborhood, for this. Swallow your pride, Jordan."

"I don't belong at your house!" Fury burns in her eyes. "And *this* is where I come from, thank you. Cole is going to be back, eventually, and he's your son. How do you think that's going to work out with both of us there? I have no right."

"We'll deal with it."

"No," she fires back. "This isn't any of your business. This is my home."

"It's not a home! You don't . . ."

I open my mouth to finish, but my heart is pounding so hard, and I'm afraid of what I was going to say.

I breathe shallow and fast, turning my eyes forward again and away from her. I lower my voice. "You don't have anyone who cares about you in this shithole."

"And I do at your house?"

I shoot my eyes to her, the answer to that question coming so easily and so heavy on the tip of my tongue that I want to tell her.

But I don't.

And she stares at me, my unsaid reply hanging between us. She falters, realization softening her eyes.

"Just get in the truck," I grit out, "and let's go home."

"But—"

"Now, Jordan!" I slam the steering wheel with my palm.

She sucks in a breath, her eyes flaring. I don't know if I scared her, or if she's worried about making a scene, but she quickly pulls herself into the truck and slams her door. She's tense and pissed and probably thinks she'll deal with me away from prying eyes later, but I don't care. I've got her, and we're out of here.

I shift the truck into gear and pull ahead, swinging around and then reversing to do a U-turn. Finally facing back the way I came, I lay on the gas and get us out of there, driving back down the lane and pulling onto the road leading back into town.

I have no idea what her stepbrother or stepmother was thinking, and I really don't care about that, either. Let them think what they want for the next five minutes, because that's exactly how long it will take them to forget she exists again.

No wonder she moved out of there in the first place. I don't think she was abused or anything—I never heard talk like that about her father—but she was definitely neglected. She deserves better.

The trees loom on both sides of the dark highway, and I roll my window down for some much-needed fresh air.

She doesn't say anything, just sits there frozen, and I could kick myself, because I should've just talked to her at the house instead of going through all this. I knew how this was going to end. There was no way she was staying in Meadow Lakes. I wasn't seriously helping her move tonight. I was finding my mettle.

But what if she wanted to move in with her sister? Or stay with a friend? I still would've fought her. I know I would've.

It's not that she can't take care of herself. I know very well she can.

I just don't want her to have to. Somewhere along the line I got invested.

No one else in her life can give her what she deserves, and until she can provide it for herself, then I'm taking that responsibility. Screw it. She deserves the best. She's getting the best.

I stare ahead and lean my elbow on the door, running my hand through my hair. *It's not my decision, though. Is it?* Pushing her around doesn't make me any better than anyone else in her life.

And I don't want to be someone else who stifles her. She'll end up resenting me, too. If there's one thing I've learned about relationships—any relationship—it's that no one should wear the pants. You have to know when to come on strong and when to back off. Both of you.

Give and take. Share the power.

I ease on the brake and slowly veer to the right side of the road, coming to a stop as a car speeds past me.

Her eyes shift, but she still won't look at me.

God, what she must be thinking.

"I'm sorry," I say, my tone quieter and calmer now. "I didn't mean to command you like that." I drop my hands from the wheel and try to slow down my heart a little.

"Cole is staying with . . ." I trail off, knowing she knows who he's staying with. "For the time being," I finish. "You'll have space, and you can have the other spare room. It's your space. You like my house, right?"

She takes in a breath, searching for words. "Yes, but . . ."

"I like having help around the place," I explain. "And it's nice to come home and not have to make dinner every night. We keep the same arrangement."

She pauses, and fear creeps up. Maybe I read her wrong, after all. Maybe she's just trying to find a way to get me off her back. Maybe she really doesn't want to stay at my house.

"Will you be happy? At my house? Honestly?" I ask. "Happier than back there?"

The silence stretches between us, and I'm beginning to feel stupid. Like I misread everything and she wasn't getting comfortable under my roof.

But all the times I caught glimpses of her this week—lighting her candles, working in the garden, having a morning swim, or cooking in the kitchen and bobbing her head to whatever awful hair band she's listening to this week—it seemed like she was at home. She was smiling so much, we'd gotten comfortable enough to joke around, and she was even getting mischievous on me, adding stupid sprouts and avocado to the turkey sandwich in my lunch the other day.

I smile a little, thinking about it.

I don't want her to trade down because she thinks she's unwanted at my house or she's imposing. I want to make sure she knows that she doesn't have to leave.

I blink long and hard, suddenly weary. And I fucking hate the idea of her in that shithole with no one there who's going to appreciate anything she does.

I drop my eyes and my voice. "Please don't make me leave you there."

I see her head turn in my direction, and I know how I must sound.

"Please," I whisper again.

She's staring at me, but I refuse to look at her, because I'm afraid my eyes will say something more or give away something teetering on the edge of my brain that I don't want to face yet.

She's happy at my house, she's safe there, she has a bed, and there's no fucking mice. It's that simple.

Yeah. It's that simple.

After a moment, I hear her draw in a calm breath as she reaches over and grabs her seat belt, fastening it.

I swallow.

"*Fright Night* is streaming on Netflix," she says. "Half pepperoni and half taco?"

I break into a smile. Turning to her, I see her blue eyes looking at me with the same easy humor she had when we were cutting watermelon the other night.

I shift the car into gear again and nod. "Call it in," I tell her. "We'll pick it up on the way home."

15

Jordan

We come to new terms.

I'm a tenant now, essentially, and while the end goal is to live here to save money for my own place eventually, I can't live off him like I was. Maybe I could've made excuses when I was Cole's girlfriend, but now this needs to be fair. No matter how much he balks.

"I don't need your forty bucks a month for the gas bill, Jordan."

"Then let me pay the electric bill."

"Why would I tell you to stay here to save money and then ask you to spend more money?"

"I am saving money. And I can keep saving money while paying at least one bill, Pike."

"Or you could not pay any bills, save even more money, and just be out of here faster."

And then that pissed me off, like maybe he really didn't want me here, after all.

"No, wait." He flinches. "I didn't mean it like that. Just . . . I don't need your money, okay? Let's stop talking now. Please?"

But we didn't. We kept bickering until he finally relented and let me have the gas bill and the grocery bill, although he did make me promise to not replace his snacks with anything organic or fat-free, to which I agreed. If he catches me sneaking in fair-trade coffee and almond milk, I'll just tell him I forgot.

Taking the broom out to the front porch, I lift up the welcome mat and shake it out before hanging it over the railing. Rain pours down outside like a torrent, and the street looks like the whitewash of ocean waves as the falling raindrops kick up and spatter against the ground.

I wonder how well Pike will be able to see the roads on his way home. It's still only about one in the afternoon, though, and it's still light out, although pretty gray, so it might stop raining before he's off work.

I swipe the broom across the wooden porch, the overhang protecting it from getting wet. The air is balmy and thick, my skin feeling damp even though no rain is hitting me under the awning. My T-shirt sticks to my stomach a little, and I tuck my hair behind my ear because it's tickling my arms. Looking up, I see Kyle Cramer pulling his BMW into his driveway, covering his head with his briefcase as he dashes to his front porch.

He notices me and flashes a smile. I give a little wave.

I wonder why he and Pike aren't friendly.

He disappears inside, and I finish cleaning up the tiny amount of dirt and thistles on the porch before laying the welcome mat back down.

In addition to the gas and grocery bills, I've taken on responsibility for the downstairs of the house: dusting, vacuuming, sweeping, mopping, keeping the kitchen tidy, although he has to do the dishes when I cook, and I only have to do them when he cooks. Which, actually, he hasn't done at all in the three days since I've come back to stay here. I kind of realized at some point over the last few weeks that he really only makes meals from the frozen food section in the grocery store—or canned soup and stews—so I've just taken over meals completely and he does the dishes, and I'm cool with that.

I also do the garden, while he handles the lawn, pool, and sprinklers. Our rooms are our own responsibilities, but I clean my bathroom, and he keeps the basement in order.

Setting up the individual chores was almost too good to be true. I thought for sure he'd flake, and I'd end up cleaning up crap he left in areas that I was tasked with keeping tidy.

But it hasn't happened. He tosses his boots in the closet after work, picks up the T-shirts he discards if he gets too hot, and I never have to bug him to get his clothes out of the dryer. I realize I've never lived with a man who lived on his own before me.

Until now, that is. Pike's used to taking care of himself and his things, because there was no one else to do it for him. It's like a whole new world.

Walking back in the house, I stick the broom into the closet and head upstairs to sort my dirty clothes. Cole's old bedroom—our old bedroom—sits vacant, since he hasn't been back since he left. I'm not sure what he's been wearing the past few days, and I don't know if he's talked to his dad, but one thing is for sure. He'll be back eventually.

I put up with as much as I did because Cole was a friend and not just a boyfriend. Most girls—if they're smarter than me, and that wouldn't be hard, mind you—get tired of deadbeats real fast. Knowing he and Elena probably won't make it is the only consolation for the hurt. He jumped right out of my bed and into hers, didn't he?

But maybe he did me a favor. Would I want him back? No. I don't want to hate him, and I know he's better than this, but we pushed it because we needed to grab onto something once upon a time. We forced what wasn't there, not because we needed each other but because we needed someone. We were always better friends.

I feel like I can breathe now. And if he has a problem with me being here, I'll let his dad deal with it.

Across from Cole's room, I open the door to the other spare room—my new room—and pull my collapsible laundry basket out of the corner.

I love my new space. There was already a daybed in here, so I just went out and bought a new bedding set. I could've moved my old one from Cole's bed, since it's mine anyway, but I wanted to start new. Nothing to remind me of who I was with him. I moved the rest of my stuff out, closed his door, and haven't been back in.

Pike and I went to IKEA and picked out a dresser—which I paid for but we needed his truck to move—a bedside table, and a cushioned chair. I had a little fun decorating, since I didn't need to consider anyone but myself. There's twinkle lights weaved into my wrought-iron bedframe, some fun pillows and a lamp, and a painting I bought from a street vendor in New Orleans when I went with my sister. Pike's pal Dutch even brought by his old vintage Panasonic cassette boombox radio for me that he found cleaning out his parents' garage a couple days ago. I guess Pike told him about the tapes.

"Jordan!" a bellow comes from downstairs.

I drop the white shirt I was sorting and jerk my head, hearing the screen door slam against the frame downstairs.

My heart thuds a little harder.

Leaving the room, I jog down the stairs. Pike's by the front door, pulling out his jacket from the closet. Water streams down his face and the golden skin of his tattooed arms, and his hair is stuck to his scalp. He pulls his jacket over his head and his soaking wet T-shirt.

I walk up to him. "What's wrong?"

"The riverbank is flooding," he says, charging into the kitchen and toward the fridge. "They're calling anyone who's able to come help sandbag before it reaches the streets."

Got it. I pull my Chucks out of the closet, hopping on one foot as I slip each one on. "Did you call Cole?"

"Yeah, but he's not answering." He grabs an armful of water bottles. "Why don't you try?"

I yank my raincoat off the hanger and close the closet, grabbing my baseball cap off the hook on the outside. "If he didn't answer for you, he definitely won't for me."

Pike reenters the living room, five bottles pinched between his fingers. He raises his eyebrows, silently asking me again, and I roll my eyes.

"But I'll try in the car," I tell him, opening the door. "Let's go."

We get down to the inlet in no time, Pike having already loaded up as many of his sandbags as he had left in the back of his truck. The city has a hefty supply, though, and they were already down here with their trucks.

With the rain being so bad this summer and every last inch of snow finally melting farther north, the river has been a time bomb. I remember it flooding the homes on the west side a few years back, but the city got prepared after that. Police, firefighters, city crew, and citizens are now scattered among the rocks of the flood barrier already in place. Piles of sandbags are set up all the way from the water, up the incline of the boulders, and to the dirt and grass up here. There's little more than a hundred yards of weeds, trees, and railroad track to cross before the dilapidated houses of the old west side that was the first part of Northridge to be settled. The water is rising, but slowly, so hopefully if the flood barrier isn't enough, the sandbags will be. The people in this neighborhood can't afford to leave, much less lose their houses.

The river runs south, growing in speed, and I shiver a little, every inch of me soaking wet. Drops of water fall from the bill of my cap, and rain runs down my legs.

"Water?"

Pike holds a bottle out to me, and I peer up at him from under the brim of my hat and smile, snatching it up. "Thank you."

He moves around me without another word, grabbing a sandbag and tossing it to a guy down the line. We've been here for three hours now, and we haven't been able to reach Cole, although I can't say I tried very hard. I don't want to see him right now, so I gave it three rings and then hung up.

I look down at the bottle of water in my hand. My mouth is like a desert.

Unscrewing the cap, I suck down half the water, take a breath, and swallow two more gulps. There's only about an inch left, so I stick it in my jacket pocket to finish later.

"Hey, Jordan," a chipper voice calls, passing by.

I look to see April Lester pulling on a pair of work gloves and heading down the rocks toward Pike, dressed in jeans hugging every inch of her legs and a cute camouflage T-shirt and hat. A black ponytail hangs out the hole in the back.

She looks kind of cute. I'm so used to seeing her in her "going out" clothes at the bar.

I pull out a sandbag from the truck bed and heft the forty-pound burlap sack to the next guy in line and turn back to the bed, repeating the task. Each bag makes its way from one set of hands to the next until it reaches its place on the riverbank.

I notice April in another assembly line, directly across from Pike, and she's talking to him.

I try to keep my eyes averted because it's not my business, but I find myself stealing glances, and I don't know why.

Liquid heat rushes through my chest, and I feel a cool sweat breaking out on my forehead.

Does he know her? Have they ever talked? I don't think they've ever been out. They can't have been. Pike's like a priest. He's so uptight, and that woman comes on stronger than a hammer over the head. She'd scare him.

I wet my lips, handing off another bag and unable to keep myself from watching them. She smiles brightly, saying something, and he looks over at her, listening with amusement. One of his rare, outstanding, and gorgeous smiles flashes on her—*on her*—and my heart skips a beat.

I scowl and grab another bag.

Is he fucking blushing? He actually looks a little shy, but he doesn't look turned off by her flirting.

I groan.

Get over it. He's a man. A young one still and, I'm sure, a pretty healthy one, too. He's had sex with women—Cole is proof of that. It's unrealistic to think he's going without. He's going to bring a woman home sometime. Everyone has needs.

I drop my eyes to his torso, the thin black pullover rain jacket molded to his body like a second skin. His sleeves are pulled up, showing off his forearms, and I swear I can see the rain falling down his neck from here. He's tall and broad, and I love the way his T-shirts fit and he wears his jeans.

When a man looks that good in clothes, you know he looks good out of them.

And if he looked half this good in high school, every girl must've wanted him. I'm curious to know what he was like then, but then there are some things I don't want to know, either.

April passes him a bag but fumbles, and he darts down to grab it before it falls from her arms.

They're smiling and leaning in close to each other, and my lungs hurt.

And, as if he senses me watching him, his eyes suddenly dart up, meeting mine, and for a moment everyone else disappears.

I stop breathing. *Shit.*

I look away, quickly grabbing another bag.

I don't look back, even though I can feel him watching me.

Once the truck is empty, I take out my water bottle and drink the rest, walking over to Pike's truck and tossing it in the bed.

"Ready?" I hear him say.

I spin around and see him coming over and pulling off his soaked jacket. His T-shirt rides up with the movement, and I tear my gaze away from his stomach.

"Are . . . are we all done?" I ask.

He throws the coat into the back and digs another water out of the cooler. "This is about all we can do, I guess. We just need to hope it's enough and it holds."

I take one last look around, noticing everyone has moved on to one thing or another. Some are climbing into their cars and some are still positioning bags or chatting.

I whip off my jacket, too, toss it into the bed of the truck, and climb into the passenger seat.

I pull the door closed, and he starts the engine, the wipers immediately kicking into gear from where they left off on the drive over.

I look out the window.

"Oh, shit," I breathe out, gazing out in the distance. He follows my gaze.

The truck sits higher up, and we have a full view of the river beyond, all the way to the other side. A small set of islands that sit in the middle is now almost covered with water, and houses on the opposite bank are threatened as the river rises halfway up their stilts.

It still has a long way to go, and the rain has already slowed down a little. Hopefully it will be fine.

"I can't believe how high it is," I say. "Surreal."

He turns to me. "You're smiling again."

I meet his eyes, my face relaxing. Was I smiling? "Well, I'm trying not to," I tell him, breaking into another one. "I mean, I hope no one gets hurt and no one gets flooded, but . . ."

"But?"

I shrug, feeling a little guilty. "I kind of liked helping today, I guess. It's fun to get dirty."

He laughs under his breath and shifts the truck into gear. "You haven't been dirty yet," he teases. "Fasten your seat belt."

A half hour later, I'm yelping and gripping the handle above the door as he speeds down the muddy canal. He jerks the wheel so we vault up over the side and back onto high ground, and I laugh, bouncing in my seat.

Oh, my God, this is fun. I feel like I'm going to die. My eyes water, I'm laughing so much.

"I can't believe you've never done this before," he says, looking over at me like I need to surrender my Small Town Girl card. "In my day, this was the place to take a girl to show her how badass you were in your truck."

I tumble left and then right as the truck navigates all the muddy dips and puddles. He's let me have complete rein of the stereo and Bruce Springsteen's "Glory Days" plays from the tape I put in. I turn up the volume and grip the dash for support. "It still is," I inform him. "In my day, though, it's becoming harder and harder for guys you date to keep a valid driver's license."

He chuckles. "I believe that."

Rain and mud kick up around us, and I can see splatters of both hitting the sleeve of my raincoat nearest the door and my bare thigh. Pike insisted we roll down the windows, not caring in the least that his interior might get dirty. He said it would heighten the experience.

"Did you bring your dates here?" I ask.

"From time to time."

I quirk the corner of my mouth into a knowing smile. "And then you took them to Hammond Lock to make out after?"

He darts his gaze to me, looking surprised. "What do you know about Hammond Lock?"

I shrug. "Oh, I heard that's where the old folks took their dates back in the day is all."

He feigns a scowl and revs the gas, barreling us down into another ditch. My stomach drops into my feet, and I yelp again, laughing.

"Stop!" I plead. "You're going to tip us!"

The front fender crashes into the bottom, kicking up a wave of mud and water in front of us. My body jerks forward into the seat belt, and I scream in excitement, squeezing my eyes shut.

Shit!

But I can't stop laughing. He's right. How have I never done this before? I've been missing out.

Cool rain falls lightly through the window, misting my leg, and I open my eyes again and wipe off my cheek, seeing streaks of mud on my hand.

Turning to him, I see his eyes meet mine, both of our bodies shaking with quiet laughter.

"Okay, it's my turn!" I blurt out excitedly.

Unfastening my seat belt, I pull the door handle, moving to get out.

"No, just slide over," he tells me. "I'll get out and come around."

I stop and turn, seeing him open his door, and instead of stepping down, he pulls himself up and swings around into the bed of the truck behind us. I quickly slide across the seat and in front of the steering wheel. The perk of his truck being so old is that it has a bench seat. I don't need to hop over a console.

I fasten my belt and gaze out the windshield, a surge of heat coating my stomach as I smile.

"Watch out for the mud!" I call out the window to him.

I have no idea how deep it is outside the passenger-side door.

But I wait as the truck rocks with his movements in back, and then the passenger-side door opens, his hand appears at the handle, and he leaps inside, never once touching the ground.

Sliding into the seat next to me, he slams the door and runs his hand over his now-drenched hair.

My eyes fall to his T-shirt, molded to his chest, defining his collarbone and the muscles of his pecs and broad shoulders.

He turns to me. "What?"

I blink and clear my throat, recovering. "Nothing. You're just still pretty nimble for your age, huh?"

His eyes flare. Swiping his hand outside the door of the truck, he brings it back in and whips it at me, mud slicing across my face.

I gasp, closing my eyes on reflex and twisting away. "Stop!" I laugh, holding my hands out as more mud comes flying. "I'm just kidding!"

"Since when did thirty-eight become a goddamn senior citizen?" he growls, but I can hear the amusement in his voice.

More mud flies at me, and I cower with my back turned to him, trying to protect myself. "I'm sorry! I didn't mean it!"

But I can't stop laughing.

Two hours later, the sky is dark, and I'm blissfully relaxed. I can't think now even if I try. Cole's and my bills sit in my room, the tuition that I'll go further in debt with student loans to pay is coming due in a couple months, and the nudge I feel at my back, knowing I can make more money if I just have the guts . . . Everything is miles away right now. I've been smiling nonstop the entire afternoon.

"That was fun," I tell Pike, both of us veering around his house toward the backyard.

We're muddy and don't want to track it in through the living room, so I suggested cleaning off with the hose in the backyard a little first.

Glancing up at Pike, I see mud on his neck and his eyes staring off, unfocused, as if he's lost in thought. A small smile plays on his lips.

"What?" I ask him.

He finally blinks, taking in a deep breath and shaking his head. "I just realized I never do anything," he says, pushing the wooden fence door and holding it open for me. "I haven't laughed like that since . . . I don't even remember when."

My heart leaps. I'm glad I'm not the only one who enjoyed it. I'm glad he liked spending time with me, because . . .

Because I'm getting used to him.

I find myself looking at the clock and getting more excited the closer it gets to five every day. I look forward to him, and I wish I didn't. I'm going to leave eventually. I don't want to get attached.

The shower flashes through my mind, and I remember his loofah, and my cheeks warm.

I feel good with him, and I'm glad he feels good with me. I just can't feel *that* good.

We come around the back of the house, toward the back door, and I bend down to twist the faucet. Water pours out of the hose, and I pick it up off the ground.

Standing upright, I run my hand under the hose, thankful the water is a little warm.

I hand it to him, and he takes it.

"Thanks for coming today," he says quietly. "We needed the help."

I nod, pulling off my sneakers and hat. "It's my town, too."

He rinses off his face, arms, and construction boots, and I notice the water pouring down his clothes and still leaking mud.

We're just making it worse.

"There's some towels in the dryer," I say absently as I dash through the back door and into the laundry room, and dig out a couple. I set them on the porch stairs as I come back out.

He pulls his shirt off over his head, and I take it, twisting it in my fists to force out the water, while he runs the hose over his shoulder and down his back.

"Is all the mud gone?" he asks.

He turns around, still holding the hose and showing me his back, and all of a sudden, I can feel the heat of his body next to me. My blood starts heating up under my skin, and I'm afraid to look at him.

"Yeah," I say, barely audible.

I pull out one of my rubber bands and start to take apart a braid; my skin is burning. He's looking at me.

I close my eyes for a moment, absorbing it.

I want him to look at me.

I hear him chuckle, though, and I open my eyes to see him reach over and take my other braid in his hand. He raises the hose and rinses off the tail.

Oh, the mud . . .

"Yeah, thanks for that, by the way." I force a sarcastic tone.

"You asked for it."

Yes. I did. He's fun to tease.

My scalp tickles at his touch, and while I'm no longer relaxed, I'm smiling again. He's only touching the ends of a few hairs, and I'm light-headed.

I swallow the lump in my throat and slowly turn, whispering, "Would you check my back?"

I wait a moment, my pulse racing in my ears and the sound of the water spilling from the hose onto the ground.

But then I feel him. The soft, barely there brushes of his fingers across my shirt and the cool water seeping through the fabric as he clears away the mud.

He's so quiet, and it's so loud, it's throbbing in my ears.

At first, he's quick. I hug my arms to the front of my body, nervous like this is the first time I've ever been touched.

But then it gets slower, his hand staying on my shoulder blade longer and growing in pressure as he presses into my curves and runs his fingers down the slope of my neck, my spine, and then my hips.

The pulse between my legs begins to throb, and my eyelids flutter.

His hand hits bare skin at my hip, lingering for a moment, and I breathe out, so nervous right now but excited.

I'm not imagining this. I'm not imagining the way his touch feels.

Gulping, I slowly look to the side, seeing his form over my shoulder, and I reach down, grabbing the hem of my shirt, hesitating only a moment before I pull it over my head. Then, quickly, I reach over and pick up a clean towel off the stairs, hugging it to the front of my body.

I want him to look at me, but I'm so scared he'll push me away.

I drop my soaked shirt and stand there, fear and desire eating away any rational thought. For a while, the steady stream of water just falls, burrowing a hole into the grass below.

And then, it's on me. Cascading over my shoulder, down the blades of my back, as his hand follows its fall, clearing away any dirt still lingering. I close my eyes, dizzy.

It's warm at my back, and I realize he's closer now, towering over me from behind.

I hear him swallow. "Towel's going to get wet," he says, his voice raspy.

A smile pulls at my lips, but I don't let it out.

Opening my eyes, I pull the towel away from my body and toss it back on the stairs, excitement like an electric current under every inch of my skin. I don't remember ever wanting something this much.

He cleans my back, my arms, and tilts my head for me from side to side to make sure there's no dirt there, as well. I finish unbraiding my hair and comb my fingers through it, feeling some wet strands mixed with the dry ones.

I want to see him and know what he's thinking, but I'm afraid to break the spell, and if I look at him, we might both get scared off.

And this feels so good.

"Are my legs clean?" I ask over my shoulder.

I know I'm being wicked, but I don't want him to be done yet.

It only takes a moment, but then I feel the water hit the backs of my legs, and slowly, he takes a knee, trying to get a better vantage point.

I close my eyes again, diving deep into my head where everything I want in this moment but am too afraid to voice is safe. It's not only his touch. It's how he does it. The long, languorous caresses down my thighs and the way the tips of his fingers trail just a centimeter higher than they probably should. And how he tries to avoid the insides of my legs, but he keeps flirting close like he wants to go there and is struggling to hold himself back.

He finishes my calves and my feet, and I finally look over my shoulder and down at him.

"My turn," I say.

He raises his gaze, his chest moving up and down in shallow breaths. His lips are parted, and there are a hundred different emotions in his eyes. But I recognize the same ones I'm having. Fear and longing, turmoil and need.

We want it, but we know we shouldn't.

I turn and take the hose from him, and his gaze falls to my breasts right there for him and only covered by my thin, pink lacy bra with roses on it.

I'm a girly-girl at heart, and I think he likes that.

Without a word, he rises and stares at me, unflinching as I bring up the hose and start to rewash him. Neither of us had much mud on us in the first place. We could easily make it into the house and to the showers, and we both know it.

I run my hand over the smooth skin of his chest, tracing the mural he has inked across his shoulder, pec, and down his arm.

I don't look into his eyes, but I know he's watching my face.

"Did you get all these tattoos when you were younger?" I ask quietly.

"Most of them," he says, raspy. "Back when I didn't have other things to spend my money on."

"Do you regret any of them?" I see mud under his ear and arch up to my tiptoes, putting us chest to chest.

"No, I . . ." He stops, his heavy breath falling on my cheek as I hover close.

"You have some mud," I explain, looking up at him with my body pressing into his.

I fall back to my feet and continue. "You were saying?"

He clears his throat. "Uh, yeah. I'm a . . . I'm a little tired of some of them by now, I guess, but at one time," he tells me, "they were exactly who I was and what I needed to say about myself."

I nod, understanding. I trail around to his back and wash off his neck, his shoulder blades, and let my fingers fall down his spine. He shifts under my touch, and heat filters through my hand, rising up my arm, and I'm so turned on. I don't want to stop touching him, but using my hands doesn't feel like enough anymore. I want to feel his again.

What is Pike Lawson like when he takes?

He turns his head, asking softly, "Aren't you going to ask me what the tattoos mean?"

I step back around to his front, watching my fingers as they graze his muscled arm. "Someday," I whisper back.

I do want to know. I want to know everything about him. But maybe, I figure, we'll keep having a reason to find each other if we save some things for later.

And right now, I'm desperate to see what else his mouth can do other than talk.

Touch me. Please.

Kiss me.

I drop the hose to my side and drag the fingers of my left hand down his abs, my heart pounding so hard it hurts. They tighten as my nails slide across the muscles, and I'm so afraid to look at him.

This is wrong. I know it's wrong.

But God, he feels good. I can feel his eyes on me, and every thread of my bra is chafing my skin, and I just want to be bare right now. I want him to see me.

I close my eyes. *Oh, God.*

"Jordan . . ." He grasps my hand, and I can hear him breathing hard.

I nod, opening my eyes but still unable to meet his. "I know," I breathe out. "I'm sorry."

I'm parched, my eyes sting with tears and I don't know why, and there's a need between my thighs that is almost painful.

Slowly, he tips my chin up. I finally raise my gaze, but he's not looking at me, either. His eyes are cast down, and his brow is pinched in pain. "You're just out of sorts," he says quietly. "You miss Cole, and I just happen to be here. It's okay."

I remain still, my fingers on his stomach and his hand on my chin. His chest moves up and down, and for a moment, I think I'm going to turn tail and run. He's making an excuse for me. An easy one to hide behind. It would make sense that I'm feeling lost and in need of someone else to escape into.

But what's his excuse? I know he looks at me. I know he does it when he thinks I don't see it, but I do.

My eyes sting, filling with tears. "That's not why I was apologizing," I tell him.

I raise my eyes, meeting his, and while I'm afraid, I have to dive. I can't hold back.

"I'm sorry because," I whisper shakily, "this isn't the first time I wanted you to touch me."

And his gaze freezes on me.

He holds my eyes, unmoving except for the rise and fall of his chest, and I have no idea what's going through his head right now, but I don't think I'm sorry. No more excuses that this is about me being distraught over Cole.

The attraction was already there.

He slowly lets his fingers fall from my chin, both of his hands balling into fists, and he clenches his jaw, suddenly looking angry.

On reflex, I take a step back, but I don't get any farther. Grabbing my waist, he hauls me into him, snaking an arm round me and gripping my jaw in his hand between his thumb and four fingers. I gasp, loving the feeling of his body hard against mine but scared, too, because he looks so mad.

"No," he growls, baring his teeth and looking at me with fury in his eyes. "Do you understand? It's not happening. You're not getting that from me."

Tears fill my eyes, and I can barely see him anymore as my body shakes with a silent sob.

His arm is like steel around me, and I can feel the heat of his rage coming off his skin.

He shakes me. "You wanna get laid, then you go hunt somewhere else."

I suck in air and twist away from him, pushing his body away.

He's right. What am I doing? Why would I do that? I feel so stupid, and I crouch down, quickly gathering up my shirt and shoes.

But I wasn't imagining it, was I? There was something between us, and it was coming from him as much as from me. Did I just see what I wanted to see?

I want to scream. Tears stream down my face, and he still just stands there, glaring at me.

"Go to your room," he orders.

I break out in a laugh, the bitter sound dripping with disbelief.

"Go fuck yourself!" I stand up, hardening my voice. "I'll find another bed tonight, thank you. Anyone will do for a slut like me, right?"

I whip around and run for the back door, but he grabs the inside of my elbow and hauls me back into the wall of his chest. I drop my shirt and shoes, and he forces us forward into the wall of the house. I shoot out my hands, crashing into the siding.

Jesus.

I shake, sucking in short, shallow breaths as my heart races and my blood runs hot under my skin.

What the . . .

He reaches around, taking my face in his hand, and his hot breath is in my ear. "Don't threaten me with shit like that. If you want to act like a brat, then maybe you should get grounded like one, huh?"

I almost laugh through the tears drying on my face. "By all means," I taunt. "I'm dying to see how you try to take control of me. You can't even get Cole to do his chores, and when was the last time a woman got hot in your bed? You're not even a man."

He growls and slams his palm into the house in front of me.

I jump.

And the next thing I know, his hand is in my hair, and my head is being twisted to the side as his lips crash down on mine.

I whimper, the feel and taste of him flooding me so hard my clit pulses between my legs. *Oh, shit.* My eyelids flutter closed, the heat and adrenaline diving from my chest to my groin in the span of a second.

He pulls back. "Fuck." And his fist tightens in my hair.

But he comes back in, his mouth covering mine, demanding more, and I can barely catch my breath. I'm hot all over.

He tastes so good. Feels so good. It only takes a moment, but my brain finally kicks in, and I reach around, taking the back of his neck and kissing him, too.

His hand grips my waist, and I can feel his fingers slide under the red silk strap of my panties peeking out, winding his hand once in the fabric like he's getting ready to yank it off.

My pussy throbs at the thought. His tongue is hot and demanding, flicking in my mouth and playing with my own, and when he pulls back just a hair to nibble my bottom lip, I shift on my tiptoes, feeling the warm slickness ache between my legs.

Oh, God.

He moves from my lips to my cheeks, leaving kisses along my jaw and back down to my neck. I can only arch it to give him free rein.

And I smile on the inside. He does want this. He wants me.

My skin buzzes, the hair rising on my arms, and I break out in chills at the feel of his hands starting to explore as much as his mouth.

I press my ass into his groin and feel the ridge of his cock, hard and tempting. He pulls his mouth away, groaning at my nudge.

"Jordan," he gasps, his eyes closed and brows etched in pain. "Fuck, we can't do this."

I turn around, arching up on my tiptoes and matching my forehead to his with my hands at his waist. "I know," I say. "I know."

God, why did this have to happen?

I hover over his lips, feeling for them as his warm breath makes me want to wrap myself up inside of him. "I know," I whisper again. "I ruined it, didn't I?"

We're victims of circumstance. At least I can feel confident that I would've liked him no matter what. If he were any other guy who came into my bar, sat down, and talked to me, I would've wanted him. He can be gruff, and he's way out of practice dealing with people, but I'm happy around him, and I like that the only thing he seems to need from me is my presence. He's happier with me here.

"You need to not fight me, okay?" I tell him. "I'll go to my sister's tomorrow, and I'll be more than fine. You don't have to worry about me. I never should've stayed—"

Suddenly, though, he grabs the backs of my thighs and lifts me up, forcing my legs to wrap around him. Planting me against the wall, he peers up at me and shakes his head. "You're not going anywhere."

And then he darts in, capturing the underside of my chin in his mouth. I gasp, my head falling back and my lids closing, as he bites and kisses, sending tingles down my arms.

I grip his shoulders and give in, squirming against him and craving the friction of him between my legs.

One of his arms holds me up while the other trails to my bra strap, pulling it down so he can kiss the skin on my shoulder.

I pant, desperate. "Take it off. Please."

His hand goes to my back, but instead of unhooking me, he yanks at the strap and pulls it down. I'm only bare for a moment, though, before we both hear a door slam inside the house and startle.

"Dad?" Cole calls. "You up?"

"Shit," Pike hisses under his breath.

"Oh, God." I squirm out of his hold, and he releases me. I dive down, gathering up my shirt and shoes again, holding them up to cover myself. I see the kitchen light pop on through the back door, and I swing around the side of the house, hiding just out of sight.

My heart is pounding in my ears, and I can't swallow. I peer around the corner at Pike, and he's looking around like he's not sure what to do, but he finally grabs the hose, still running water, and continues washing off his already clean arms and hands.

"Yeah, out here!" he calls, his Adam's apple bobbing up and down.

I hear the screen door creak open, and I slink back, making sure I'm out of sight.

"Hey, what are you doing?" I hear Cole ask.

I hurriedly fix my bra and pull on my damp T-shirt again.

"Just cleaning off," Pike answers. "The river nearly flooded the harbor today. I tried to call you."

"Yeah, sorry."

There's a moment of silence, and all I can hear is the running water spilling onto the now-flooded grass.

"Where's Jordan?" Cole says.

"I don't know . . . inside?"

My eyes fall and guilt hits me like a stab. He had to lie to him.

I mean, of course he would. I would've, as well. But the reality sinks in that I can leave Cole and walk away and life will go on. Pike can't do that. That's his son.

"You staying?" Pike asks him.

"Just picking up some stuff," Cole explains, sounding solemn. "I don't think she'll want me around for a while yet. Thanks for letting her stay here."

Pike's voice is barely above a whisper. "It's not a problem."

There's more silence, and then I hear the water shut off and some shuffling.

"She really took care of me when . . ." Cole trails off and then continues. "When I couldn't stand to have anyone else around. I never wanted to hurt her."

Needles prick my throat. Everything is so messed up, because I don't know how angry I'm allowed to be.

He did it right under my nose. For weeks.

But in my heart, I wasn't faithful to him, either.

Somewhere down deep, we always knew this was finite.

"You can come home," his father says quietly, almost pleading.

But Cole doesn't respond, and I wish I could see his face. Is he looking at his father? He can't meet people's eyes when he's upset or sad.

"What are you doing?" Pike asks him, so much sadness in his voice. "What are you doing with yourself, huh?"

I hear a sigh and then Cole says, "I'll talk to her. Eventually."

And then the screen door falls shut, flapping against the frame, and I slowly peek around the corner, seeing Pike standing alone in the spot where I left him.

His brow is etched in pain, and he's staring at the ground. His head turns slightly toward me, though.

"He doesn't treat you right, and he should," Pike says, his face ridden with guilt. "But this can't happen, Jordan."

I press my teeth together, tears lodged in the back of my throat.

I know.

I know.

16

Pike

I can feel her. Her warm legs snaking through and over mine between the sheets, and she's hot and wet between her legs as she grinds on me. I grab her by the hips and flip us over, yanking down her panties and diving down, taking her in my mouth.

God, her moans are so sweet, and I don't want to ever leave this bed. I want to do nothing but feel her and taste her and smell her, make her smile and sweat and come. She's mine.

But suddenly, my eyes pop open, blinking into the early morning's dim light.

I'm alone, and I breathe in through my nose, chasing her smell in the dream.

I close my eyes. "Jesus," I pant, licking my dry lips.

I fist my hands, still feeling her ass in my palms, and I need her. I need the same soft body I had in my arms last night so badly my jaw aches from clenching it.

Rubbing the sweat off my neck, I peer down and see my dick tenting the sheet.

Fuck.

I need to get laid. That's all there is to it. Jordan isn't special.

She's not.

She's a hot young woman living in my house and constantly in my face, walking around in her short shorts with her long legs, perky ass, and lips that taste like a fucking peach. It's like putting a steak in front of a starving pit bull and saying "don't touch."

I groan as my dick swells with blood, growing even harder.

God, if I called her in here right now, would she come? I'm tempted to take back what I said last night, I want back what I had in my hands that much.

But no.

I'm already aching with guilt, and losing control and going further with her would do a world of hurt. Last night was simply the result of not being fed in too long. Nothing more.

Christ, she's a kid. If she were two years younger, I could go to prison for what I almost did to her last night.

I need to get this out of my system.

Throwing off the sheet, I get out of bed and pull on some boxer briefs and jeans. After I've thrown some cold water on my face, brushed my teeth, and run some gel through my hair, my dick has calmed down enough for me to leave my room. I pull on a T-shirt and the rest of my stuff that I'll need for work and walk out of the room.

If Cole hadn't come home when he did . . .

I jog down the stairs, pushing it out of my head. I just hope she doesn't think she needs to leave on account of this. It probably would be for the best, but I don't want to be another person she can't count on.

In the kitchen, I pour myself a cup of coffee and open the fridge, looking for the milk.

I pinch my brows together, shifting cartons around and finding only almond milk. I take it out and wrinkle my nose, studying it. Almonds produce milk?

Jordan. I roll my eyes and uncap it, sniffing it. "Hmm . . ." It doesn't smell bad.

I shrug and pour it in the coffee.

Picking up the mug, I slip my other hand into my pocket and lean against the counter, blowing on the coffee.

I hear Jordan's footfalls on the stairs, and my stomach twists as I blink long and hard to brace myself.

She breezes into the kitchen, lifting her eyes and meeting mine long enough to give me a quick, curt half smile before trailing around the table and pulling her book bag off a chair.

She seems in a hurry.

I force the words out. The sooner we deal with it, the sooner we can get back to normal. "I'm sorry about last night," I tell her. "It was my fault, and it shouldn't have happened. Okay?"

Her hands slow, and I see her eyes shift as she digs in her pack, but she doesn't look at me.

She pulls the zipper closed and straightens, heading toward me and pulling open the fridge.

"I gotta go," she says.

I watch her warily. She doesn't seem mad. She just seems nervous. Maybe she was waiting for me to take the lead to see how to handle this.

Or perhaps she wants to act like it didn't happen at all. Maybe she regrets it.

Do I regret it?

Yeah. Yeah, of course I do.

But I enjoyed it, too. The need to take her up to my bed and savor every second and every inch of her was like looking forward to heaven last night. I wanted it. I couldn't wait.

And I wouldn't have stopped. My muscles hurt just thinking about what I was going to put my body through to enjoy every moment with her.

But even without Cole, she's still half my age. Nothing about this is right.

"You're a beautiful girl, Jordan," I say in nearly a whisper, "but you are just a girl."

She pauses at the fridge next to me, and I see her swallow. She's so pretty. Hair clean and flowing, makeup subtle with just a hint of pink on her lips . . .

"My head wasn't straight," I explain. "We're both lonely, and I've loved having you here so much the boundaries got blurred. It won't happen again."

She nods, and her gaze drops. I wish I knew what she was thinking. It's not like her to be so quiet. Does she hate me?

"It's okay," she says gently.

But I shake my head. "It's not. I don't expect that from you. I want you to know that."

God knows she gets enough of that shit at work.

Taking her apple and bottle of water, she turns and walks for the table, picking up her bag. She can't have class this early, but I'm not about to question her like it's my business. I've done enough to her the past twenty-four hours.

I watch as she leaves the kitchen and enters the foyer, pulling her house keys off the hook. She reaches for the door but stops, pausing.

"My hands were on you, too," she says.

And then she pulls the door open and walks out, closing it gently behind her.

I stare after her, the empty space making me suddenly want her back.

"Don't say things like that," I mumble to an empty house.

If I know you want it, too, how will I be able to resist you?

"You sure you don't want to come?" Dutch asks.

I shake my head, tossing my gear into the bed of the truck. "Nothing sounds worse than a bar full of people and prefrozen mozzarella sticks right now," I tell him. "I have a date with a left-over calzone in the fridge."

Todd passes by, laughing. "I'll bet calzones taste even better with a certain barefoot blonde making them, too."

My neck heats up from the teasing. I don't think anyone knows Cole isn't staying at the house right now, but Jordan's and my interactions haven't gone unnoticed. Poker night, the lingerie show, her bringing me lunch . . . The guys are drawing their own conclusions, I'm sure.

And actually, the calzones were takeout from a couple nights ago, but yes, Jordan's not working tonight, and I'm anxious to see how she is. And to—hopefully—get back to normal with her.

Not too anxious, though. I kept the guys an hour later today on purpose, because while I'm dying to see her, I don't *want* to be dying to see her, and I needed to prove that I have some control over myself.

Dutch pulls on his baseball hat, shooting me a half smile like he agrees with Todd, but I just frown and climb into my truck. I don't need the mental image of Jordan walking around my kitchen in her bare feet, bending over counters to grab things, and doing that cute thing she does where she blows her hair out of her face, but it just falls right back into the same spot again.

We can live there, and our lives will continue until she gets her own place. She'll go to school and work and once in a while a guy just may come by to pick her up, and I'll carry on, too. I'm a single man. She has to expect I'll be out with a woman here and there. It's fine, and it's as it should be.

If she were ten years older, though . . .

I smile to myself, finally feeling like I got my head back on straight. I twist the key, starting the engine, and pull out of the lot, making my way home.

I'm glad I didn't try to get out of the site right away at five. And all in all, I did well. I was the one who stopped things last night, right? Twice? I have a moral compass, and while it wavered, it found true north. Eventually.

And I'm only human. Would anyone not notice how beautiful she is?

I blow out a breath, turning on the radio as I coast into town and wind through the neighborhood streets.

I need a date. I'll just twist, wind, and mold what happened with Jordan last night into some six-minute fluke under the full moon and go back to being . . . her, like . . . elder and shit. Just a responsible adult she relies on for guidance. That's it.

She's not a woman, she's not experienced in the world, and I'm not the man who's going to marry her or give her kids. I have no right to her.

I take a deep breath, feeling ready, and pull onto my street and up into my driveway. It's just after six, Jordan's VW is here, but that doesn't mean she is. I told her not to drive it yet, but she could be with her sister.

I park and grab my lunch box before climbing out of the cab. Reaching into the back, I pull out my tool belt and swing it over my shoulder, walking across the lawn to the porch stairs.

But I spot something out of the corner of my eye and turn my head, seeing Kyle Cramer's house. Jordan is stepping out of his front door, followed by Kyle, who hands her a piece of paper and smiles down at her.

She continues to inch away, but she smiles back and jerks her thumb toward my place, and they both exchange a few words and nod. Turning away from him, she walks my way, and my gaze flashes to him still standing behind her, seeing his eyes roam her backside.

My lungs fill with heat, and instinct starts to kick in. *Don't even try it, asshole.*

She approaches, looking up and slowing for only a second when she sees me.

I jerk my chin, keeping my tone even. "What was that all about?"

She blinks, walking up the porch steps. "Oh, he, uh . . . he has his kids tonight," she says, "but he forgot he had a baseball game, so he asked me to watch them. I said yes. He was just running through the house and procedures with me."

"Why you?" I follow her.

She glances back at me, and I realize that sounded rude.

"I mean, he must have babysitters lined up already," I add. "I was just curious why he asked you."

"I don't know." She shrugs and grabs her bag, checking to make sure she has what she needs. "Probably because I'm right next door, and he thinks I'm still into pocket money," she jokes. "It's fine. Really. I have nothing else to do. I'll be back late, okay?"

Late? The games are over by ten.

He must be joining the team at the bar afterward.

And then the degenerate's going to come home drunk, to a barely legal, hot babysitter.

Fuck no.

She moves for the door, swinging the pack on her shoulder, and I take a step.

"Wait . . ." I say.

She turns, but her eyes only drift over me, never staying too long.

She's trying to avoid me.

"If you want," I broach gently, "you can just bring the kids over here. They can swim."

She finally meets my eyes, and I notice hers are red. She's unhappy, but she's trying to hide it. *Jesus.*

She shakes her head, looking apologetic. "You just got off work. You want to relax, and they'll be noisy."

She drops her gaze again, looking nervous.

Is it me or is it something else? I did the right thing last night. I don't want her to feel rejected, because she'd make any guy the luckiest man in the world.

Someday.

Maybe she's not angry I stopped it, though. Maybe she's upset it happened at all.

I take another step, lowering my voice like I'm afraid the neighbors can hear us. "Are you mad at me?" I ask her.

She pops her eyes up, answering quickly. "No." And then she searches for her words. "I'm just trying to sort through some . . . things in my head."

I can see tears welling in her eyes, and I hurt everywhere. Why do I always want to hold her so much?

She bows her head, trying to hide the tears she can't stop, and I step up to her and only hesitate a moment before putting my hand on the side of her face. My fingers wrap around the back of her head, and she doesn't push me away.

"I'm here, okay?" I whisper. "Nothing's changed. I still love the smell of your candles and the sound of your music in the house." I pause and then add, "Although I'm not a huge fan of the cucumber wraps you snuck into my lunch yesterday."

She breaks into a quiet laugh, her shoulders shaking.

I rub her cheek with my thumb. "I'm not going anywhere."

And I pull her in, hugging her to my chest and just wanting nothing more than to protect her and give her every damn thing she doesn't have.

I wrap my free arm around her, and after a moment she gives in and snakes her arms around me, too, melting into me. We hold each other so tight that I don't know if I'm holding her up or she's holding me up, but for a moment, I'm afraid I'll fall if I let her go.

"Bring 'em over," I tell her. "It'll take the pressure off you having to entertain them. I'll get the floaties ready and order some pizza."

She pulls back, sniffling, but there are no more tears pouring out of her eyes and she quirks a half smile.

"Kids like cheese only," she says, an air of peace settling back into her expression.

"Yeah, I remember." I think Cole still likes cheese only, actually.

She drops her bag by the door where it was before and casts me a look before leaving, an understanding settling between us. I'm not here to hurt her.

And providing I can stay the hell off her better than I did last night, then I won't.

I can't do it!" Jensen yells, water dribbling off his lips.

The seven-year-old treads water, the goggles huge on his face. Below him, three dive rings stand upright on the bottom of the pool, and after I got him brave enough to hold on to my neck while I dived down to retrieve them, I thought it was time he try.

Cramer is a twat, but his kids aren't bad.

"Try to go feetfirst, then," I tell him. "Here, put your face in and watch me."

The pool only goes to six feet, but I swim anyway, putting myself above the rings. Jordan is in the shallow end with Ava, who's only two, and showing her how to blow bubbles in the water. I was relieved to see her come out in a more conservative bikini than that damn seashell one, but I'm not finding the no-cleavage halter top of this one any easier to take, unfortunately.

"Ready?" I say, tearing my eyes off her soaked hair plastered to her back and looking at Jensen.

He nods, like his head is too much weight for his body, and I suck in a breath, launch up, and then fall feetfirst to the bottom of the pool, releasing air as I descend and pushing the water up with my hands.

My feet hit the floor, I grab a ring, and I push myself back up to the surface, taking in another deep breath. He pops his head out of the water, sputtering a little.

"Did you see?" I ask, wiping my eyes. "I let out bubbles and pushed the water up above me, and it helped me sink to the bottom."

He nods again.

"Wanna try?"

He shakes his head.

I laugh, slicking my hair back. "Okay. Another time, then."

Just then, a stream of water pummels my back, and I look over my shoulder, seeing Jordan shooting me with a squirt gun. The little girl on her hip laughs, and Jordan scrunches up her nose, making a battle-ready face and aiming the water at my head. I jerk away, hearing the little girl cracking up behind me.

"I want one!" Jensen rushes for the side of the pool and grabs one of the Super Soakers Dutch left when he brought his kids over one day last summer. I grab the other one, and all of us start filling up our weapons, Jordan giving hers to the toddler and getting another for herself.

For the next ten minutes, we barely stop to take a breath as we laugh, attack, and dart around the pool to escape the onslaught. Everyone turns on each other, the baby shooting Jordan right in the eye, and Jensen hitting me in the head.

I grab the baby, using her for mock cover, and Jordan squeals, diving under the water to escape shots coming from Jensen, Ava, and me.

The boy eventually pushes himself up on a step to sit, and both Jordan and I are breathing hard from the exertion. I set the baby on the deck, and she walks over to the picnic table and starts munching on watermelon. Jensen joins her, taking another slice of leftover pizza.

Déjà vu hits me. I'm surprised I still have the energy for this. Seems like ages ago I was trying to teach Cole how to swim and letting him bring his first girlfriend over in middle school while I covertly kept an eye on them from inside the house. This wasn't as stressful as I remember it being, though. Maybe because I'm older.

Or maybe because it's easier when there are two adults wrangling the kids instead of one. I actually had fun tonight.

I watch Jordan as she hops up onto the pool deck and sits with her legs still dangling in the water. Taking each water gun, she empties and shakes them out, setting them aside.

The duality of her swimsuit has the coils in my brain twisting tighter and tighter, and I'm so confused. She wears black on the bottom. Adult, sexy, and beautiful against her tanned skin. And pink on the top. Innocent, sweet, and entirely Jordan, because she can be such a girly-girl.

Her thighs, toned and smooth, and the cute, studious expression on her face as she furrows her brow and concentrates on her task. Everything about her is young.

Except her eyes.

Eyes that can be so patient, because she's had years of practice being disappointed, but eyes that can also be angry, because you know shit has been hitting the fan in her life since day one and hasn't eased up one bit.

You can see her brain working through every decision and every interaction, because she's so good at assessing consequence and danger by now that it's become second nature.

She knows that time always passes and her day will come. Just hang tight.

She has the smooth skin and body of a young woman, but the eyes of someone who's seen decades.

My eyes fall to her mouth, remembering the feel of her kisses, and another rush of heat coats my chest just under my skin. I turn away, running my hand through my wet hair.

It wasn't a fluke. I want her.

I love the smell of her in the house, the way she sits next to me, either here or in the movie theater that first night, so easily and comfortably, like we're two peas in a fucking pod, and how I'm excited to wake up every day, knowing I can see her.

"Jesus Christ," I say under my breath.

I'm having my first fucking crush in like twenty years.

"What?" I hear her ask.

I lift my head, turning toward her. Did I say that out loud?

"Nothing," I shoot back.

She peers up at me as she empties the last gun, and I pull the noodles out of the pool and toss them up on the deck to evade her eyes.

I want more of what happened last night, and I don't know what I'm going to do.

A phone starts ringing on the picnic table again, and I look over at her.

"Your phone's ringing again."

She nods, a slight frown crossing her face. "Yeah, I know who it is."

My eyebrows rise a little. Who's she trying to avoid?

The phone has rung several times since I've been home, and to my knowledge, she hadn't answered it.

She looks over at me, seeing me staring at her with a questioning look on my face, no doubt.

She just laughs to herself, explaining, "Guys in town think I'm easy picking now that Cole and I are over." She runs her fingers through her hair, fluffing the wet strands. "They're swooping in to *comfort* me."

She says the last with air quotes, and my armor instantly steels. Comfort her?

But I force myself to back off. It's actually just what I need to put things in the proper perspective. She should be going out with her friends.

"Well, maybe you should give one a chance," I tell her, forcing the words out. "I want you and Cole to make up and be friends again, but you should get out and have some fun."

The words taste like shit in my mouth, but I feel good that I did the right thing. She'll date someone. I can start seeing someone. We'll get distracted and invested in new people.

"I will," she answers, cutting off my train of thought. "Carter Hewitt invited me to go tubing this weekend, so I said I'd go."

My face falls. I don't know a Carter Hewitt, but . . .

"Tubing?" I say, trying to keep my cool. I approach her at the edge of the pool. "Uh . . . no," I tell her, shaking my head. "No."

"Huh?" Her eyebrows pinch in confusion.

"Six hours of drifting on a river with nothing else to do but drink your ass off?" I blurt out. "By the time he gets you back to his truck, you'll be three sheets to the wind, and then you really will be easy picking." I let out a bitter laugh. "Absolutely not."

Her eyes round, and her jaw clenches in anger.

Oh, shit.

"You are so . . ." she whisper-yells, so the kids don't hear, "old-school!" She scowls up at me, her lips tight. "This alpha, possessive, keep-your-daughter-locked-up-with-a-shotgun thing is insulting! I'm not an idiot, and you . . ." She bares her teeth. "Are not my father."

I arch an eyebrow as she pulls her legs out of the water and stands up, huffing. I fall back, floating through the water. *Yeah, believe me, I know that. The thoughts I have about you aren't the least bit fatherly.*

"Wrap up the pizza in tinfoil before you put it in the fridge," she orders me. "Don't just slap it on a plate."

I lock my jaw to hide my amusement at her orders. Like I haven't wrapped up leftovers before in my adult life.

Grabbing the kids' bags and towels, she takes Ava's hand in hers and leads Jensen toward the back gate. "I'm going to run them home and get them in bed," she tells me and then turns to them. "What do you guys say to Mr. Lawson?"

"Thank you!" the kids say in their slurred voices with mouths full of food.

I step out of the pool and grab a towel, drying off my hair.

"Mr. Cramer said he'd be home by eleven," Jordan says. "But I know the team usually stops for beers at the pub after the game, so I might be late. I have my key if you lock up."

"I'll be up," I reply under my breath. I'd trust a junkie to hold my wallet more than I'd trust Kyle Cramer.

I hear the wooden door swing open and the kids shuffle through.

Then I hear her voice. "Oh, and you're a jerk," she says.

I peer over at her. "You'll thank me when you're not getting date-raped."

She makes a face and pulls the gate closed, slamming it hard.

I stare after her, laughing quietly. She's so fucking adorable.

And then my face falls, realizing I'm almost giddy. I'm not a smiler, and I've far exceeded my quota since she's come into the house.

I finish cleaning up the backyard as the sky slowly turns black overhead, and I make sure to wrap the pizza in tinfoil, as instructed. The pool is cleared, the toys and floaties put away, and the picnic table is cleaned. Grabbing the damp towels off the deck, I trail into the house and lock the back door, turning off the pool light, as well.

Tossing the towels into the washer, I leave the lid open so I can put more in after my shower.

As I head for the stairs, though, the doorbell rings.

Crossing the living room, I pull open the front door and see a young man through the screen. My guard rises a little, but I push it open, forcing him to back up.

"Hey," he says.

I nod, taking in the posh wannabe frat boy who looks slightly familiar, although I can't remember from where.

"Remember me?" he says, holding out his hand. "I'm Jay McCabe. Cole's friend."

I shake his hand, studying him. *Jay* . . .

"Is Jordan here?" he asks. "I was told she was staying here still."

Jordan? What does he want with . . .

And then it hits me.

"Jay," I say, realization dawning as my spine straightens steel-rod straight. "Her ex-boyfriend?"

The corner of his mouth tilts up in a smirk and a light hits his eyes. "Yeah, we went out."

But I'm not even listening anymore. I run my fingers over my thumb, itching to fist my hands, as my chest starts rising and falling with heavy breaths.

I step out of the house and walk straight for him, only about an inch taller, but I make sure he knows it.

His face falls when I don't stop, and he stumbles back to avoid me walking into him.

"Hey," he protests.

But I keep going. I walk until he's forced backward, down the stairs and to the fucking grass.

Alarm sets in his eyes. "Jesus, what the hell?"

I step up to him and cross my arms over my chest. "I don't normally throw my weight around a kid like you, but I want to make this clear," I bite out. "You may have your own little posse of followers who are enamored of you or scared of you, but I"—I pause for effect—"am not. I know who you are and what you like to do. Keep away from Jordan, and I'd really appreciate it if you'd fuck off around my son, too." I start walking into him again, forcing him off my lawn. "Don't step foot on my property again, or I'll put you in a hole under some wet cement and make you part of the foundation of the next house I build, never to be seen again. Now, take a hike."

And I gesture with my chin for him to leave.

"Wha—"

"Did I stutter?" I cut him off.

He's breathing hard, his Adam's apple bobbing up and down, and he digs into his pocket for his keys, I assume.

"Jesus," he says and climbs into his car.

But all I can see is red. I want to tear him apart. How can my son call that guy a friend?

He took it upon himself to put his hands on her. He'll never even set his fucking eyes on her again if I have anything to say about it.

I watch as he speeds out of the driveway and into the street, taking off as fast as he can. In a moment, any fear he might be feeling will turn to anger, and he'll talk himself into believing I'm not capable of the threat.

And part of me hopes he tries his luck again just to give me an excuse.

I glance over at Cramer's house, seeing all the lights on but no movement at the drapes, so hopefully she didn't see him come here.

Walking back inside, I lock the door but then think better of it and unlock it again. You know, just in case she's outside and he comes back and she needs to get into the house quickly or something.

I roll my eyes. *Jesus.*

Heading upstairs, I veer into my bathroom and pull open the shower door, turning on the water. It quickly fills with steam, and I pull off my swim shorts and step in, closing the door.

The hot water hits my skin like a thousand needles, but it quickly follows with warmth that feels so good I'm almost lightheaded.

Planting my hands on the wall, I dip my head under the spout, letting the water cascade down over the back of my head, my neck, and my back.

What a clusterfuck.

I can't get ahold of my kid, and when I can, he doesn't want to talk to me. And it certainly doesn't help the situation that I'm drooling over his latest girlfriend like I've never done for any other woman in my life.

And even worse, now that she's single, I'm going to have every little asshole in town sniffing around my front door, just dying to get his hands on her.

I know I can't have her, but it still won't stop. The desire.

I close my eyes, emptying my lungs and feeling her everywhere. "Jordan," I whisper.

My dick immediately swells, and I feel it growing hard at just the sound of her name. She kissed me back last night. She's attracted to me, too. Does she fantasize about me?

I harden even more at the thought of her in bed, thinking about me. Wanting me.

I fist my cock because it's aching so badly, but I stroke it by accident, and I groan at how good it feels.

She fills my head, and I swear I can smell her. She's so close.

I stroke myself, giving in to the fantasy.

I'm in bed, and it's pitch-black in the room. A knock sounds on my door, and I stir, sitting up.

"Yeah?" I say, bending one leg at the knee and resting an arm on it.

Jordan pushes open the door, and I can only tell it's her by the glimpse of her golden hair.

"What's wrong?" I say gently.

I'm naked under the sheet, but she can't see anything.

"It's storming," she says, lingering at the doorframe. "Can I sleep with you?"

Lightning flashes through the windows, lighting up her body, and I catch glimpses of her naked legs and sweet face. The water continues to pour over me, and my cock in my hand gets longer. Reality slips away as I dive, chasing the only thing I'll be able to have of her.

Whatever's in my dreams.

"Come here," I whisper.

She hurries over to the side of the bed, and I peel back the covers for her.

Sliding in, she huddles close to me, and I put my arm around her, feeling her leg come over mine. My hands roam, and all I feel is bare tummy and thighs. She's barely wearing anything.

"Jordan . . ." I pant.

God, her skin is so soft, and she feels so good.

"I'm cold," she says, her breath caressing my jaw. "Is this okay?"

My thigh sits between her legs, and I can feel the heat pouring out of her. I tuck her closer. "Come here."

I rub her thighs and hips, up her back, and keep her nose buried in my neck. Every inch of her is like an electric current to my dick.

I stroke slower but hold it tighter, like I imagine her.

"Is that better?" I ask her.

She nods, her lips inches from mine.

"Your mouth is even warmer, though," she tells me, feeling my breath on her. "It's the warmest part of you."

I fight to hide my smile. Who am I not to give my girl what she needs?

Turning her over onto her back, I keep running my hands up and down her body, but I start hovering my mouth over her skin, too. Breathing out hot breaths across her neck and through her black half shirt, over her breasts and the hard nipples through the fabric calling to me, but I resist. I trail down her stomach, running my lips over her belly button, and for a moment, my teeth come out, dying to take a piece of her in my mouth, but she moans, and I look up, seeing the mounds of her breasts peek out from under the bottom of her little shirt.

Shower water spills over my face and streams off my chin, and I want this to be real. I want her in my fucking bed.

"Better?" I ask her.

She nods, her eyes still closed. "Mm-hmm," she says. "Can you keep doing it, though? I'm still cold."

Hell yes. I take her thighs as I roll over onto my back, bringing her on top of me.

"Come here, baby."

I can't have all of her, but I'll take this.

I rub her thighs and slide my hands farther up her body, teasing her just under the shirt.

She wears a black top and black panties, and I joke, "I thought you liked pink."

I can't see her smile, but I hear it in her voice. "You want pink?" she taunts.

And then she pulls up her short shirt, settling it just above her beautiful breasts. She grazes the nipples, showing me where her pink is.

I shoot up, wrap my arm around her waist, and take one in my mouth, tugging on it and then sucking it into my mouth.

I feel the blood rushing to my cock, and I'm so close already. I open my mouth, like I can actually feel her soft skin between my teeth.

Jesus, I want to know how she really tastes.

"Warmer?" I ask, knowing damn well her skin is hot now.

I feel her nod and know I have to stop this. I let it go on too long.

"Jordan, we have to stop."

But I can feel that she's soaked.

She starts grinding on me, rolling that ass as her words fall across my forehead. "It's okay," she whispers. "No one has to know."

She starts dry humping me faster, her pants growing louder and heavier, and we're alone in here, it's dark, and no one has to know.

"Jordan," I gasp, the world tipping on its side with the fucking pleasure. "Baby, we can't. What are you doing?"

"I'm making it hard."

Yeah, no shit.

I jerk myself harder, heat flooding my groin and fire spreading from my stomach and thighs.

She digs her nails into my shoulders, and I squeeze her hips as she rides the hell out of me.

"Baby, you have to stop," I beg. God, I'm gonna come.

"But it feels good when it's hard."

I shake my head, whispering against her lips. "I'm not for you. Some other man's going to . . . We can't."

"I can't stop," she whimpers. "Please don't make me stop."

Her tits stand out at me and her hips roll in and out, and she's the sexiest goddamn thing I've ever seen.

Fuck, yes.

"Fine," I finally growl and fall back to the bed, still gripping her hips as the ridge of my cock rubs against her. "Give your cunt what it wants."

She mews, closes her eyes, and plants her hands back on my knees and takes what she wants from me.

I squeeze my cock for dear life, feeling her jutting hips in my hands, and I shoot, jerking harder and harder as I spill.

"Oh, fuck. Fuck!" I yell. "Shit!"

Oh, my God. I drop my head to the shower wall, the cum spilling out, and I slow my hand, the muscles burning as I release the rest.

I see spots behind my eyes, but I can still smell her sweat, and I don't want it to be over. I want more.

"Goddammit," I mouth, licking my lips and forcing a swallow. "Shit."

I want more.

I can't remember the last time I came like that, but still . . . it wasn't enough.

I take my hand off my cock and fist my fingers, aggravated. That was supposed to help, dammit. That was supposed to get her out of my system.

I feel my dick start to warm again, and I push off the wall, growling. I hit the faucet hard, turning the hot water to cold, and rinse off.

I just need to fuck a real thing. Not her. Just someone else. I'll lock myself in a motel room with a box of condoms and get it out of my system.

Yeah. That's what I'll do.

This week. I'll get it done.

I reach up to the rack and put my hand on my regular hook, grabbing for what I need to finish washing, but there's nothing there.

It's been missing for days, in fact, and I furrow my brow, looking around. "Where the fuck is my loofah?"

17

Jordan

"You made the taco dip, right?"

I nod, scrolling through my Instagram in the passenger seat. "Yeah."

"And the bacon-wrapped jalapeño poppers?" Pike asks.

"Yes," I hiss. "You only asked me like ten times."

He's quiet for a moment, driving through a neighborhood not far from ours.

I mean, his.

Ours.

"I just like them, is all," he says.

A lazy smile tugs at my lips, and I feel a hint of pride. I love that he's not just nice about things. He actually truly likes what I contribute. Whether it's a meal or a snack I'll leave on the counter for him after work or the new rock pad I made for the backyard yesterday, which he loved.

I'd had the idea after mudding and noticing how the hosing off made more mud, so I decided it would be fun to put a box of smooth stones by the hose, so now we can stand on that to hose off and keep our feet clean at the same time. It also drains the water exceptionally well, and it'll be handy. When we go mudding again.

It's been a few days since that night, and I've tried to morph what happened between us into just some freak accident because I was on the rebound and vulnerable for attention or something, but it hasn't stopped what I've started to feel for him from growing. It's a crush. We're alone together too much, and it's understandable we'd form a bond.

Hopefully, this block party potluck, and getting out of the house and around other people, will put things in perspective again.

"And it's not turkey bacon, right?" he suddenly blurts out.

Huh?

"On the poppers?" he clarifies, and I can see him looking at me out of the corner of my eye.

Jesus, is he still thinking about the food?

"And you didn't sneak in anything weird like wheat germ or use cauliflower instead of actual potatoes in the potato salad like some of those low-carb bullshit diets call for, right?" he goes on.

I burst into laughter, letting my head fall back, my phone drop in my lap, and my eyes close. *Oh, my God.*

"Jordan, I'm serious," he scolds. "I've been looking forward to this all week."

My body convulses as I shake my head at him and smile. He's so weird.

And I'm amused he's craving the stuff I made so vehemently.

I finish chuckling quietly and bury my nose in my phone again. "Everything is fatty and savory and delicious," I tell him. "Don't worry. I'm letting you have a cheat day today. You can clog your arteries until the cows come home."

I feel him nod. "Good." There's a brief pause and then he speaks up again. "If you feel uncomfortable, though, let me know. I can take you home."

"I'll be fine," I reply. "I talk to people all the time at work. I know how to make conversation."

Dutch and his wife invited Pike, Cole, and me, but Cole said he had to work an extra shift today and couldn't make it.

But as I'm scrolling my feed, I happen upon a shot of Patrick's Last Ditch, the super-convenience store just outside of town, and I recognize Cole's car at the pump. It's his post.

headin outta town for the dayyyyy! whoop!

Working, my ass. But it does seem unusually ambitious of him. Taking a road trip on his day off. Surprisingly, I don't scan for Elena or any other girls who might be with him, but I do feel a pang of resentment that he's just carrying on like I never existed. I mean, it's not like I'd answer the phone anyway, but it would be nice to know that he's tried to call. To know he's at least concerned about how I'm doing. I guess dating each other ruined whatever friendship we had, too.

I don't know why I care. My dad, my mom, my ex-boyfriends . . . There's something to be said for keeping your circle small, I guess. I have Cam and Shel.

We turn onto Owens and immediately see the street ahead blocked off with a couple barricades. Pike swerves over to the right and parks along the curb. It's only a little after two in the afternoon, and while the party started a couple hours ago, Dutch's wife said it would go well into the night, so the kids could have some fun with the sparklers.

We climb out and slowly stack the food in our arms, Pike taking his precious trays of poppers and taco dip, while I roll the small cooler with drinks inside and the potato salad propped on top.

"Hey, man," Dutch says, heading for Pike with a beer in his hand, which is slipped inside of a Koozie that reads *I PEE IN POOLS*.

"Hey, Pike!" someone else calls from inside the barricades.

Pike nods at whomever, and I stop alongside them, Dutch casting me a smile. God knows what conclusions he's drawing as to why I'm here with Pike. Why I'm always with Pike. Not sure if he knows Cole and I broke up.

A pretty woman with dark auburn hair comes up and takes the trays from Pike, leaning in to kiss him on the cheek.

"How are you?" she asks, smiling up at him.

He reaches down and takes the potato salad off the cooler for me. "Good. How are you?"

"Oh, we're kickin' it now," she jokes, leading the way into the party. "Although, this one"—she gestures to Dutch—"had to beer up every time he was forced to move one picnic table this morning."

Pike chuckles, and I gather this is Dutch's wife.

"This is Jordan," Pike introduces me. "Cole's, um . . . friend. He couldn't make it."

I laugh to myself at his stammer. I guess it's a better explanation than "this is Cole's ex-girlfriend who still lives with me and constantly argues with me, and I really hate her music, but look . . . taco dip!"

"I'm Teresa," she says, rolling her tongue over the *r* and looking over her shoulder at me with a smile. She gestures with my trays. "Are these cream cheese?"

"Oh, yeah."

"Yay," she singsongs, leading us over to the tables of food.

Everything is set up like a buffet, three long tables lined up together and filled with food. There are several coolers at the end. The smell of charred hamburger hits the back of my throat, and my mouth waters. Groups of people lounge on chairs in their yards or in the blocked-off street, and kids run everywhere, playing tag or rolling down the hills of some of the lawns. A few teenagers not much younger than me sit around, playing on their phones, while the adults laugh and talk, occasionally stopping to bark orders at one of their kids. It might not be technically summer yet, but the heat beats down and is lessened only by the sporadic cloud cover. It's a beautiful day.

"Come on," Dutch says, nudging Pike.

Pike glances at me, probably to make sure I'm all right, and finally sets the salad down before walking away. He trails off, shaking hands with some friends and twisting off the cap of a beer someone hands him.

I shuffle next to Teresa as she places everything on the table. "How long have you and Dutch been married?" I ask.

She sighs. "Fourteen years." She looks over at me. "And three kids later, I still want to kill him every day, but he makes good spaghetti, so . . ."

I snort. I'm sure she's just trying to be funny, because I doubt she can explain them. She looks pretty put together, while he's got on a flannel and shit kickers.

"This looks so good," she says, removing the Saran wrap. "Thank you for bringing so much. It won't last long."

Just then, an arm comes between us, the hand swiping up four poppers by the toothpicks and stealing them away. I recognize the ink on the arm right away.

"Hey," I scold Pike, but I can't shake my smile.

He peers down at me under heavy lids, looking entirely too sexy. "Excuse me," he whispers and turns away, heading back to his friends. He glances back at me, smirking, and I cock an eyebrow at him. Should have known he'd be all scared they'd get eaten before he had a chance.

"I hear you and Cole are staying with Pike for a while," Teresa says.

"Yeah." I swing our cooler over with the others and grab a water bottle out of it. "It seems paying for our own apartment was too adulty for us," I joke.

She nods knowingly. "Take your time. I wanted to get away from my parents so badly, and then when I found I had no money, because bills were way more responsibility than I bargained for, I ran back home." She picks up her Solo cup and holds it up to her lips, gazing out at the guys. "I'm glad Pike's got some company, though. That house is too big for one person."

I take a drink of my water, following her gaze. I'd hate to think of Pike living in that house alone after I leave. He really should be sharing his life with someone.

"I know a few single women who wouldn't mind changing that if given the chance," I remark, thinking of April, my sister, and half the moms on our block, who flirt with him when they pass his house on their "jogs."

"Yeah, but he's a loner," she replies.

I nod, smiling in agreement. "Yeah, I'm starting to understand that."

"He wasn't always like that." She glances at me, taking a sip of her drink. "He was a lot like Cole back in the day. Partying, laughing, speeding, breaking rules . . . He even spent the night in jail once."

My eyebrows dart up. Really?

I turn my eyes back on him and watch him pull the baseball cap out of his back pocket and pull it over his light brown hair, the muscles of his tattooed arm bulging against his T-shirt.

"But then Cole was born," I say, guessing the story from there.

"Yeah." Teresa sighs, rocking from left to right to the music playing from some speaker in one of the houses. "Someone had to be the adult, and Lindsay . . ." She trails off and then straightens, clearing her throat. "I'm sorry. I don't mean to gossip."

"It's okay," I tell her. "He certainly doesn't give up much."

I've seen Cole's mom here and there, and it's hard to picture her with Pike. She's pretty ostentatious, and I feel like the Pike I know would get whiplash trying to keep up with her.

At least, I know from what Cole has told me that it didn't last long between his parents, and if he didn't have some of the same mannerisms as his father, I'd wonder if Pike was sure Cole was his son. She's had at least four boyfriends whom I've seen in the past couple years.

Teresa exhales a breath and lowers her voice. "Pike is proof that we learn when we're forced to and maturity is more the result of experience than age," she tells me. "He was the only twenty-year-old I knew working two jobs without even a second thought to all the friends he was losing because he could never hang out."

I look over at her, suddenly wanting to know it all. I want any insight into who he was before I knew him.

"All of his friends were buying hot cars," she continues, "but he's been driving his dad's old pickup ever since I've known him. It was never a sacrifice to him, and there was never any question about taking care of Cole. It takes conviction to do what you know you're supposed to do regardless of what you want."

Her words hit me, and I let my gaze drop. *Conviction to do what you know you're supposed to do . . .*

And I suddenly feel like shit.

He wanted me the other night. And if it weren't for Cole, I have no doubt we would've slept together.

But Cole *is* there, between us, and we can't change that. Not ever. It's wrong, and no matter how much I want him, he would only hate himself afterward. His son will always be more important than anything else.

"He's a good man," she says.

Then she turns to put a serving spoon in the salad and open the chips for the taco dip, and I stand there, feeling like a truck is headed for me, but I can't move.

He is a good man.

I can't ruin that.

I suddenly feel like I need to get out of here. Pike's not my family, and as natural as it feels to be where he is, it's on borrowed time.

Over the next couple hours, I keep my distance from Pike. Teresa gives me a tour of her house, I sit with her and a few others, eating and talking, although I don't say much, and one of Dutch's kids wrangles me into dodgeball in someone's driveway. I help kids light sparklers, although it's not yet dark, and help Teresa take empty tins to the garbage and clean up soda cans and water bottles.

I'm not sure if Pike is paying me any mind, because I haven't looked at him to check his whereabouts, but once in a while, I feel the back of my neck get warm or a tingle spread up my spine.

"Oh, hey, Jordan," someone says, hopping over my legs, about to trip. "Didn't see you there."

He laughs, and I look over from where I lay on the grass to see Carter Hewitt smiling over his shoulder at me. Another guy and girl stand around him, but I don't remember their names even though we all graduated together.

Carter and I were supposed to go tubing today, but he canceled due to this block party his parents asked him to be here for. Luckily, too, because I was having a hard time talking *myself* into not canceling. I didn't want to let Pike win that argument, but he was right. Tubing is an excuse to get drunk, and I wasn't in the mood.

I sit up and dust the grass off my arms, which I was using for a pillow to watch the stars start to come out. "Hey, what are you guys doing?" I ask.

"Anything but this." He sighs. "There's a shitload of people at the A&W. Wanna come? I'll buy you a float."

I chuckle under my breath and stand up. That actually sounds really good.

"I haven't been there in so long," I remark. "Why not? Let me just tell my ride."

He and his friends head to their cars up the street, and I jog over to the lawn chairs full of guys in the center of the road. Pike sits with his back to me, while Dutch lounges next to him with his wife on his lap, and a few others around the circle I recognize from Pike's poker games.

"Hey," I say, coming up to Pike's side. "Some friends are heading to the A&W. Root beer floats and that. They invited me to come."

I'm not asking permission, but it kind of comes out like that.

He doesn't look at me, just tips up his bottle of beer and takes a sip. "Root beer float?" he repeats sternly. "What are you . . . five?"

Jerk.

"Noooooo," I say, "but that's how you like to treat me sometimes."

Dutch laughs quietly next to him but speaks up in my defense. "Hey, I still love floats, man."

I roll my eyes at Pike and look to Teresa, smiling. "Thank you so much for having me," I tell her. "This was nice."

"Thanks for coming, sweetheart. And thanks for the food."

"How you getting home?" Pike interjects, still avoiding my eyes.

"I'll bring her."

I look over to see Carter stepping up next to us, and Pike turns his head just a hair to see him before turning away again.

I lift the corner of my mouth in a little smirk and bend down, speaking a few inches from his ear. "Do I have a curfew?"

Dutch snorts, and I see a little snarl flare on Pike's mouth before it disappears.

"Have fun," he says tightly.

I stand up again and turn, following Carter to his truck as amusement lightens my mood again.

Pike is jealous.

And while I don't want to be thinking about him, I really like knowing he's trying not to think about me.

How much of what he wants is he hiding or burying or trying to suppress? What does it look like when he doesn't control himself anymore?

"Oh, my God, did you hear about Jillian?" Selena Gardner gestures to another girl, intermittently chewing on the end of a straw. "She tells Dean and Matt that one of them is the father, they go to get paternity tests, and neither one of them is the dad!" She laughs.

"Oh, my God!" The other girl's eyes bug out. "Shit, does she even know whose it is?"

"Who cares?" Selena furrows her brow, leaning back on the car again. "I'd be more concerned about catching something other than a baby. I don't leave the house without condoms anymore. You never know when you're going to need them. Like, really . . ."

Everyone laughs, and I fake a half smile in an effort not to be awkward, but I'm sure I am, since I have barely said two words in the last ten minutes.

We got to the A&W an hour ago, and as expected, the place is full of teenagers and families with truck beds full of kids. The moonlight and crickets compete with all the headlights and car stereos, and the smell of charbroiled burgers and hot asphalt fills the air as engines rev and car doors slam.

There's not a single person here I've talked to more than twice since I graduated over a year ago.

"I love this," someone says to Selena, reaching over and handling her small Louis Vuitton purse. "Where'd you get it?"

"Isn't it cute?" Selena lifts the strap over her head, showing the girl the purse. "I feel kind of bad. I owe my dad so much money, but I just had to have it."

I drop my eyes to the purse, equal amounts jealous and aggravated. Sure, I'd love a purse like that, and I'd love to have her problems where she can mooch off family, because that's what family's for when you're nineteen.

Part of me wishes I could ever be like that.

But even after I finish school, I'll be so strapped with student loans, frivolities like designer handbags will still be a long shot. And strangely enough, I'm okay with that. I'd rather have a decent car. A house. The ability to pay all of my bills in the same month.

Selena and I are living through completely different problems, and I relate to her even less now than I did in high school. I'm sure the feeling is mutual.

Without making up some excuse to escape, I just turn and walk toward the side of the building, digging out my cell phone.

"Hey, Jordan. You okay?" I hear Carter call.

I turn my head, seeing him stand with some others, and I nod.

Once I reach somewhere slightly quieter, I dial Cam and hold the phone to my ear, tossing my empty cup in the trash can.

"Hey," she chirps, knowing it's me.

"Hey," I say, her voice instantly soothing me. "Are you working? Can you come and get me?"

"I am working," she tells me, "but I can split for a half hour. Where are you? Is everything okay?"

I notice music in the background.

"Yeah, everything's fine." I tuck my hair behind my ear. "I'm at the A&W. I just want to go home."

Home.

I pause every time I say it, knowing full well it's not really my home, but it feels weird to say "Pike's house" or "Cole's dad's house," too.

After I hang up with Cam, I hit the bathroom first and then let Carter know I'm catching a ride home. There's momentary disappointment, but I'm pretty sure it's because he's lost his hookup for the night. Although, I'm not sure how he thought I would be anyway, especially after ignoring me to talk about cars and then being all too happy to let me get wrangled into "catching up" with a bunch of girls I never did any catching up with before, even in high school.

It's not that there's really anything wrong with Carter or Selena or anyone else here. But when they talk, you can tell they have nice things, like money in their pockets. And their moms. They have this lightness to their voices where you can hear that they haven't been evicted from an apartment before or are trying to decide if they should trade in their smartphone for a flip phone because it's cheaper.

I'm different from them, and I always have been. Being here tonight just brings those feelings back, the feelings I hated having in high school, and when I'm around Pike, I . . .

I knit my brow, thinking.

When I'm around him, I'm in my element, I guess.

And more than anything right now, I just want to go home. Or wherever he is.

Cam arrives in less than fifteen minutes, and I climb into her car, not protesting as she speeds through town toward Pike's neighborhood. Her boss is lenient, but the longer she's away, the more money she loses, so I let her rush.

"Thank you," I tell her. "Sorry to pull you away."

She's in a thigh-length black coat, tied at the waist, and I'm pretty sure she's not dressed in much underneath, just slipped something on to walk through the parking lot without getting molested.

"You sure you're okay?" she asks again.

I grab the dash with one hand as she makes a sharp right. "Yeah."

"Everything going fine with the dad?" She glances over at me. "You know you can come to my place anytime. You're welcome to stay."

"I know."

Nothing is wrong. In fact, I'm now realizing everything that's right, and it's not at the A&W. I know what I want, and I know why it can't be with Pike. I just need to find someone exactly like him.

I clutch the root beer float I bought for him as a gag as my sister winds through the streets and finally pulls up in front of Pike's house.

I groan, my stomach still somersaulting. "Thank you."

I climb out of the car, hooking my wallet on my wrist and closing the door.

"Is that April Lester's car?" Cam asks through the open window.

I turn my head, seeing a red Mazda Miata convertible parked behind Pike's truck, and my stomach sinks.

What the fuck? It's late.

I dart my eyes to the house and see that it's dark, no lights on anywhere. What would they be doing in there with no lights on?

A lump swells in my throat, and I feel like I'm going to throw up.

"She's probably selling Girl Scout cookies," Cam jokes.

But I'm seething. "It's not cookie season."

"Oh, honey, for some of us, it's always cookie season."

And I turn to my sister who makes a V with her fingers in front of her mouth and sticks her tongue between the two fingers, wiggling it.

I push off the door, mumbling, "Bite me."

But she just laughs, kicking her car into gear. "Goooooood luuuuuuck."

It takes two tries to swallow as I look up at the house. What is she doing here? What is she doing *in there*?

Yes, it's his house, and to my knowledge he hasn't hooked up with anyone since I came here weeks ago. He's young, single—he has every right to bring women home.

But it doesn't stop my heart from beating a mile a minute or my stomach from hurting. I'm here. Couldn't he go to her house instead? Or to a motel?

I walk up the steps of the front porch, my heart pulsing in my ears, and turn the knob, but it's locked. Pike almost always leaves the door unlocked for me. Even if I'm at work until two in the morning.

I try to keep the float stable in my left hand as I dig in my shorts for the key. Pulling it out, I unlock the door, dread weighing me down as I open it. If I walk in on them doing something, I'm not sure I won't burst into tears or start screaming.

Please, don't, Pike. Please don't do this.

I step into the house, softly closing the door behind me and locking it. I look around the dark living room, and my ears take in the silence, listening for anything that will confirm my worst fears.

Slowly trailing into the kitchen, I see my candy-apple candle lit on the table, its soft glow brightening the darkness. I didn't light it, though.

I clench my teeth. Was he going for ambience or something?

I look out the window over the sink and into the backyard, seeing the pool lit up but no one out there.

Walking back for the living room, I head toward the stairs, but then I hear muffled laughing, and I stop. Heading for the basement door, I gently twist the knob and quietly pull open the door, immediately hearing their clear voices.

"I want to hit the black one," April whines.

"Black one is last," Pike explains, his voice deeper and more playful than usual. "You put it in a pocket now, you lose the game."

"What do I get if I win?"

"What do you want?"

She laughs softly, and I hear shuffling. I can't see them as they're around the corner at the pool table, but she's doing something, and I squeeze the doorknob in frustration.

And then I hear his hushed, low voice. "I think that's if I win," he answers to whatever she's doing, and I can hear the smile in his voice.

"Mm-hmm," she moans, and my eyes go round, not sure if she's doing something to him or he's doing something to her.

What the hell? Is he serious? How long have they been here already? He knew I could be home anytime.

I'm a kid, for crying out loud. How am I supposed to get schoolwork done and sleep if they're going to go at it all night?

And this is what he was planning, I'm sure. If they wanted to play pool, they could've gone to The Cue. He brought her here for sex.

I march back through the kitchen and into the laundry room, ripping open the washer door and dumping the root beer float into the bin, paper cup and all. I slam the lid shut again and start the machine and then tear open the dryer door, pulling out his shit and slamming that door, too. If he wants to treat me like a kid, then here we go.

I jog up the stairs and swing into my bedroom, turning on my boombox and blaring "Bad Medicine" as I slip off my day clothes and pull on a pair of sleep shorts and half T-shirt.

Grabbing the handle of the tape player, I saunter back downstairs to the kitchen table and slide into a chair in front of the latest landscaping model I'm working on for school with the music still booming beside me.

It's barely ten seconds before I hear Pike's heavy footfalls on the basement stairs, and I tense my jaw, bracing myself.

He walks into the kitchen and comes right up to the table, hitting the *Stop/Eject* button on my player. The house immediately falls silent, and I pop my head up, feigning an innocent look on my face.

"Oh, I'm sorry," I say. "I didn't think anyone was here."

Pike stands up straight, pinning me with a look that says I'm a terrible liar.

"Hey, Jordan." April enters the kitchen behind him. "How are you?"

I give a tight smile. "Fine." And I return my attention to my model, messing with some fake grass.

Pike is still staring down at me, and there's a long, awkward silence as April probably tries to figure out what's happening now.

"I'll . . . head out," she finally says.

Pike hesitates a moment, and I can see his fist tighten around the chair on the other side of the table, but I won't meet his eyes.

I know I just acted like a brat, and I'm a little embarrassed, especially since I didn't fool him, but . . .

He could've taken her anywhere. He brought her here in hopes I'd see them together.

He walks her out, and I can't hear the few muffled words they exchange, but as soon as the door closes and I hear the lock click, I exhale.

She's gone.

He walks back into the kitchen, to the fridge, and I notice he's still wearing the navy blue T-shirt and jeans from earlier, with his work boots still on. He's not the slightest bit undressed, so that's a good sign.

"Sorry if that was awkward," he tells me, pulling out a soda. "We actually just got here ourselves. She stopped by to—"

"It's your house. I don't care," I tell him, faking concentration on my task. "Do what you want."

"Are you sure?" he asks, amusement in his tone. "You were slamming the washer and dryer doors and blaring music at ten at night. You seem . . . irritable."

I shake my head, shrugging. "Of course not. I wouldn't expect you to change your lifestyle just because I'm here. Go for it."

He's silent, and I can see him out of the corner of my eye just standing there a moment. I feel bad that I'm now elated he's going to bed alone. I want him to have someone. Someone to love him and make him feel good.

But . . .

Not her.

And not anyone else, actually.

I'm falling for him. I want him to have me.

And he's so stubborn, he pulled that tonight just to prove how much he doesn't want me.

"But I did think you'd have some damn taste, for crying out loud," I remark, gluing on more grass under the fake tree.

"Excuse me?"

I look up. "Did you know she broke up Marcus Weathers' marriage?" I ask him. "She hangs around the bar, waiting to see who's going to take her home on any given night, and she's not picky. Married, taken, whatever . . ."

"Good thing I'm not taken, then," he fires back. "There's no problem."

I lower my eyes and recap the glue, realizing I lost that round.

"You can do better," I finally mumble.

It's not that I hate April. I didn't care what she did to whose marriage before. It takes two to tango, doesn't it, and Marcus Weathers was also to blame.

But I care now that it's hitting too close to home. Pike *is* taken.

"What business is it of yours?" he challenges, walking back over to the table. "I'm a grown-ass man who's been having sex since before you were born. I'm used to getting it whenever I like, and I don't answer to you, you hear me?" His words bite, and I feel small. "I'll keep doing whatever I want, regardless of the opinions of some *kid* living under my roof."

The word "kid" hits me like a hammer, and my heart sinks. I grind my teeth, twisting the hurt into anger.

"Got it." I look up at him. "I'll go to my room, then."

I rise from my seat, and his eyes immediately drop to my bare stomach. The T-shirt falls well above my belly button, and I revel in the way his body freezes and he has to tear his eyes away.

I circle back around the table, toward the living room, but

remember the candle burning. Turning back, I make a show of leaning across the oval table, arching my back and feeling my shorts sink lower to expose the red strap of the same thong I wore when we made out in the yard a week ago.

"Forgot about the candle," I say, raising my heated eyes to him. "But I can leave it burning if you want. I know the red's your favorite."

Red candle or red thong? Doesn't take more than one guess to tell which one his attention is on.

He swallows, his timid eyes glancing at the red silk peeking out. I quirk a smile, and his eyes dart to mine, thinning.

"You're pissing me off more by the second." His raspy growl sounds dangerous. "You ruined my night, and I've still got a lot of steam to blow off, so tread carefully."

I close my eyes, making my wish, and blow out the candle before standing up straight again.

"This 'kid' is the reason you have so much steam to blow off, isn't it?" I taunt. "You're such a liar."

He squares his shoulders, breathing hard. "Go to your room, Jordan."

"Happily." I back away, teasing him. "I have a vibrator up there with bigger balls than you."

He rushes me and lifts me up, tossing me over his shoulder, and I grunt as the air is forced out of me and his shoulder digs into my stomach.

What the hell?

He pounds up the stairs, and I feel like I'm going to fall the higher we get.

"Pike, stop it!" I yell.

"Then stop pushing me!" he bellows, and a slap lands on my ass.

I yelp, the burn spreading across my left cheek. *Son of a* . . . I reach back and try to cover my behind in case he spanks me again.

It sounds like he kicks open my bedroom door, and the next

thing I know, I'm flying off his shoulder and crashing back onto my bed.

My elbows dig into the mattress, and my head jerks forward, my hair flying into my face.

"Now go to bed!" he barks.

I blow the hair out of my eyes and see him walking out. "Tuck me in?"

I see him drop his head, and he's breathing so hard, like he's almost out of fuel. He turns, calming his voice just a hair. "What the hell has gotten into you tonight?"

Is he kidding?

I shoot off the bed and stand in front of him. "You brought her here, that's what."

"It's my house!"

I shake my head. "She won't satisfy you," I tell him. "She's not what you want."

"So, you're jealous?"

I lower my voice, approaching him. "You have everything you need in this house. There's no reason to look elsewhere for"—I drop my head, suddenly a little embarrassed—"for anything you *need*," I tell him.

I'm all he needs.

His chest rises and falls in front of my eyes, and I inhale his scent that's unique to only him. Sun, wood, and the faint fragrances of his bodywash, shampoo, and the Tide his clothes have been washed in. He smells like a hot summer night and how I wish my first time had gone, and I soak it up while I can, because any minute, he's going to storm off.

"So, you had a little tantrum on purpose, then?" he says, not really asking. "Because you wanted to be the one in my bed tonight?"

I dart my eyes up, narrowing them. "Because you invited her over to hurt me, but I know your game, and you'll be the one who loses," I retort.

I close the inch between us, my shirt brushing his. His chin drops as he looks down at me, and my heart pounds against my chest.

"Because even if she stayed and she rode you to kingdom come all night long," I tell him, "you'll still wake up thinking about me before you even remember she's in bed next to you."

His breathing grows heavier, and I can see him weakening.

I continue. "You'll be wondering what I'm doing in my bed alone, if I'm awake and warm, or"—I push up on my toes and hover my mouth over his jaw as I whisper—"if I'm touching myself and dreaming about you coming in and eating me out through my panties."

He sucks in a breath, closing his eyes, and I can feel him get hard through his jeans. "Jordan, please," he begs, sounding desperate. "Fuck."

I try to keep my smile to myself, but I'm so happy. I know he wants me.

I hook my fingers on the waist of his jeans, nudging his chin with my nose to taunt him. "I know you want to," I whisper again. "You want to grab me so bad."

I stay right there, up on him, but I take my hands off him and slide my fingers into my own waistband instead, gently and slowly slipping off my shorts. They fall down to my feet, and I fist my fingers, my body so alive with fear and desire and need.

Look at me.

Touch me.

"I'm dying to taste you," I tell him. "And to feel you. Every day it's getting harder and harder to ignore what my body wants. I wake up so wet, Pike." I move my mouth over to his, layering our lips. "I want you to want me. I want to *see* you wanting me and getting off on me."

I can feel the slickness between my legs, and his breath is so hot. I lower myself to my feet but keep my eyes on his.

"I love how you worry about me and want to protect me," I say. "But a girl has needs, too, and eventually, I'll have to find another man who can do your job better."

Rage burns behind his frozen stare, but he doesn't blink.

"Another man will kiss me," I breathe out, "and take off my clothes and go at me in his bed, in his shower, and spread me wide over breakfast on his kitchen table . . ."

Pike's lips are almost twisted in a snarl, and he's breathing hard—in and out, in and out—as he glares down at me.

It's there. I can feel him. It's like we're wrapped up together, the heat between us almost suffocating, and all he has to do is reach out and pull me into his arms.

Take me.

I wait.

I'm yours. Just reach out and take me.

But he doesn't.

He just stands there, and tears burn at the backs of my eyes as he hovers, unmoving.

Unwilling.

My heart is breaking.

I shake my head. "You don't have a clue what to do with me, do you?"

I scoff and push away from him, but then suddenly, he grabs my arms, hauling me back to him. I gasp as he puts his hands under my arms and lifts me off my feet, bringing me face-to-face with him like I'm five years old.

"Oh, I may be out of practice, little girl," he bites out in a threatening tone, "but I think I'll figure it out."

And he brings me in, kissing me and stealing my breath so hard, all I can do is wrap my legs around him and hold on.

Fuck yes.

18

Pike

Goddamn her.

Goddammit. I'm not stopping. Fuck it. I can't.

She just kept pushing and pushing, hitting all my buttons, everything she knew would bring me to this, and I wanted her to. In the back of my mind, I always knew I couldn't *not* have her.

I grab her ass in my hands and drop us down to her bed. She unlocks her legs and straddles me, our lips never breaking contact. I love her mouth. Hot and sweet, and she teases me with that tongue—flicking and brushing in ways that drive me insane.

"I hated feeling like that," she pants.

"Like what?" I run my hands all over her, gripping and squeezing as she breathes over my mouth and grinds on me, making me painfully hard.

"Jealous," she says.

It takes me a moment to remember we were fighting about April being here. Slipping my hand up her shirt, I take her breast in my palm, and she lets out a little gasp. I groan at finally having her in my hand.

"I know," I say. "When you left the party with that little shit tonight, I was so pissed." I bite her bottom lip between kisses.

"Like I was fucking seventeen again and someone else was taking what was mine."

My cock swells, and God, I can't stop touching her. She's so damn beautiful. Her smooth skin and mussed hair. The little triangle of red fabric between her legs where I can already see she wasn't lying about being turned on. She's wet, and I'm fucking starved to taste her.

Another man who can do my job better . . . Bullshit.

I brush the hair out of her face as she grinds on me, and we hold each other's eyes. Hers say everything I'm feeling, and we're both falling.

Dammit.

"What do you see in me, girl?" I ask, shaking my head. I couldn't keep a nineteen-year-old woman happy when I was nineteen. Does she think I can do it now?

"You have no idea, do you?" She cups my face, kissing me. "When we first met and we watched that movie together at the theater, I felt so guilty"—she kisses me again—"because when you mentioned the *Poltergeist* showing, I . . . I was tempted, because I wanted to see you again," she confesses. "There was something there even then."

I sink into her mouth, kissing her long and deep, as I wrap an arm around her body and press her into me. Curling my fingers around the silk at her hip, I feel an urge to bury myself inside her right now.

But no. To her, I'll end up being a fling, but I'm gonna make damn sure it's the best one she ever has.

I kiss her neck, sucking and nibbling all the way up to her chin and running my thumbs over her hard little nipples.

"Pike . . ." she pleads. "Please tell me you have condoms."

I nod, coming back to her mouth. "In my room."

"More than one, right?"

I smile. "Yeah."

"Go get 'em."

I wrap my arms around her and stand up, taking her with me. "I have a better idea."

She locks her ankles behind my back, and I carry her out of her room and down the hall to mine. We need a bigger bed.

She doesn't stop kissing me the whole time, and I almost close my eyes with the pleasure, because I don't think I've ever felt this damn good. She's going to spoil me so much that no one else will ever do again.

We enter my room, and I kick the door shut behind us, lowering her to the bed. But when I pull away from her and rise, she protests. "No . . ."

I back up toward the door, watching her—finally having her on my bed—and I feel like I just won the fucking lottery.

Reaching behind me, I lock the door and stare at her, the moonlight streaming through the window lighting her up. She's sitting with her knees bent and her hands planted behind her, propping herself up. Her lips are swollen from the kissing, and I'm already imagining her naked between my sheets.

"God, you're so sweet," I say under my breath.

A coy smile plays on her lips. "I'm really not."

I arch a brow at her challenge. "So, what do you like, then?"

"What do you do?"

Such a little shit.

Crossing back over to the bed, I lean down over her and fist her panties in my hand. "You said you wanted me to eat something," I remind her. "What do you want my mouth on?"

She drops her eyes, staring at my lips. "Um . . ." She swallows and caresses her inner thigh, moving her hand up to the V. "Down here."

"And what's down there?" I play with her, staying just out of reach every time she moves in for a kiss. "Use your adult words, Jordan. What do you want me to kiss?"

"Um," she stammers, turned on and dying for it. "Um, my . . ."

My . . . ?

She comes in for my mouth again, but I pull away, making her bare her teeth in a quiet little growl.

"My . . ."

"Yes?"

"My, um . . . my cunt," she whispers.

My eyebrows shoot up; I'm surprised. I wasn't expecting that word, actually, but okay.

"I want you to kiss and suck on it," she breathes out, begging. "Make me come?"

And I squeeze my eyes shut for a moment, my dick fighting against my jeans for room to grow.

Fuck.

Anything you want.

Tightening my hand around her panties, I yank and rip them off. The fabric tears clean away and I throw them across the room as she sucks in a breath.

And then I throw my own shirt off and dive down, taking her pretty pussy in my mouth.

"Pike," she whimpers, clutching my head to her body and falling back on the bed.

Jesus, I'm fucking high. I've wanted this for so long, and I finally have her, legs spread on my bed, body begging for me.

I suck on her clit first, stretching it into my mouth and going back in again and again, making her squirm and desperate to come. I lick her up and down, swirling my tongue around over her nub and getting drunk on her scent and taste. After a minute, I lose control, though, and I'm kissing and nibbling her everywhere. I curve my arm under her thigh and grip it for support as I feed off her, doing it as much for me as for her. Her back arches off the bed when I flick her with my tongue, and she moans.

I keep doing that until she's panting so fast I know she's ready to come apart. Palming one of her breasts, I keep my head buried between her legs until I feel her stomach start to shake and then she sucks in a deep breath and freezes as the orgasm takes hold.

She cries out, letting it go, and I tongue her, not stopping until she starts to calm.

"Jordan," I whisper against her skin. I don't know why I say her name, but I think I'm fucking afraid she's not really here and this is all a dream.

Her fingers thread through my hair, and I come up, hovering over her. Brushing the stray lock off her forehead, I stare down into her, taking in her flushed cheeks and bright eyes, her little shirt that has ridden up, exposing her beautiful breasts and pert nipples.

I dip down, taking one in my mouth, sucking and dragging it out just like her clit. She whimpers, her hands coming back to wrap around the back of my neck. I switch to the other one, trailing one hand down her body and trying to take in as much of her as I can.

I know everything we're doing is wrong, and I don't know how I'm going to explain this to anyone, but right here—right now—I don't want to be anywhere else. I wish I could die as happy as I am right now. In here, in the dead of night, in this dark room, behind a closed door, we don't need to explain anything to anyone.

For just this moment, it's ours.

I climb off the bed and stand up, unfastening my belt and opening my jeans. I reach into the bedside table and pull a condom out of the box, rising again and staring down at her. Her legs are closed, one knee slightly arched up, and her hands at her sides, fisting the comforter as she watches me.

"You sure about this?" I ask her.

She nods.

I kick off my boots and slide the rest of my clothes off, standing up straight again. Opening the package, I look down at her, but her eyes have lowered to something else, her breathing growing shallow. I feel a smile tug at the corners of my mouth, wondering how many other adult words she knows.

But I don't get a chance to ask. She sits up, swinging her legs over the edge of the bed, and goes for my cock, taking it into her mouth.

I groan and gasp at the same time, her tongue wet and hot as she draws back and sucks in the tip.

"Jordan, please." I fist the back of her hair, gently trying to pull her away. "That'll put me over the edge, and I want you to come again."

Pushing her back on the bed, I come down on top of her, melting into her mouth and kissing her deep. I nestle between her legs, and she bends her knees up as she runs her nails down my back.

Slipping my hand under her, I grip her ass and press our bodies together, the world spinning behind my closed eyes. Having her under me, skin on skin . . . my cock is so hard, I can't take it.

This is mine.

Leaning back on my heels, I roll on the condom, never taking my eyes off her.

"I'm a little scared," she says, worry creasing her brow.

I halt, trying not to squeeze the fist around my cock too hard.

Scared?

"What if I make too much noise?" she whispers.

And I exhale, relieved she's not having second thoughts. I stroke my cock and come down on her again. "Pull up your shirt, Jordan," I whisper back. "I want to see your tits when I fuck you."

Her breath shakes and an excited smile plays on her lips, but she lifts up her shirt for me, and I dive down quickly and snatch up a nipple between my teeth again.

She gasps and spreads her legs wide, and the tip of my cock finds the wet heat of her tight cunt like a fucking magnet.

I come up, propping myself up on one arm, and lean down,

nibbling her lips. "Try to be quiet, okay?" I whisper, teasing her. "Can't have Cramer finding out what I'm doing to his babysitter."

She laughs, kissing me back. "Yes, Mr. Lawson."

Reaching down, I hold her eyes as I fit my tip at her entrance, and then I grab hold of her hip and thrust inside of her, immediately overcome with the feel of her and my body shaking.

She arches her neck back and closes her eyes, moaning, and her breasts bounce with the movement.

"Oh, fuck, fuck . . ." she cries. "Pike . . ."

"I know, baby." *You feel so good.*

I thrust again and she clutches my waist to hang on as I slowly pick up the pace, sinking deeper inside her and mesmerized by her body underneath me. I dip down, sucking on her breast as she moans and whimpers.

Coming back up, I kiss her mouth, and she does that thing where she licks my tongue, and I'm spiraling.

"Jordan, fuck," I breathe out, thrusting faster and harder until the only thing I hear is our bodies coming together.

Her moans fill the room, growing louder, and I kiss her, muffling the noise as she comes apart again, her pussy tightening around my cock as she orgasms.

I look up and see us in the dresser mirror, turned on by the sight of her legs around me. She follows my gaze, mischief flashing in her eyes.

She leans up, whispering in my ear, "I want to see."

I wrap my arm around her waist and flip us over so she's on top. Her T-shirt falls below her breasts again, and her hair tumbles around her in beautiful disarray. I grab her hips just so I can feel her body move as she takes me on. She stares down into my eyes, her hips rolling, her stomach waving, and her ass jutting in and out as she rides me.

Then she looks up, an instant curve to her lips, telling me she likes what she sees in the mirror.

"You're so tight," I groan.

She puts her hands on my chest and digs in, baring her teeth and breathing hard as she fucks me faster.

"Yes," she breathes out, her eyes falling closed. "Yeah, God, please . . ."

I grab her ass and arch up, taking a nipple in my mouth again, sucking and tugging and then moving to the next one in a frenzy. She leans into me, never slowing her pace, and I can feel the sweat gliding down the small of her back.

I suck in air through my teeth, my muscles tensing, and I'm close. I flip her back over, hungry to be in control again, and her head falls at the side of the bed, too close to the bedside table. I grab the edge of it and whip it away, sending it toppling over, lamp and everything crashing to the floor.

She whimpers and kisses me, caught up in the madness of the moment, too.

"Don't stop," she pants. "Don't stop. I'm gonna come again."

I press my forehead to hers, both of us damn near hyperventilating as I thrust over and over again, trying to think of anything that won't make me come, but she feels too good, and I'm too fucking lost.

"Oh, Pike," she cries. "Right there. Yeah . . ."

My muscles are burning, my head is spinning, but I don't break pace, because if I fucking die right now, this is how I want to go out.

"Ah," she moans, her body tensing and her breathing shaking.

She falls silent and then . . . she throws her head back and cries out. "Oh, God!"

I kiss her, seeing her come again enough to send me over the edge. I thrust hard, squeezing my eyes shut and spilling, diving deep inside her again and again as the orgasm racks my body and exhaustion and euphoria set in at the same time.

White-hot heat streams from my thighs, and my cock pulses,

and everything about her is heaven. Everything feels like it's the first time.

I come down, resting my elbows on either side of her head, and smooth the hair away from her face.

She gazes up at me, her face flushed and shiny with a light layer of sweat. "You didn't kiss her, did you?" she asks softly.

I chuckle under my breath. "And that's what you're thinking about right now?"

She twists her lips in embarrassment, but she presses anyway, "You didn't, right?"

"No," I tell her. "And she wouldn't have spent the night. I was trying to forget about you and how much I wanted this, but it wouldn't have happened. You were right. I wanted you."

I kiss her, surprised that even though I've come, I'm not done with her. I could stay here all night.

"And that little shit from the block party?" I question her. "Nothing happened, right?"

Her faint dimples grow deeper.

"Jordan," I warn, furrowing my brow.

She laughs. "No," she finally answers. "He doesn't have your body"—she gives my cheek a peck—"or your tattoos"—she kisses my jaw—"or your mouth"—she kisses my lips—"and every word that comes out of it that gets under my skin and drives me crazy in all the best ways."

I sink into her, kissing her long and hard. The fucking damage is already done. I'll feel guilty tomorrow.

"One thing, though," she says, pulling her mouth off mine to leave a trail of kisses across my cheek. "I know you have work tomorrow and probably want to get to sleep, but I'm kind of hungry. Can we get some ice cream downstairs and then do it again before bed?"

I drop my head into her shoulder, shaking with laughter.

Anything you want, baby.

I roll my neck under the hot spray, every muscle in my body tight and sore. I don't really exercise, but I'm hardly ever sitting on my ass, so I thought I was in good shape. She shot that idea to shit last night, though. I can't help but indulge in the fantasy of having her here every day, as many times a day as I want, just for the sake of my muscular health, of course.

But I know I can't. We did it again last night and then crashed, and as much as I want her even more this morning, now that I know what I've been missing, we can't let this become normal. It'll be painful enough when it ends.

I shut off the water and step out of the shower, pulling my towel off the hook and drying my hair. The bathroom is dark because I wanted to delude myself that nighttime still wasn't over, but it's just after five in the morning, and I have to be at work in an hour. When I see her again, it'll be in the bright light of day, and I'll have to face how I did something so fucking shitty last night.

I finish drying off and wrap the towel around my waist before walking to the sink and brushing my teeth. And trying not to think about the hot young woman still asleep in my bed in the other room.

I mean, how wrong is what we're doing? She's single, I'm single. We're both adults. Yeah, there's the age difference, but it's not unheard of.

And I fucking liked her before I knew who she was. No one else was a factor in that. We're not trying to hurt anyone.

Stepping back into the bedroom, I look over at her in the bed. Asleep on her stomach, hugging one of my pillows under her head, and her hair fanned out behind her. She wears one of my T-shirts, and although I love her naked, I can't complain. I love her in my clothes, too.

Walking over to her side of the bed, I pick up my watch off the bedside table—the one not toppled over on the other side—and fasten it to my wrist as I stare down at her.

We've known each other less than a month, but I feel like she's always been there. Like I was saving that side of the bed just for her.

I don't know if I love her, but I've never wanted anything or anyone this bad.

Her foot peeks out from the sheet, and I smile at her pink toes. So very Jordan.

She moans and turns her head, and I raise my eyes, seeing her turn over in her sleep, resting her hand on the pillow next to her face.

The sheet is down at her waist, and the shirt has ridden up, showing a sliver of her stomach, and I let instinct take over. It's still dark outside.

The night doesn't have to be over yet.

Peeling down the sheet, I see her hot-pink panties, and I don't mind that she doesn't sleep naked. It means I get to undress her.

Gently pulling down her underwear, I climb over her, putting one knee between her legs and sliding her shirt up with one of my hands.

I touch her and kiss her softly, moving across her cheek to her ear and back toward her mouth.

"Good morning," I whisper, nibbling at her.

She moans again, arching to meet my lips, which are trailing down her body, tasting her stomach, her hips, and back up to her breasts.

"Isn't it?" she says, joking.

I chuckle.

Reaching over to my nightstand, I dig out another condom and rip off my towel. "Just a quickie, okay?" I tease. "To get me through the day."

She moans again, stretching her arms above her head. "'Kay."

And I dive in.

Several minutes later we're both panting and sweaty again, and I need another shower, but I don't have time.

Fuck, that was good. Is it me or does she feel better in the morning?

I look over at the clock. "I gotta go."

I don't want to, though. How awful would it be if the boss called in sick, so he could stay home and fuck his hot little live-in all day?

Reluctantly, I climb off her and walk to my dresser, pulling out some jeans and a T-shirt. "Do you have to work tonight?" I ask.

She pulls the sheet back up over her and gazes at me sleepily. "Maybe."

I shake my head. Always playing games.

"Maybe I'll be home," she explains, "or maybe you'll have to find me."

I close the dresser drawer and open another, grabbing socks.

I turn to her, fixing a stern look on my face. "I'll be home at five. Be here," I order her. And then I start to walk toward the door but turn and soften my voice, adding, "Please?"

She grins and turns on her side, hugging my pillow under her again and looking at me with the sweetest eyes. "Miss me."

I do already.

I leave, closing the door behind me and closing her bedroom door, too. Just in case Cole comes home, sees her empty bed, and starts to wonder where she is.

Jogging down the stairs, I feel an urge to smile even as the guilt knots my stomach. I almost feel normal.

But luckier than any guy I know. The girl of my dreams is in my bed right now, and I get to come home to her, too. She was right. I have everything I need under this roof.

Except my son. This is his home, and he's not here, and Jordan makes me forget him.

For nineteen years, it was always him. Sacrificing to build my business to be able to give him a good home and education, and either being scared of relationships after what I went through with Lindsay or losing relationships because other women didn't want to have to deal with the mother of my child for the rest of our lives. My life revolved around him, but no matter what I did, it all still went to shit. She twisted him up and used him against me, and he doesn't know whom to trust.

Letting myself be happy with a woman isn't wrong, but that woman being Jordan is what could break whatever faith he has left in his parents. Why can't I stop? Why does my heart hurt so much every time she smiles? Or chews on her thumbnail or stands on her tiptoes to reach something in the kitchen or fucking blinks, for Christ's sake?

I walk into the kitchen and pour coffee into my travel mug. I fasten the lid and grab my lunch out of the fridge, throwing in some extra chips since I don't have time for breakfast.

The doorbell suddenly rings, and I turn, scowling. Who's showing up this time of morning?

Leaving everything on the counter, I walk to the front door and lean over, peering out the front window.

And speak of the devil . . .

My ex stands out there in nylon workout pants and a matching tank top. Her hair is up in a messy brown bun, but she has a full face of makeup on. She's the only person I know who gets made up to go to the gym.

Of course, she probably only goes to meet guys.

I pull open the door, trying to be quiet, so Jordan doesn't stir.

"What do you want?" I say, holding open the door.

"Well, you're nice," she sneers, keeping her arms crossed over her chest. "Ever the asshole, huh?"

And without waiting for an invitation, she walks in, pushing past my arm.

"If you're showing up at my door at five in the morning, it can't be good," I say, closing the door. "Are you drunk?"

She walks into the kitchen, tosses her keys on my counter, and spins around, facing me. "Why is my son living at some random girl's house and not with you?"

I fight the urge to roll my eyes at her fake concern, which is just an excuse to be invasive. "He's welcome to come home anytime," I explain, heading for the stool and grabbing my T-shirt. "He's the one who left."

"Because you're allowing Jordan to stay. Why?"

I pull the garment over my head. "If you want to know what's going on with Cole, ask Cole. As for who I rent out a room to, that's none of your business."

I comb my fingers through my hair, having forgotten to style it. She's quiet for a moment, and I don't look at her as I pull my phone off the charger and stick it in my pocket.

She steps up to my side and takes my chin, forcing me to face her.

I jerk away. "What?"

"You're flushed."

"It's warm out," I retort.

But underneath my skin, my blood warms and my heart pounds harder. I pick up my coffee, taking a sip to conceal my nervousness. The woman is a shark. She can smell blood across an ocean.

"I know what you look like after you come," she charges. "So, question is . . . is it the sweet piece of teen ass upstairs or someone new?"

I slam my mug down, glaring at her. "That's enough."

Goddammit. I forgot how smart she is. I haven't even left the house yet, and I can't even get what I'm feeling by the one person I've run into. *Awesome.*

Heading over to the table, I sit down and pull on my socks and boots and gather up everything I need for the day.

"Cole quit his job," she finally tells me. "Three days ago."

I look up, stopping what I'm doing. *Three days?*

"Let me give you a tip," she condescends. "Parenting didn't stop when he turned eighteen and you no longer had to pay child support. He still needs you."

"Forgive me if I don't take parenting lessons from a woman who got pregnant so she'd have a meal ticket for the rest of her life." I turn to her, pinning her with my stare. "Maybe he quit so he wouldn't have to work for nothing, since you guilt him into giving you half of his paychecks."

She slaps me across the face, and my head jerks to the side.

But I just laugh.

Of course I'm worried. He's been out of work and hasn't been home, but I'm not taking a lecture from her. She's used him, and I've had enough of her bullshit.

"That's the reason you don't let him come work for me, isn't it?" I ask, not backing down. "Because in exchange, I was going to pay his bills and give him a stipend to make sure you didn't get your hands on his whole damn salary. You only care about him when he comes bearing cash." I gather up my shit and walk for the door, yanking it open. "You know who I'm really jealous of? All the men who got away before you trapped them with a kid. I'm not sorry I had Cole, but I am sorry it was with you. Get out."

I'm proud I kept my voice down and was able to muster some control, but I'm seething inside. She comes into my house, accusing me of being a bad parent, and then hits me. She's not my wife and never has been. I have to put up with her, but not with everything.

She stands there, looking almost amused, and finally walks up to me. "Yes," she says, about to leave, but she turns and taunts me over her shoulder, "because your house is the only area of your life you can get me out of."

And then her eyes flash up my stairs and back to me, a sick smirk playing on her lips.

She walks out, and I remain still, everything I felt in my bedroom minutes ago completely gone. Cole is spiraling, and he needs me now more than ever.

And Lindsay knows about Jordan. She may not know anything for sure, but her suspicions will be enough.

She'll tear Jordan apart. There's no way I'm putting her through that.

I just wish I could've had her for more than seven hours.

19

Jordan

I press the stones onto the step with my pick and grab the glue, squeezing it into the crevice to fasten the pieces to the model. I feel an urge to glance at the clock on the microwave again, but I refrain, knowing it hasn't been more than two minutes since the last time I checked.

It's after six, and Pike is late. He's hardly ever late.

As the minutes go by, though, I feel my temper rise, because he hasn't called, either, and he specifically asked me to be home. This isn't like him, but it's damn well like every other guy I've known. I'm that girl they can treat like garbage and make wait, because I take it.

For a while, anyway.

The pizza I ordered, half pepperoni and half taco, was delivered an hour ago and is keeping warm in the oven, while my salad is in the fridge, staying chilled. *The Lost Boys*, continuing our eighties horror movie marathon, is on the TV, ready to play, and I'm alone.

Again.

Okay. He could be in the middle of something, still at work. Understandable, and I'm an adult. I don't need my hand held. He could've also been in an accident, but that's extreme, and I don't want to be that girl who calls, either. He'll think I'm . . . getting attached or something.

I glue the glass balls onto the bed of what will soon be the stream, letting the minutes tick away his chances as I sit there, wait, and get angrier.

The day has been so great. I woke up sore but hardly even noticing, because the memories of last night had me blushing constantly. He was not out of practice at all, and I couldn't stop smiling as I cleaned up the broken lamp and fixed the nightstand again.

And cleaned the remnants of the A&W cup out of the washing machine from when I dumped the ice cream float in it last night. Thank God he didn't find out about that or he'd change his opinion on whether or not I'm an adult.

After tidying up the house, I really didn't want to wash off his smell, but I desperately needed a shower. I cleaned myself up, and then I called Cam and borrowed her car to go get my paycheck at Grounders and run a few errands. I got sideways looks from my sister and Shel, both probably wondering why I'm practically fucking skipping around everywhere, but I didn't care.

Because in a few hours, his eyes were going to be on me again, and I really love when his eyes are on me. Maybe we'd go swimming tonight or throw some pillows and blankets into the back of the truck to go make out somewhere. Or maybe I'd pick a fight so he'd bend me over the kitchen table for another spanking.

Stupid. Fantasies and expectations that never measure up in reality. I should know better. Here I am, sitting here waiting for whenever he happens to show up, ready to be at his beck and call.

After a while, I pick up my phone again, checking to see if I have any messages.

Still nothing.

I look at the time, and it's nearly seven now. Two hours late.

He'd know I was expecting him. If he didn't call, then maybe something did happen.

I dial him, about to feel either really pathetic if he's *not* sitting in the ER right now or really bad about all my doubts if he is.

The call goes to voicemail, though, and I hang up, hesitating only a moment before I get up and walk to the refrigerator, drawing my finger down Pike's list of contacts. I see Dutch's number and dial it, thinking of something to say that won't make me seem desperate.

The line rings three times before he answers.

"Hello?"

"Hey, Dutch," I say quickly, adding some pep to my voice. "It's Jordan. Sorry to bother you. I know Pike doesn't always keep his phone on him and thought you would. I'm about to leave for work, and I lost my key to the house." I lick my dry lips, my heart hammering. "Are you all about done at the site? I didn't know when Pike would be home and didn't want to just leave the door unlocked."

"Oh, we closed up shop two hours ago, honey," he tells me. "I'm home already, and he went with the guys for a beer at Poor Red's. I'm sure if you call him he'll run home and lock up."

My throat constricts and tears burn.

He went out.

I force a tight smile, hoping it disguises the anger inside. "Yeah. Will do. Thank you."

I hang up and close my eyes, forcing myself to calm down. He went out. Without even letting me know. He just left me sitting here.

I blink away the burn, refusing to be hurt. I cared about him, and I fucked him. But I don't love him, and he clearly doesn't give a shit. He got what he wanted.

All that possessiveness and a need to watch over me and protect me. It was just to keep me here so he could get in my pants. He resisted me because he felt bad, but he was simply biding his time until he could talk himself into it. Taking me to bed was always the plan. Now that he's had his piece of ass, the monkey is off his back, and hey, maybe April is at Red's tonight, too, and they can pick up where they left off.

I growl, kicking a chair.

This doesn't happen to me. Not anymore. It ends now.

I hold up my phone and dial Cam, remembering what tonight is.

"Hey, what's up?" she answers.

I curl my lips, feeling suddenly bold. "I feel like I want to see my first wet T-shirt contest."

She gasps and then squeals into the phone. "Yes!"

20

Pike

I pull into my driveway a little after nine and look up at the house. She won't be asleep yet, and I'm in no better condition to deal with her now than I was four hours ago when work ended. But I can't put it off anymore. We need to talk.

I see a small light on in the kitchen that I know is probably the one over the stove, but the rest of the house is dark, and part of me hopes she actually is in bed, because I don't want to do this.

Jumping down out of my truck, I slam the door and walk to the house. Slipping the key into the dead bolt, I twist it and open the door, stepping into the dark living room. There's no light streaming in from anywhere, and I don't hear her music playing. I know my standing her up didn't go by unnoticed. She called a couple hours ago but didn't leave a message. She's undoubtedly angry.

I take in a breath and instantly smell warm cheese and spicy meat. *Pizza.*

Walking into the kitchen, I pull open the oven and find the large box from Joe's and take it out, setting it on top of the stove.

I flip the lid. Every piece still sits in the box, untouched.

My stomach knots, and I feel like shit. Of course, I knew she would have something for dinner. Heading back into the living room, I pick up the remote and turn on the TV, seeing the dark glass come to life and the cover of *The Lost Boys* (1987) appear on the Netflix screen. She had everything ready for a night in.

Trailing upstairs, I stop at her bedroom door, not seeing a light from inside streaming underneath.

I knock twice and wait. When there's no answer, I twist the handle and open the door.

Through the moonlight coming in through her window, I see her bed still made and an empty room.

My pulse quickens. She doesn't have a working car yet. Where did she go?

Did she have to work, after all? I check my phone again for texts, but I don't see anything.

Maybe her sister gave her a ride.

But she would've told me if she had to work.

Dialing Jordan, I jog down the stairs as the line rings and turn the television off again.

When the line picks up, a blast of music hits my ear and I flinch, pulling it away just a hair.

"Hey," she says, and I'm surprised she sounds so . . . calm.

"Where are you?"

"Out," she replies. "I'll be home later."

"Are you working?"

She laughs, and I hear another woman's voice and a string of chatter in the background. "Uh, no," she finally answers.

Then I hear a bellow of what sounds like forty men cheering in the background, and I straighten, trying to figure out what the hell's going on.

"Jordan, I'm sorry I was late," I tell her.

"Huh?"

"I'm sorry I was late!" I shout into the phone. "Work had to be done, and I had to stay."

"Then why didn't you call?" she replies, her voice growing louder. "You weren't at work. You were at Red's, and I don't wait.

Not anymore. I'm out with my friends, and I'm having fun. I'll be home later."

And then all the music in my ear and the DJ's voice in the background falls dead and the line cuts off as she hangs up.

Hangs up *on* me.

I lower my phone and stare at the ended call. Okay, so she's mad. *I think.* She didn't sound mad, though. Or drunk. She just sounded indifferent, and for some reason, that feels worse. I can deal with anger, but not with a girl who sounds like she's perfectly content with whatever conclusions she's drawn. Shit.

Then it occurs to me what the DJ in the background was announcing.

Wet T-Shirt Night at The Hook.

My eyes widen. She wouldn't be that stupid, would she?

Goddammit. What the hell am I supposed to do? Is she out having some fun like she said or is she checkmating me? Is she trying to entice me to come get her by threatening to do something I won't like, or do I stay right where I am, call her bluff, and see what happens? This is why women and I don't get along and my relationships don't last. I don't have the head for this bullshit.

But the fact that she went out at all is because of me. If I had come home when I told her I would, she'd be curled up next to me on the couch right now, taunting me with her eyes, her hands, her smell, and that sexy-ass way she arches her back when she stretches.

I sigh and shake my head.

I want her so badly.

Sticking the phone in my pocket, I pull out my keys and head for the door. As soon as I open it, though, I see Cole standing there with his hand out like he was just about to open it.

I halt, my eyebrows shooting up.

"Hey," he says, his voice unusually pleasant.

I open my mouth to speak but it takes a minute to find my voice. "H-hey," I stammer, a little shaken at seeing him suddenly. "I've been trying to get ahold of you all day. I was even out to a couple of your usual haunts during my lunch break. Where the hell have you been?"

"Yeah, I know, sorry." He walks in and heads for the kitchen. "I had some things to tie up."

He goes for the fridge and pulls out a soda, then turns and leans against the sink as he pops the top.

"So, what's going on with you?" I stand at the island. "Your mom shows up this morning, saying you quit your job?"

He flashes me an amused look like I'm overreacting.

"If you kept me posted, I wouldn't nag," I burst out but try to make it sound like banter.

He glances behind him out the window, seeing something, and pushes off the counter, heading through the laundry room and into the backyard. I follow him.

"I'm fine," he calls over his shoulder. "I actually have a new job. That's why I quit."

He walks over to the pool and starts pulling the tube for the vacuum up. I'd completely forgotten about it. It had been going since yesterday afternoon.

"A new job?" I ask, taking his slack from behind him. "Where?"

"It's a surprise."

"I don't like surprises. Where's the job?"

He starts laughing, and I scowl.

"Why are you laughing?" I demand. Does he know how worried everyone is about him, and now he acts like he's got everything together, and we're supposed to not ask questions?

"Because I'm excited," he says. "I'll tell you soon. I promise."

"Is it legal?" I pull the tube, feeling the weight of the vacuum as it starts drifting across the pool toward us.

His back shakes with another laugh.

I quirk an eyebrow.

"I promise, this job is as legal as it gets," he tells me, a private joke in his words I don't understand. "I've got a steady paycheck coming, medical, dental, retirement, the whole works." He glances at me. "I'm not on drugs, and I'm not in trouble. I'm absolutely fine. I'm sorry I haven't been around. I just didn't want it to be awkward for Jordan."

I drop the tube, having reached nearly the end.

"So, you're fine, then?" I ask, for clarification.

"Yeah."

"Will you come home?"

But he shrugs, looking unsure. "It would be uncomfortable, I think. I want Jordan to stay here as long as she needs."

I approach him. I'm still a couple inches taller than him, but I'm always surprised at how much bigger he seems every time I see him.

I hesitate to say it, because I don't want her to go anywhere, but I know Cole's place is here. "I can find a different arrangement for her," I tell him.

I can figure something out to make sure they're both taken care of.

He doesn't seem to need to think about it, though. "No." He shakes his head, squaring his shoulders. "It wouldn't be worth it. I'll have my own place soon anyway."

"Really?" Now I am worried. This new job seems a little too good to be true. "You're making me nervous again," I tell him.

But he just starts chuckling again, and then he turns his attention back to the vacuum, and I join him in hauling it up.

"Listen," he says, "I wanted to get my first tat before this job starts. I was thinking we could get one together. Would you want to?" He flashes me a nervous look, and I can tell it was hard for him to ask. "Like next weekend?"

A tattoo?

The last one I got, he was two, I think. It's not really what I'm into anymore, but I'd definitely do it for him. I'm just grateful he's even asking to do anything with me.

"Yeah." I nod. "Sounds good."

I even know what I want to get, too; the idea pops in my head so fast.

"Come on," he nudges, pulling on the vacuum. "I'll help you with this, and then I'm gonna go meet up with friends, okay?"

"Yeah." I pull on the last of the tube, and the vacuum emerges, draining water.

I have a little errand to run, too, actually.

I don't even think anyone under twenty-one is allowed in this place unless they're an employee, and Jordan better not be. I have a fleeting thought on the way over to call and report Mick Chan for letting a nineteen-year-old in his strip club, but it's not like I didn't take advantage of lenient bar owners when I was nineteen, too. Plus, it would just piss Jordan off more. I can hear her now. *Oh, I'm old enough for you to go down on but not old enough to have a drink?*

Well, yes, legally speaking. If she wants to get technical about it, anyway.

Sliding my keys into my pocket, I head across the parking lot and pull open the door to The Hook. The music bounces off the walls and vibrates under my feet, and I inhale the familiar smell of the orchid-scented shampoo Mick always uses for the carpets. It smells like the flood of perfume you get walking into a high-end casino that's trying to cover up the odor of cigarettes. It's been a long time since I've been in here, but all of a sudden, I'm nineteen again.

I pay the cover and walk in, stopping as I pass the bar and see the sea of people in the place. Young guys, older men, a few women and couples, purple lights under the white stage . . .

Apprehension takes hold. I shouldn't have come here.

I should leave before she sees me. She's an adult, she's taken good care of herself for a long time, and that little voice in my head is right. If I can take her to bed and keep her up half the night going at it, then she's old enough to make her own choices. She should be able to go out with her friends. I *want* her to go out with her friends.

I just don't want her here, because I know Mick wants her, she needs money, and I made her situation in my home feel shaky tonight. She's upset, and what if she starts thinking she needs to move out? What if she has a few drinks and decides she needs to make some extra money?

I run my hand through my hair, feeling the gel I put in it and remembering how I got cleaned up for her. I even changed my clothes.

I glance down at the navy blue suit I bought last year for Cole's graduation, but I left off the tie tonight. Just a white shirt, open at the collar, and some black shoes. I don't know why I put it on, because I'm feeling fucking stupid now, but I think I just want her to know that I'm not an open book. I can be different. I can still surprise her.

I back up to leave, praying she hasn't seen me, but the crowd in the club cheers and bellows, and my attention is drawn to the stage, where a group of girls stand in a line.

They're dressed in everything from jeans to skirts to thongs, looking nervous but giggling and playful. A couple women have already started the contest, and it seems the will to win three hundred dollars now calls for more extreme measures than back in my day. Two women are already wet, some older woman coming by and dumping pitchers of water all over them as they reach inside their drenched shirts and jiggle their breasts and then turn around, straddling the floor as they shake their asses for the roaring crowd. More water gets dumped all over their backs. Heads of wet hair fly, and they may as well be fucking naked. They practically are.

Some of the guys have their camera phones out, and I'm pretty sure that's not allowed, but no one cares. These women are not amateurs, are they? Jordan can't do that shit.

Can she?

Just then, a gang of women pull a young blonde onstage, and I see Jordan resisting them, laughing but shaking her head nervously.

What the . . .

I can't hear her, but I see her lips mouthing "no" over and over again as she digs in her heels and tries to pull her arms away from her sister.

Someone from behind reaches in front of her and unzips her little white sweatshirt, and I launch forward, but then a pitcher of water is dumped all over her chest, and I halt, momentarily frozen.

Her eyes go wide, her mouth falls open, and she looks like she's in shock from the undoubtedly cold water as she just stands there with her hands out in front of her and her sweatshirt now draping down her bare arms.

The ends of her hair are wet, but her long, sexy layers wisp around her face, and water streams down her stomach, making her skin glisten.

Where did she get that lingerie top? It's cream-colored and lacy, thin straps over her shoulders, and damn near see-through. Her dark nipples are visible from here, as are the curves of her breasts as the wet fabric clings to her body.

And my eyes burn as they drift around the room to every guy watching and catcalling her. She should be wearing that in my fucking bed. Not on a goddamn stage. I ball my fists.

She seems to break out of her shock, because she suddenly hugs her arms to her body and darts offstage, leaving her sweatshirt behind. She launches down the steps and runs along the wall, toward the hallway where the bathrooms are. Some girls at a table grab for her, calling her name, and she keeps going and turns her smile back at them, blushing to her friends. Or her sister's friends.

Suddenly, she looks up and locks eyes with me, coming to a halt. The girls at the table see her stop and follow her gaze, glancing between the two of us.

The two vertical dips in her stomach on both sides of her belly button glimmer, covered in drops of water, and the sight of her skin makes my cock fill with blood.

She wore that. She purposely put it on, which means she was considering going up there. I raise my eyes from her body and stare at her, taking a step forward.

Mine.

She backs up a step.

I move again. And so does she.

"It was an accident," she snaps, her eyebrows pinched in a scowl. "She was just playing around. I don't need any crap about something that wasn't my fau—"

I rush up to her and wrap my arm around her waist, taking her face in my hand and pulling her mouth to mine.

She whimpers, surprised, and I don't care who sees us at the moment. Without breaking the kiss, I walk her backward, into the hallway, and around the corner.

She tears her mouth away. "What are you doing?"

But God, I'm so hungry. I dive for her lips again, tasting her tongue and threading my hand through her soft hair.

"No." She pulls away from me.

I drop my arms, my heart pounding and my fingers still buzzing with the feel of her skin.

"I'm not going to fight with you," I tell her, breathing hard, "and I'm not going to ask you to come home. I just want to say I'm sorry."

She lifts her chin, feigning ignorance. "About?"

"The pizza, the movie . . ."

"Forgetting me," she adds.

I approach her, trying to stay calm and keep my hands off her. "I didn't forget you. I can't . . . forget you."

She's quiet, holding my eyes, and I'm not sure what's going on in her head, but I just needed to say it to her face. I don't want her acting out because she thinks I was being careless with her.

Without another word, she twists around and heads down the hallway, pushing through the exit.

"Where are you going?" I follow her.

"My sister has a change of clothes in her car," she answers, still sounding impatient with me. "I'm fine, and I'll be home later, okay?"

She reaches Cam's white Mustang in the crowded parking lot and goes to the driver's side.

"Stop." I come up behind her, putting my hand on the door in front of her. "Just let me explain."

She twirls around, a sympathetic look on her face. "Oh, I'm sure you have an excuse. A really good one. No worries."

She turns back around and reaches for the handle, but I need her to listen. Just for a second.

"Stop. Please." I breathe hard, staring at the back of her head. "Jordan, I . . ."

I swallow, just wanting her to turn around and look at me with her sweet smile and gentle eyes again.

I drop my voice to barely a whisper. "I can't lose him," I tell her.

She stills, and all I can hear is her breathing. Did she have any regrets when she woke up this morning?

She finally turns and looks up at me, nodding calmly. "I know," she says softly. "So you have to lose me. I get it. I don't want to hurt him, either."

She spins around again to open the door, but my head falls forward into her neck, and my eyes close. She's like water slipping through my fingers, and I'm dying here.

"I'm falling for you," I whisper.

Slowly, she turns around again, and I don't know if I should've told her that, but I raise my weary eyes, taking in her quiet expression. Her eyes look equally floored and something caught between desire and the struggle to hold back.

"I knew you were out there somewhere," I tell her, quirking a sad smile. "The girlfriends, women I dated, Cole's mother . . . I never wanted to marry anyone, because they weren't what I was looking for. I had started to think I had my sights set too high and you didn't exist." I clasp the back of her neck and run my thumbs down her throat. "Turns out my dream girl belongs to the one person it would kill me to hurt."

Tears well in her eyes, and I bring her in, my lips meeting her forehead.

"I don't mean to scare you," I go on. "But you kind of scare me, because I want you like I need air, and . . ."

She nods. "And complications," she finishes for me.

Pulling back, she looks away, and neither one of us is sure what to do next. The problem is there to stay.

"I needed time to think tonight," I explain. "I'm sorry I stood you up."

"And what did you figure out?" She drops her eyes, pulling at my fucking heart. "With all your thinking?"

I don't hesitate, because I know I can't stop. "That I can put off feeling guilty until tomorrow."

I snatch up her lips and kiss her hard, feeling her slowly melt into me and pressing her body to mine. Heat floods through me, and I grow hard, moving my hands around her back, gripping her ass and lifting her leg by the back of the knee. I trail kisses over her cheek and down her neck, and she lets her head fall back, giving me free rein as I press her into the car and nibble her throat and collarbone.

"Pike, someone will see us," she pleads.

But I'm so damn hungry for this. The strap of her top falls down her arm, and I pull the cup off her breast and dive down, taking a mouthful of her flesh, nipple and all, in my mouth.

She gasps. "Pike. Oh, God . . ."

She moans as I kiss and suck on her, nibbling on the pebbled skin of her nipple.

"Jesus, we gotta get home," I groan. "Or I'm going to fuck you right here."

"Hey, Pike," someone calls.

I pop up, Jordan yelps, and I wrap my arms around her as she tucks herself into my chest, trying to hide her barely clothed body.

"Shit," I growl and turn my head, seeing Ben Lovell in his police car, idling right next to us. How did we not hear him drive up?

"Ben," I say, breathing hard. "What the hell?"

He's doing a lousy job of hiding his amusement as he answers. "Just doing my rounds, man," he says. "Is that Chip Hadley's girl you got there?"

"None of your business." I shift, trying to make sure Jordan is out of his view.

But he still tries to peer over at her. "You okay, honey?" he asks, still smiling.

She hugs her arms to her body, covering her nakedness as she folds her smile between her teeth. "Um, yes, sir."

He chuckles to himself and shakes his head. "Goddamn," he mumbles under his breath, shifting his car into drive and slowly moving on.

I wait for him to leave the parking lot before I turn to Jordan. "Don't worry. He'll keep quiet."

Lovell isn't a gossip.

She quickly pulls up the strap of her top and crosses her arms over her chest, looking around nervously.

"Come on." I take her hand, leading her to my truck. "Let's go home and go for a swim."

"Naked?" she taunts.

I pull open her door for her, shaking my head. "No," I reply.

"Wear the shells. I've been dying for the chance to peel that suit off you."

She smiles and climbs in the seat, and I walk around the car, opening my door. She takes out her phone, probably texting her sister to let her know she's leaving, and I start the engine, kicking it into gear.

Before we're even out of the parking lot, she crawls up next to me and starts nibbling on my neck.

"Speaking of suits . . ." she says, sliding a hand inside my jacket and caressing my chest. "I could get used to this look on you."

"Don't," I warn. "It's only for special occasions."

"And I'm a special occasion?"

"I think you know you are," I tease. "I don't widen my comfort zone for just anyone."

I flash her a smirk, not the least bit annoyed she's flipped my whole carefully constructed, boring world upside down. I'm doing things I wouldn't normally do just to please her, but she's also making me feel things I haven't felt in a long time. Some of them, never. I actually found myself entertaining a list in my head today of all the things I want to do with her. Take her to baseball games and on road trips, and I actually sifted through fucking eBay today for eighties cassette tapes I thought I could surprise her with, like I'll still be around for the holidays and her birthday next year, for crying out loud.

She makes me excited for everything to come. Whatever that is.

I turn to her, trying to keep one eye on the road and kiss her at the same time, but I just end up laughing.

"Buckle up. You're gonna get me in trouble."

She plops back on her ass and scoots over, pulling on her seat belt.

"Oh," I say, glancing at her, "and I know Mick wants to hire you. You're not working there. You got that?"

She rests her head back on the seat, staring out the windshield. "Oh, are you laying down the law now?"

"I don't like worrying. This gets settled now."

I don't really think she's serious, but I like things carved in stone.

She just shrugs. "My sister makes good money. She's not hurting anyone, and I'm not letting anyone support me." She pauses and then continues. "I guess I'll do what I have to do. I don't really need your permission, you know?"

I dig in my eyebrows, the irritation of this situation crawling up my back.

But then I remember how hard she had to be pulled onstage tonight, obviously deciding that a wet T-shirt contest was not for her, no matter if she had gotten dressed for it or not.

I let out a little snort, remembering the way she protested. "I don't even know what I'm concerned about," I say, my voice thick with humor. "You're a good girl. You don't have what it takes to work there."

"I'm not a girl."

I press my lips together to stop smiling, but it's hard. I know, I know, she's a *woman*.

"And if Dutch or that little prick Jay or any of the guys who work for me come in?" I press. "You gonna be able to wear a bikini behind the bar and serve them drinks, or even worse, take off your clothes and dance for them? Let them use you to get off? Sit in their laps and rub up on them for forty bucks?"

I can't help but laugh under my breath at the ridiculous notion. If she actually thinks about it and mentally puts herself in that situation, she'll know it's absurd.

She turns her head toward me. "Are you laughing at me?"

"I'm saying I know you," I tell her, evening out my tone. "You and I both know you don't have the guts any more than I would, so let's stop wasting time arguing about something that will never happen."

She faces forward and turns silent, but I see her jaw tense as she stares out the windshield. Assuming I know her mind more than she does is probably condescending, but she's acting childish, keeping up this pretense. She has more common sense than that, and I don't like games. She knows she would never be able to deal with those customers, and she definitely can't strip and dance naked. She'd probably be so embarrassed to be stared at, she'd break into tears.

Seven minutes later, though, I pull into the driveway, and she hops out before I've even killed the engine.

"Jordan?" I call, swinging my door open.

What the hell? We're not fighting again, are we?

But she glances over her shoulder as she walks toward the porch. "I'm just gonna get in my swimsuit."

I stand there, twirling the key ring on my finger. Oooookay.

Awareness pricks on the back of my neck, and I turn my head, scanning the neighborhood for Cole's car or his mother's. Then I dart my gaze over the windows of nearby houses for peeled-back curtains or movement.

I'm sure there's talk on the block by now.

People notice things, and Cole is rarely here, while his girlfriend and I are constantly together. It won't take long for people to come to their own conclusions.

By the time I make it into the house, Jordan is nowhere to be seen. Trailing upstairs, I pass her closed bedroom door and head to my room to change into swim shorts. She's still in her room when I come out, and I head back downstairs to grab some water bottles and turn on the backyard lights. The pool lights up, and I turn on the radio affixed underneath the cabinet, some chick singing about "Guys My Age" already playing on the station Jordan has it tuned to.

My phone beeps with an unfamiliar ring, and I walk over to the island and pick it up.

Jordan. Why is she FaceTiming me?

Answering, I see her appear on the screen, but she's looking down at me, like her phone is propped up on something lower than her. Like her desk. Her hair drapes around her, and I can't really see anything else other than the glow of the overhead light.

"What are you doing?" I ask, carrying the phone into the living room.

But she remains silent.

I sit down on the couch, leaning my elbows on my knees and watching her. A small smile plays on her lips, and she moves her head left and then right, and I can tell she's toying with me. She stands up straight, and I lose sight of her face, but her beautiful body comes into view, and I see that she's wearing the shell bikini.

My heart skips a beat, and I have to fight back a smile. Her breasts bulge outside of the little pink fabric, and the thin strings look so delicate on her tan skin. I want to ask her to turn around, but I'd rather just have her down here.

The screen jostles, and I see she's repositioning the phone farther back, and when she comes into view again, I can see part of the desk, her body, and her face now. She leans into the desk, eyeing me with a flirty look, her arms pressing into her body and, coincidentally, her breasts, too.

I quirk a smile. "Yes, Jordan?"

"I'm not a kid," she says, her smile suddenly disappearing.

A feeling of trepidation courses through me, and I knew this was too good to be true. She's teasing me, and she's not coming down now.

I sigh and lie back on the couch. "Then stop acting like one," I reply.

She stares down, pinning me with her defiant eyes. "I'm not a kid," she says again.

And I watch as she reaches one hand behind her neck and the other behind her back and pulls both strings, the pathetic little pieces of fabric falling off her body and to the floor.

I swallow a hard lump at the sight of her. *I was going to do that, dammit.*

Her hard nipples stand out at me, and the skin on my palms buzzes with the memory of her in my hands. My stomach flips, and my cock is swelling with need already.

Please don't do this to me.

But I can't look away.

I can't hear the music in her room, or maybe she's hearing mine in the kitchen, but she starts swaying a little bit and rocking her hips, closing her eyes and running her hands up, down, and all over her body, face and hair. She looks like dessert.

Biting her bottom lip, she plays with me, caressing her tits and slipping her hands down her stomach and playing with the hem of her bottoms, threatening to pull them down.

She taunts me with her eyes and the promise of seeing something good. Like a stripper.

Realization hits, and I finally know what she's doing.

I shake my head, my body on fire for her. "You can't do it," I tease.

She can't take off her clothes and dance.

"You're right," she says, turning around and looking at me over her shoulder. "I can't do it. I'm just a little girl, right? A silly little girl."

She faces me again, giving me a coy smile as she tilts the screen down, and I notice that she's straddling the rounded corner of the desk. Still standing, she places one hand on the desk and the other one up on the wall, I think, with the corner of the wooden desk resting between her legs.

And I watch as she slowly starts humping it. Her hips roll and her stomach fans in and out as her ass moves and grinds over the tabletop, and I can hear the friction of the fabric over her pussy rubbing against the wood.

Oh, Jesus. My chest rises and falls faster as I watch her do the most beautiful thing I think I've ever seen. God, I love watching her. Her tits sway with the movement, bouncing a little when she starts going harder, and my mouth has gone so dry I can't swallow.

"You wanna see me do this?" she teases, her big eyes telling me she knows damn well I like what I'm seeing.

"Stop fucking around and get down here."

She drops her head back instead, running her fingers down her face and body, cupping a breast and squeezing it before trailing the hand down her stomach.

"I told you I had a vibrator," she says, looking at me again. "I don't use it, though." She increases her speed, and I can hear that the grinding has gotten harder. "I like to be in control. I like to work for it, like I'm fucking a real one."

I lick my lips. "Jordan . . ."

"Shhh . . ."

She opens her mouth and moans and then lifts a knee, placing it on the desk to widen her legs. Sweat cools my brow, and I sit up, leaning forward again.

"I like you watching me," she says. "You've always watched me, haven't you? Always wanted to have your fun with me."

I falter, knowing what she says is true. I've wanted her since the first time I saw her.

"It's okay," she whispers. "I always knew, and I always liked it. Keep watching me, Mr. Lawson."

I swallow, my mouth still so dry. "I am," I breathe out.

"Oh, God," she moans.

My eyes burn, and I'm desperate to blink, but I can't take my gaze off her. I can almost feel it. Like the corner of the desk is my fingers she's fucking, and her soft flesh is grinding on my hand. Or my fucking mouth, I don't care. I've never been so jealous of an inanimate object.

"Move the phone to the bed," I tell her. "I want to see you from behind."

She slows her movements, shaking and breathing hard, and I can tell I caught her just as she was chasing her orgasm.

Oh, well, she'll have to work harder to get it back again.

Walking the phone to the bed, she props it up against something and quickly looks back and forth between the screen and the desk to make sure I have her in view, and then walks back to the desk corner.

Running her fingers through her hair, she glances at me over her shoulder, smirking. I tighten my fist, anxious for the feel of that perky ass.

But before she lifts her knee again, she slips her fingers under the hem of her bikini bottoms and slides them down just below her ass. And she leaves them there. Planting her hands on the desktop, she leans over it, lifts her knee, and arches her back for me, jutting out her ass as she starts dry humping the corner of the desk again.

Her behind, her hair falling down her back, her way of moving and taunting . . . I reach down and adjust my cock, now painfully stiff and ready. To have this view of her, I'm dying.

"Mmmm, that's what I like," she pants, meeting my eyes over her shoulder. "Watch me. Watch me fuck for you. I'll do whatever you say. It's all for you."

She goes harder, stronger, and faster, and I'm not sure if I want her pussy in my mouth or around my dick first. I'm taking her from behind tonight. I have to have her like this.

"Jordan . . ." The phone cracks in my hand.

"You like it?" she taunts. "You like when I play with myself for you?"

"Baby." I rise from the couch.

I need her.

"Mmmm, I like you watching," she groans. "Am I being good now?"

I don't take my eyes off her as I climb the stairs.

"I wish there were ten more of you watching me," she says, "wanting me."

If there were any more of me, she'd have a huge problem tonight.

"Pike, I'm so wet. You could slide right into me."

My dick jerks and pulses, and I reach her door and twist the handle.

"You like it?" She pumps faster. "I'm so hot and wet for you."

The door's locked, and I jiggle the handle, dying to get inside.

"Jordan?" I call, my patience nonexistent. "Open the door."

"Oh, Pike. Oh, God."

I look down at the screen again, seeing her hair damn near touching her ass as she throws her head back and fucks the desk. God, her ass . . .

"More, more, more, more . . ." she whimpers. "I'm coming. Oh, God. Yes!"

"Jordan, shit . . ." I yank at the door, ready to knock it down. "Open the door."

Don't come without me.

"Fuck me!" she cries out, moaning and whimpering. "Yes! Yes . . . yes . . . yes."

Her voice gets lower and calmer as she rides it out, coming on the other side of the door and finishing without me.

"Jordan?"

Goddammit, I don't want her satisfied yet.

But the door doesn't open, and when I look at the phone, her movements have slowed, just the barest grinding and little sounds out of her as she finishes herself off. I'm going to bend her over that fucking desk right now.

"Jordan, Jesus, open the door," I growl.

She straightens, putting her foot back on the floor and pulling her bikini bottoms back on. Walking over to the bed, she leans down and meets my eyes, a dreamy look on her face.

"I love seeing you enjoy that," she says, the sweet look of contentment on her face. "I love seeing that I can hold your attention. And not only *can* I do it, Pike, but I think I liked it."

She curls her lips in a little grin.

I jiggle the door handle again. "Jordan, open the door."

She just tsks. "I'd like to, baby, but . . ." She sighs. "The dance is over, and you're not allowed to touch the girls." And then she winks at me. "Night, sugar."

The light on the screen disappears as she ends the call, and the whole hallway suddenly goes dark. I stand there, trying to figure out if she's actually doing what I think she's doing, when the light under the door disappears, as well, and I realize she's shut off her lights.

She's going to bed?

I yank at the door. "Jordan," I bark. "What the fuck?"

I hear a drawer open and slam shut and then the bed creak with weight. After a few moments, there are no sounds, and my worst fears have come true. I have a raging hard-on. What would she do if I broke down the door right now? Shit!

I let my forehead fall into the door, and I'm about to throw up my man card and cry.

"When I get ahold of you, it won't be pretty," I warn her. "That's a promise. You're in for it."

My phone beeps, and I look down, swiping the screen.

Go to bed, the text reads.

My stomach twists, and I'm halfway between going downstairs and blasting music so loud she can't sleep while I work off some steam doing laps in the pool or picking another fight to get her out of bed again.

It's late, though, and if I work out now I'll be up for hours. I have my hand and the Internet, don't I? Although I don't need porn when just the memory of her a bit ago hasn't left long enough to let me get soft yet.

Trailing down to my room, I slam the door shut behind me and crash to the bed, rubbing my aching groin.

Another text beeps in.

And don't jerk off, it says.

I clench my teeth and whip the phone off to the side, hearing it hit the dresser and drop to the floor.

I better wake up and find her on my dick in the morning or no one is safe tomorrow.

21

Jordan

It didn't take as long to fall asleep last night as I thought it would. Moments after I sent my last text, I heard something hit a wall in Pike's room, and I kind of felt a little bad but also smiled, feeling a little powerful, too. Playing games with him wasn't my goal, although I do love that we're good at getting under each other's skin.

I simply wanted to show him I'm capable of more than he thinks I am, and I don't appreciate people telling me what's in my own head.

Then, when he tried to get in the room, I wanted him so badly—his hands, his mouth, his words—but I always forgive too easily, and I don't want to be that girl anymore. Even if Pike is one of the good ones—and I'm pretty sure he is—I needed to prove to myself that I'm worth the work and the wait. It was necessary to raise the bar for myself and not give everyone what they want from me so easily. I've been a pushover long enough. Jay, Cole, my parents . . .

And I fell asleep, proud of being stronger.

Now today, on the other hand . . . He can have me as much as he wants, because I can't wait anymore, either. After telling him to keep his hands off himself last night, I forced myself to do the same today, and the first thing I'm going to do when I see him is pull off his shirt, because I love the way he looks in just jeans.

The weather is warm today, but there's a little cloud cover, keeping the heat at bay, and I lie outside on the grass on my stomach, listening to Don Henley on the cassette player as I flip through the fall catalog of courses at my university. I've already registered for next semester, but I'm thinking of adding another class.

My legs, crossed at the ankles, swing back and forth in the air behind me, but then my phone rings, and I reach over and pick it up off the grass. Looking at the screen, I knit my brow.

What does Dutch want?

I answer and hold it to my ear. "Hey," I say. "Everything okay?"

My suspicious mind is immediately drawn to Pike and some god-awful accident with any one of the machines he works with.

"Uh, yeah, sorry to bother you," he tells me. "Do you know what's wrong with Pike today?"

"What do you mean?"

"Well, he's been in the worst mood," he whines. "Everyone's afraid to go near him. He's barking at everyone, he punched about eighty nails into every single piece of Sheetrock he hung, and then he accidentally accepted the wrong shipment of lumber, which prompted a really interesting tantrum reminiscent of my twelve-year-old daughter. It's been weird."

I snort but then clamp my hand over my mouth to stifle it.

"Um . . ." I search for words, my throat thick with laughter. "No idea, actually."

Actually, I have a very good idea.

"Well, take cover, honey," he says. "He's on his way home, and I don't know what the hell his problem is."

My body shakes with silent laughter, and just then, I see Pike's truck come roaring down the street. Even his engine sounds pissed.

"Okay," I tell Dutch. "Gotta go."

I hang up, not waiting for his goodbye, and watch as Pike

barrels into the driveway, the truck coming to a screeching stop. Glancing at my phone, I see it's only about four in the afternoon. He's way early.

He looks over at me on the grass, and his eyes zone in, anger and intensity pouring through like I'm about to get the big, fat spanking I deserve.

I fix a coy look on my face and arch my back, pushing up my ass, and then slow the swinging of my legs for good measure to draw his attention to my body.

He steps out of the truck and slams the door, and I can't hide my smug smile as he approaches, neither of us able to look away.

"I'm not laughing," he points out sternly. "Now, get inside and take off your clothes. I've had a whole day to dream up the theme park I'm going to make of your body tonight, girl."

A rush of excitement lodges in my lungs, and I can't breathe. I can see all the promises of what's to come in his eyes, and I can't lie or play with him anymore. I want it, too.

Holding his gaze, I stand up, and his eyes rake down my body as I slowly back up toward the house.

And he moves forward, following me.

But then a voice carries over his shoulder, interrupting us. "Pike, hi!" a woman calls.

We both halt, and I see Mrs. Taft, one of the neighbors, standing behind him.

"How have you been?" she asks.

He bares his teeth, closing his eyes, and he looks close to hitting something. My stomach shakes with amusement that I don't let out.

He quickly turns around, affixing a fake smile. "Constance, hi," he says, almost sounding chipper. "I'm good. Just . . . busy."

She nods and peers around his shoulder. "Hey, Jordan."

"Hi, Mrs. Taft."

I walk over to Pike's side, sliding my hands into my pockets.

She smooths a hand down her brown ponytail, holding the leash of the King Charles spaniel she's been walking since I came out to lie on the grass a half hour ago. She looks up at Pike. "Haven't seen your boy around much."

"Oh, yeah. He's . . . um . . . busy, too," Pike stammers, trying to make up some excuse. "What's up?"

"Well, I heard Jordan might do some babysitting." She peers over at me. "Any interest? There's a housewarming party across the river at the Kuhls' place," she tells Pike. "You should come with me. Relax. I just need someone to watch the kids, though."

"Tonight?" he blurts out.

But she doesn't answer him, just glances at me again. "Jordan, how about it? I know you're not fifteen anymore but thought it was worth a shot."

"Yeah, sure—"

"No," Pike cuts me off.

I close my eyes for a moment. *Jesus, Pike.* That was real smooth and totally not obvious.

Constance looks at him, surprised.

"She has class in the morning," he quickly explains.

Yes, I have class on a Sunday.

"And, uh, chores to do around the house," he adds, casting me a stern look, "that she's been *bad* about not taking care of."

Yes, Mrs. Taft. After I do the dishes, I have to do Mr. Lawson, so . . .

"Sorry," he tells her.

She glances between us, and she knows something is up, because he's being fucking weird right now, but she handles it with class.

"Oh, no worries," she chirps. "Maybe another time."

I give her a smile and nod, trying to recover from my embarrassment and thankful when she finally moves along.

Pike and I stand there a moment, and I'm trying to gauge how, if they're not talking about us yet, they will be after that.

"Mr. Lawson . . ." I chide, shaking my head.

I turn and start walking for the house, and when I look back, he's following me, his eyes pinned on mine.

"People are watching," I say. "You better not follow me in. It'll look weird."

I see his eyes shoot left and right, taking in the various neighbors working in their yards, playing with their kids outside, or sitting on their porches. I don't really care, but I know he does.

With his long stride, he's at my back in no time, and I tingle all over as I hurriedly open the door and step inside. His body forces me in, the door closes behind us, shielding us from the outside world, and he spins me around and pulls me into his arms. I have only a moment to take a breath before his mouth is on mine, one of his hands holding the back of my head, and the other arm wrapped around my waist, pressing me to him so tightly that I can hardly breathe.

But God, I don't care. I'm warm and surrounded by his smell, and he feels so far gone that he's carrying me with him. Circling my arms around his neck, I spread my legs as he lifts me up and I lock my ankles behind his back.

"Shit, baby, I'm dirty," he says, still devouring my lips. "I should take a shower."

"We'll take one after," I moan, pulling away only a hair.

He carries me into the kitchen and sets me on the table. I pull his shirt up and over his head, breaking the kiss for only a moment before our arms are around each other again. He leans into me, forcing me back a little as he deepens the kiss.

"I couldn't wait to get home," he whispers. "You don't know how hard I was trying to control myself today."

"How hard?" I work at his belt, frantic to get it off.

"I was in the worst fucking mood," he growled. "I couldn't get you out of my head. All I wanted was this." And his hands scale down my ribs, and he pushes me back and forces my shirt and bra up over my tits. I fall to the table, and he dives down, biting and tonguing my nipples.

I close my eyes and moan, squirming under him and arching my back, not sure if I'm trying to get closer to his mouth or if it's too much to take. I can feel his lips all the way to my toes.

Heat fills my wet pussy, and I watch as his hot tongue flicks over the hardened bud of my nipple, my clit throbbing so hard I can't breathe. I shake, an explosion of pleasure racking me and warming my insides. My eyes roll into the back of my head, and I cry out.

Shit! Shit, shit, shit . . .

I shudder, opening my eyes, a little in shock.

I look down, seeing Pike staring up at me. "Did you just come?" he asks, his eyes rounded in surprise.

I swallow, my mouth suddenly parched, and nod. "Yeah. I think so."

His eyebrows shoot up. "You like your breasts kissed, huh?"

"I like it when you kiss anything on me."

He rises and pulls me up to my feet, holding my eyes as he unbuttons my shorts. "You were so amazing last night."

My eyes light up. "So, I was good, huh?" Maybe I have a performer in me, after all.

But he just cocks a brow. "Don't get any ideas. It won't be like that with anyone else."

My shorts drop to the floor, he whips me around, and I plant my hands on the table to support myself. I hear a wrapper crinkle and then the clank of his belt as he opens his jeans. My thighs shake, so turned on by what's coming. Thank God the blinds are closed.

Arching my back, I open my legs for him and look over my shoulder. "I'm sorry I did that to you last night," I say.

He pulls his cock out of his jeans and rolls the condom on, and then comes in, wrapping a hand around my neck and kissing me hard.

"Well, not really sorry, I guess," I pant against his lips. "This makes it worth it."

Hell yes. He's so hot right now. Well, he always is, but . . .

Pulling down my panties, he grips me where my thigh meets my hip and guides his cock to my entrance. Once it's crowning me, he pulls my hips back to him, and I'm sliced in two, gasping and shuddering as his dick slides deep inside me.

"Oh, my God," I whimper, my head dipping because I'm shaking so hard.

He doesn't give me any time to recover, and all I can do is hang on as he holds me tight in his fists and fucks me. I raise my right knee to the tabletop and lean forward a little more, his cock sliding deeper and making me moan.

He pants hard, grunting in my ear, and his hands are all over the place as he reaches around, one hand squeezing my breast and the other dipping between my legs to rub my clit.

"You can go again later, right?" I ask over my shoulder.

"You're insulting me," he growls in my ear. "You think I can't keep up with you?"

"I just really want to . . ."

"Want to what?"

I open my mouth, whispering against his lips as our bodies meet again and again. "I want to suck you off." I rub my lips over his, taunting him. "I want to feel you in my mouth."

He exhales hard, baring his teeth and closing his eyes. "Jordan . . ." He shakes his head almost as a warning.

I kiss him, our lips hovering over each other as sweat glides down my back. "You want your cock in my mouth?" I whisper.

He bites my bottom lip gently and lets it go. "Say it again."

"I want to suck your dick," I say again.

His cock pounds me like a hammer, and I curl my toes, feeling my orgasm crest.

"I want to lick you," I whisper, "and taste you and make you come."

His fingers dig into my flesh, and the tops of my thighs ache from where they keep hitting the table, but he's making me come again, and nothing in the world has ever felt this good. I'm almost there.

I flick his lip with my tongue, feeling fire spread through my thighs and rock my insides. "Please?" I whisper, backing up into his dick and chasing it, too. "Fuck my mouth tonight?"

"Jordan, Jesus!" he cries out, and he grabs my shoulder at the neck and pounds me so hard, I can't speak even if I want to.

We both come, my knuckles turning white as I dig my nails into the wooden table, tensing, and tightening every damn muscle in my body.

"Pike!" I cry out. "Oh, God."

I lower myself to the table, hugging my arms to myself, closing my eyes, and feeling him pulse inside me. His hand is planted next to my head, and he hovers above, breathing hard and jerking into me a couple more times.

I want him to come inside me. I want him spilling out of me, and I want to feel it. I'm on the pill, and I'm healthy. Once I know he is, I'm telling him the damn rubbers can go in the fucking garbage.

I might taunt him via video again if his pent-up frustration gets me off like that.

A few moments later, my breathing has returned to normal, and I'm spent.

"You know I'm teasing, right?" I tell him. "I'll only ever perform for you."

His hand glides down my damp back, and I hear him inhale like he's about to talk, but then a pound hits the door.

"Jordan!" a voice yells. "Jordan, you here or not?"

We both pop up, my heart skipping a beat. *Cam.*

Pike pulls out of me, and I slide my panties up, hurriedly scrambling for my bra and shirt. I hear the garbage can lid slam closed, and then Pike is by my side as he hurries back into his T-shirt and me into my clothes.

But just then the front door creaks open, and I hear Cam's voice. "Jordan!" she calls into the house.

"What the fuck?" Pike growls under his breath, throwing me a freaked-out look just as Cam wanders into the kitchen.

Pike takes a couple steps away from me, running his hand through his hair as I zip up my shorts.

Cam stares at us, her eyes darting between Pike and me and clearly taking in our disarray.

"Hey," she says, a suspicious tone in her voice.

I lick my dry lips, trying to catch my breath. "Hey," I say back. "So, you're just walking into people's houses now?"

"I was banging on the door and ringing the bell," she points out, her shock gone and now replaced with amusement. "I saw both cars outside, so I knew you were home."

An uncomfortable silence follows as she looks at Pike with a smile in her eyes and at me with raised eyebrows.

Pike looks like he wants to escape. He straightens, jerking his thumb to the backyard. "I'm gonna throw some hot dogs on the grill for dinner."

And he quickly grabs a package out of the fridge and heads into the backyard.

As soon as he's gone, Cam's mouth drops open, her eyes widening on me. "Oh, my God!" she mouths.

"Shhh . . ." I tell her, casting a worried glance in the direction where Pike left.

"Are you serious? How was it?" She comes over to me and swipes her thumb over my damp forehead. "That good, huh?"

I can't help but let out a small laugh, because I don't know what else to do. I can't think straight right now.

I'm sure I'm blushing.

"Aw." She looks at me with love, rubbing my arm. "I'm happy for you. It's mind-blowing, isn't it? Screwing someone who's actually good at it."

Yes. Not that Cole was bad, per se. It's just different with Pike. He's in my head more than anyone's ever been.

"Well, have fun," she tells me, sauntering over to the fridge and removing a soda. "Just don't get knocked up, okay?"

"Why?" I blurt out, but then I realize how that sounded. "I mean, not that I'm planning to. I'm nineteen." I move over to her. "But you didn't say that with any of my other boyfriends. Why Pike?"

"Because you're having fun," she says, closing the refrigerator and turning toward me. "And that might be all he's having, too. Just be careful."

The words kind of stab. Is she right? Is that all we're doing?

"You get to enjoy a stable male who has a job and an active driver's license at the same time," she explains. "And he gets to have a hot young girl in his bed. Enjoy it while it lasts. Until the cows come home." She nudges my chin like I'm five. "Just don't get your hopes up. Stay sharp."

Don't get my hopes up.

But I think they already skyrocketed when I wasn't paying attention.

I smell the grill in the backyard, but I'm not hungry anymore.

22

Jordan

The following Thursday I have my summer class, and Pike lets me use his truck. He's been catching a ride with Dutch to and from work all week so I have a reliable vehicle to get around, and he even mentioned buying another car for himself under the guise that he should have something nicer for "going out," but I know it's just his excuse to get me in something better than the VW.

I refused. He almost has my car running, so I'll make do with however much longer that will last and cross that bridge when I come to it again.

I pull up alongside the curb and park the truck out of the way, seeing Dutch and Pike in the driveway, working on my car. Actually, Pike is working on it, and Dutch is camped out in a nearby lawn chair with a beer in his hand.

I grab my backpack and stroll across the street and up our driveway.

"Hey, guys," I chirp. "How's it going?"

Pike glances over his shoulder at me, his eyes trailing up and down my body. I bite back my smile and so does he as he quickly turns back to work under the hood.

I woke up to his mouth trailing down my stomach at two o'clock this morning, ending between my legs and remaining there until I came twice.

And then we didn't get back to sleep until four. The man has more energy than I can take, and I'm so tired today, but in the best way possible. Every inch of my body is being well used, and it's hard to concentrate on anything else except the need to be with him when I'm not with him. I don't want to fall for him.

I mean, I want to, but not until I know exactly what's happening here. Cam could be right and this is just a fling.

"We're good, honey," Dutch replies, his beer can resting on top of his knee. "Just about got you ready to go here."

I walk past the car and the guys, seeing Pike tightening or untightening something with a wrench.

"Really?" I pinch my eyebrows together. "It's nearly done?"

Pike shoots his eyes up. "Soon."

Well, yay. It'll be nice to not have to bum rides. For a while, at least.

"Thank you," I tell them and then look to Dutch. "What can I do for you? Sandwich? Beer? Free babysitting?"

He just chuckles. "Aw, that's okay. I saw how nice the house looks, so Pike must be working you pretty hard already."

"Oh, you have no idea," I tease. "I'm working up a sweat way past my bedtime lately."

The wrench in Pike's hand falters, and he loses his grip on the bolt, shooting me a look.

I fold my grin between my teeth and turn around, walking up the steps and disappearing into the house.

I carry my bag into the kitchen and set it next to my model on the table, and then I grab a bottle of water out of the refrigerator and head upstairs. Taking a towel out of the hall closet, I walk through Pike's bedroom and into his bath. The main bathroom is finished being retiled, but I still haven't moved my stuff out of this one, and I don't have any plans to.

Closing the door, I strip down to my bra and panties, start the music app on my phone, playing “Hurts So Good,” and wet my toothbrush before swiping some toothpaste on it.

The door opens, and I jerk upright, momentarily startled until I see it’s Pike.

He closes it behind him. “That wasn’t funny,” he says, looking at me sternly.

“I wasn’t trying to make you laugh,” I mumble over the toothbrush.

His lips curl with mild amusement as he comes up behind me, turning me around and pressing me back into the sink. “Trying to shock me out of my comfort zone, then?”

I smile.

“You do that a lot,” he accuses, but I know he’s not angry.

I shrug and turn around, spitting out the toothpaste and rinsing out my mouth.

“I can’t help it,” I say, drying my mouth with the hand towel on the sink and looking at him in the mirror. “I don’t like your comfort zone. It’s too tight in there for the both of us.”

His hands trail around my stomach, and he hugs me to his bare chest as he kisses my neck. “But I like tight places,” he whispers.

I twist around and hold his eyes as I unfasten his belt. “You need a shower,” I tell him. “Is he still here?”

He grabs my hands, stopping me. “Yes, unfortunately . . .”

I walk over to the shower, opening the door and turning on the water.

“You know,” I tell him, “if I’m too much trouble, I can get out of your hair. April called me today. Made me an offer.”

He turns and crosses his arms over his chest, leaning back on the sink. “April?” he repeats. “How did she get your number? And what kind of an offer?”

I unhook my bra, letting it fall to the floor, and push my

underwear down my legs. His eyes scale down me, resting on my breasts—his favorite part—and I go on.

"Her brother owns a house he hasn't had any luck renting out," I explain. "She thought it would be great for me to move in. The rent is cheap in exchange for cleaning up the place. A whole house all to myself."

I step into the shower, but when I try to pull the door closed, Pike is holding it open.

"Well, that was nice of her," he says, not looking at all happy.

He then starts unbuttoning his jeans, suddenly deciding to join me, I guess.

I nod innocently. "Mm-hmm," I say. "She's an angel. So selfless."

"Right." He quirks a brow and steps in, closing the door.

We both know damn well I ruined her night when she was here last, so she can be "helpful" all she wants, but what she's really doing is helping herself by getting me out of her way.

"And what did you say?" he asks, leaning his head back under the spray and wetting his hair.

"I said I'd think about it."

"But you can save more money staying here for a while," he points out. "I think that's best. Don't you?"

I laugh to myself, soaping up my loofah. His motives aren't exactly selfless, either.

"She was concerned I might be uncomfortable," I explain. "Us here alone together . . ."

He pushes me back against the wall, and I suck in a breath, dropping the loofah. His hand dives between my legs, and he lifts up my knee, opening me for him. He softly and slowly rubs my clit in circles, making me pulse and go weak in the knees.

"You uncomfortable?" he asks, his voice low and husky.

"No." My breath shakes. "But maybe you miss having the place to yourself? Maybe she thought I was in your hair."

His heated eyes bore into mine, and he shakes his head slowly. "If you leave, I won't have everything I need in this house."

He increases his speed, hovering his mouth over mine, and then he slips a finger inside me.

I gasp, closing my eyes, and his lips sink into mine, kissing me soft and slow as he enters my body again and again.

His tongue flicks my top lip, and then he whispers, "How can I not want to come home to this every day? So fucking sweet."

He pulls out of me and then slides back in, two fingers this time, slow and gentle, as he pins me to the wall. I let my head fall back, whimpering as he watches my face.

God, he's good. I reach down between us and stroke his cock.

"She's right to watch out for you, Jordan," he says, biting my bottom lip. "You're too young for all the fucking stuff I want to do to you."

"I'm not that young," I taunt. "I'm old enough for lots, in fact."

"Yeah?" He groans, growing big and hard in my hand. "Hold on, baby."

He pulls his fingers out, grabs the backs of my thighs, and lifts me up, pressing me into the wall. His cock is long, hard, and ready, and I feel it teasing my entrance.

Yes.

"Hey, Pike!" Dutch shouts.

We both lift our heads up, Pike drops me to the floor, and he turns his head, looking out the frosted glass.

"I'm in the shower!" he barks, shielding my body from view.

"Yeah, duh," his friend jokes. "Your phone rang a couple times. Looks like Lindsay. I'm gonna set it on the counter here."

Pike presses his body into me, so Dutch only sees one body in here if he looks at the glass. "Yeah, thanks," he says curtly.

I bite my bottom lip, feeling naughty. I lean into him, kissing his jaw and stroking him.

"Jordan . . ." he growls through his teeth.

I laugh quietly.

"Shhh . . ." I hear him chide me.

"I'm gonna turn on the game," Dutch calls out. "I'll wait for you downstairs."

"Okay."

There's a pause and then Dutch speaks up again. "So, uh . . . where did Jordan go? I didn't see her down there."

"How am I supposed to know?" Pike fires back, losing patience. "Would you get out of here?"

"Okay, fine," he says. But then he adds, "Just tell her not to forget to pick up all her clothes off the floor when she gets out of the shower with you, okay?"

My eyes go wide, my mouth falls open, and I bury my face in Pike's body just in time to stifle my laughter. *Oh, shit.*

The bathroom door closes, Pike's head drops to my shoulder, and the heat of the moment has left the building as embarrassment warms my cheeks.

Thanks, Dutch.

I wake up late, being jostled out of my sleep and feeling like I'm about to fall. I open my eyes, seeing that I'm in Pike's arms. He raises me up, one arm under my back and one under my knees.

"What are you doing?" I ask, closing my eyes again and curling into him.

"Sleep with me?" he says.

Sleep with him? Does he even need to ask? A few nights I've fallen asleep with him, but for the most part, I've tried to spend my nights in my own bed in case Cole comes home and starts looking for me. Or worse, comes into his dad's room and finds me there. I want Cole to know—I don't want to hide this from anyone—but we both agreed that he doesn't need to find out like that.

He lays me down in his bed, and I pull the sheet up over my underwear and tank top.

"You want me naked?" I tease.

"No, please don't." He locks his door and then walks around the end of the bed and climbs in the other side. "I actually do need some sleep, and it's going to be tough enough not getting hard right now without you naked, too."

He lifts up his arm, signaling me to come in, and I curl up next to him, resting my head on his shoulder.

A wave of peace settles over me. This feels so good.

I run my fingers down his chest and stomach and then circle my arm around him, looking up at him in the dark.

He and I are at two completely different places in our lives. He asked me once what I see in him. I could ask him the same thing.

"What are you staring at?" he asks.

I tip my head back down, rubbing my lips over his skin and thinking. "I envy you."

"Why?"

I shrug. "You just have yourself figured out, and I don't," I tell him. "I worry about everything. Will I make it through school? Will I be who I want to be? Will I have friends and contribute to the world or just wind up doing work I hate like my sister and my father and everyone else I know?" I glance back up at him. "Everyone except you, that is. You give the impression that you're right where you want to be with yourself, and you don't regret anything. I regret everything."

I breathe out a little laugh. "Well, not everything," I correct myself. "I feel stupid a lot, though. About words I speak as soon as they come out of my mouth. Things I do. Decisions I make. I'm always second-guessing myself. Like maybe I'd just be happier if I stayed quiet and kept my damn mouth shut and my head down."

His arm tightens around me. "Happier or safer?"

Aren't they the same?

But no, I know what he's saying. *A ship at harbor is safe, but that's not what ships are for.*

"I think you're scared, because people have worked hard to make you think you're not worthy of their attention, Jordan," he says. "Your parents, that ex of yours from high school . . . even Cole. You gave people a chance, and they abused it. That's their fault, not yours." He tips my chin up so my eyes meet his. "Don't think it has anything to do with who you are. And don't let anyone make you afraid of yourself. You're incredible."

My smile peeks out, and even though a thousand doubts about where he and I are headed run through my head, I'm taking tonight for tonight. I needed to hear that. The only other person who talks me up like this is my sister.

But Pike is better, because I can kiss him, too.

"And I became who I am because I had no choice," he points out. "If things had been different, I would've liked to go to college. Travel. Maybe wear a suit to work." His body goes rigid. "I envy *you*. You're still growing, and you can still be anyone you want. You have all the choices in the world ahead of you."

I hadn't thought about that. How different his life would be if Cole had never come along.

"The memory of you in that suit," I muse. "You should take me on a date in it. You've never seen me in a dress."

He's silent, his thumb rubbing up and down my arm, and I know what he's not saying. He can't take me out unless we go somewhere out of town.

I take a deep breath, pushing the concern to the back of my mind.

"When I first saw you, I felt like I'd been punched," he whispers. "You have a body that makes me feel like I'm on a roller coaster when I touch it."

I smile and slide off my panties before swinging a leg over him, straddling him and sitting up.

He exhales, gripping my hips. "But really, it wasn't until the buildup of every little thing you do—bringing me lunch, serving me my own ass in that supply room at the bar both times, and even telling me to get that backsplash and making me laugh with your innuendo about how I'm like a cave." He laughs. "You make my heart pound so hard it hurts, Jordan. You, your mouth, and who you are, it all makes me want to touch you. It makes me not want to stop this."

He meets my eyes and tucks my hair behind my left ear. "Do you regret me?" he asks.

I shake my head.

"It's okay," he prompts. "You can be honest, even if it's just a small part of you. I'll understand."

I lean down, planting a hand next to his head. "I regret the way I couldn't stop staring at you the day I moved in when you carried some of my boxes into the house," I tell him. "How I love the way you don't say much and how you like to watch movies with me. I regret the way my stomach flips when I hear you moving around in your room in the morning, and I know I'm going to see you soon." I rub my hand up his chest and over his neck. "And I regret that I look for you when I come into a room and how, after you leave for work in the morning, I have to get myself off in the shower again, because I can't stop fantasizing about you and it gets me too turned on to wait for you to come home."

His abs flex as he arches up a little, pressing his cock against me.

"And I regret that I would do nothing different," I go on. "I couldn't not feel this."

I swing my leg back over, turn around, and climb on top of him again, this time reverse cowgirl. I lift my T-shirt over my head, letting my hair fall down my naked back, and cast my gaze over my shoulder, flirting with him.

His cock swells underneath me, and I start rolling my hips, grinding.

"You're trying to kill me," he groans.

I run my fingers through my hair, feeling his hands run all over my body and reach up to cup my breasts.

"How many women have you slept with?" I ask him.

"How many men have you slept with?" he shoots back. "No, never mind, don't answer that."

I grin, answering him anyway. "Before you? Two."

"More than two," he retorts with his answer.

"Is there anything I'm not doing that you want to do?" I keep rolling on him, his eyes frozen on my ass as it moves.

"Why are you asking that?"

"I just wonder how I measure up to a man with a lot more experience," I explain.

He meets my eyes. "First of all, it's not *a lot* more experience. And second of all, there are lots of things we haven't done yet, which I have every intention of doing with you once we can calm down and stop ripping off each other's clothes the second I step into the damn house after work every day," he growls jokingly.

I lay back on him, my head next to his and one of his hands reaching down between my thighs.

"Stop feeling so good, and I'll control myself," I say.

He kisses me and then holds my eyes, something serious in his. "Don't think about the other women," he tells me. "I don't."

My chest caves as I stare at him, and I'm filled with things I can't say. *I . . .*

I open my mouth. *I . . .*

I kiss him, feeling the stubble around his mouth, his smell feeling like home. *I can't love you. I don't love you, do I?* It's an impulse. That's what he'll say. He'll say I'm a kid. He'll say it's not real.

I love you.

"Jordan, God," he gasps, kissing me deeper. "What are you doing to me?"

The same thing you're doing to me.

His phone starts ringing, and we try to hold on to the kiss and ignore it, but reluctantly, he finally sighs and pulls away.

Picking up the phone, he looks at the screen.

"Shit," he hisses.

I kiss his cheek and nibble at his jaw.

"Baby, just a minute." He sits up, and I scoot off him, letting him take the call.

He swings his legs over the side of the bed and answers the phone. I pull the sheet up, covering myself.

"Hey," I hear him say.

I hear a loud male voice on the other end, and I think it's Cole.

"Yeah," Pike answers, straightening his back and running his hand through his hair. "Yeah, sorry, I've been swamped. Didn't realize it was urgent."

Cole talks again, and I don't think Pike is breathing.

"Cole, I—"

Cole cuts him off and Pike is still as he listens.

"No, I don't think that's a good—"

He's cut off again as Cole speaks.

After a moment, I see him heave a breath and nod. "Yeah," he says. "Okay . . . yeah. Fine. See you tomorrow."

He hangs up the phone and tosses it on the bed, falling onto his back and rubbing his hands up and down his face.

"What's wrong?" I ask.

"You mean more than being on the phone with my son while his ex-girlfriend is naked in bed next to me?"

I frown.

He tips his head back and eyes me. "We've got a bigger problem than that, actually. Brace yourself."

23

Pike

I put sheets and blankets on the couch," I say, walking into the kitchen. "Fridge is full. Make yourself at home."

Cole and his mother follow me in, the front door closing and anything but hospitality pouring out of my voice. Cole is more than welcome, but I'd love to put her in a hotel if I could.

He's giving me a guilt trip, though.

"I'm not sleeping on the couch," Lindsay informs me, plopping her purse on my counter. "I need privacy. I'm a grown woman."

Jordan trails in behind them quietly, crossing her arms and leaning against the doorframe. Her eyes are downcast, and I don't think she's looked at me since last night when Cole called. I had to work today, and she took the day shift at the bar, and between her moving all of her toiletries back into her own bathroom and being holed up in her room doing who knows what tonight and me putting the finishing touches on her car, we haven't said much. I guess I don't know what to say any more than she does.

I look at Lindsay, her thick red lipstick matching the red lace bra peeking out of her black silk top, and for about five minutes twenty years ago I thought she was hot and confident. Now, it's not attractive at all, because I know what's inside.

Hopefully, I only have to put up with her for a night or two. Cole moved back with her the past couple days, but they're replacing the storm windows in her apartment, so they needed somewhere to stay while the workers finish.

"You can have all the privacy you want at a hotel," I remind her. "I offered to pay."

"Dad, come on," Cole mumbles, walking to the fridge for a soda.

He glances at Jordan, but she's not meeting anyone's eyes.

The room turns silent, and it's so uncomfortable.

I clear my throat. "Well, unless you want to share a room with Cole," I tell Lindsay, "there's nowhere else, except the basement."

"What about the spare room?" she shoots back.

"That's Jordan's room."

"Jordan shouldn't even be living here," she says, almost a hiss. And then she turns to Jordan. "Can you please share a room with my son for a couple nights, so I can have the spare room?"

"It's not a spare room anymore," I bite out, my heart suddenly thumping. "It's her room."

There's no fucking way . . .

"This is ridiculous." Lindsay glares at me. "I'm the mother of your son, and I need a room." She glances at Jordan again. "You've spent plenty of time in a bed with Cole. Another night or two won't kill you, right?"

I move forward, planting my hands on the island. "She's not sleeping with Cole. They're not together anymore. It's unfair."

"It's a bed," Cole finally speaks up, sighing. "It's just sleeping. We can handle it."

I look to Jordan, waiting for her to put up some kind of fight and help me out here, but all she does is raise her eyes, meeting mine and saying nothing. Like I'm the one letting this happen, and she's waiting for me to do something.

If she's not going to back me up, then I look stupid, fighting for her honor. She's a big girl. They won't understand why I'm the only one protesting.

And I'm scared now.

I want her and Cole to reconcile and be friends again eventually, but I don't want them together, alone, all night. They were a couple, dammit. He knows her body as well as I do. What if they start feeling what they felt when they first got together and everything was good? What if she starts thinking she needs someone . . . younger? They have history.

I'm not going to be jealous of my son. We're not competing. But he's known her a hell of a lot longer. What if they talk and reconnect?

It's on the tip of my tongue to just blurt it out. *She's mine, and she's not sharing a bed with another man.*

But I look at Lindsay and the train wreck she's been, and how, in the last six years, he has repeatedly taken her side. She always played the victim and guilted him into standing up for her, and he will stand with her again, because he knows I can stand on my own. It would make her year to find out I was screwing Jordan behind his back. She's just looking for something to hate, and I'm not putting Jordan in the middle of that.

I drop my eyes, barely able to unclench my jaw. "Jordan, there's blankets on the couch," I say quietly. "Let me know if you get cold."

I start to walk out of the room, but then I hear Jordan finally speak up. "No, Cole's right," she replies. "It's a bed, it's sleeping, and it's only for a night or two. I'm cool with it."

I stop and look over at her, but she's just focused ahead, calm as can be. I squeeze my right fist and stalk out of the room, heading upstairs. It's barely seven and a Friday night, but if I don't get space, I'll do something stupid.

Like pick the fight I so desperately want with her right now in front of everyone.

Sometime after midnight I fall asleep. I was on the verge of giving us away half a dozen times tonight, but the risk of regretting coming clean was too great. Not now. Not in front of my ex.

This is a fling. A dirty, sordid fling, right? At least that's what everyone will think.

And it would break Cole's heart. I'm sure he expects her to move at some point. He hasn't been too concerned with her since he left, after all.

But knowing I swept in, played with one of his toys, and knowing there's a chance I might make her happier . . . Yeah, speaking from experience, there's always a part of you that feels you have more of a right to a former girlfriend than anyone else, even after the breakup. He'll see this as a betrayal. As me taking her side and trying to do better where he couldn't.

And he'd be right. Every feeling he'd have I would understand.

I'll come clean. Eventually. She'll realize I'm too old—too settled—and she'll want more. It won't last.

Knowing that, though, doesn't stop me from wanting her. From missing her and needing her.

The bed dips behind me, and I blink my eyes open, realizing someone else is in the room. It takes me a moment to register, but then relief floods me, and I reach my hand back, pulling her into me.

Jordan.

But then I furrow my brow, my heart jackhammering as Victoria's Secret's Heavenly wafts through my nostrils, and I feel a leg that doesn't have the same curves and tone I've grown to crave every day.

Popping up, I turn my head and see a familiar outline at my side but not the one I want. "What the hell?"

I whip off the covers and turn on the lamp, sitting up and staring at Lindsay. She's wearing a red silk nightie.

What the hell does she think she's doing?

"Are you serious?" She pins me with a surprised look like that wasn't the reaction she was expecting. "Don't pretend like you don't remember the drill, Pike. When a sure thing shows up half-naked and horny in your bed, you don't turn them down."

She leans in, pressing her body into mine and going for my neck with her mouth.

"Stop." I rise from the bed and grab my jeans from the chair, sliding them on. "I'm not that fucking desperate."

"It doesn't have to be that way, Pike." She sighs, scooting closer onto her knees and tucking her dark hair behind her ear. "I was young. I was stupid. And I was selfish," she pleads. "I didn't see what a good man you are. How lucky I was to have someone ambitious and responsible and steady. I want you." She cocks her head, playing me with her eyes. "It wasn't all bad. You remember that, right? You remember how hot we were."

I reach into the drawer of my nightstand, seeing the new box of condoms I had to buy because Jordan and I went through the last one faster than I expected. I quickly grab a cigar out of the box and my lighter and slam the drawer shut so Lindsay doesn't see it and start being nosy.

"I didn't have much of a frame of reference back then," I spit out. "I do now."

"You're lonely," she states. "I want to try again. For Cole's sake. You know how much he would love to see us together? He was too young to remember."

I let out a bitter laugh. *And thank goodness for that.* Coming home from a double shift and shelling out sixty bucks to a babysitter before spending the rest of the night catching an hour's sleep where I could between Cole waking up for feedings while she was out partying.

"Aren't you tired of going out alone?" She climbs off the bed and steps up to me. "Seeing all our friends with their families and homes and vacations? We can be that. I've grown up. I could be here for you, taking care of you, and taking care of this house."

This house. She means *our house.* She wants to live here.

The idea of her in my house, walking around like it's hers, makes me sick. This isn't her house. It'll never be hers. *It's* . . .

I stop myself, not needing to put the thought into words. There's only one woman I see living in this house.

I walk for the door. "And, let me guess . . . in exchange, I'd financially support you in this arrangement, right?"

"I could make you happy," she tells me. "I have before."

I drop my eyes, barely even needing to ponder that statement. A month ago, I might've agreed with her. Once upon a time, for a very short spell, we were happy. Days here, hours there.

But now I know, it didn't even come close. She doesn't even compare to what I've had the past few weeks.

"Go back to your room." I walk out, leaving the door open and then adding over my shoulder. "Jordan's room, I mean."

I charge down the hallway, slowing when I pass Cole's door and so fucking tempted to push it open. That's mine in there. What kind of a man puts his woman in that situation? What kind of a man doesn't fucking own up and take what's his?

I need to think. I jog down the stairs and make my way through the kitchen and then the laundry room, every moment I wait bringing me closer and closer to not being able to take this. I know she won't let anything happen, but I need her out of there.

But as soon as I step outside, I see that the problem is already solved. For the moment, anyway. She sits on the edge of the pool, her legs dangling in the water, and glances over at me as I step outside.

I pause momentarily, her blue eyes cold and distant. Awareness pricks at my back, knowing Lindsay's room—Jordan's room—faces the backyard, and she could possibly be watching.

Casually, I walk to the lawn table, light my cigar, and set the lighter down, puffing and inhaling until the end burns bright orange. The sweet scent fills my nose, and I blow out smoke, immediately feeling a tingle in my head. I walk over to the side of the pool opposite her and look down at her, seeing she's dressed in some sleep shorts and a black tank with no bra on.

The hard points of her nipples are visible from here.

I tense my jaw. "You're sleeping in that?" I mumble, barely moving my lips and keeping my voice as low as possible.

"He's seen me in less."

I pinch the cigar and flick the end with my middle finger. "And?"

"And what?"

I arch an eyebrow. "Did he touch you?"

I hear her breathe out a laugh. "Maybe." And then she thins her eyes on me. "And maybe I let him. He's a chip off the old block, after all."

My jaw aches, and she shakes her head, turning away from me.

I know she's angry. I know why she's angry. And I know we all do stupid things when we're angry. She's pushing me away, and I just need time to think. Just some time.

"Don't do this," I tell her.

"Then don't ask me stupid questions."

Her chest rises and falls with shallow breaths, and she looks miserable. I don't know what to do.

"This is killing me," I whisper, shooting my eyes to her window to make sure Lindsay isn't watching. "Fucking killing me, knowing you are in his bed."

"Then you should've told them the truth," she fires back. "That she could use my room all she wants, because I sleep in your bed now."

She pushes herself to her feet, dusting off her ass, and I can't look at her in the eye anymore. *She sleeps in my bed now.* Yes, she does.

And I want her there more than anything right now.

"If you want me, we're going to have to face him sooner or later," she says. "You can't keep me cooped up here, Pike. I want to do things with you, go out with you, go to dinner, kiss you, and not have to worry about being behind closed doors when I do it."

I'm quiet for a moment, and she doesn't wait for me to find my tongue. She stalks off toward the house, and I frantically glance up at her window again before shooting off to go get her. Grabbing her hand, I pull her around the corner of the house and back her up against the wall.

"We can't," I plead, staring down at her. "Not yet. What we're doing isn't right. Everyone will talk. Cole won't understand."

Her eyes glisten with tears as she stares up at me, but her jaw tenses with anger.

I back up a step, running my hand through my hair. "What if this ends in two weeks, and I've destroyed what relationship I do have with my kid, because I couldn't keep my dick in my pants?" I tell her. "I should've just kept my hands off you! Why couldn't I resist? Huh?"

It's a rhetorical question, but it's the truth. I should've kept my hands off. Who the hell knows how Cole will take this? How much deeper could Lindsay sink her claws into him over this? Everything I've done in my life was for him. I didn't go to college because she wouldn't work and we needed money. I worked my ass off so I could afford everything he would need. He's finally coming around, and this could ruin everything.

She's quiet for a while, and I hate it. I want to know what she's thinking, and when she's angry, at least I know she wants to fight. Right now, her breathing is slow and steady, and she just stares at me, too calm.

She nods to herself. "It's not worth it," she deciphers. And then she starts to walk away. "I know you're right."

"Jordan . . ."

"No, it's okay." She stops. "I get it. I knew my sister was right. This was never going to happen."

That's not . . .

But it is what I meant, isn't it? If I can't tell him now, was I ever planning to? When would it be easier? After they've been broken up a couple years?

When I don't respond, she glances at me. "I'll see you in the morning."

She walks for the back door, and I feel like I've been kicked. I feel like I'm never going to see her again.

I race after her, catching her hand and stopping her. "Don't," I beg. "Jesus, I didn't mean that. Jordan, I . . . you are worth it. I just . . ." I shake my head. "I don't know."

"It's okay," she says, sounding so calm I'm scared. "It really is. I should thank you, actually. I've been trying for years, it seems, to be the kind of woman I admire, and all of a sudden I feel like I am that woman now. I know I'm worth it. You're just not."

She moves to walk away, and I stop her again. "Jordan."

This time she whips around, holding her head high and yanking her hand out of my grasp. "Tell him now, then," she demands.

The air rushes from my lungs with the ultimatum.

"Tell him with me now," she says, "so I can go get in our bed, and we can go to sleep, and tomorrow we can start to move forward, because it will all be done, and we won't have to worry about it anymore." Her eyes challenge me. "Tell him now."

I open my mouth to speak. To tell her I will. I'll march up right now and tell my son the truth. That I think I love her, and I'm sorry, and I didn't mean to hurt him.

But I know I'm right. She'll be back to school full time in two months, meeting guys who are educated and have their whole lives in front of them. I'm not upsetting my family when I don't know what this is yet. She has no right to ask that of me.

She starts to back away, the blue in her eyes like ice.

"It's so incredible how fast it can happen, isn't it?" she says as she slowly leaves me. "How I feel absolutely nothing for you now."

24

Jordan

"You don't look so good, sugar."

I look up from the cooler where I'm loading beer bottles from a case and give Grady a weak smile. "Nothing a box of Thin Mints won't fix," I tell him.

Or a vat of ice cream or Pike walking in here right now, taking me in his arms in front of everyone, and telling me he loves me.

God, I'm so tired. And weary. I couldn't stand to look at him last night, and I wanted nothing more than to be away from him and out of his life.

I took my newly repaired VW and crashed at my sister's, and then I came to work at ten to get ready for the lunch shift, and I've been here for twelve hours now, staying long after the schedule dictated.

My anger and resolve are still there, but so is the sadness now. I miss him.

But I hate myself more.

I love him and want him, but . . .

I can't be around him.

He makes me laugh, and when I'm with him, I'm home. Like he's the only thing in my life I understand.

But I don't understand myself anymore. Someone has to fight for me for a change.

I'm not going back.

"You clocked out without closing the tab before you left last time," Grady says, pulling cash out of his wallet. "Here's your tip."

He slides a couple twenties across the bar, and I close the cooler and laugh under my breath, my eyes feeling heavy with fatigue.

"Grady, it didn't even occur to me," I tell him. "Don't worry about stuff like that. I'm just happy you're here."

Which is the truth. He saves me from having to force conversation with anyone else while I'm working. He doesn't flirt or make crude comments, and he likes my music on the jukebox.

I leave the money and clear off his empty bottle, popping the top of a new one and setting it in front of him.

"Hey, can I have two Buds?" someone calls, holding out money at the bar.

I head over, hearing the phone ring and seeing Shel grab it.

Opening the cooler, I pull out the two Buds.

"Jordan?" Shel repeats into the phone.

I glance over at her, setting the two beers down in front of the guy.

"Who's calling?" she asks.

I keep my eyes on her, my breathing going shallow as I take the guy's money and ring up his drinks.

"Pike?" she says.

She casts me a look, and I shake my head. It's late, I've been gone since last night, and I'm actually surprised he hasn't come looking for me, making his pushy demands as usual.

"Yeah, she's not here," Shel lies. "Her shift ended. Try her cell phone."

She hangs up, probably not waiting for him to say anything else and definitely not knowing that Pike has already called my cell a few times today. He didn't leave messages, though, and he hasn't texted.

She approaches me. "What is going on?"

"Nothing."

She cocks her head, not believing me. "You look exhausted." She gently pushes my hair behind my ear as I wipe down the bar. "Have you eaten anything today?"

"I'm fine," I tell her. "Just tired."

"Is Cole causing you more problems?"

I sigh, feeling my stomach grow shaky. I want to talk to someone, but I'm sick of being the girl with guy problems. I'm tired of Shel worrying about me, and I don't want her to know. She already thinks Pike is an ass, and for some reason, I hate that. I don't want to give her more ammo.

"Why is his father calling you?" she presses me.

I avoid her gaze, drop the dishcloth in the bucket of hot water, and grab a fresh one, wiping off the same liquor bottles I already did this afternoon.

I feel her eyes on me. "Jordan, what have you gotten yourself into?"

My chin trembles, and tears sting the backs of my eyes. "Nothing," I say, still not looking at her. "I'll be okay."

A server comes out of the kitchen with food, and I step around one of the other bartenders coming back with a new bottle of Captain from the liquor closet. I think for a moment, trying to figure out what I can do next, and finally bend over to retrieve a package of napkins from a cabinet. Tearing it open, I start to refill one of the containers on the bar.

"Go home," Shel says, putting her hand over the container. "Get some sleep."

"I'm fine. I'd rather be here."

"If you don't go home, then go to your sister's," she suggests.

"Just please get some rest. You work any more hours today, you're not going to be able to drive yourself home at all tonight. I'll see you tomorrow."

I open my mouth to argue, but she just shakes her head at me, knowing what I'm about to say.

"I'm not your mom," she points out, "but I'm as good as. You need sleep. Get some food from the kitchen and go. Please."

I do as Shel says, make myself a sandwich I don't feel like eating, and climb into my car, turning on the engine. An Alice Cooper song is playing on the eighties station I'm tuned to, but I turn it off, not in the mood at all for the escape I usually crave.

Home. It takes me a good twenty minutes of driving aimlessly around town, lost in my head, before I commit to whose home I'm going to. I need clothes and my schoolbooks, and even though I don't want to see Pike, Cole, or his mother, I can't use my sister's makeup for another day. Everything has glitter in it.

As I pull onto Windy Park Place, I take in the stream of cars and trucks lining both sides of the street, as well as Pike's full driveway. Some vehicles I recognize, some I don't, but I slide into a slot between two cars in front of Cramer's house, spotting the lights coming from over Pike's fence in his backyard.

Cole must be having a party. *Super.*

Leaving my purse in the car, I take my keys, lock it, and walk toward the house, wanting to be anywhere but here, but knowing I need to do this. My skin buzzes with awareness, and the hair on my arms rises as the music floods my ears. But I charge up the porch steps, still dressed in my backless blouse from work. I tighten my high ponytail and just hope with all the people here, Pike and Cole don't notice me come and go.

I enter the house and look around, seeing the back door bob closed as someone walks out, and then I hear the bathroom door close in the laundry room. The light under the door to the basement is on, and the chatter outside is almost as loud as the music. At least Cole is keeping people out of the house, for the most part. Pike is most likely not sleeping through this.

Gently stepping up the stairs, I walk quietly down the hallway, seeing Pike's bedroom door closed and the light off inside. Cole's door is also closed, and I open mine, peeking inside and seeing it empty. My bed is unmade from Cole's mother sleeping in it last night, and I look around, using the light streaming in from outside to see. None of Lindsay's things are in here, so maybe her apartment is done, then. Leaving the light off, I grab my leather book bag and stuff in books and notebooks from my desk and start loading a duffel bag with clothes and anything else I'll immediately need.

"Thought I heard someone come in," a voice behind me says.

My heart stops, and I hesitate, instantly recognizing the voice. I close my eyes, willing him to go away.

Cole wouldn't have invited him. He must be crashing the party.

Scissors sit on my desk in front of me, and I eye them, instinct kicking in.

"Cole broke up with Elena," Jay tells me. "You gonna take him back?"

Broke up? Were they really together? I look down at my thumb, seeing the small scar in the darkness and barely feeling anything anymore. How he could always tug at my heart, but now, it seems like ages ago that Cole gave a damn about me. I can't even muster an ounce of longing tonight for the connection we once had.

Survival mode has kicked in. My brain is in control now, and it won't give me the keys to my heart until it's sure it can take it.

"You want a little revenge first?" Jay taunts, and I can hear his voice growing closer. "Come on, Jordan. I'll give you a good fuck right now, right here."

"As opposed to the terrible lay you always were?" I retort.

He says nothing, but I can just imagine the little snarl playing on his lips and the tingle he's feeling in his hands that's begging him to make me pay for that remark.

Taking the scissors in my hand, I turn and twist them around in my fingers, playing with them as I look at him.

He stands just inside my doorway, dressed in his jeans and T-shirt with his cold eyes glaring at me under dark brows.

"What you must have told yourself to convince that pea brain inside your head that you made me come so good," I say coolly. "The three times we did it were so bad, I would lay there confused, and then amused, before finally breaking into tears that there was nothing about you that wasn't absolutely pathetic."

His top lip twitches, and right now, he's gauging how likely he is to get away with what he wants to do to me with a backyard full of witnesses right outside my window.

"Now I'm simply terrified for every woman I see you with," I continue, "but also secretly smiling, because I know after they fake how much they love your cock in bed, they're in the bathroom, fingering themselves to a mental image of any guy in town who's not you."

He lurches forward a step, and I straighten, dropping my hands and squeezing my fist around the scissors. His eyes flash to the tool, and he stops.

"Get out of my room," I tell him, my tone calm and even, "and don't ever speak to me again."

He hesitates a moment.

"Now," I state.

His chest caves with heavy breaths, and I can hear the anger fuming inside of him.

He wants to rush me so badly.

But I'm not even scared. I feel nothing.

It takes his pride a moment to realize he won't get far if I decide to scream, but after a moment, he backs away and finally turns, disappearing down the hallway. His footfalls hit the stairs, and I wait to hear the back door slam closed before I risk moving again.

He may not stay out of my way for good, but he has a track record of deciding I'm worth minimal effort before he moves on to someone else. Let's hope he keeps doing that.

I finish packing my clothes and slip into the bathroom, collecting my toothbrush, razor, and shampoo, stuffing everything into my bag and zipping it up. Swinging both bags onto my shoulder, I leave the room, resisting the urge to look back, and head down the stairs and into the living room.

Pike stands just inside the front door, though, and I stop, both of our gazes locked on each other.

Shit. I was almost out of here.

"I was out looking for you," he says. "Just wanted to make sure you were okay."

His gaze drops to my bags, and his fist curls around his keys. His voice drops to a whisper. "Don't. Please."

"Don't what?" I step forward. "Don't leave or don't tell Cole?"

The party rages outside, and we stand in the darkened room, locked in a no-win battle. It's simply a question of who gets hurt, and it's a choice he still thinks he can get out of making.

He wants me, but he's a coward.

"This had to end, right?" he chokes out, speaking only loud enough for me to hear. "In ten years, I'll be nearly fucking fifty. I'm not going to saddle you with that. This was going to end. You know it always was."

I do now. My eyes burn, tears welling, but it's strange. I'm not sure I'm sad. What he says is almost a comfort, because I know this story. I'm used to it.

I walk for the door.

"I'm not ready to let you go," he tells me, stepping in front of me. "Just not yet. I'm not done . . ." He searches for the words. "Talking to you and . . . loving you." He takes my shoulders, moving us behind the front door, my back against the closet. "Let's go somewhere. Just us. There's a midnight showing tonight. Let's go. Get out of here and away for a couple hours, and we'll talk."

I peer up at him. "Somewhere dark, right?"

In a theater where we won't be seen?

He looks at me like that's exactly what he was thinking, and he's sorry for that, but it's the way it is. "We'll figure it out." He plants his hands on both sides of my head on the door behind me and leans in. "Just not yet. Don't leave yet."

The numbness I've been feeling since last night wavers, and I hear him in my head. *I'm not going anywhere. I'm not going anywhere. . . .*

I have no doubt that's true. And will always be true. Pike doesn't walk away from his responsibilities. He'll always look out for me.

And I can't think of anything I'd rather be less to him than an obligation. I can't be like Cole or his job, his house or his bills. I'm not a duty.

I'm everything else.

"Do you love me?" I ask. "Are you in love with me?"

He holds my eyes, and even in the dark, I can see his eyes are red, tired, and hurting. But when he opens his mouth, no words come out.

I shake my head. "It doesn't matter, I guess." I give up. "You have no courage, so you won't be forever." I stand up straight, tightening my hand around the straps of my bags. "And in the end, you'll wind up being nothing more than a waste of my time."

His face falls, and he looks so completely deflated. He doesn't have the conviction to do anything. All he knows is he doesn't want me to go.

"Oh, this is too good," someone says. "So that's your kink, huh, Jordan?"

Pike and I jerk our heads to see Jay has just come out of the kitchen and stepped into the living room. Pike drops his hands and stands up straight, fixing Jay with a hard look.

"Come on, baby," Jay taunts me, and I can smell the beer on his breath from here. "I'll be your daddy and you can open your legs for me, too, for a little rent money."

Pike lunges for him, and I gasp. He grabs Jay by the collar and whips him around, sending him flying through the storm door. Jay barely even flinches, probably because he knew what he was doing.

My heart stops, seeing him stumble onto the porch and Pike charge after him.

They both barrel down the stairs, a few people scattered around the lawn as they leave the party from the back gate or come in from their cars.

Jay shoves Pike away, but Pike grabs his arm, throws his fist back, and comes down like a hammer, pounding Jay in the face and sending him collapsing to the ground. I walk onto the porch, seeing the bystanders stop and watch, while others call out.

"What the hell's going on?" I hear Cole's voice.

Glancing over, I spot him coming out from the side of the house. I step up to the railing and watch Pike, pulling Jay up off the ground and throwing him into a car.

"Dad!" Cole shouts, rushing up.

But no one else seems to notice him.

"Don't worry." Jay laughs at Pike, blood trickling off his lip. "We can share the little whore."

Cole turns to me. "Did Jay hurt you?"

I guess it wasn't hard for him to figure out who the "whore" he was referring to was. I say nothing.

Jay turns his gaze on me, shouting, "Why don't you tell Cole how cozy you and his dad have been here without him?"

"What?" Cole looks between us, confusion etched on his face.

"I'll see you again, Jordan!" Jay calls out, shoving Pike's hand away and pulling out his car keys. "You'll be working at The Hook just like your sister, and I'll come in there and buy your ass. That's a prom—"

Another fist lands across his face, but it's not Pike this time. Cole has rushed over to him and sent him tripping backward to the sidewalk.

Jay growls, spitting on the ground and bringing his hand to his lips and pulling it away, inspecting it.

"You knocked out one of my teeth!" he barks.

"Get out of here!" Cole yells, throwing out his arms. "Go!"

Sweat glistens across Pike's brow, and he looks at me with the same eyes he had the night we first slept together. When I straddled him on my bed and he gazed up at me, giving in and giving me everything he had.

Everything else around us disappears. He grinds his fists at his sides, and his body is rigid, like he's about to charge me and pull me into his arms and carry me away.

"You two?" I hear Cole say.

I blink, Pike drops his gaze, and the spell is broken. Cole stands between us, looking back and forth at us as people slowly disperse, and I see him start to connect the dots with the way we were just looking at each other.

"Jordan?" Cole nudges for me to say something, but I just lower my gaze, unable to look at him.

Pike swallows, breathing shallow. "Cole—"

"Oh, fuck you," Cole tells him, cutting him off and backing away.

Pike takes a step but Cole spins around and charges away, out of the yard and down the street.

Pike doesn't follow. He knows his son at least as well as I do, and Cole won't hear anything tonight. And what would Pike say to make it better, anyway? Damage is done.

Pike stands there, staring after Cole and looking like the life has been sucked out of him. What does he have now?

Pulling out my keys, I head down the porch stairs and walk to my car, not stopping or hesitating as I pass Pike Lawson.

And he doesn't follow me, either.

I now know he meant what he implied last night. I'm not worth it.

I know everything is a mess, I type on my phone. Please know it wasn't about revenge. It just happened, and I'm sorry.

I've been staring at my phone for twenty minutes, trying to figure out what to say to Cole. I'm logging off social media and only talking to my sister and a select few others for a while. I need space and quiet. I just didn't want to go silent without something.

I'm not sorry it happened, but I am sorry if it hurt him. I reasoned with myself that he cheated on me and I don't owe him anything.

But I don't want it to end like this. I'm fine with leaving. I'm fine with not seeing him right now.

I just needed him to know. . . . It wasn't about him.

Do you love him? His reply pops up.

Needles prick the back of my throat, and I press the *Power* button on the side of my phone, shutting it down.

I force the lump down my throat and stuff the phone in the side pocket of my bag and zip it up, closing my eyes to push back the tears.

Shel enters the liquor room, where I'm standing in front of a stack of beer crates, and instead of handing me my paycheck she went to go get, she takes a wad of cash and slips it into my bag without letting me see it.

After I crashed at my sister's again last night, I came here today to collect my pay before leaving. But judging by the stack of bills she just hid in my bag, she no doubt slipped me a lot more than what I've earned.

If I fight her, it would just be a waste of energy. I make a mental note to work extra hours when I come back. Whenever that is.

"What are you going to do?" she asks, resting her hand on her hip and peering at me.

"I don't know."

"Where are you going?"

"I don't know."

She sighs, and I pull my bag up, swinging it over my shoulder.

"Normally that would scare me, but . . ." I trail off, thinking. "I don't want to keep doing anything I've been doing. I just want to wake up tomorrow and not recognize anything about my life." I raise my eyes, looking at her. "And please don't give me some lecture on how I'm running away, floundering, letting others control what I feel . . ."

She takes my shoulders, speaking firmly. "Run," she tells me flatly. "Run far away. Just go. Call if you need anything, okay?"

I nod, thankful she understands. "Can you tell Cam not to worry? I'm fine, and I'll call her."

"You're not going to see her?"

Tears threaten, and I veer around Shel and out of her grasp, walking out of the liquor room. "I can't."

If I think too long, or I look at her face, I'll chicken out. Pike told me once, "hit the ground running." I'm sure this isn't what he meant, but I'm going for it.

Jordan Hadley doesn't leave her job. She doesn't jump into a run-down, unreliable vehicle and hit the road with nowhere to go. And she's certainly too afraid to ever be alone.

If I think, I won't do it. I'm going. No turning back. Maybe I'll come back tomorrow, the next day, or next week, but the longer I keep my foot on the gas, the farther I'll be from who I was.

I stop at the bar and pick up my sweater, which I laid on a stool.

"I know it hurts," Shel says, coming up behind me. "You were happy."

"I'll be fine." I hook the sweater over my bag, avoiding her eyes. "He wasn't my first."

"Yes, he was."

I stop and look over at her, the knots in my stomach tightening.

"You don't have to say anything, but you know . . ." She continues. "You didn't feel this with Cole or Jay or anyone else."

I look away again, biting the corner of my mouth to keep my feelings in check.

I'll get over him. And very soon, every memory will fade, all his words and how every touch felt. It'll all fade.

"But let me tell you something, girl," she goes on, speaking low and discreet for the few customers in the place. "What you feel for him or anyone else isn't what you need. This"—she taps my chest over my heart—"what you're feeling right now, is the best thing that can happen to you. Because when all the pieces of your heart start to come back together, and they will, they'll be stronger. And much tougher for someone to pierce." She pushes my hair behind my ear in the way she always does. "So you can be sure that when someone finally does, he'll have worked for it. We don't need food to survive this life as much as we need our hearts broken at least once. But the best part is, the first break is always the worst. It'll never feel this bad again."

And for that, I'm glad.

But it also makes me wonder. . . . If my heart will never break this badly again, then will I love anyone like I loved Pike Lawson?

25

Pike

I pull up in front of Lindsay's, scanning the parking lot around me for Cole's Challenger. I don't see it, but I can barely see anything through the rain right now. I've called him and Jordan nonstop for the past twenty-four hours, but I can't take it anymore. If he wants time, I can do that. If he needs space, I'll give it to him.

But I need to apologize to his face. I need him to know I love him and I didn't mean for this to happen.

Not that he'll listen or probably even hear me through his anger, but I can't sit around anymore.

Climbing out of my truck, I run to Lindsay's door, under the covered porch, and pound with my fist. It's been raining all day, and while I let the guys have the day off, I still went to the site and took care of business just to kill time until Cole got off work today. If he started his new job already, that is.

Lindsay opens the door, still in her pencil skirt from her office job but barefoot and her shirt untucked. She sees me and crosses her arms over her chest, pinning me with a smug look.

"I want to talk to him," I tell her.

"You've done enough," she sneers, pulling out her tight ponytail. "Jesus, I thought I was the bad parent. What were you thinking? Taking his leftovers like there isn't any other woman in this town you can pound?"

"It wasn't like that."

"Spare me the details." She reaches over to a nearby table and grabs a glass with what's most likely vodka and orange juice. "She's no different than you thought I was. She used you, Pike. Used you for a place to live and utilities, and oh, what else did you do? Fix her car, too?" She shakes her head, smiling bitterly. "She lucked out with you, and all she had to do was open her legs. Christ, you men really are dense when it comes to a pretty face."

My jaw tenses. *Jordan isn't like that. She's nothing like you.*

I'm not here to talk about her anyway.

"You don't know anything," I grit out.

"Aw, were you two in love?"

My heart thumps twice as hard, and my face falls, an image flashing in my mind of her standing by the pool just three nights ago, asking me to tell Cole and then to take her to bed—to our bed.

My stomach sinks. I miss her so much.

"Oh, my God, you do love her," Lindsay says, staring at my face and looking like she's about to laugh.

But before she can say anything else, I steel my spine. "Where is he?"

"Gone," she says, leaning on the door and taking a sip of her drink. "For the next eight weeks."

"What?"

"Well, maybe if you were paying more attention to your son than his piece of discarded trash, you would know he went up to MEPS over a week ago for his physical and other tests," she tells me, all too pleased to rub everything I don't know in my face. "He enlisted in the Navy, Pike. Seems he was desperate for the guidance he's clearly not getting from you. He shipped out this morning."

My eyebrows nose-dive. "What?" I yell this time.

The Navy? You don't just join the Navy. It takes months to enlist. I should know. I almost did it when I was his age.

As if sensing my questions, she goes on. "He's been planning it for a while. He's lost, wants some direction," she says as if reciting her grocery list. "He was afraid to tell anyone, because he has a habit of not following through with things. He wanted to surprise us when he was sure. After he went to MEPS, took his test, got his physical, and committed, though, he was going to tell you, but I guess he never got a chance."

My lungs empty, and I drop my head.

Needles stab my throat, and my eyes sting. This isn't right. He wouldn't have done something like that. Cole's not . . . disciplined. Would he willingly put himself through that? What was he thinking?

"He's at Naval Station Great Lakes," she says. "He'll be back in a couple months. Check his Instagram if you don't believe me. He made a final post this morning."

Instagram? I don't . . .

Jesus Christ.

She slams the door, and I immediately hear the lock turn.

I stand there, outside her door, the rain pouring around me with the past several days running through my head as I try to connect any clues Cole left about his plans. Quitting his job, telling me all the perks of his new one . . . He wanted a tattoo.

This secret new job was a big deal.

Did he really join the military?

Heading back to my truck, I climb in and slam the door against the downpour, and check my phone for any messages or texts again.

But still nothing. Not from Cole or Jordan.

Did she know about this?

No, she would've told me.

Remembering what Lindsay said, I type **Cole Lawson Instagram** into the search bar, and I immediately see a few different accounts pop up. Clicking through them, I find one with his picture and notice the first post is the most recent. It's just a picture of the open doors of a bus that it looks like he's about to board with a caption that reads **I should've taken the blue pill.**

What does that mean? Then I remember *The Matrix*. One of his favorite movies when he was younger.

I run my hand through my hair, ready to crawl out of my goddamn skin. How could he not at least send a text? I understand if he won't talk to me, but he has to know I'd be worried. To leave me for months with all these questions . . .

I sit in the truck, spending the next half hour searching websites and parent blogs, trying to figure out how I can talk to him. He isn't allowed a cell phone during training, and I can't call him unless there's an emergency, and even then I have to go through the Red Cross to reach him.

Fuck. I feel like I'm in the twilight zone right now. He's gone. With no way to immediately reach him for eight weeks.

We haven't spent much time together the past few years, but he was still only a phone call away. I can't let things be left like this for two months.

I search the local recruiting station in the area and call the office. I might be able to get his address through them once he receives his assignment.

There's no answer, so I'll track the recruiter down tomorrow and find out how I get ahold of him.

Goddamn it. "Shit!"

I feel so fucking helpless.

Knowing his cell phone has probably been confiscated by now, I dial him anyway and hold the phone to my ear. It goes immediately to voicemail.

"Cole," I say, swallowing a few times to wet my throat. "I . . . I . . ."

I shake my head, closing my eyes.

"I love you," I tell him. "And I'm always here for you. I know I . . . I know I have no excuse. I just . . ." Tears well in my eyes, and I don't know what else to say but the truth. "I tried not to fall for her. I did try. I'm sorry."

Hanging up, I throw the phone down, feeling empty. I don't want either of them out there without them knowing that I love them.

I'm alone again, and I just want them back. They're everything.

Jordan was right. I should've just told him, gotten it over with, and got him moving toward accepting it. I was never going to give her up willingly. How long was I planning on lying to him? Even if she and I didn't end things, I would've had to tell him at some point.

I start the engine and shift into reverse, backing out of the parking space and speeding out of the lot. Getting back onto the road, I head across town, periodically checking my phone for any messages.

Jordan left nearly everything at my house. She took some clothes, her books, and a few personals, but her models, her bed and furniture, and the painting are still there. She'll be back for that stuff, right? All hope isn't lost yet. I'll see her again.

But I haven't seen her in town anywhere, she hasn't been at work, and I haven't spotted her car. Where is she?

She was so calm the other night. Eerily calm, actually. As if she didn't care anymore.

I'll hate myself forever if I ruined her. My beautiful, happy, sexy girl who kills me with her smiles and jokes.

Pulling into The Hook's parking lot, I hop out of the truck and walk through the rain, into the club.

There's no one at the door, taking covers, but I doubt I'd stop anyway. I walk in and halt, déjà vu flooding me. The same song from Jordan's little FaceTime dance is playing as two women twirl around poles up on the stage. The picture of her beautiful body performing for only me hits me, and I'm almost sick with how fucking stupid I am and for what I lost.

Spotting Cam to the left, I walk over, not even caring she's on top of some guy right now. She straddles him, her arms resting over his shoulders.

"Where is she?" I demand.

Cam shoots her eyes up, arching a brow as she grinds on the guy, not skipping a beat.

"Look, I just want to talk to her, okay?"

Cam finishes the guy, whispering something in his ear, and rises from the chair, brushing past me.

I follow. "Can I at least know if she's all right?" I ask, my tone firm. "It's been days. Is she staying somewhere safe? She left nearly everything behind, so I know she doesn't have her own place."

Cam keeps walking, and I'm a little uncomfortable with the fishnet wrap she has around her thong-clad ass, but I keep pursuing. She gestures to the bartender, who reaches into a cooler and pulls out a bottle of water for her, sliding it across the bar.

But instead of stopping, she takes the water, turns, and keeps walking away from me.

"Cam, Jesus!" I blurt out, taking out my wallet and fishing out money. "Here's a hundred bucks for five minutes of your time!" I slap it on the bar. "I don't want a dance from you. All I want—"

She spins around, and I don't have any time to react before her knee jams right between my legs, sending me falling forward.

I growl, gasping as white-hot pain fires like bullets through my groin, thighs, and stomach. I squeeze my eyes shut, dropping to one knee, and a cool sweat breaks out all over my body.

I faintly hear her voice in my ear. "I wouldn't dance for you if you were worth a billion dollars and your dick tasted like a cherry Tootsie Pop," she bites out. "Stay away from me and my sister. Forget she exists."

Sickness coils through me, and it takes a while before I can breathe regularly again. By the time I'm able to rise, my legs shaky, Cam is gone.

And so is my hundred bucks.

You don't love her, do you?" Dutch asks.

I finish stacking the boxes in the garage, my fourth project in the past week to keep busy when I'm not at work.

Dutch sits on a lawn chair just outside, leaning forward, his elbows on his knees, and watching me like I'm a bull in a china shop, about to break shit any second.

It's been nine days now since I've seen my son or Jordan, and every day that passes feels like they're getting farther away from me. Like he's moved on and like I never existed to her.

Any hope I had is quickly being depleted.

I've called, texted, and left messages for both of them, and the only lead I have is an address to write to Cole that I harassed his recruiter into getting for me. I mailed my first letter yesterday.

As for Jordan, the only assurance I've been able to get that she's okay is from Dutch, who heard from his wife, who got it from Shel that Jordan is out of town visiting friends and she's fine.

Is she coming back?

I stopped calling after a few days, because she clearly doesn't want to talk, and I'm trying to respect her wishes, but . . . If she called right now, I'd go get her from anywhere she was and give her anything she wants. For the rest of my life she can have anything she wants.

"Pike, you can't marry her," Dutch states like he knows where my head is at. "You know that, right?"

I keep my back to him, rehanging discarded tools on the workbench and slowly clearing off the table.

Nine days ago I would've agreed with him. I would've said he was right.

People will talk. They're probably already talking. They'll make it dirty and wrong, and her friends from high school will joke about her, and no one would take us seriously. All they would see is her age and how she moved from son to father, and it would be the talk of the town.

But now I'm not so sure. Who cares what they think? We'd get through it, and Jordan's circle of friends is as small as mine. She won't give a damn what strangers have to say about it.

We'd be fucking happy, and eventually people would move on.

She wanted me. She wanted to love me.

She was ready for us.

I shake my head, arguing, "She's different."

"No, she's not," Dutch retorts. "She's young and full of hope. Like we used to be."

I turn slowly and look at him. It's not like him to stand against me.

But I listen as he goes on.

"Everything is new and fresh to her," he says. "She's excited about life, and she makes you remember what that felt like. Before we grew up and realized we weren't going to be fighter pilots saving the world or kings of Wall Street riding around in stretch limos." He laughs under his breath, sitting back in the chair. "Before there were bills to pay and responsibilities piling higher as the years went on."

His eyes fall, and I can see everything I'm feeling on his face. He doesn't hate his life, and he adores his wife and kids, but if we could go back and do at least one thing differently, I know we both would.

Here we sit, and we're not sure what we have to look forward to anymore.

"Look, man." He raises his eyes to me. "You had fun with her. I'm not saying you did anything wrong. If the sex is good, then enjoy each other. But you have to think about the future, and you know it won't always feel like this." He pauses, knitting his brow. "She'll wake up in ten years and see a picture of a high school friend online who's trekking through Nepal or some shit, and she'll look around at her own life and think about how she's saddled with two kids in this small town and married to a man nearly fifty years old whose life is more than halfway over."

I remain silent, the weight of his words sitting in my gut like bricks.

"You think she won't regret choosing you, knowing that her best years are almost gone?" he asks.

But I don't have to answer. He knows he's right.

In ten years, she'll still be young and beautiful, and I'll deserve her even less than I do now. I can't give her everything she wants no matter how much my ego thinks otherwise.

She was built for big things. She's smart and strong, and she deserves the world. She deserves a life that passed me by a long time ago.

Another man will be to her everything I'm not and never will be, and even though that idea is like acid in my mouth, she'll be happier for it. And above everything else, that's what I want. She'll grow with someone else, and that's the life she deserves.

Dutch leaves, and I close up the garage, heading into the house and immediately up the stairs. I stop at Jordan's bedroom, the door open and the light breeze outside her window blowing the leaves on the tree in the backyard.

Her faint smell lingers, and the dent her body made is still etched into the pillow propped up in her chair.

I don't go in, though. It's not my room, not my girl anymore, and she's out there somewhere, moving on with her life, and I need to do the same.

Enough. Do the right thing.

Reaching for the knob, I inhale her perfume one last time.

And I pull the door closed.

26

Pike

Two Months Later

Threading the thin white rope around the wheel, I yank on it, seeing it move toward me on the pulley. I move over to the other wooden post I've cemented into the backyard and pull on that rope, as well, testing it.

I have no idea why I'm putting in clotheslines.

All I know is I'm running out of ideas. I already built a wooden picnic table with a built-in beer tub in the middle, stained it, and added benches. I've also put in a fire pit, a stone pathway leading from the back gate to the back door, mulch in the flower beds, torches around the pool, a pergola, a hammock, and a small pond with a rock garden. I keep moving from one project to another, so I don't have time to think about how I'm not using any of it. I'll enjoy it when I'm done, I guess.

"Looks different back there," I hear someone call out.

I look up, seeing Kyle Cramer standing on his bedroom balcony and looking down into my backyard.

Does this guy have a hard-on for me or something? Why's he always trying to talk to me?

"Got some time on your hands, huh?" he gauges. "I noticed it's been a lot quieter here the past several weeks."

I cast him another look, giving him a curt smile. Maybe if I acknowledge him, he'll leave me alone.

And yes, it's been quiet. Until now.

"So, um," he starts, and I silently groan. "I saw you and Jordan one night."

I stop and shoot my eyes up again, glaring at him. Heat rises to my neck at hearing her name. I haven't talked about her with anyone for months now.

"My kitchen faces yours," he explains, "it was late, and you two were at the sink."

My body warms, remembering that. The sight of her walking naked to the kitchen one night, and how I wouldn't let her get a midnight snack until I got mine. She was so beautiful.

I straighten, clenching my teeth. "You watched?"

"No," he blurts out like he would never. And then he shrugs. "I mean, I might have if you two hadn't eventually taken it to the floor and out of my line of sight."

He follows with a laugh, and if I could fucking fly, I'd be over this fence right now, strangling him.

He seems to notice my anger and tries to placate me. "Listen, I didn't mean to see anything, okay? You could try to stay away from the windows, you know?" He shakes his head. "I'm just saying, I think it's the first time I ever saw you smile. It certainly seems like she made you happy. I can't imagine she wouldn't make any man happy, actually."

"Shut the hell up," I mumble, bending down and picking up tools, dropping them into the small box.

Really? How could we have been so careless? He's the last person whose eyes I want on her.

"So, where'd she go?" he asks. "It didn't work out with you two?"

I ignore him, gathering my shit so I can escape inside.

"How'd you fuck that up, man?" he laughs out, taking a swig of his beer. "You get a woman like that—young and hot with a body in that good a shape—you don't lose it."

I toss my wrench down, charging forward with nowhere to go. "I'm gonna kick your ass. Shut the fuck up."

"So, she's available now, right?"

"Son of a bitch," I growl.

He just snickers. I must be so amusing.

"You are definitely sad," he says. "Women aren't that hard to make happy if you have half a mind to."

"I'm not incapable," I snap. "But that's not the point. Teenage women belong with teenage guys, and don't you fucking forget it next time you run into one. She deserves someone her own age."

He nods, thinking. And then he pins me with a look. "So, your son was her age, right? Did he treat her better than you did?"

I breathe hard but stay silent. He gives me a smug half grin and backs away, walking back into his house.

That's not the point, asshole.

Yeah, I can safely say her relationships with guys her own age weren't winners, either, but . . .

But what? I'm not going to be able to give her everything she wants? I'm not going to grow with her? I'm not going to start over and build a family anymore at my age?

Two months ago, those all seemed like viable arguments, but over time, they feel less convincing now. Like maybe who I am and where I'm at in my life isn't carved in stone. It can still be subject to change.

I shake my head. *I don't know.*

No, I did the right thing. It's been months, and I haven't heard from her. She's clearly moved on.

But God, I fucking miss her. It's like I'm constantly sick with hunger, but food won't satisfy me. There's an emptiness inside me that I can't fill on my own.

I pick up the toolbox and turn toward the house, but when I look up, I see Cole standing in the open back doorway to the house.

I halt. *Jesus.* How long has he been standing there?

The box dangles from my fingers as we just hold each other's eyes, and I'm completely stunned to see him here.

"I saw you at the graduation," he says, a hand in his pocket.

His graduation from boot camp was yesterday, and I'd been writing him and hounding his recruiter all summer for any contact. I had to see him, though. I couldn't miss it. It's a huge accomplishment.

Slowly, I drift toward him, unable to tear my gaze away. He looks incredible. Taller and bigger, a long summer at boot camp having tanned his skin and lightened his now buzzed blond head of hair. He wears his green camouflage uniform with his hat in one hand as he leans against the doorframe.

"I just wanted to see you," I tell him. "I wasn't sure if you put me on the list or your recruiter did, but you didn't respond to any of my letters, so I wasn't sure you wanted me there."

After the ceremony ended, I wanted to talk to him, but his mom was there with her latest boyfriend, and he was joined by a couple friends who'd driven up to see him. I didn't want to ruin it, so I left. He'd have his cell phone back now, so he would see all the calls, texts, and voicemails. He'd let me know when he was ready.

He drops his head, scanning the ground in front of him. "I got all your letters. Thanks for the phone cards."

You mean the ones you didn't use to call me? I quirk a smile, not blaming him. It was a long shot, but I am glad he got everything. As long as he knew I was thinking about him . . .

"How are you?" I step up and set the toolbox down, pulling the shop cloth out of my back pocket and wiping off my hands.

He's quiet and takes a deep breath. Finally, he raises his blue eyes to me. "Got a beer?"

I nod gently and lead the way back inside and into the kitchen.

The air-conditioning hits me, cooling the sweat on my back, and my nerves make it hard to breathe, but I'm not as nervous as I thought I'd be when this moment came. He's not yelling yet, so that's a good sign.

I pop the tops of two Coronas, the late afternoon sunlight vanishing from the kitchen table as it dips behind some clouds.

He takes a seat, and I do the same. When he remains quiet, though, I realize the ball's in my court.

"So, are you happy?" I ask him. "In the military?"

I've had time to get used to the idea, especially after getting assurances from his recruiter, but I need to hear it from him.

"Yeah." He sets his beer on the table, keeping his fist wrapped around it. "I don't know—I guess it's what I needed. To be torn down and rebuilt better."

I wait for him to go on.

"I can't sleep in," he says, "I can't show up drunk, I can't call in sick because I'm feeling lazy that day. . . . It sucks, but I've also got a job and money in the bank. A career. That feels pretty good." He finally raises his eyes to me. "I've got a future, and for someone who never knew where the fuck their place was in the world, it's kind of nice to let the military decide for you and give you direction."

"You sure?" I lift the bottle, taking a drink.

I love that he's doing something with himself, but I also want to make sure he's carving his own path.

He goes on. "That's where Jordan and I never made sense. She knew her own mind, and I resented myself when I was with her, because I never did." He releases a sigh. "I wasn't her equal, never good enough for her. I would never be that strong-minded. Some of us just aren't."

My heart skips a beat at the sound of her name again, but I ignore it. I'm not confident that joining the military was really what he wanted to do with his life, but I am sure he wasn't finding answers in this town. At least he knew that much.

He was strong-minded enough to take that leap.

"You did this, didn't you?" I ask. "You made it through training. I'm proud of you."

I see his Adam's apple bob up and down, and the muscles in his jaw flex. He takes another drink, still not looking at me.

"So, where is she?" he asks, casting looks behind him to the living room like she's still in the house.

"I don't know." I shake my head. "She left after you did. I haven't seen her in two months."

His gaze snaps to mine, his brows furrowing in concern.

"I've talked to her sister," I assure him. "She's fine. Wherever she is."

He seems to accept that answer, because he takes another swig. But now I'm a little more unnerved than I was a moment ago. It's clear she hasn't kept in touch with Cole, either. Not that I thought they would stay in contact after everything, but they were friends. Lifelines to each other at one point. The more ties she cuts, the fewer reasons she'll have to come back.

"You seeing anyone else?" he asks.

"Nah, not right now." I take another drink. "Just concentrating on the house and the business."

"Yeah, I ran into Dutch on my way into town, and he told me you guys are like two years ahead of schedule."

I chuckle. "Not that much . . ."

Although, we're doing damn well. You can get a lot of work done when you're not racing home every day to a woman who sets your body on fire.

"So, did she break it off with you or you with her?" Cole asks, bringing up Jordan again.

I stare at him. I don't want to talk about this. I just want him to be okay. I want him to talk about anything else with me.

But mostly, because I'm not proud of my answer. If Jordan hadn't left, I would've kept her as long as she was willing to stay. I should've given her up for him, and I didn't. And I'm not sure I would've if she had left the choice up to me.

"I'm sorry," I tell him instead. "You'll never know how sorry I am."

His eyes are locked on mine, a flood of emotions I'm not sure I want to face crossing his gaze. Pain, disappointment, confusion, loneliness . . . But also calmness, resolution, and acceptance.

"When I saw you at graduation yesterday, I wanted to still be mad at you," he says. "And I was aggravated that I wasn't."

He drops his eyes, the wheels turning in his head.

"There's something to be said about time and distance, I guess." He gives a sad smile. "You get a lot of perspective. A lot of time to think about things."

Yeah.

"When I was six," he goes on, "you lost a contract because you came to my Little League game that day instead. On my tenth birthday, you moved my party and paid for everyone to go to the go-kart place, because Mom and one of her boyfriends started fighting at the house and embarrassing the hell out of me in front of everyone. When I graduated high school, you took out a second mortgage to pay for my college, which I just pissed down the drain."

My throat swells. He remembers all that?

"Doing what you could to make me happy, no matter the sacrifice, never seemed like a tough decision for you." He peers over at me, his voice thick with emotion. "So, I think, doing something you knew could hurt me was definitely not an easy choice," he says. "I know you love me."

I grind my teeth together to keep my breathing even, and relief washes over me.

"I don't know how okay I am with all this, but . . ." He nods. "I know you love me."

I'm speechless. It's a little heartbreaking to look at your son and wonder if you had anything to do with how good he turned out. I can't believe he's sitting here right now when I wasn't sure he'd ever look at me again.

"Do you still love her?" he asks.

I hesitate a moment, searching for the words. Yes, I still love her, but . . . "She's better off," I tell him.

He leaves it there, not pressing further. "I have to be back tomorrow night. Is it okay if I stay the night?"

"Of course."

He rises, carrying his beer toward the living room with him. "The Twins are playing the Cubs tonight," he says. "You want to watch?"

I inhale a deep breath and release it, feeling like my body is relaxing for the first time in months. "Sounds good. I'll order some pizza."

"Cheese," he specifies.

I laugh quietly. "Yeah, I remember."

I take my phone out of my pocket and start to dial Joe's, but then I hear his voice.

"And, Dad?" he says.

I look up.

"I love you," he tells me. "But no one's better off without you."

That night, I wake up to thunder rolling somewhere in the distance. I don't open my eyes, the weight of too many long days at the jobsite heavy on my lids. I turn on my side, knowing I'll fall back asleep if I give it a minute.

The inside of my right arm burns with the tattoo I got earlier tonight. Cole and I decided to go to Rockford after the pizza and get those tattoos he mentioned. He chose an anchor in the middle of his back, accompanied by a compass and a fisherman's knot with the motto "Forged by the Sea" around it. It's all just outlined, though. He said he'll get it colored in after he's earned it.

I'm guessing that means after his first six months at sea.

The candle etched on my skin feels like it's actually lit, the smoke from the wick drifting up the inside of my arm all the way to my elbow. I've known since Cole first mentioned tattoos two months ago that something that represents Jordan was the only thing I wanted on me for the rest of my life. The birthday girl and her wishes. She'll always be a part of me.

I inhale a long breath, and even though I've washed the sheets several times since she left, I can still smell her hair on the pillows.

And if I concentrate hard enough and keep my eyes closed, she's there next to me.

I snake an arm around her body and pull her into me, burying my nose in her cool hair.

"Was I snoring?" she whispers.

I smile, trying not to laugh. "No."

She's so self-conscious, and it's adorable. I hug her to me, feeling so filled, because everything I need is in my arms right now. Her curves fit every inch of mine, and I'm whole. My chest fills with something almost too much to contain.

She breathes calmly, and I run my hand over her naked stomach, my body coming alive for her. So easily, like it always does.

Suddenly, her small voice pierces the quiet room again.

"You got me pregnant," she whispers.

I still. What did she say?

No, that can't be right. We've been careful.

When I don't say anything, she turns around and faces me, her guarded eyes on mine. "I missed my period last week," she says timidly. "I took a few tests earlier today. Best I can figure is I'm about a month along."

I close my eyes. Oh, my God. A baby?

My baby.

"I hope she has my eyes," she tells me.

I open mine. "Your eyes?"

"Well, she'll be a mix of both of us, after all," she explains, "and I want her to have your smile. It evens out, right?"

I touch her face. "You're sure? There's a baby?"

She nods. "I'm sure." She looks at me warily and asks, "Is that okay?"

I open my mouth, no words coming out. A baby? I picture myself waking up with an infant in the middle of the night, car seats, and cartoons, and I'm overwhelmed, but strangely, I feel . . . so fucking in love with her and the idea of her body growing with my kid.

But I wanted her to have choices. Does she really want this?

The only thing I know is that I want her. I want everything with her, and I wish, for her sake, it wasn't yet, but I wanted this eventually.

"I love you," I whisper. "I love you so much."

She exhales and smiles as if she were holding her breath that whole time, and climbs on top of me, straddling me.

"I love you, too." She kisses me, her naked body molding to mine. "I was so nervous. I didn't know if you'd want more kids, or—"

"Shhh, baby," I tell her, kissing her and holding her face. "I love you. I just . . ." I pause and then continue, looking up into her eyes. "You're stuck with me now, aren't you?"

She gives me a little smile, and I take her ass in my hands.

"I've seen lots of bad love, Pike," she says. "We both have, haven't we?" And then she does the barest of grinds on me, awakening my body immediately. "This is the good kind. When you find it, you keep it. Nothing is more important."

I grow hard as she moves against me, and I hold her face, staring up into her eyes.

"Do you love me?" she asks.

"I'll never stop loving you."

She dives in, kissing me and hovering her lips over mine. "Then I'm so lucky," she whispers. "We're so lucky."

I dig my hands into her and pull her closer, but there's suddenly nothing there, and I blink my eyes open, seeing that my arms are empty. It was a dream, and I can't slow my breathing. Whipping off the sheet, I sit up, swing my legs over the side, and bury my head in my hands.

"Fuck," I choke out, my forehead covered in sweat.

I'm still hard, blood pulsing through my cock, because I can still feel as much now as I could two months ago. I'd give anything to have her in my arms right now.

Standing up, I pull on my jeans and head out of the bedroom. I pass Cole's room, where he's asleep inside, and quietly open Jordan's door. Her room's been closed up for eight weeks, and I'm overcome as soon as I inhale. She's everywhere, and I close the door and switch on the light.

Her home-and-garden magazines lie at the bottom of her bed, and I look over to the desk, my eyes falling on its corner and remembering how beautiful she was that night. The boombox Dutch gave her sits on top, and I walk over, turning down the volume and pressing *Play.* I recognize Bruce Springsteen's "I'm on Fire" coming out of the speakers, and I adjust the volume again, not wanting to wake Cole.

Walking over to the bed, I sit down and listen to the song, looking around.

I can't get away from her, and I never want to. I thought I was in love with Lindsay at one time, but I wasn't. It wasn't like this.

And I never even told her. She doesn't know that I love her.

I never thought I'd say this, but Cramer is right. I would've loved her with everything I had. She was it for me. I would've gone to any length to make her happy for the rest of her life.

But I blew it.

Looking over, I spot a jar sitting on her bedside table, the label on the front reading *Dreams*. I reach over and take it, studying the few dozen little scrolls of paper, all different colors and tied with gold string, piled inside.

My heart thumps in my ears—I don't want to invade her privacy, but I need to know. I need to know her dreams don't include me or things I can give her. Her love clouds her mind. What she wrote here will be the truth.

Unscrewing the lid, I dump the scrolls on the bed and pick one up. I slide the string off, my stomach rolling with nerves as I unroll the first scroll.

Invent my own
Christmas tradition.

I smile weakly, something like that sounding right up her alley. She's creative, and I'd love to see what she comes up with.

Setting it down, I pick up another one and pull it apart, reading it.

Drive a convertible with
the top down in the rain.

Yeah, I can just see her dragging me out for something like that, trying to get me to have some fun.

I pick up another scroll, my smile falls, and my mouth goes dry, readying myself again to see something I might not like. The pulse in my neck throbs as I unroll it.

Have a library in my house someday. Built-in bookshelves, leaves blowing outside, and a cushy chaise with cozy blankets.

I dig in my eyebrows and drop the paper, quickly picking up another.

I wonder if I can get Pike to stay in bed all day on a rainy day to watch movies.

I guarantee you, girl, watching movies won't be all we do if we stay in bed all day.

I unroll another.

Ride in a hot-air balloon.

My breathing quickens as I keep unrolling scrolls, one right after another.

Adopt a dog.

How do you make your own beer? I'd like to try that.

Take my kids for trips to the lake in the summers.

Install a clothesline in the backyard of my future house. No one has those anymore!

I blink. I just installed a clothesline. She has that now.

I keep going.

Run a marathon.

Keep a blanket in the trunk for spontaneous picnics.

See a parade.

Learn how to make chili.

Go four-wheeling.

Swim in the ocean.

Fill Pike's truck bed with blankets and pillows and go stargazing.

I keep reading scroll after scroll, finally unable to take any more and pushing them away.

"Fuck," I breathe out, my eyes stinging.

I can give her all this. Every single one of these things—her dreams, the life she wants—I can give it to her. All of it.

What did I think? She wanted wealth, power, and fame? What did she say on one of her first nights here?

I really don't care about the wedding. I just want the life.

She wants a home. She wants people to love.

She wanted me to want her. That's all she wanted.

Tears I won't let fall spring to my eyes. "What the fuck did I do?"

27

Pike

I take a deep breath and hold it in as I grip the door handle to Grounders. I tried calling Cam, and I even went to The Hook again, but I can't find her. So Shel it is, I guess. I'm sure this is a waste of time—the woman has hated me since she met me—but I'm desperate.

Pulling the door open, I step inside, music and the smell of fried food instantly swarming me. Shel stands behind the bar with only three customers in front of her, and I look around the place, seeing a few tables filled but most empty. It's a pretty quiet Monday night.

I crack my neck, bracing myself as I step up to the bar.

She sees me instantly and stops drying a glass as her back stiffens. "Cam, can you serve this guy?" she calls.

I glance at the other end and notice Jordan's sister leaning over it. She must be covering Jordan's shifts while she's gone.

Her head rests in her hand as she talks to some patron, but as soon as her eyes lock with mine, she stands up straight, her smile falling.

Shel starts to walk away.

"Wait," I say, stopping her. "I'm not staying."

"Good."

"I just—"

"I'm not going to tell you where she is," she cuts me off.

I see Cam watching us, and I take another breath, squaring my shoulders. "I just need to know she's okay."

"She's fine," she replies curtly. "And she'll be even better if she stays away from you and this town."

I move in, dropping my voice. "I need to see her. Please."

"You had her."

Her eyes are nearly covered by her long black bangs, but I can see the hatred in them well enough.

I don't want to bother Jordan. She's stayed away, and I haven't heard from her, so that tells me I think I did the right thing. She's doing fine, and she'll be happier.

But I'm not. This isn't over for me. You need your heart to get out of bed, walk, talk, work, and eat, and she took it when she left. I wasn't much before she came along, but what I did have inside me, she left with. I'm fucking miserable.

"Please tell her . . ." I pause, admitting out loud what I was afraid to face. "That I love her."

Shel doesn't say anything, and I can't even look in her eyes and see everything she's thinking that I know is true. I fucked up.

I'm about to leave when Cam moves in.

"It's been two months," she says to Shel. "And he still looks like shit."

"That's not Jordan's problem."

"And we're not Jordan's keepers," Cam retorts. "She walked away once, she can walk away again if that's what she chooses. We don't need to protect her."

Shel hesitates, shoots me a glare, and finally gives up, walking around Cam to the other end of the bar.

Cam turns to me. "Look, we don't know exactly where she is," she says. "She calls and checks in every few weeks. But she has a friend whose family runs some motel in eastern Virginia. She's been trying to get Jordan to come visit and even offered her a job there one summer." She hesitates and then shrugs. "Without a lot of money, I can't imagine Jordan has anywhere else to go."

Virginia. That's a twelve-hour drive. Would she have done that with the VW?

I guess if Cam says she's calling, then she's safe. And this is as good a lead as I'm going to get. Her fall classes start in a week, and if she were returning, she'd be doing it by now, wouldn't she? She'd want her things out of my house, and she'd need to figure out where she was going to live. Was she planning on coming home at all?

I need to find her. I can't wait.

I turn to leave but then stop. "What's the name of the motel?" I ask Cam.

But she just sighs. "Hmm, can't remember," she says, playing with me. "I guess if you want her bad enough you'll find her."

And then she walks away, pleased with herself that she's making it more difficult for me. I could call around, I guess, but if I do happen to find her, she might just hang up on me. I need to go find her in person.

I need to at least see her one last time and tell her that I love her and that she's everything.

And that I'm dead without her.

28

Jordan

I click the mouse, moving the red six of hearts and everything underneath it to the black seven of clubs. Then I turn over the new card, clicking it twice and watching the ace automatically slide up to a free cell.

After nine weeks I've gotten pretty good at this game. Danni keeps suggesting I learn poker or blackjack or maybe even get into some online gaming with people from around the world, but I'm not that cool. I like playing alone. Just something to keep my brain occupied. It's been an eventful summer vacation, too. I've won about three hundred fifty games out of four hundred, and I only lost that many because I kept playing too late and would fall asleep, letting my battery die.

I actually feel quite pathetic when I let myself think about how I've spent hours and hours over this gorgeous summer. But then I just start a new game, and I stop thinking about it.

The bell on the lobby door chimes, and I look up, seeing a young man in a black pullover and jeans walk in, heading for the front desk.

I slide off my stool and stand. I'm always nervous when we get customers this late. The motel sits on an old highway without a lot of businesses or lights. Most people stick to the interstate, especially when it's dark out like this, and those who don't kind of make me wonder.

But hey, it's business.

"Hi." I smile. "Welcome to The Blue Palms."

He steps up to the counter, and my smile falters, seeing the huge wing tattooed on his neck with the words *The Devil Doesn't Sleep* etched in black ink. This is a pretty conservative area. He can't be local.

"Hi." He meets my eyes but only for a second. "How many vacant rooms do you have?"

"Um . . ." I look in the cubbies and count the keys to make sure. "Six," I tell him.

He nods, reaching into his back pocket for his wallet, I assume. "I'll take five. For one night, please."

Five? I don't think we've been this close to *No Vacancies* since I got here. What does he need all those rooms for?

Not that I'm complaining, though. We need the business.

The Blue Palms, owned by my friend Danni and her family, sits on a nearly deserted road, the new interstate put in twenty years ago making business very hard to come by these days. The only people who seem to know we're here are the townies, the relatives of townies traveling in to visit, and bikers looking for a more authentic experience by riding the old highways.

I'm glad I came to help out, though. Danni's been begging me for years to visit, and it's been a throwback to spend another summer with her. She and I won scholarships to a sleepaway camp when we were twelve and have been keeping in touch long-distance ever since. I've always wanted to match the place where so many of her quirky and sexy stories come from with my mental picture.

The customer hands me his ID, and I take it.

"Thanks," I say, propping it up on the keyboard to register the rooms to him.

The door suddenly swings open again, the bell ringing, and I hear a demanding voice bark, "We need food!"

I look up, seeing three women standing at the door, and notice a few more outside. I don't see any other men. My eyes fall down their attire, and next to them, my sister's clothes at The Hook seem prudish. Hair, makeup, heels . . .

I shoot my eyes to the guy and see him blink long and hard, looking aggravated. He picks through the paper menus stuffed in the board on the wall and takes out a few from different places.

"Do these restaurants deliver?" he asks, setting them down and pulling a wad of bills out of his wallet.

"Yeah, all of them."

He holds up the menus with the cash, and one of the girls jogs up and snatches everything out of his hands.

"I want receipts and change," he orders, not looking at her.

She makes a face at him behind his back and then she disappears outside with the others.

I feel compelled to warn him. This place has an unofficial code of conduct, and Danni's pretty strict about shenanigans. They've scraped by here for a long time, but the town is looking at developing this property. She doesn't want to give them an excuse to want this place gone.

"This is a pretty quiet, family-oriented place," I tell him, slowly typing in his name and address. "Parties aren't allowed, so just an FYI . . ."

He looks at me, his dark sandalwood eyes almost amused. "They're my sisters," he says.

I bite back my smile and focus on my work again. *Sure.* If those are his sisters, then I'm his mom.

But he certainly seemed pretty annoyed by them like a brother would be, I guess.

I place the keys on the counter—with the old-fashioned, rounded diamonds for key chains—and print off the contract to sign.

"The pool closes at ten," I tell him. "The ice and vending machines are between the two buildings, and there's a laundromat across the way there." I glance at him and point behind him, outside. "Front desk is open twenty-four hours. Let us know if you need anything. And that'll be two hundred eight dollars and forty-two cents, please."

But as I place a pen on top of the contract and wait for his response, I see that he's not even listening to me. He's staring at the neon sign on the wall to his right and the quote written in script . . .

Well, they're nothing like Billy and me . . .

His stern expression breaks into a small smile all of a sudden as he stares at the sign, a mixed look of wonder and confusion on his face as if a memory is playing in his head. I glance at the sign again, Danni's obsession with nineties music the bane of my existence all summer. It's a quote from a Sheryl Crow song, and I never asked her if it meant anything, because then she'd play the song, and I'd suffer.

"Sir?" I say.

He blinks, turning to me, still seeming disoriented for a moment.

"Are you okay?"

He shakes it off and opens his wallet again. "How much is it?"

"Two-oh-eight forty-two," I tell him.

He hands me three hundred-dollar bills, and there's a sign that says we don't take bills larger than fifty, but seeing the unnerving pile of cash in his wallet, I don't feel like ruffling his feathers. I take the money and get his change.

He taps on the counter as he waits, and I realize he's matching the rhythm of "The Distance" by Cake, which Danni has playing on the speakers in the lobby.

"Oh, don't do that," I joke, handing him his change. "You'll encourage the owner. I'm trying to convince her the playlist is driving away customers."

He takes the money and shoots me a look. "Nineties music is the best. It's when people told the truth."

I curl the corner of my mouth, not arguing further. He clearly drank the same Kool-Aid as she did.

"Thanks," he says, swiping up the keys.

I hand him back his ID and watch him leave. Outside, he doles out the room keys to all the ladies, and after a moment, they all make their way to their rooms. I'm half-tempted to go to the window and see if he goes in with one of them. Or five of them. Very curious.

"Was that a customer?" Danni says behind me, and I glance back, seeing her walk into the office. Her apartment, where she resides with her grandmother, sits behind the office, so it's easy to run and check on her when she needs.

"Yeah," I tell her. "He got five rooms for the night, and he's traveling with at least half a dozen women, so have fun on the night shift."

She snorts and walks up, picking up the contract. "Tyler Durden?" she reads his name, squinting through her glasses.

I nod, pulling a stray brown hair off her flannel shirt. She even dresses nineties.

"Didn't you get ID?" She makes a face at me. "It's a fake name."

"His ID said Tyler Durden," I shoot back. "Why do you think it's a fake name?"

"Tyler Durden is a lead character in *Fight Club*," she spits out like I'm an idiot. "The best movie of the nineties, and one of the best books ever. It's disturbing that you don't know that, Jordan."

I laugh, shaking my head. We might be the same age, but we're worlds apart in interests.

Fight Club.

My smile falls, and I drop my eyes, turning back to the computer. I've seen the movie, but the name didn't register. And I've seen it recently, too, with Pike . . .

I swallow, my chest growing tight. *Dammit.* I've done really well the last few weeks, turning my attention elsewhere so I don't think about him. It was hard at first, but not seeing him every day made it easier. It was right to leave like I did.

But every once in a while, he'll pop up in my head when I make taco dip for Danni during a long Saturday shift or hear a song or when I see my raincoat and the splatters of mud still on it from him and me playing around. I haven't even lit any candles, because I don't know what to wish for when I have to blow them out.

To wish to feel like I did with him gives him power over me again, but deep down, that's all I still really want.

To feel that good again.

It'll just have to be with someone else now.

"So . . ." Danni pulls up another stool. "Don't your fall classes start up soon?"

I click off the *FreeCell* game, avoiding her gaze. "Yeah."

She waits for me to say more, but I'm not really sure what to say. My financial aid came in, so classes are paid for, and I have enough to get an apartment back home, but it almost feels like taking a step backward. He called when I first left, but after a few days it stopped, and there's been nothing since.

I hate to admit it, but I wonder far too often what he's doing, if he's seeing anyone, if he misses me . . .

If I go home, I may run into him. What will that be like?

I'm proud of myself that I've stayed away, but I still feel ashamed that he's there in my head, lingering all the time. I'm not over him, and until I can blow out a candle and have something better to wish for, I don't think my head is in the right place to go back yet. I'm scared.

"You know you can stay forever," Danni goes on. "Seriously. My college isn't bad at all. You can transfer."

"Thanks," I tell her. "But I need to go back. I know I do. I've just been putting off thinking about it."

"You don't want to see him."

I meet her eyes, her black-rimmed glasses falling down her nose again.

"I don't want to be who I was when I left," I clarify.

"You're not." She leans an elbow on the counter, resting her chin in her hand. "You're allowed to hurt. But you didn't allow it to keep you down," she points out. "That's what makes us strong. You haven't called him, and we had some fun. He didn't ruin your summer, because you didn't let him."

Yeah. We got drunk at the pond, rocked out to bad music as we raced around town in her '92 Pontiac Sunbird convertible, and had some pool parties here. I laughed a little.

"And it's not like he tracked me down, either, so . . ." I tell her. "I guess we both knew it was borrowed time. It was just a fling. He was right."

A fling.

A cool story I'll have fun looking back on when I no longer love him, and I can appreciate it for the sex it was.

I feel her eyes on me, because she knows I'm lying to myself, but like a friend, she lets me dive into my delusion. We need lies to survive sometimes, because the truth hurts too much.

Maybe a transfer would be a good idea, after all.

I stand up. "The printer needs paper," I tell her.

And without looking at her, I walk into the back office, blinking away the burn in my eyes before she sees. I'm not going to cry. I can't hide here forever, after all. Northridge is my home, my family is there, and I have to go back at some point. I can do it.

"Hi," I hear Danni singsong. "Welcome to The Blue Palms."

I laugh to myself. "The Blue Palms" are a set of neon palm trees outside that aren't real and certainly aren't native to Virginia. But I like the tropical colors of this place, the retro pinks and blues, and the old-style, beachy charm. It might not have the amenities of the larger hotels, but it's private, clean, and nostalgic. It has character.

"Uh, thanks," a male voice says. "Um . . ."

I open the cabinet, grabbing a ream of paper, their muffled voices carrying on in the lobby. I hope he only needs one room, because for once, we're about sold out.

"Jordan Hadley?" Danni says more loudly, as if repeating him.

I halt with the paper in my arm and the cabinet still open.

"Yeah," the man says, and I inch closer to the doorway to better hear. "I'm sorry to bug you. Does she work here? I was told she worked at a motel in the area, and I've been almost everywhere."

The vein in my neck throbs, and I can only manage short, shallow breaths.

"And you are?" Danni probes.

"Pike Lawson," he answers. "A friend."

My arms give way, and I nearly drop the package of paper.

"Pike . . ." she repeats. "Like in *Buffy the Vampire Slayer*?"

"Huh?"

"Nineteen ninety-two cult classic?" Danni explains. "Luke Perry? His name is Pike in the movie?"

Normally I would laugh at her verbal diarrhea, but my head is swimming and my stomach is doing somersaults. He's here? He's really here?

There's silence for a moment, and then Pike asks, "So, does Jordan work here? I really need to see her."

He sounds vulnerable, his voice making me realize I missed him even more than I thought I did.

But somewhere inside, my strength grows, and I steel my spine, ready to show him I'm not going to hide from him. I don't know why he's here, but if he tries to make demands again like when I tried to move back with my dad, I don't feel like it will be hard for me to stand up and stay defiant. He won't tell me what to do.

No matter how hard he tries.

Stepping out from behind the corner, I enter the lobby, seeing Pike standing on the other side of the counter. His gaze immediately locks on me.

He inhales a breath and just stares, his body rigid.

I take in his black T-shirt and deeper tan, like he's had a full summer working outdoors, and my heart flutters at the sight of those piercing and warm hazel eyes and big hands that have picked me up and carried me half a dozen times. He looks taller, but I know he hasn't grown, of course.

Danni hops off her stool. "I'll just . . . go check on my grandma," she says and quietly walks past me, to her apartment.

Pike stands between the front door and desk, fisting his hands at his sides and looking like he's about to move forward but not doing so.

I walk to the desk and set the paper down. "What?" I ask.

But again, he just stands there like he's in a trance.

The back of my neck breaks out in a sweat, and I'm getting nervous. Why is he just standing there, staring at me? "What do you want?" I press, my tone curt.

He opens his mouth but then closes it, swallowing.

"Pike, Jesus—"

"The day you left," he blurts out, and I stop.

I wait, listening as a look of fear flashes in his eyes.

"The house was so empty," he continues. "Like a quiet that was never there before. I couldn't hear your footsteps upstairs or your hair dryer or anticipate you walking into a room. You were gone. Everything was"—he drops his eyes—"gone."

A ball lodges in my throat, and I feel tears threaten, but I tense my jaw, refusing to let it out.

"But I could still feel you," he whispers. "You were still everywhere. The container of cookies in the fridge, the backsplash you picked out, the way you put all my pictures back in the wrong spot after you dusted my bookshelves." He smiles to himself. "But I couldn't rearrange them, because you were the last to touch them, and I wanted everything the way you had it."

My chin trembles, and I fold my arms over my chest, hiding my balled fists under my arms.

He pauses and then goes on. "Nothing would ever go back to the way it was before you came into my house. I didn't want it to." He shakes his head. "I went to work, and I came home, and I stayed there every night and all weekend, every weekend, because that's where we were together. That's where I could still feel you." He steps closer, dropping his voice. "That's where I could wrap myself up in you and hang on to every last thread in that house that proved you were mine for just a little while."

His tone grows thick, and I see his eyes water.

"I really thought I was doing what was best," he says, knitting his brow. "I thought I was taking advantage of you, because you're young and beautiful and so happy and hopeful despite everything you'd been through. You made me feel like the world was a big place again."

My breathing shakes, and I don't know what to do. I hate that he's here. I hate that I love that he's here. I hate him.

"I couldn't steal your life from you and keep you to myself, you know?" he explains. "But then I realized that you're not happy or hopeful or making me feel good because you're young. You are those things and you're capable of those things, because you're a good person. It's who you are."

A tear spills over, gliding down my cheek.

"Baby," he whispers, his hands shaking. "I hope you love me, because I love you like crazy, and I'm going to want you the rest of my life. I tried to stay away, because I thought it was the right thing, but I fucking can't. I need you, and I love you. This doesn't happen twice, and I'm not going to be stupid again. I promise."

My chin trembles, and something lodges in my throat, and I try to hold it in, but I can't. My face cracks, and I break down, turning away from him. The tears come like a goddamn waterfall, and I hate him. I fucking hate him.

His arms are around me in a second, and he hugs me from behind, burying his face in my neck.

"I'm sorry I took so long," he whispers in my ear.

"You did," I cry. "You took so long."

"I'll make it up to you." He turns me around and clutches my face, pressing his lips to my ear. "I promise."

He holds me for a while, and my pride tells me not to give in. Not to let anyone in and no more second chances.

But I'm not completely certain I wouldn't do the same thing if I were in his shoes. Cole, Lindsay, Shel, my sister, Dutch, the whole neighborhood . . . they'll talk. Some will judge him for this. His fear is justified.

But they don't know. They don't know how lucky we are and how good it is.

I love him.

I pull away and wipe at my teardrops on his T-shirt. "And I didn't put the picture frames back in the wrong spot," I tell him. "That's where they belong."

He laughs, wiping away the tears on my face, and brings me in, kissing me. Everything floods back—his mouth, soft but strong, and his taste—and I kiss him back, rising up on my tiptoes to deepen it.

"Need a room?" someone chimes in. "You came to the right place."

I pull away again, and Pike clears his throat as Danni walks in and sits back on the stool.

"Pike, this is Danni," I say. "Danni, Pike."

"Nice to meet you," she says.

"Yeah, you, too." He holds out his hand, and they shake.

"So, do you guys want a room?" she asks again. "On the house?" She pulls the last room key out of the cubby and holds it out.

He leans over, taking it. "Thank you. Really. That'd be great."

She shifts her gaze to me, and I can tell she's looking for confirmation that everything is okay. I nod, assuring her.

"Well, have a good night," she tells us. "I'll see you in the morning."

Pike takes my hand, and we walk outside, the humid August air already damp on my arms. He clutches me like he's going to lose me as we walk to his truck and retrieve his duffel bag and a little package. I laugh, seeing mud still all over his door and the tires.

Walking to the room, I pass the five I doled out to "Tyler" and his ladies, and I can hear music, chatter, and laughing from inside several of them. We pass another room with curtains drawn, but light from the TV pierces the fabric.

Up the sidewalk, one of the regulars, Peter, walks to the Coke machine with a sword strapped to his naked back and wearing his usual black leather pants.

"What the hell is that?" Pike mumbles to me, looking at him.

"That's Peter," I say, admiring the black hair that drapes damn near down to his waist. "He's here every weekend, LARPing."

Pike pinches his brows together and looks at me.

"Live-action role-playing," I explain. "Sometimes he brings a beautiful elvish princess and they get kinky. You can hear it through the walls."

He snorts as we reach our room, and he unlocks the door. I step inside and walk over to the nightstand, turning on the lamp as he shuts and locks the door.

"Can I take you home tomorrow?" he asks. "I'm anxious."

I peer up at him. "Anxious for what?"

He just quirks a smile. "Everything, I guess."

He tosses a little box at me, and I reach up, catching it.

"What's this?" I ask.

"Open it."

I walk to the sink and face the mirror, tearing off the tape. Ripping open the box, I dig out three cassette tapes and immediately start grinning.

"I found some eighties music for you I can stand," he says, coming up behind me as I inspect the new additions to my collection.

"AC/DC," I read the labels. "Metallica . . . Beastie Boys."

I look up at him, and he dips down, kissing me. I close my eyes, feeling like I'm dizzy. I wonder how much trouble he went through to find these. I hope it was a lot.

I flick his tongue with mine, the kiss turning heated and strong, and I reach around, clasping the back of his neck, not letting him go.

He sucks in air through his teeth, and I can feel him harden through his jeans.

"Baby, I've been all over fucking Virginia," he pants. "I need a shower."

"We'll take one after," I say, reminiscing about our kitchen table foray two months ago when he wanted a shower first then, too.

I drop the tapes to the counter and press my back into him, moaning.

He kisses me and pulls back just a hair to look into my eyes. "There hasn't been anyone else since you left," he tells me.

I blink up at him. "I know. I can't say the same, though."

His face falls, and his jaw tenses.

I pin him with regretful eyes. "I missed you, so I had a few drinks on the Fourth of July and had a little tryst with the desk corner in room 108," I tell him. "It was pretty hot."

He breaks into a laugh, his body shaking behind me.

I actually didn't do that, but I felt tempted a few times. When I close my eyes, though, I only see him, and it felt pathetic to masturbate to a guy who I thought didn't want me.

So, I've been chaste, and now I'm ready to go wild.

Turning me around, he picks me up, and I wrap my legs around his waist as he carries me to the bed. Letting me fall back, he pulls his shirt over his head and stares down at me as he unfastens his belt.

All of a sudden, though, a very loud and fast pounding hits the wall behind our bed, and shrill moans and whimpers pierce the walls. We both stop and listen as Peter and his princess go at it in the next room, banging their headboard against ours and sending it bobbing back and forth.

His eyes go wide. “Oh, they *are* loud.”

Yup.

Then he looks down at me, an air of mischief in his eyes. “We can take ’em.” And then he grabs the back of my knees, yanking me down to the end of the bed, and I squeal as he comes down on top of me.

29

Jordan

One Year Later

"I'll learn on my own if you stop micromanaging me!" I scold, trying to push Pike's hands off my handles.

He sits behind me on my new four-wheeler and revs the gas, vaulting us up out of the ravine and out of the mud. I gasp, leaning back into him, my stomach dropping to my feet as I clutch his forearms to steady myself. I laugh.

"Well, if you'd wear the helmet . . ." he says.

"But I can't see in the helmet."

We're mudding. It's not like we're cruising at thirty-five miles an hour out here. I don't need a helmet for this. And plus, I'm just learning how to use the quad today. He'll be lucky if I top out at twelve miles an hour.

But if I won't wear the helmet, then he won't let me drive it alone until I've been given proper instruction. Hence the driver's ed lesson.

We race across the bank, mud splattering all over my new red ATV, my boots, and my jeans. I also feel a few drops of something cold periodically land on my hair, held out of my face with a baseball hat, and on my shirt.

My finals just ended this week, and I've had lack-of-sleep headaches nonstop, but I feel so much better today. I'm glad he surprised me with this. A day of him, fun, and fresh air is all I needed.

He's been so great through my bad moods the past couple weeks as I study, making me snacks and doing well to not distract me while I get work done.

Although he did come into the library—my old bedroom—and tempt me with a quickie here and there under the guise that I needed a study break.

Yeah, okay.

I smile, remembering him walking in while my nose was buried in a book, pulling off his shirt, and telling me he's going to get a shower, but I know what he really wants, because he knows the sight of him in only jeans is my frickin' porn. I didn't put up a fight. I never do. I want him just as much as he wants me.

But now finals are over and so are classes until next fall, and I'm all his.

His truck is parked ahead, and his ATV still sits on the attached trailer, clean and shining just like new.

He pulls to a stop and turns off the motor, burying his lips in my neck and kissing me.

"I have a present for you," he teases.

I turn my head, grazing my lips over his cheek. "You already gave me my present." I run my fingers over the handles of my new four-wheeler, also remembering the orgasm I got at six this morning. It's been a very good birthday so far.

"The four-wheeler was just an excuse to get myself one, really," he explains.

I nibble his jaw. "So, what is it, then? More antiques for my collection?"

"Cassette tapes aren't antiques, Jordan," he states firmly.

I laugh. "You're right, you're right. They're considered *classics*. Like cars over thirty years old. Like you!" I chirp. "You're a classic."

He clamps his hand over my mouth, stifling my laughter and

shaking his head. He's not offended by my running joke. I only tease him about his age because he still thinks it's an issue, and I'm trying to lighten the mood.

And to a few people around town, it is strange. But they mean nothing to us. Cole, my sister, and Shel have all come around, albeit Cole a little slower than the others, but they're all that matters.

I bite at his fingers on my mouth, playing, but suddenly, he holds up a small black leather box in front of me, and I stop.

My face falls, and I'm no longer laughing.

Lowering his hand from my face, he remains silent as I stare at the case, a million different thoughts running through my head right now, but I can barely hear them, because the pulse in my ears is deafening.

Oh, my God. It's not a . . . ring, is it? I mean, we haven't talked about this.

I always hoped it would come to this, but Pike doesn't take big steps without a little help. I had no idea . . .

Slowly reaching out, I take the box out of his hand and open it, my mouth going as dry as a desert when I see the diamond ring inside.

Tears sting my eyes, and my mouth falls open.

It's a rose. Like the ones on the birthday cake he got me last year and the flowers I planted around the house this spring. A large diamond sits in the middle of platinum petals, adorned with little stones themselves, and it's unlike anything I've ever seen. Beautiful and special and completely me.

He wants to marry me?

I let out a little sob, overwhelmed. "Are you kidding me right now?" I snap. "I'm covered in mud!"

He's doing this now? When there were hundreds of dinners and breakfasts in bed this past year when I was pretty and clean?

His chest shakes with a laugh behind me and he wraps his arms around my waist. "You're beautiful."

I rub my thumb over the large stone. It's real. All this is real.

"I've been planning this for a long time," he says. "You think I'd know what I wanted to do or say, but I can't think right now." His breath falls across my hair as he whispers. "I guess I should've gotten down on one knee, huh?"

"No, don't let go of me." My voice shakes.

I swallow the hard lump in my throat and pull the ring out, setting the box down and trying it on. The cool band slides on perfectly, and I take his hand, putting it on the handle again with mine on top of it.

His finger doesn't yet have a ring as I entwine our hands.

But it will.

My heart swells like it's too much for my chest to hold, and I'm speechless. He certainly surprised me. I can't believe he did this without giving me one clue what he was up to.

I stare at our hands together, leaning back into him and even more excited now for everything that's to come. I think part of me—a small part—was still waiting for him. It was always in the back of my mind, that fear that he might still see me as too young or not ready for this or him, but he has to know . . .

I'm happy every day. There's nothing that feels better than him.

A few raindrops hit my arms, the clouds overhead darkening, and I finally find my breath, inhaling deeply.

"So, you going to say yes or . . ." He trails off.

I smile at the small ounce of fear I hear in his voice at my silence. "Yes." I turn and kiss him. "You make me so happy. I love you."

He presses his forehead to mine. "I love you so much it hurts, baby."

His mouth sinks to mine again, and he takes my face in his hands, kissing me and teasing my tongue to where I feel it everywhere. My breathing turns ragged, and I'm about to suggest we take this to the truck, since we're all alone out here, but the rain picks up, hitting my body much faster now.

I break the kiss and look up, squinting against the rain to see the storm clouds overhead. Summer storms are starting early this year.

He climbs off, helping me, and we both jog to the passenger side of the truck, him opening my door for me.

"Can we do it today?" I ask, taking my brand-new, unused helmet off my seat and setting it on the floor.

"Get married?" he asks. "You really don't care about the wedding, do you?"

I look over to see him grinning at me as he pulls off his muddy shirt and tosses it into the bed of the truck.

I stand in the open door and shrug. It never occurred to me growing up to care about a party and fancy clothes. When other young women dreamed up their theme colors and bridesmaids' dresses, I just wanted everything after that. The husband, the kids, the home with the smell of cookies after school, picnics and road trips . . .

I climb the step, about to get into the truck, but he pulls me back around and into him. I fall into his naked chest, my feet still planted on the step, and wrap my arms around his neck.

"I kind of do care about it," he admits, flinching a little as if in apology. "I've never been married before, either, you know? I'd love to see you in a dress."

Now, how can I say no to that? I nod, kissing him again. It might be fun, actually. Engagement photos in the mud? *Yes, please.*

"I was thinking Mexico," he tells me, peering up at me. "A beach on the Sea of Cortez and just you, me, and our close and personals?"

I smile. "Hell, yes."

Sounds right up our alley. Quiet, private, and perfect. And I'd be lying if I didn't say it excited me to go somewhere I've never been. I've barely been out of this town, and the idea of having to get a passport thrills me as much as now having to shop for this dress Pike is going to die when he sees me in.

I'm already bubbling with excitement at the look I hope to see on his face.

He looks up at me, growing quiet, his eyes serious. "You gonna want kids?" he asks.

My heart thumps, knowing this is a potentially sensitive subject.

"One, at least?" I broach, timid. "Is that okay?"

I understand that starting over is a lot to ask of him, but I would love to have his baby.

Eventually.

To my surprise he barely hesitates before nodding. "I'm okay with it," he answers. "Can't wait too long, though, or I'll be getting the senior citizen discount at the kid's graduation dinner."

I break into a laugh.

"After you get your degree, though," he tells me, "it's on, okay?"

"Okay."

I sit down in the seat and pull off my muddy boots, throwing them in the bed with Pike's shirt, and I take off my hat, my hair falling around my face.

"You know . . ." I start, "I'm a little nervous."

"Oh?"

I shake my head, tsking. "Marrying an older man with so much more experience . . ."

He comes up to me, grabbing my hips and pulling me to the edge of the seat and into him. I run my hand up his naked chest.

"I don't need my wife to know what other men like," he states. "Just what I like."

My eyebrows shoot up, getting an idea. Slowly, I unbutton the flannel shirt I'm wearing and watch his eyes go round when he sees I have nothing on underneath it. I open it slightly, inviting his eyes to rest on my bare breasts.

"And what do you like?" I taunt like that night in the kitchen when I put a Band-Aid on his finger.

His gaze is locked on my chest, and I let the shirt fall down my arms, my nipples hard from the chill of the rain in the air.

I drop my voice to a whisper. "I think I need more practice."

His eyes grow dark and full of desire as he looks up at me. Pulling himself up on the step, he dives into the truck and out of the rain, his body coming down on top of mine. I fall back on the seat, opening my legs for him as I work to open his belt.

Our lips hover over each other.

"Whatever the birthday girl wants," he whispers.

EPILOGUE

Pike

Nine Years Later

A crack of thunder pierces the silence, and I blink my eyes awake as lightning flashes through the room. I sigh, sticking my thumb and a finger in my eyes, rubbing.

More rain, dammit.

Nope. It's not my job to worry about it for the next two weeks, so I'm not going to. Dutch can handle it. (I have to believe that.)

Jordan and I are out of here in the morning, and he's in charge while I'm gone. I promised her she and the boys would have my complete attention while we're away as long as she leaves her laptop home and doesn't try to sneak in any work, either. The problem with her is that her work is also her hobby, so I kind of felt bad asking her to stay away from something she loves for that long.

But she's right. The kids need to see us without our eyes buried in some screen.

I turn my head, looking down at her next to me. She's curled up on her side, her nose and lips buried in my arm with one hand draped over my chest and shoulder. Her shoulder-length hair is swept over the top of the pillow, and I reach down and pull the sheet back up over her bare legs and white panties. She wears the yellow T-shirt she got on our honeymoon in Mexico, and I still can't tell she's four months along with our second kid. Our first,

Jake, is asleep in his room down the hall. *Jake Ryan Lawson.* She named him after some guy in a teen movie from the eighties, but I don't tell people that. She can tell them, but I'm certainly not going to.

I rest my hand on her thigh and stare up at the ceiling.

I'm forty-eight years old. What business do I have with a six-year-old son and another kid on the way?

But fuck, I'm happy.

The pitter-patter of the rain hits the windowpanes, and I feel Jordan breathing so peacefully next to me. I close my eyes. *Mine.* My house, my wife, my family . . . *mine.* Sometimes I'm so overwhelmed by how lucky I am that I can't wrap my head around this all being real. I still can't stop reaching for her when she's close or stop being anxious to crawl into bed at night, knowing we're finally alone.

I suddenly remember the wash drying out on the line in the backyard and pop up and out of bed. "Shit," I mumble, pulling on some lounge pants.

Leaving the room, I walk down the hall, stopping at Jake's door and quietly cracking it open. He sleeps in his bed, while Cole's son, Parker, is passed out next to him. Both of them look like a spiderweb of arms and legs, and I laugh under my breath. We've explained to them that Jake is Cole's brother, which makes him Parker's uncle, but it's hard for them to make sense out of something like that when they're the same age.

My chest tightens every time I see them like this, though. My son and my grandson are more like brothers, and I really don't give a shit if it seems weird to others, because we're a lucky family.

Cole met his wife, Kotori, when he was stationed in Okinawa, and both of them are currently attending some convention her company sent her to in Las Vegas. We invited Parker to join us for a couple weeks, so they could go on their own.

Closing the door, I jog down the stairs, passing all our family pictures on the walls, most of which I'm in, and walk through the kitchen to the laundry room. I grab a wicker basket off the dryer and make my way into the backyard. The rain is small, but it hits my back like little darts, sharp and fast. I run over to the clothesline and start yanking beach towels and any other last-minute clothes Jordan wanted washed in order to throw in the suitcases. We probably have more than enough packed for the road trip north, but my luck, we'll get to the lake house and she'll be pissed off for two weeks because she doesn't have her other-other pink shirt that goes better with the sneakers she got that time on that one trip.

I clear the line, stuffing all the pins into the bag, and carry the basket back inside. Opening the dryer, I stick everything in and turn on the machine, making sure it's ready for when we wake up in the morning.

Heading back upstairs, I close the door to our bedroom and climb back into bed, Jordan immediately finding me in her sleep and snuggling up. I wrap my arm around her.

"Everything okay?" she asks softly.

"Yeah." I kiss her forehead, pulling the covers up over us. "Go back to sleep. Big day tomorrow."

"You know I can't sleep during thunderstorms."

My chest shakes with a laugh, because she's such a liar. This issue of sleeping during storms has never been an issue in our bed. She sleeps like the dead next to me, and I take a lot of pride in that fact.

I suddenly want to see her face, so I reach over with my free hand and take the matches, striking one and lighting the candle on the bedside table. I blow out the match, the room glows with a soft light, and I look down at her face, still in shadow but a little more visible now.

Her long lashes and beautiful skin. Her pink lips that I've kissed thousands of times for thousands of hours. Her body that I've loved for ten years and in a million different ways. You think I'd be used to her by now, but my dick starts to stiffen at just the thought of her on top of me again.

Her head pops up and she looks around, startled. "Oh, the clothes," she bursts out.

"I got them," I tell her, patting her leg to calm her down. "Don't worry."

She relaxes, nodding and yawning at the same time.

"Kids okay?" she asks, putting her head back down on my chest.

"Yep. Sleeping like logs."

I rub her back, trying to soothe her back to sleep, and feel her leg drape over mine. I clench my teeth, the warmth between her thighs seeping through to my own now. My groin pulses.

"Are you nervous?" I whisper.

"A little."

She's giving a presentation at the opening of the botanical gardens she designed for the new museum in Rockford tomorrow. After college, she worked for a firm for several years but decided to start her own last year. The museum was her first big solo project, and not only are the clients extremely pleased with her work, but word of it has brought in several new projects already. She's an artist.

But one who hates public speaking, so I'm thinking it'll be painful but short tomorrow.

"Just remember." I kiss her hair. "We get to climb in the car and hit the road afterward."

Her arms tighten around me. "Can't wait."

After the presentation, we're driving up to Minnesota, where we rented a lake house for two weeks. Her sister, Cam, and the latest in a string of wealthy boyfriends also rented a house nearby, so they're bringing her son with them, and we'll have company when we feel like it.

And someone to take the kids off our hands for a night when we don't.

Her fingers trail down my chest, and she drags her nails lightly down my stomach. My body starts to come alive under my skin, and I don't think I can sleep until I get it out of my system.

"So, you awake now?" I tease.

She nods. "You?"

"It's hard to sleep when you do that."

She laughs and raises herself up, sliding a leg over my body and straddling me. "Oh, goodie."

She lifts her shirt over her head, and I immediately touch her stomach, feeling the hard little mound where my son or daughter sits.

She smirks down at me, cocks her head playfully, and I still see that girl crawling on the floor of the movie theater every time I look at her. She had me even then.

"I love you," I tell her.

Coming down, she hovers over me, looking into my eyes as my hand goes to her breast.

"Oh, wait." She pops up and leans over to blow out the candle.

"No, leave it on," I groan, rolling my hips up into her. "I want to see you."

She looks down at me. "Did you lock the door?"

I make a face. "Shit."

Why do I always forget that? I've only had kids for over half my life.

"Can't have them getting an eyeful, can we?" she scolds but smiles at me.

Leaning back over, she closes her eyes, pauses a moment, thinking, and then opens them again, softly blowing out the candle. The room goes dark except for the moonlight making the rain shimmer on our bedroom wall, and I see her outline come back down on top of me.

I squeeze her hips, feeling her grind on me. "You ever going to tell me what you wish for?" I ask.

She kisses me, whispering against my lips, "It's bad luck to tell."

She moves down my neck, and I arch my head back and close my eyes, letting her in.

"But I will say," she goes on, nibbling my jaw, "I always wish for the same thing, and every day it comes true."

BIRTHDAY GIRL BONUS HALLOWEEN SCENE

This scene takes place a couple months after
Pike comes to get Jordan from the motel
but before he proposes to her on the four-wheeler.
She's back in college and living in his house.

Jordan

I love this car. I grab my water bottle and the receipts I'd stuffed into the drink holder, fold back my visor, and take my backpack from the passenger's seat. I step out of the new Chevy Blazer Pike bought me.

I mean, bought us.

Technically us. That's the story he's sticking to anyway.

I swing my backpack over my shoulder and head for the garage, turning around to walk backward as I gaze at my new car, dark red with black wheels. I smile. It just matches the leaves falling from the trees onto the sidewalk, perfectly complementing the jack-o'-lanterns on the curb. I want to jump up and down at how pretty it is.

And then I roll my eyes at myself and toss the garbage into the trash bin as I turn back around.

Pike still drives that old, beat-up truck, and while this new car is nice for "nights out or road trips" like he said, I know he bought it for me. *Safe and reliable*, he said.

Because I can't take care of myself, and I'm just one expense after another for this guy. Not that he gives any impression it bothers him. I just don't want people thinking he's my meal ticket. He gives me so much, and I just . . .

I catch movement to my right and stop, looking out over at Kyle

Cramer's house. His screen door swings open and Cam steps out, him trailing behind her as she laughs at something.

My shoulders fall as I freeze. *Shit.*

Her long hair shines in the light, and she slips her hands into her dark skinny jeans pockets, her skin exposed in her off-the-shoulder shirt as she turns to look at him. He has a towel wrapped around his waist as he uses another one to dry the back of his head. She leans in and kisses him, long and slow, moving over his mouth soft and passionate.

Like a promise of more to come.

Like how I kissed Pike in the shower this morning.

I dart my eyes over my shoulder, scanning the neighborhood for noses stuck to their windows or peeled-back drapes.

Cam heads toward me, and Kyle disappears into his house again.

"Hey!" she says, smiling.

But I'm not smiling. "What are you doing?"

Her face falls, and she straightens, rolling up her sleeves. "You know I've been trying to fit in more cardio, Jordan."

But her joke doesn't breach me. Cardio? We go to the gym for that.

"Seriously, Cam," I whine. "The whole neighborhood is already whispering about what a tart I am behind my back, and you're only adding fuel to it."

"Tart?" She looks at me, amused.

Yes, tart! Ever since Pike brought me home from Virginia, word has certainly gotten around. *They're sleeping together! How long has it been going on? She's doing it because Cole dumped her. What kind of man wouldn't lose control with* that *living in the house? Poor guy—her attention will certainly cost him a few bucks.*

I mean, Jesus. Almost no one understands our relationship or how we have anything to talk about, so of course they assume it comes down to sex and money.

I walk toward the kitchen door in the garage, finding the door key.

Cam chases after me. "Don't put me in a bad mood. I just spent a very enjoyable afternoon next door, getting—"

"Lalalalalalala . . ." I sing to drown her out as I unlock the door.

Picturing Kyle Cramer getting exactly what he wants from my sister aggravates me. He doesn't deserve her.

"And I am not going to feel guilty," she goes on over my singing, "just because the Northridge housewives are jealous."

I throw her a look and push through the door, hitting the button to close the garage on my way in.

She adjusts her sweater and lifts her chin. "If they had a lick of sense, they'd take a few notes from me, drop to their knees, and give their men something to watch tonight other than the TV."

Oh, for God's sake . . .

But I honestly don't know why I'm worried. Or angry. Cramer isn't evil. I still watch his kids here and there—partly because I love watching Pike with them, but . . .

I don't know. He's sleazy, and he likes to mess with her head at the strip club. Making her give his friends dances or paying other dancers to get on him when he knows she's watching.

But it's Cam and not me, and Cam is different.

She approaches, softening her voice. "Stop worrying, okay?" she pleads. "I'm already growing bored with him."

Well, thank God. I'm sleeping with the single dad here, she's sleeping with the single dad there. We'll get reps.

I plop down at the kitchen table, letting out a deep breath. I'm overreacting.

"Why are you so worried about everything lately?" she asks.

Why? It takes a moment to find my words, but with my sister, I know I can just be straight.

"He pays for everything," I mumble what's really bothering me. "My education, the new car, allllllll the bills . . ."

I went back to Grounders last month, but with school and his unpredictable work schedule, we hated being apart any more than necessary.

So I quit, and he was beyond thrilled. He supports us entirely.

Cam pulls out the chair and sits down next to me. "You're his future, and he's investing in it," she tells me. "Your college debt would be his as your husband anyway. What's the difference if he helps you now or gets saddled with your debt later?"

"Husband?" I laugh, even though flutters hit my stomach. "Slow down, now."

"Oh, please." She levels me with a sarcastic gaze. "He closes his eyes when he kisses your forehead, for Christ's sake. He's not letting you go. Ever."

He closes his eyes? Really? My cheeks warm.

"You've made his house a home," she continues, "you love him, you're honest, loyal, and genuine, and you're completely devoted to him. He's the luckiest man in the world and he damn well knows it."

I chew the inside of my lip to keep the tears away. Leave it to Cam to put things in perspective. I love him good, don't I? It's enough?

"Those bitches had their chance." She tries to pinch my cheek, but I swat her hand away. "They're just bitter that a kid was smarter than them and snatched him up while they were snoring."

Yeah, okay.

Part of me still feels like Pike will wake up and realize he's taken a step backward in life and want someone his own age.

But she's made me feel a little better. I'm doing my best. I know that much. It won't be like this forever. I'll graduate, get a job, and contribute more.

Cam rises and adjusts her jeans. "Now I have to go get my puddin' and get ready," she says. "I'm the Harley to his Joker tonight. Woohoo."

Oh, that's right. Halloween. Pike and I won't be home tonight, so I can't pass out candy. I'll leave some candy on the porch. Hopefully the teenagers don't take it all.

I walk over and dig a bag out of one of the cabinets, opening it. I pull out a handful of chocolate and quickly stick it into a baggie.

I give it to my sister. "Give him his first candy of the night from me," I tell her. "And have fun."

She takes the baggie but notices something and stops, picking up my costume on the hanger as it lies draped over the island barstool.

"Yeah, you, too," she says and holds up the costume, looking at me.

I shrug. What?

It's the Little Red Riding Hood costume from the movie *Trick 'r Treat*.

She starts to move her body, moaning and rolling her eyes into the back of her head. "Oh, Grandmother," she pants. "What . . . a big . . . dick you have!"

Her mock sex sounds fill the house as she thrusts against my costume, and I grab a cookie from the plate on the counter and throw it at her, snatching my outfit out of her hands.

She rears back, shielding herself from any more attacks as she laughs.

Moron.

"See yaaaaa," she teases.

And then she turns and leaves.

I hold up my costume and look at it. I'm pretty sure Pike won't be wearing his, but it doesn't matter.

Wearing this tonight, I'll have plenty to fear from him anyway.

And I can't wait.

My hair blows, and I look up at the night sky, spotting the dark clouds even at night. I hold a small basket of snacks, the air caressing my chest through the thin fabric of my short-sleeved, low-cut peasant blouse. I wore a red cape for public.

And no bra under the thin white shirt for Pike in private.

I look over, seeing him approach with a picnic blanket under one arm as he slips his car keys into his jeans pocket and heads for the entrance where I stand. He had to work late, so we decided to meet here.

I smile, laughing under my breath. His long-sleeved gray T-shirt peeks out from the bottom of his black pullover jacket. God, he's so hot.

But no costume, I guess.

He shakes his head at me, clearly seeing my expression. "You know I love you . . ."

"And I love how predictable you are," I tease, coming in and wrapping an arm around him. "It's okay."

He was supposed to dress as Principal Wilkins from the same movie I'm dressing from. I guess he decided the suit and glasses were just too silly, but I couldn't care less. I'm still calling him Principal Wilkins.

All night long.

He slides an arm around my waist and lifts me up. I press my lips hard to his, just holding him and breathing him in. I love how he smells. Like wood and wind and warmth.

I suddenly want to be somewhere where I don't have to let him go.

"And I'm loving this," he says, looking down at my outfit as he sets me back on the ground. "You sure you want to see a movie?"

I catch the insinuation in his tone and toss him a look. We're not going home. Yet.

"It's supposed to rain," he quickly explains. "We could watch it at home."

I laugh again, threading my fingers through his and walking us both into the park.

"Nuh-uh," I tell him. "We've been cooped up long enough."

Between my second year of college starting and that site two towns over he's been working on, we've been busy. If he's not working and I'm not studying, then we're too wrapped up in each other to make it out of the house much.

But . . .

I don't know. It feels like something else is holding us back, too, and it could be my paranoia stemming from why I left last June, but I can't help but feel like he's still nervous sometimes.

Like they can't judge us if they can't see us? We go to the store together, Home Depot, the movies, but . . . if we go out to eat, he makes some excuse to try a new place in the next town or grab takeout instead and have a picnic. Which is awesome. I haven't complained.

But still, we're not going home yet.

We head through the park; the open, wide lawn spreading before us has a huge blow-up screen already set up and a sea of people—couples and families—parked on the grass with their blankets and coolers. It's after nine, so trick or treating is done, and kids run around, ready to see a classic horror movie. Albeit a PG one.

The surrounding trees hug the crowd in shadows as Pike leads me over to the concession stands. "Two, please," he says to the kid and then looks down at me. "Butter?"

I nod.

"Both with butter," he orders.

Poltergeist is showing tonight, and the screen plays a bunch of retro movie trailers as everyone finishes trailing in, getting their snacks, and getting seated. As soon as I heard which movie was playing, I knew we had to come tonight. It was the date we almost made the first time we met watching *Evil Dead* last May. It was the date he tried to make a month later when I left his house—and his bed—and ran far away, because I knew if I stayed, I wouldn't be able to resist wanting to be with him.

Two months later, he came and got me, and now, more than

two months after that, we're inseparable unless we can't be. I wake up with him, I go to sleep with him, and I get to touch him anytime I want. He's always looking at me, never goes anywhere except work without me, and for some reason, doesn't think I know how to undress myself for bed every night, so he helps with that, too.

Such . . . a sweetie.

I feel his eyes on me, and I look up, seeing his downcast gaze scowling at my breasts. I look down at them bulging out of the top, the cool air coaxing my nipples through the fabric. He pulls my cape closed, and I laugh to myself.

We pay for our popcorn and Pike takes both cups, both of us heading for the lawn.

But then suddenly, Dutch is there. We stop, seeing him exit the line next to us, grumbling, "They're not serving." He rolls his eyes at us. "Some bullshit about being family-friendly. Beer *is* the reason I am friendly to my family."

He walks off and Pike lets out a small laugh.

We watch Dutch head back to his family, and Pike and I start to move.

But then I hear my name.

"Jordan?"

We halt again.

I turn my head, following the voice, and see Mr. Jarchow holding a tray of nachos with two sodas tucked in his arm.

My old principal. Not nearly as good-looking as Pike would've been as one but still a good guy.

"Mr. Jarchow." I reach up for a quick hug.

Pike releases my hand as I do, and I pause but shake it off.

I come back, looking at my old high school principal. His light brown hair has turned dusty, and he looks like he hasn't been home from his workday yet, still wearing the same kind of slacks and shirts he wore to school when I attended, minus the tie. But who are we kidding? The tie was always gone by lunch period anyway.

"How are you doing, sweetie?" he asks.

"Good," I tell him. "I'm in my second year at Doral State."

"Studying . . . ?"

"Landscape design."

He snaps his fingers. "I knew it."

I laugh. Yeah, I was the president of the Garden Club. Not a difficult feat, though, when we only had three members.

Mr. Jarchow's eyes gleam at me but then they rise, seeing something behind me, and his lips turn tight. "Pike?" He nods in greeting. "How's it going?"

"Joey." Pike reaches out his hand.

"Joey?" I repeat, turning to Jarchow. "May I call you Joey now that you're no longer my principal?"

He laughs under his breath, but he looks straight at Pike when he says, "And no longer your fifth-grade teacher or your eighth-grade science teacher. Why not? You're an adult now."

I force the smile to stay on my face, but it's a struggle, because I can hear the disdain in his voice.

"Legally, anyway," he adds as an afterthought.

I close my eyes for a moment.

So I guess he knows. Pike and he are about the same age. One is in love with me and the other raised me, in a way that teachers do. Well, this is awkward.

And Jarchow isn't pretending otherwise.

Thankfully, Pike keeps his cool.

"You know, watching you grow up," Jarchow says, "I always knew you'd do something creative career-wise." His look is gentle and fatherly again. "It's good to hear I wasn't wrong."

His heartfelt demeanor never failed. He's one of the people I was lucky to have during those years.

But I can't feel or hear Pike's breathing next to me, which tells me he isn't.

"Well, have fun," I tell Jarchow.

"You, too, sweetie."

And he walks off, carrying his food to his three daughters seated not far away.

Pike takes my hand again and leads us off, but I can see the silent rage all over his face.

"It wasn't that bad." I clutch his hand. "He saw me grow up. It's weird to know I'm dating someone . . ."

"His age?" Pike finishes for me.

But I can tell he's aggravated. Mr. Jarchow just became principal five years ago, and he and Pike clearly knew each other well. Jarchow probably taught Cole.

"Dating . . ." Pike shakes his head as we walk, my word not sitting well for some reason.

"You sure you don't want to go home?" Pike teases, laying out the blanket. "We could make out."

I snort, setting the basket down. We can make out later. We *will* make out later.

Oingo Boingo's "Dead Man's Party" plays on the screen, and I look up, seeing Bentley with a few other people I know. He waves, and I wave back, the couples all laughing and joking together. I saw them less after high school but still at the bar sometimes. When I worked there.

I turn around to sit and meet Pike's eyes, his gaze darting quickly between my high school friends and me before he looks away again, fixing the blanket. I don't need those friends. We weren't close anymore anyway.

But seeing the couples together makes me realize Pike and I don't really have mutual friends, do we? At least not yet.

"You know, I was thinking . . ." he says, taking my hand and pulling me down into his arms. "You're going to need an internship senior year, right?"

"Yeah."

"Well, if you want . . ." He threads a lock of my hair through his fingers. "De Kalb is coming in to assess the property next week. You should be with me during the walk-through. Start networking."

I smile wide. Really? De Kalb is a major developer. I mean, interning with them would open so many doors, especially since we don't live in a metropolitan area.

"Convince your mom to let me host either Thanksgiving or Christmas, and I'll be with you during any walk-throughs you want."

He gives me a little snarl. "Fine, but if I have to eat a tofurkey, I will never have your back in front of her again."

Whatever. His mom likes my cooking. She's just a control freak about the holidays and loves for her house to be home base for all the family. Fine by me, but I'm cooking.

"You had tofurkey in the tetrazzini last week," I retort. "And you didn't notice."

"What?" He grabs me and digs his fingers into my waist.

I jerk, squealing at the tickle.

"Excuse me?" he plays, feigning anger. He tickles more, and I giggle as I try to squirm away from him.

But he pulls me back into his chest, both of us calming. "Actually, I did notice. I just didn't say anything."

"Sure."

He tosses me a look, and I try to hold back my smile. I'm not really changing what he eats on purpose, but if I'm cooking dinner that night, then he'll eat what I eat.

We look at each other, holding each other's eyes, and before I can help it, my gaze drops to his lips. Smooth and strong and have touched almost every inch of my body. They even have their favorite places on me.

And suddenly, I can't stop the heat rising to my cheeks. There's no one around us, we're in our bedroom, and everything is in slow motion. Our breathing quickens, and just as the lights around the field suddenly extinguish and the crowd cheers for the movie about to begin, his mouth lands on mine, and we kiss.

He doesn't use his tongue at first. Just cups my face as I tilt my head back and dive into our own little world. I love him so much. These stupid little kinks we continue to work out are nothing compared to this and how well he loves me. His tongue touches mine, and I'm on fire, almost sorry we came tonight after all.

But even after the movie later, I know we won't make it home before we have to pull over somewhere. I'll just have fun with the foreplay until then.

He snaps the ruffled band on my shirt at my cleavage. "You're enjoying this, aren't you?" he asks in a whisper.

I grin as I settle back against him and he kisses my temple. "A little."

Like yesterday morning when I made him breakfast in my underwear and half shirt.

But then when he insisted I sit in his lap to eat my breakfast, it was my fault when he wanted something other than his own food. He'd pulled me back against him like this, stuck his hand down the front of my panties, and fingered me before he went to work. I'll happily take those punishments for taunting him.

A breeze picks up, sweeping through the crowd, and people fumble to keep their blankets on the ground. Ours lifts, too, and I dart over, away from Pike for a moment, to dig a soda can out of the basket and plant it down on the blanket to hold it down.

"Pike?" a woman exclaims.

I look up and see a brown-haired woman in jeans, a tight pink Henley, and cat ears standing a few feet away. She holds out her hands, fixing a look of surprise on her face.

"Oh, my God, hey!" she says, charging over with her shiny, straight hair cropped to the shoulders and her eye makeup flawless.

Pike rises, and I still.

"Dee," he says, both of them embracing. "Jesus . . ."

I stand up, immediate insecurities rising, but I push them away.

She pulls back, and I watch as her hands drift down to his upper arms, holding him. I narrow my eyes.

"What's it been?" She looks him up and down. "Fifteen years?"

"Just about."

A gleam hits her eyes. "You know, I convinced myself every boy I went to school with was some beer-bellied baldy by now," she goes on, "and that was incentive enough to stay away from this town, but here you are, looking like someone I'm going to develop a teenage crush on before the night is over."

He laughs nervously, and I stand there, waiting for him to introduce us, but neither of them looks at me.

"How are you?" she asks. "Not married, right?"

And then she grabs his left hand to check for a ring, I presume. She sighs in relief, seeing his hand is bare. "Oh, thank God."

Pike takes a step back, and her arms fall away finally. "Are you still living in Arizona?" he asks.

"Yes, but it's so fucking hot—still." She laughs, and I go to fold my arms over my chest in aggravation but stop myself. "I needed a more cooperative temperature to feel festive. I'm just back for the weekend." And then she fixes him with a look. "Long enough to break your heart if you let me."

Um, no. The image of two high school friends falling in bed together, getting all hot after years of pent-up sexual attraction, makes my stomach roll. I let my eyes drift up and down her body. She's pretty.

I visibly turn my head to Pike, and he finally looks over at me.

So does she. As if I just appeared out of nowhere.

"Oh, I'm sorry," she says, wincing. "Excuse me, sweetie. You didn't hear me swear." She playfully puts her hands over my ears. "My bad."

Excuse me? I fist my skirt at my sides.

She pulls her hands away, shaking her head at herself. "She

looks exactly like you," she tells Pike. "I knew about Cole, of course, but I didn't know you had a girl, too."

My stomach sinks. Oh, my God.

Pike is dead silent for a few moments, and when I finally open my eyes, he chokes out a laugh. "You're so funny," he says. "Dee, this is my, um . . ." He swallows, forcing the word out. "Girlfriend, Jordan Hadley." And then he looks at me. "Jordan, this is Deanna Mansano. We graduated together."

I exhale. Fucking finally. Was that so hard?

I hold out my hand as Dee looks between the two of us, her eyes wide. Hopefully, she's not appalled at anything but her own assumptions.

"Hey," she finally says, taking my hand. "Wow, I'm so sorry. Nice to meet you."

"You, too."

I can still see the shock playing on her face as she probably reprocesses everything she just said that I was right in front of her to hear.

"And he's being kind," she tells me, finally recovering. "I barely graduated."

There's an awkward silence, but she holds out her hand, gesturing to both of us. "You should both come to Red's with us after the movie," she tells us, looking at Pike. "You and I can catch up, see some of the old crew, and I'm sure you won't have to guard the door while I pee this time."

I glance at Pike.

He nods, remembering. "Dutch ripped the doors off the stalls when someone gave him a sugar cube that he thought was only a sugar cube."

They laugh, sharing in the memory.

She knows Dutch, too. An emptiness settles inside me, but it hurts.

Of course she would know him. If she grew up here, she's known Pike and everyone else a lot longer than I have.

Pike's eyes look happily lost in thought for a moment. "I forgot all about that night."

"You were my hero." She touches his fucking arm again. "You should come, though. Both of you."

He looks over at me. "Actually, I have work early in the morning," he tells her. "Wish I could. Thank you, though."

He has the day off tomorrow. I can't go into the bar because I'm too young, and he doesn't want to tell her that.

"Well," she trails off, looking a little disappointed. "It was nice to see you. You both have a good night." She starts to move away, but she looks back at me. "And I'm sorry again for my mistake. I'm drunk. And an idiot."

I force a small smile. I guess I can't blame her. She's interested. Who wouldn't be?

And at least she backed off once she realized her mistake.

She leaves, and Pike and I stand there for a moment, watching her walk back to her friends.

Their friends.

"She's only in town for the weekend," I remind him. "You could go and hang out with your friends."

I trust him, even though the idea ties my stomach into knots. What if he realizes what he's missing? Conversations with someone on his level. Someone mature. Someone who's maybe done wanting kids and has been a few places and had a few experiences.

But he just replies, "They're not my friends, Jordan. Don't worry about it."

And he sits back down.

The movie starts, and I reluctantly join him, but not in his arms.

And he doesn't reach for me, either.

What the hell is happening? Is this on me or him? I'm not sure if I'm mad or mad that he's mad.

I let out a breath. I guess he had a point about keeping us secluded the past couple months. Jarchow pissed him off, and Deanna unnerved him. Deanna unnerved me. I wasn't jealous of Lindsay, mostly because Pike seems to dislike her vehemently.

But Pike has good memories with Dee. A history. Something I don't really have with him yet.

And my God . . . I do not look like him. She just humiliated him. Us.

"Pike—"

But he shakes his head. "Just watch the movie, baby."

He fiddles with my cape, putting it over my legs to cover me against the chill, and I fall silent. We sit there, the movie playing, but I don't think either of us is watching. The popcorn sits uneaten, as well as the snacks in the basket.

I drop my eyes, doubt swamping me. What's he thinking?

We burned hot for a few amazing months, but reality is seeping in, and he's going to start seeing this as a step back.

I'm not what he needs. This doesn't make him happy.

A joke passes in the film. We're silent. A scare pops up, we don't react.

We shouldn't have come tonight. This was a bad idea. Another bad idea from me and my stupid expectations.

Only now, I'm scared. I can't lose him. I walked away once, but . . . I can't walk away again. I don't want anything more than I want him, and if he ever didn't want me anymore, I'd . . .

"What's wrong?" I hear him ask.

The movie plays, the breeze quickens, and I blink at the sudden break in silence, seeing him leaning back on his hands out of the corner of my eye.

He knows what's wrong. I can barely manage more than a whisper, because my throat is filling with tears. "I love you more than anything."

He doesn't move, and if he were home, and I were sad, he'd pull me into his arms. But he can't do that now. Which is probably good.

"You're embarrassed," I tell him.

some people, this is no problem, but others have an idea of where they want to be at a certain point in their lives and they have to make a decision. Thankfully, Pike decided he wanted everything with Jordan. Absolutely everything.

Will you ever write a sequel to *Birthday Girl*?

I feel like Pike and Jordan are really happy! This is probably the best ending for a couple I've ever written. We basically got two epilogues. I think I'll leave it with that.

If you could write a spin-off, who would you write about?

Probably Cam—Jordan's sister. I wrote a scene, and it's available on my website. She seems like a lot of fun, and the dynamic intrigues me!

horrible decisions, because we're still developing emotionally. We get selfish. Mean. Arrogant. We get tunnel vision. We regress into small thinking. We get caught up in drama. Who a person is in their younger years is absolutely no indication of who they will be later. At least that's my opinion. I think Cole has had a lot of strain, with his mother especially, and we don't know his experience yet. I believe he's forgivable.

And if you, like Cole, are a person who regrets past decisions, just remember that every day is an opportunity to do better. You are under no obligation to be the same person tomorrow.

You're closer to Pike's age than Jordan's. Did you relate to his problems and the guidance he tries to give Jordan?
Oh, sure. I think that's one of the things I loved about writing this. I could relive two different times in my life. Jordan grew up faster than she maybe should have owing to her upbringing, but Pike did, too, under different circumstances. She strives for a life she'll never have to take a vacation from, and he's still waiting to start his life at all. I remember going through both of those times, wanting to escape the cycle at home and still not feeling like I'd found my calling even years later.

Pike makes a big deal out of his age, but thirty-eight isn't old by most people's standards. Why did you make it a big deal for him?
Good question! Pike is certainly not too old to get married and have more children, but I also think it's fair and practical for Pike to pause at the idea of starting over.

He had to consider that Jordan would change in her twenties. He worried she might not still want him later in life. He also worried about being an older father. I know a husband and wife who couldn't have children. When they looked into adopting a baby and realized the process could take five years, he said no. He didn't want to be forty-five and waking up for midnight feedings. For

TITLES BY PENELOPE DOUGLAS

The Fall Away Series

BULLY

UNTIL YOU

RIVAL

FALLING AWAY

THE NEXT FLAME
(includes novellas *Aflame* and *Next to Never*)

Stand-Alones

MISCONDUCT

BIRTHDAY GIRL

PUNK 57

CREDENCE

TRYST SIX VENOM

The Devil's Night Series

CORRUPT

HIDEAWAY

KILL SWITCH

CONCLAVE
(novella)

NIGHTFALL

FIRE NIGHT
(novella)

PRAISE FOR THE FALL AWAY SERIES

"Douglas follows *Bully* with a gritty, racy new adult tale peppered with raw emotions. This smoking-hot, action-packed story is a powerful addition to the edgy side of the genre, and readers will eagerly anticipate the next installment." —*Publishers Weekly*

"*Bully*, the first book in Douglas's new adult romance Fall Away series, was a self-published sensation, and *Rival*, the latest installment, is bound to capture even more readers with its intensely emotional writing, angst-driven plot, and abundance of steamy sex scenes."

—*Booklist*

"*Bully* was a wonderfully addictive read that kept my heart racing from start to finish. I could not put it down! 5 stars!!"

—Aestas Book Blog

"A heated and passionate novel, full of feeling and intensity that will appeal to the reader seeking an emotional rush."

—IndieReader

"I love, love, love, love, love, love, love this book! What a wonderful debut novel by Penelope Douglas! This book had me hooked! So addictive! So witty! So devastating! So amazing!"

—Komal Kant, author of *The Jerk Next Door*

"Jaxon Trent was so worth the wait! Penelope has masterfully combined the best of new adult with all of the scorching intensity of erotica to make *Falling Away* the best installment in [the] series."

—Autumn Grey, Agents of Romance

"What?"

"You're embarrassed."

He doesn't hesitate long. "I'm not."

The leaves on the trees rustle, and the blow-up movie screen sways, pulling at its stakes in the ground.

"I just wanted us to get out for the night," I tell him, pushing my hair out of my face to look at him. "We never go anywhere really public. You didn't even want to say I was your girlfriend."

"Like you rushed over to invite your friends over here or drag us over there?" he snaps back. "I mean, you're not at all afraid of what they'll think, I guess."

A crack of thunder pierces the air, and I feel a drop of rain hit my arm. But I barely register the commotion around us as people start chattering and rising from their seats.

So he thinks I'm the one who's embarrassed?

"The rain's starting." He sits up and pushes himself to his feet. "Let's go."

I rise. "I was thinking of you," I tell him. "Your comfort."

He leans down, pulling up the blanket and forcing me off.

"Because you worry too much what people think," I go on. "You just stood there while Jarchow acted like an ass."

"He acted like I was a child molester, Jordan!" he whisper-yells, glaring at me.

My spine goes steel-rod straight. I thought we'd settled this. We're not doing anything wrong.

But he apparently hasn't gotten over it, and I knew. I knew this was a problem in June, and it's still a problem for him.

I glare at him. "I told you. Didn't I tell you? Why did you even come for me in Virginia?"

Pain hits his eyes, but he doesn't answer me.

"People think you only want me for . . . That I'm good for one thing, because what else would you want from a bubblehead nineteen-year-old? Are they right?"

"Are you serious?" he growls, breathing hard as he inches closer. "You know that's not true. You're overreacting."

"Yes, teenagers do that." I dip down and swipe up the basket and popcorns, tossing them in the trash.

He shakes his head, like I'm oh so immature. "Let's just go."

"I have my car."

"Leave it!" he barks.

But I charge off, following the crowd to the parking lot. Maybe he's right. Maybe I'm overreacting.

But it seems I'm telling myself that a lot lately. Like today with Cam.

I never want to let him go, but what if this isn't the life he wants? It would kill me to make him unhappy.

Am I making him happy? Is this too hard?

"Jordan?" he calls after me.

"I need to be alone."

"Jordan!"

I whip around, fat drops of rain hitting me now as people go running to their cars. "I need to be alone."

Why are people so awful? What makes them have any right to judge us? I just wanted a night out. We should be able to do that. I should be able to walk out of the house in the morning without the neighbors looking at me like Pike is keeping a dirty little secret inside.

Rain pummels the gravel lot, kicking up dust and drenching my hair as I whip open the car door and put the basket inside. Untying my cape, I remove it and toss that inside, as well.

"I'm not embarrassed," Pike says, throwing the blanket into the back of the truck. "I'm pissed off."

I stand in my open door, watching him over my shoulder.

"I wasn't hiding you or embarrassed by you," he explains, anger creasing his brow. "I was hiding us."

Rain soaks my clothes and hits my mouth as cars peel off around us, parents getting their kids home.

"I'm fucking happy," he barks.

The words make my heart fly, but the rage on his face and the harsh tone of the words almost make me laugh.

"I'm fucking happy, and I hate everything they don't see in you," he tells me. "Looking at us like they know what goes on between us when they know nothing!"

I turn around slowly, watching him—his eyes intense and piercing me.

"Of how I'm ten times more entranced and obsessed with you—your whispers in the morning, the sight of you in my house, the feel of you in my arms, your smile, and your body—than I've been with all of the women in my life combined," he says. "Fucking looking at us with their snide smirks when they don't know what this is. I don't want anyone invading it, because I'm not going to be made to feel like this shouldn't be happening. I won't live without you."

My throat swells as tears fill my eyes, and I can't fucking breathe.

"Now, get in the goddamn car," he orders. "Don't make me come after you."

I swallow the needles in my throat as I watch him round his truck and pull off his jacket, tossing it inside.

But I don't move. I can't wait until we get home.

I don't take my eyes off him as the rain hits my blouse, soaking through. Pike goes to climb into his truck but stops, seeing me.

He comes back around the door, looking at me over the hood. He doesn't blink as his chest rises and falls steadily.

How does he do it? I've never been more afraid of losing something, because I've never loved anything more. But he always knows what to say to make it all go away.

I breathe hard, fisting my hands because they're aching for him,

and tip my face up to the rain, feeling the fabric stick to my nipples like a second skin.

He's going to marry me. This is it. It's forever.

"Wanna make me come after you?" I hear him ask.

And I smile, all the doubt washing away. I open my eyes and meet his again, seeing he's slowly stepping around the front of the car with a look in his eyes.

I nod, stepping around the front of my own vehicle and backing away from him as he inches forward. Raindrops stream down my legs, and water slips into my flats, but I barely notice. The way his eyes take me in, I may as well be naked.

Cars spin their wheels around us, one by one emptying the lot, and I carefully back up around them. Pike won't give chase with so many around us, so I don't need to run yet.

I hold his eyes as he cocks his head, looking at me like I'm asking for it.

A horn honks behind me, and I go to look over my shoulder to see who it is, but then I see Pike shoot off, darting toward me. I gasp, breaking into a laugh.

And run.

Scurrying through the mess of cars, I haul ass into the trees, digging in my heels, because I know he'll be on me any minute.

I can't believe he did that. People are probably wondering if I'm in danger or something, running away from him.

I dash into the woods, seeing the old Donahue barn, and swing open one of the doors, not bothering to close it.

Horses peek out from their stalls, the smell of hay hitting me as I race to the other side. Instead of seeking refuge, like he thinks I will, I run out through the other doors, exiting the barn, and quickly close them again. Heat swirls in my belly, and my heart is in my throat, but I keep my laughter quiet as I peek through the slits in the board and watch Pike enter the barn.

His T-shirt is already soaked, and I watch him glance from side

to side, looking for me inside the barn. I bite my bottom lip to keep from laughing.

He moves down, checking stall after stall, and I trail around the side of the barn, finding a hole here or a slit there to keep an eye on him. Once he goes up into the loft, I'll go inside, hide, and jump his ass when he least expects it.

But as I move to the next peep spot, I can't see him anymore. Did he go up the stairs already? I move my eye in a circle, scanning every inch I can see, and then move to another slit to try to get a better view.

He's not there, though. He has to be in a stall and out of my view. I stand up straight, ready to head to the front of the barn, but I see something out of the corner of my eye. My heart jumps.

I jerk my head, seeing Pike standing outside at the corner of the barn.

He runs for me.

I squeal and change directions, darting around the back of the barn again and rounding to the other side, toward the front.

But before I can reach the parking lot again, he's there, catching me in his arms. My startled scream turns into a laugh, and he throws me over his shoulder, carrying us both back into the barn.

My shoes are gone, and I'm smiling. But then I feel his hand slide up my skirt and pull down my panties, the fabric ripping.

I feel them slip over my feet, and then they're gone. My toes curl. God, I want him.

He sets me on the ground, and my mouth is on him as he tries to unlace my little corset.

"I love you," he says, breathless as I pull off his shirt.

But I can't pause long enough to reply. My hands are everywhere. On his chest, his face, and finally, down his jeans, rubbing him until he's moaning.

He yanks at my laces, and I shift on my tippy-toes, because my thighs are on fire.

"Just rip it," I breathe out.

He grabs my blouse, tearing it away from my breasts, his hand immediately cupping one and kissing me hard.

"Oh, God. Pike."

He lifts me up and carries me, but I don't know where, because I'm lost in his lips, his jaw, his neck . . .

He sits me down on a table, unfastens his belt and jeans, and pushes up my skirt. I barely have time to register the cool air hitting between my legs before he pushes me to lie back and thrusts inside of me.

"Ah!" I cry out.

He pauses for a moment, savoring the feel, and then dips down and sucks on my nipple as he begins moving inside me.

"I'm so lucky," he says.

I whimper, holding his head to me.

God, this is good. He lifts up, holding my hips and looking down at me, my tits bouncing back and forth, still wet from the rain.

But I can't even feel it. I'm on fire right now.

He thrusts again and again, kissing me and my breasts, his hands roaming my hips and ass. I'm never not in the mood for this and every time it's good.

Because we're made for one another.

"They need to see us, Pike," I tell him.

I mean, I get it. I know why he wants to keep us to ourselves and not let anyone rain on our parade, but that can't go on forever.

He comes back down, sucking my breast into his mouth. "You really want Jarchow to see what I'm doing to his former student right now?"

Ew. No. That's not what I meant.

He leans back up, propping himself up with one hand and grazing my face with the other as he looks down at me.

His dick slides in and out, and I run my hands down his chest, loving to watch how his body moves when he fucks me.

"They need to see us every day," I go on, "because the sooner they trust that this isn't changing, the sooner they'll get over it." I meet his eyes again. "And they will get over it. They'll see it every day, and they'll learn."

If one thing is certain in this world, it's that it moves on eventually.

"I love you," I tell him. "They can't ruin this."

He grabs the end of the table above my head and thrusts harder, his tip hitting me deep, and I roll my hips, arching my back.

"Ugh, fuck," he groans, closing his eyes.

And I smile, because that's the sexiest compliment a man can pay you in bed.

Not that we're in a bed, but all the same . . .

I hear a creak and the sounds of rain rushing in, and all of a sudden, Pike stops, popping his eyes open. What?

I twist my neck, following his gaze. Deanna stands in the doorway with some guy, both of them soaking wet.

Uhhhh . . .

Pike pulls me up, holding me to him, so all they see is my naked back.

Her mouth hangs open a little. Both of them are stopped dead in their tracks at what they see at the back of the barn, and I'm not sure if they're just trying to escape the rain or if they're up to the same thing we are.

A faint smile plays across Pike's lips. "Barn's full," he says.

And I turn around, burying my own smile in his neck.

Yep, he's mine.

"Excuse us," I hear her finally say.

And then the door creaks closed again.

I burst into laughter, wrapping my arms around him. I thought for sure he'd grab me and have us hurrying out of here, embarrassed.

But his mouth crashes down on mine and he's not stopping.

I fall back to the table as he pumps harder and faster, and I close my eyes again, feeling him and loving him so much.

"Pike," I moan.

He spreads my knees wide, leaning over me and thrusting as my orgasm crests and he starts groaning more and more.

But then something hits me, and I gasp. "Oh, shit."

"What?"

"I think I left a candle burning in the house?"

I don't remember if I blew out the blueberry vanilla one in the kitchen or not. Dammit!

I try to push myself up, but he leans down more, getting in my face as he rubs my clit and thrusts at the same time.

"You're not seriously stopping?" he growls against my mouth.

Heat spreads down my thighs, and I wrap an arm around his neck as my hair sticks to my face.

"But the house could burn down."

"I don't care."

His hard breath caresses my lips, and I smile, falling back onto the table again.

Fine. I don't care, either. Pretty sure we're going to care in a few minutes, but . . .

I moan, arching into him and clawing his chest. *Whatever.*

ACKNOWLEDGMENTS

First and always, to the readers—so many of you have been there, sharing your excitement and showing your support, day in and day out, and I am so grateful for your continued trust. Thank you.

To my family—my husband and daughter put up with my crazy schedule, my candy wrappers, and my spacing off every time I think of a conversation, plot twist, or scene that just jumped into my head at the dinner table. You both really do put up with a lot, so thank you for your patience.

To Jane Dystel, my agent at Dystel, Goderich & Bourret LLC—there is absolutely no way I could ever give you up, so you're stuck with me.

To the PenDragons—you're my happy place on Facebook. Thanks for being the support system I need and for always being positive. Especially to the hardworking admins: Adrienne Ambrose, Tabitha Russell, Tiffany Rhyne, Katie Anderson, and Lydia Cothran.

To Vibeke Courtney—my indie editor who goes over every move I make with a fine-tooth comb. Thank you for teaching me how to write and laying it down straight.

To Kivrin Wilson—long live the quiet girls! We have the loudest minds.

To Milasy Mugnolo—who reads, always giving me that vote of confidence I need, and makes sure I have at least one person to talk to at a signing.

To Lisa Pantano Kane—you challenge me with the hard questions.

To Jodi Bibliophile—no cowboys. Got it. No pubic hair. Never. No condoms. Eh, sometimes. Eye-rolling—welllllll, I tried. Thanks for reading and supporting, and thank you for your witty sense of humor and for always making me smile.

To Lee Tenaglia—who makes such great art for the books and whose Pinterest boards are my crack! Thank you. Really, you need to go into business. We should talk.

To all of the bloggers—there are too many to name, but I know who you are. I see the posts and the tags, and all the hard work you do. You spend your free time reading, reviewing, and promoting, and you do it for free. You are the lifeblood of the book world, and who knows what we would do without you. Thank you for your tireless efforts. You do it out of passion, which makes it all the more incredible.

To Jay Crownover—who always comes up to me at a signing and makes me talk. Thank you for reading my books and being one of my biggest peer supporters.

To Tabatha Vargo and Komal Kant—who were the authors to message me after my first release to tell me how much they loved *Bully*. I'll never forget.

To T. Gephart—who takes the time to check on me and see if I need a shipment of "real" Aussie Tim Tams. (Always!)

And to B.B. Reid—for reading, sharing the ladies with me, and being my sounding board. Can't wait to climb inside your head. Wink-wink.

It's validating to be recognized by your peers. Positivity is contagious, so thank you to my fellow authors for spreading the love.

To every author and aspiring author—thank you for the stories you've shared, many of which have made me a happy reader in search of a wonderful escape, and a better writer, trying to live up to your standards. Write and create, and don't ever stop. Your voice is important, and as long as it comes from your heart, it is right and good.

Birthday Girl Q and A

***Birthday Girl* is different from your usual work. Did you worry that it would disappoint readers?**
I think I'm always nervous. Especially when my editor gets ahold of a book! She's brutal.

But honestly, I never feel like I have a choice but to be who I am. I loved the idea, and it felt really good—a nice change of pace—to write a kinder hero, someone who works hard for a living and deserves to come home to a person who loves him. I remember a reader saying, "This is the book I didn't know I needed from Penelope Douglas," and that was great to hear, because readers, I think, needed to see that I could write a man like Pike. He has his moments, but he's not a bully. He has no real trauma. He's a good man.

Where did you get the idea for *Birthday Girl*? Any real-life inspiration there?
Haha. I get this question a lot about all of my books. But just like horror and fantasy writers, romance authors also have imaginations. I dream a lot. Especially in the morning, between sleep and consciousness. My mind is rested, and I let it wander. I favor taboo stories, so I'll think of scenarios that pique my interest or intrigue me (like *Credence*, lol), and then I wonder if I can write them in a way that readers will relate to. I love a challenge.

And I loooooove taco pizza. There was plenty of inspiration there. If you ever run into a Happy Joe's, try it!

What is your favorite part of this story?

Oh, my goodness. There are so many scenes I loved. The pool party when he gave her the cake. The night she tries to move back in with her dad, and Pike won't let her leave him. The night she comes home and finds that Pike has invited another woman over. Basically every interaction between them, because he wanted her so much and I could just feel it in all of their conversations. The tension was palpable.

If you could change one aspect of this story, what would it be?

My biggest struggle as a writer—other than character descriptions—is starting a book. My stories can be slow going at first, and that's something I've tried to work on.

Do you really feel an age-gap romance like this would work in real life?

If it were my daughter, I'd have reservations, simply because Jordan is young for any kind of serious relationship. I'd want my kid to concentrate on school, travel, pursue goals, and attack every day like a demon, to only worry about finding work that fulfills them and experiencing life. Freedom is good to have early on. I wouldn't like the idea of them settling down at such a young age.

But . . . Pike isn't someone who would hold Jordan back, either. If she wanted to hike the Andes, he might groan at the idea, but he'd join her every step of the way. Jordan isn't inexperienced. She knows a good relationship from a bad one, and nothing she gets in life would be worth it if she didn't have him, too. For Pike and Jordan, it works, and that's the thing about life. We'll never know someone else's experience to accurately judge their choices.

Do you think Cole is a bad guy?

Not at all. I don't want to offend, but I firmly believe a lot of us are shit shows in our late teens and twenties. I definitely was. We make

Penelope Douglas is a *New York Times*, *USA Today*, and *Wall Street Journal* bestselling author. Their books have been translated into twenty languages and include the Fall Away series, the Hellbent series, the Devil's Night series, and the stand-alones *Misconduct*, *Punk 57*, *Birthday Girl*, *Credence*, and *Tryst Six Venom*.

VISIT PENELOPE DOUGLAS ONLINE

PenDouglas.com

PenelopeDouglasAuthor

PenDouglas

Penelope.Douglas